the

MEPHISTO
COVENANT

the Mephisto Covenant

BOOK ONE:
THE REDEMPTION OF AJAX

TRINITY FAEGEN

EGMONT
USA
NEW YORK

EGMONT

We bring stories to life

First published by Egmont USA, 2011
This paperback edition published by Egmont USA, 2012
443 Park Avenue South, Suite 806
New York, NY 10016

www.egmontusa.com
www.trinityfaegen.com

The Library of Congress has cataloged the hardcover edition as follows:
Library of Congress Cataloging-in-Publication Data
Faegen, Trinity.
The redemption of Ajax / Trinity Faegen.
p. cm. — (The Mephisto covenant ; bk. 1)
Summary: Jax, a son of Hell, and Sasha, a descendent of Eve, unexpect-
edly find love, but Sasha must sacrifice the purity of her soul to save him
while he struggles to keep her safe from his brother Eryx, whose mission
is to take over Hell and abolish humanity's free will.
ISBN 978-1-60684-170-9 (hardcover) — ISBN 978-1-60684-271-3
(electronic book) [1. Good and evil—Fiction. 2. Christian life—Fiction. 3. Supernatural—Fiction. 4. Love—Fiction. 5. Russia—Fiction.]
I. Title.
PZ7.F132Re 2011
[Fic]—dc22
2011005904

Paperback ISBN 978-1-60684-388-8

Book design by Torborg Davern
Printed in the United States of America

For Mike.
I'm your huckleberry.

"I AM PART OF THE PART THAT ONCE WAS EVERYTHING,
PART OF THE DARKNESS WHICH GAVE BIRTH TO LIGHT . . ."
—MEPHISTOPHELES, FROM GOETHE'S *FAUST*

ONE

"YOUR FATHER'S RING IS GONE! THAT SLIME, ALEX, TOOK it—I know he did."

Sasha stood in the doorway to her mother's bedroom, watching her tear through shoe boxes and dresser drawers, debating whether to tell her that Alex didn't take Dad's ring. Inside her jeans pocket, her hand curled around the now familiar circle she'd been carrying for over a week, ever since she'd taken it to a psychic in Haight-Ashbury who said she could read the souls of people in the objects they wore every day.

Another dead end. She'd been so sure Mercy Jones would be able to tell her who had killed her father, but Mercy only blathered on about Sasha's aura, that it was pure and beautiful, with the light of divinity—the most perfect she'd ever seen. Mercy said she was destined for an extraordinary life. What she didn't say was what had happened to Dad. She couldn't get a read on the ring because it had been too long since Dad had worn it, too long since he'd died.

A hundred bucks later, Sasha walked out with the cloying scent of incense stuck all over her, the ring in her pocket, the assurance she was real special, and still no clue about Dad.

Mom was swearing in Russian, off-the-charts upset, now tossing panties and boxers and T-shirts out of the drawers. "I should never have shown it to him. Thank God I put the painting in a safe place after he saw it. Had he taken that . . ."

"What painting?"

Her mom paused for a moment, as if she had to think about how to answer, then continued digging through Dad's bottom drawer, the one where he had kept his socks. "I found it in an old house in Vladivostok, years ago."

As much as anything, Sasha loved art. She loved museums and studying Old Masters. Mom knew that. If she had an old painting, why had she never mentioned it? "Can I see it?"

"Not right now." She stopped suddenly and stood straight, dark eyes narrowed while she looked toward Sasha. "You never liked Alex, said all along he was bad. How did you know?"

"It was just a feeling. He gave me the creeps." Way worse than that. Every time he came over, she got violently, horribly sick. Alex Kasamov was something evil.

Turning the ring between her fingers, she walked to the

bed, to Mom's nightstand. Opening the drawer, she moved the contents around as if she was looking for the ring, then straightened, turned, and held it out to her mother. "You must have left it in here and forgot."

With huge relief on her face, Mom snatched it from her and inspected it closely.

Sasha turned to leave, almost hoping Mom would ask where she was going. A year ago, before Dad died, her mom would have put her through the third degree before telling her no, she couldn't leave to attend a midnight meeting. Now, it didn't seem to matter where Sasha went or what she did. All Mom cared about was her job at the State Department. And Dad's ring.

Skipping the dicey elevator, Sasha took the stairs, five flights down to the lobby of their building. Outside, light fog had rolled into Oakland, and the air was damp and chilly. Shivering with cold and anxiety, she walked to the end of the block, toward a blue Toyota SUV.

Trying out a psychic was weird and desperate, but no one knew, so no one could give her a hard time. Tonight was a whole different thing, and everyone would know. Going to a Raven meeting was social suicide. Whether she joined or not, she was making a statement by accepting the invitation, and after tonight, she was either a Raven or she was nobody. Tomorrow, she'd lose friends, people would whisper behind her back, she'd be uninvited to Smith Hardwick's party on Friday, and whatever chance she had with Tyler Hudson would be toast.

The Ravens were supersecretive and tried to make it seem like a huge deal to be invited, but after Smith Hardwick said it was lame, everyone except the geeks lost interest. Nobody but the hopeless wanted to join the Ravens.

"Just so you know," she said to Missy after she was inside the car, "I'll be way pissed if you lied about all this."

Missy turned toward the Bay Bridge. "It's no lie, I swear. You won't be sorry you came."

"You've been pretty vague about it, so tell me exactly what I have to do for Eric to tell me what I want to know."

"Not Eric. Eryx. And it's simple—really no big deal. Say you agree to follow him and help him find other people to join, and he'll give you what you want. If you don't believe it's true, just look at me. I used to be fat, remember?"

Sasha didn't say yes, even though she totally remembered. Missy had been ginormous—had been ever since she came to St. Michael's in fourth grade. But when their senior year began in August, she looked like a different person. She was instantly everybody's favorite Ugly Duckling turned Beautiful Swan, invited to every party, asked out by some seriously hot guys, even Smith Hardwick. Then it got around that she'd joined the Ravens, and she'd been smacked back to the swamp.

"I lost all the weight because of Eryx. He changed my life." She glanced at Sasha before she turned onto a side street that led to the Embarcadero. "He can find out who killed your dad. All you have to do is join."

4

"How?"

"You say an oath, then—"

"I meant, how can he find out?"

Missy turned to look over her shoulder while she parallel parked. "I'm not exactly sure, but if he can tell you what you want to know, does it matter? You've got to have faith."

Since she was little, Mom had taken her to the Russian Orthodox church once a week. Her faith was reserved for God, not some strange guy named Eryx, but she didn't say so because Missy clearly wouldn't appreciate it, might even take Sasha home and renege on the invite. The Ravens weren't about God. Some said they worshipped Satan, but from what Missy said, Sasha didn't think that was quite right. She wasn't sure what they were about, but she was going to find out. If Eryx, whoever he was, had some special power that he could use to find out about Dad, she was more than willing to say some stupid oath. It was only words, and she figured God would give her a pass, under the circumstances.

In truth, it all sounded like BS, but she had to try because she had to know who shot Dad. She imagined him in his hotel room in Moscow, looking up when someone busted in, aimed, and shot. He must have been scared and, in that split second before he died, had to know he was leaving them alone.

He'd have hated that. Dad was hard-nosed and blunt on the outside—a total marshmallow on the inside. When she had friends sleep over, he'd yell across the house, "Girls, simmer down and get to sleep!" Then he'd wake them up the next morning, grinning, waving a spatula. "Chow line starts in five, *chicas.*"

He had come back to the United States in a metal box, and Mom had him buried in Minnesota, outside of Mankato, where he grew up. There was a flag draped over his coffin, because he'd been in the army for a while. He'd served in Afghanistan before he left the service and got a regular job with an insurance company.

Who shot an insurance man? It made no sense. The Russian cops called it a robbery gone bad, but the only thing stolen was Dad's cell phone. Otherwise, nothing had been taken except her father's life.

In the beginning, Sasha expected the murderer to be caught and brought to justice, but that didn't happen. Her mother said it was different in Russia, that some crimes were left unsolved because the cops got paid off by the Mafia. Mom wrote a lot of letters to people in Washington, demanding they force the Russian government to investigate, but nothing ever happened. No one knew who killed Mike Annenkova, and worse, no one appeared to care.

Out of the car, she and Missy walked toward the waterfront and down the street toward Pier 26. Missy led her through a maze of buildings, the narrow space between them dimly lit by vapor lights at the corners, until she stopped at a metal door with a sign that said NO ENTRANCE. Immediately after her knock, the door opened.

Sasha hesitated, but David Hollister was there, grasping her arm and tugging her through the doorway. "Glad you came," he said, shoving his glasses up his thick nose with his free hand. "Did Missy tell you about the Code of Silence?"

Like she'd willingly tell anybody she bought into something this silly? "Yeah, David, she told me."

He dropped her arm when the door closed behind them and turned away, switching on a flashlight. "Follow me," he said importantly.

Squelching the urge to turn and leave, she did as he said, listening while he told her he'd been appointed acting leader of the Ravens, that he was tapped to become one of Eryx's assistants. "It's unusual for anyone to make it this high in such a short time. I only joined a month ago. But I have real leadership abilities, and I'm a master of persuasion." For a guy who got pantsed on a regular basis, David was sure full of himself.

Sasha glanced at Missy, who had no expression at all, staring down at the beam of David's flashlight.

They came to another door. David sucked spit through his teeth and made a big deal out of knocking. "It's a special code, so they know it's a Raven on the other side."

Good grief. It would be pathetic if it wasn't so stupid. Sasha wondered how much more goofiness she'd have to endure before she got to meet the mysterious Eryx and ask him what he could do for her.

When the door opened, she saw a small room with no

furniture, no boxes—nothing at all but several bare candles placed in the center of the concrete floor, illuminating spray-painted figures: *66X*. The sign of the devil was 666. Did they replace one of the sixes with an X for Eryx? She wasn't sure if that was silly, or seriously disturbing. Standing in a semi-circle were twelve St. Michael's seniors, silent and solemn, all of them staring at her. Missy's hands were at her back, pushing her forward so that she stumbled out of the shadows and into the candlelight.

Feeling their hostile glares, she realized with a jolt of surprise that she was in enemy territory. Her courage faltered, and she had to fight herself to keep from turning back toward the door, away from this creepy group of people. She'd known most of them since kindergarten, but they stared at her as if at a stranger, with no hint of warmth or welcome.

Was this part of their initiation? It had to be, because why would they hate her? She was just a regular girl who was nice to people, especially the ones who got picked on a lot. Like David Hollister.

"So you want to be a Raven," Amy Lee said. "What makes you think we'd want you?"

Before she could think of an answer, Casey Mills said, "She doesn't want to be a Raven. Missy said she's only here to find out who killed her father."

"You're a phony," someone else said.

"A user," said another.

"Eryx doesn't want you unless you're all in, unless you give up God."

Then they were all talking at once, closing their circle until she was trapped in the middle, standing on the X. She could feel the heat of the candles against her jeans.

Having insults hurled at her while standing on an altered satanic symbol in a deserted warehouse office was surreal. Had Missy really asked her to tonight's meeting to see if she was interested in joining? Confused and hurt, she looked at Missy and asked, "Why?"

Her turncoat friend stepped closer and said in a dull voice, "Because of what you are."

"What am I?" She didn't get it. And last she checked, she wasn't a moron.

Missy's eyes narrowed while the others scoffed. "You're still trying to fake us out. Do you really think we're too stupid to know?"

"Know *what*?"

"You're Anabo," came a voice from behind her, a familiar voice with a heavy Russian accent.

Turning quickly, Sasha stared as Alex Kasamov stepped out of the shadows, then steeled herself against an instant wave of nausea. She guessed he was in his forties, and older ladies probably thought he was hot, including her mom, but Sasha thought he was smarmy, with slicked-back dark hair and evil eyes. "What are *you* doing here?"

"I sponsor the Ravens."

"How? Why?"

"The day Katya asked me to take you to summer volleyball practice at your school, I met Casey. He was on his way to try out for football, and I could see he needed a little help. I made certain he made the team, and he agreed to find others to follow Eryx. That's why I said I'd sponsor them. Everything I do is for Eryx."

"Including going out with my mom?"

"Yes, but Katya wouldn't cooperate, couldn't see that what I have to offer is the only way."

Had he tried to get Mom to pledge to Eryx? That'd be funny, if it wasn't so twisted. Mom was all about God.

Alex came closer and stopped just in front of her. She took a step back, but Missy's hands were there again, holding her still. "In Greek," he said, "*Anabo* means light. Before Eve fell from grace, before original sin, she had a daughter, Aurora. You're one of her descendants, called Anabo because your spirit is all light, without darkness."

Her heart beat so fast, she wondered if they could hear it. "I've never heard of Anabo, or Aurora. I'm not anybody. You're way wrong."

He shook his head. "I learned all I need to know about you from your mother and the kids here tonight. People are drawn to you, they like you, even before they really know you. You stand up for the losers. You're there for those who get into trouble, without judging."

"All that makes me is nice."

"The Anabo never give in to temptation because they're never tempted to begin with. You don't understand hate, rage, lust, greed, or jealousy. All of humanity has to resist the pull of the dark side, but you don't because it's not there. You have no concept of evil except in the abstract. From the moment you were born, you were destined for Heaven."

"We're all destined for Heaven."

The Ravens began shouting at her, but Alex silenced them with a raised hand and a shake of his head. "Those who don't succumb make it to Heaven, but it's a lifelong fight for everyone except the Anabo." Superfast, he jerked her sweater up at the same time Missy wrenched her arms behind her. "There's no doubt what you are. You have the sign of the Anabo—your birthmark." He turned her toward the group, displaying the tiny *A* on her ribcage for all to see.

The Ravens went wild, screaming, shouting, calling her filthy names. Casey Mills spit at her.

Turning her head, she glared at Alex. "How did you know about my birthmark?"

"I saw it while you were sleeping."

The little *A*, surrounded by sunbeams, was below her right breast, which meant he must have gone into her room while she was asleep, lifted her T-shirt, and looked at her. How? Why hadn't she woken up? Why had Mom let that happen?

"I had to know. Had to be sure." He let go of her sweater,

and Missy released her arms. "I suspected, because you were so afraid of me. Unnaturally afraid. It's instinctive in the Anabo to be terrified of Eryx's chosen ones."

"What I feel about you isn't fear, Alex." More like revulsion and loathing.

His eyes narrowed. "Call it what you will, I knew you couldn't stand being in the same room with me, and it had nothing to do with me dating your mother." He glanced around at the others before he moved still closer. "The Anabo are very rare, and of great interest to Eryx. As soon as the Ravens have had their fun, I'm taking you to see him."

No way was she sticking around, and for sure she wasn't going anywhere with Alex Kasamov.

Turning, she darted between Missy and David and booked it for the door, but she'd barely gotten through and made it a few steps into the warehouse before Alex caught her, clamped one arm around her neck and the other around her waist, squeezing until she could barely breathe. He dragged her backward, into the smaller room, into a chorus of insults from the others.

While Alex held her, Missy tied her hands behind her back and hobbled her ankles.

The Ravens stepped back, widening their circle, and that's when she saw the rocks. A pile of them in the corner. Single file, the Ravens went past and gathered up two or three rocks each, then returned to the circle. David sucked spit through his teeth and grinned. "Ready for some fun, Sasha? Maybe you'll enjoy this as much as I liked getting pantsed every goddamn day of my life!"

She stared at him and said nothing. He knew. He remembered. She was the one who stuck up for him.

His grin faded. "Yeah, you think I wanted that? You think I *liked* you acting like Joan of Fucking Arc, cutting off my balls in front of the whole damn football team?" He hurled a rock, and it hit her in the face, glancing off of her cheek.

She couldn't protect herself, and the next stone hit her nose, a third hit her breast, square on the nipple. With a shriek of pain, she fell to her knees, but one of the boys hauled her to her feet again. "Get up, angel."

They pelted her with the rocks, coming at her from every direction, bruising and cutting. Nothing had ever hurt this bad. One eye began to swell, but she could see Alex through the other, standing just behind Missy, laughing.

"Where's the God Squad now, Sasha?" Amy Lee shouted.

It was maybe the hardest thing she'd ever done, but she wouldn't give them the satisfaction of crying, or begging for mercy. She didn't say a word. Somewhere in the midst of awful pain and blind fear, her mind checked out and she thought of Dad, remembered his laugh, his smiley eyes, his big hands that fixed the plumbing, cooked pancakes, and petted her hair when he came to say good night.

She began to pray, desperately pleading to God. If he'd get her out of this alive, she'd be a better person. She'd work at the soup kitchen. Build houses for Habitat. Become a nun.

Please, God, help me!

Suddenly, as if someone hit a pause button, the shouts and laughter stopped. Dead quiet. Everyone in the room was frozen, some with an arm raised in midthrow, some with eyes half closed in midblink. They were each still as a statue.

Everyone except Alex. He looked as if he'd seen a ghost, his eyes wide with fright as he looked past her. Seconds later, he shifted his focus back to her. "I should have killed you the night I discovered you're Anabo."

It was like a nightmare where she had a chance to save herself, but couldn't because of her inability to move. Tied up, bleeding, with one eye almost swollen shut, she had no prayer of escaping Alex when he wove around the frozen Ravens, rushed toward her, picked her up, and threw her over his shoulder. With her head hanging down, all she could see was the back of Alex's pants as he ran for the door into the warehouse. Her whole body hurt, and bouncing on his shoulder was agony. She saw blood drip to the concrete and realized it was hers.

Jarring her, he skidded to a stop. "Get out of my way!"

Who was he talking to? All the Ravens were frozen.

"There's no way out," a deep voice said. "Give up and give me the girl."

Who was it? How did he get here? The door hadn't opened.

She felt hands around her waist, felt the tug and pull between Alex and the one with the deep voice. "Let go. *Now.*"

"Back off. I'm taking her to Eryx."

"No," the voice said calmly, "you're going to Hell on Earth, and I'm keeping the girl."

Who belonged to the voice? Where was Hell on Earth? Was it a joke? A metaphor?

Just after the hands at her waist went away, a pair of black boots and long legs in black leather pants came into her line of vision, along with a large hand holding a lethal-looking switchblade. She cringed when it plunged into Alex's back, heard him grunt, felt his hold loosen and her body slip from his shoulder.

She landed in confident arms, cradled against a very warm and broad chest. Alex crumpled to the floor. "Is he dead?"

"No, just out of commission. I'd love to kill him, slowly and painfully, but I can't. Be still and quiet now, and I'll fix you."

"Who are you?" She tried to see his face, but the way he was holding her, with her head pressed against his shoulder, she couldn't really get a good look. It didn't help that her right eye was swollen almost shut.

"My name is Jax. Hush now, and close your eyes."

She did as he said and tried to be calm, but it was no use. He was a stranger, and after what just happened, her fear factor was way over the top, making her stiff with anxiety. "The others . . . if they wake up . . ."

"They won't."

"Did you . . . was it you who froze them like that?"

"Yes. Just stay calm."

While she fought shock, a slow invading warmth spread through her, starting at her feet and moving upward, all the way to her face. She didn't need to look to know the bruises disappeared and the cuts healed. The binding rope fell away, and within a matter of moments she felt no pain at all.

"Better?" he asked.

She nodded. "Thank you. How did you do that?"

"I'm not sure. It's just something I can do." He pressed her closer to his body for an instant, then slowly set her on her feet and stepped back, allowing her to get a look at him.

Her mouth went dry. "Holy . . . "

He was young, maybe eighteen or nineteen, dressed in black from head to toe—black leather trench coat swirling around his black boots. His face was hard, square, shadowed with the beginnings of a beard; his cheeks were high, his chin firm, his hair black as midnight, messy and too long. She met his eyes—ebony, fathomless eyes—and she knew, without a doubt, he was not of this world. Inhuman. A specter of Hell. No wonder he hadn't come through the door.

As carefully as she was checking him out, he was just as obviously looking her over. "You're the most beautiful thing I've ever seen," he said in a raspy whisper.

"Ditto," she murmured. She didn't think it was possible for anything to be more bizarre than frozen Ravens and instant healing, but she was way wrong. An entire colony of butterflies had landed in her stomach, which could mean only that she was crushing on a guy whose eyes were so disturbing, he looked like he was straight from Hell.

Time to go. "Thanks for saving me, Jax, but I've gotta run. Peace out." Turning, she hauled ass for the door, slipping when she hit a puddle of blood.

Before she crashed to the floor, he caught her and set her back on her feet to face him, steadying her with warm hands. "Don't go yet. Just tell me who you are. What's your name?"

"Sasha."

"Is that short for Anastasia?"

"Alexandra. I'm Alexandra Annenkova. Everyone calls me Sasha." He smelled like cinnamon and cloves. Considering the warehouse smelled like saltwater, old fish, and something mildewed, the scent of him was incredibly inviting, and she had to force herself not to lean closer.

Startling her, five more guys appeared out of thin air, just behind him, all dressed identically, with the same eyes, the same midnight-black hair. Their faces were different, but they were obviously brothers. They looked surprised to see her, and one of them, a guy with a ponytail, said, "Well, I'll be damned," at the same time another, who wore a diamond stud in one ear, said, "Lucky bastard."

Great. A whole family of Hell Boys. She had to get out of here. Turning, she headed for the door, swearing to herself that if she made it home, she'd never, ever do anything this stupid again.

"Wait!" His hands grasped her arms, spinning her around to face him. "Don't be afraid. I won't hurt you. Please, just stay a minute and talk to me. Tell me why you came here tonight."

She shrugged off his hands and took a step back. "I was told that if I joined the Ravens, their leader, Eryx, could tell me who killed my father."

"And you believed it?"

"Not really, but I had to try."

"Is it that important to find out?"

"It's all that matters."

"Eryx won't help you. Whatever you were told about him, it was a lie."

"You know him?"

"A long time ago, he was our oldest brother."

"If he was your brother then, he's your brother now."

Jax shook his head slowly. "Maybe biologically, but not in any way that matters. He's our enemy, and our only purpose is to keep him from taking over Hell."

Sasha stared at him, wishing that he was insane, or that she could rationalize everything that just happened by blaming it on a hallucination, brought on by the stoning. But the truth was, he didn't look even slightly unhinged. And maybe she was rattled, but she was completely conscious. "Why would Eryx want to take over Hell?"

"It's his nature. He has no hope, no compassion, no light in his soul. He's like a machine, his only goal to collect the souls of people he can sucker into following him. If he ever has enough, he'll take Hell from Lucifer, and that will be an end to free will. Humanity will lose all hope, and the dark side will take over. It'll be anarchy. The end of the world."

She'd heard enough. Moving back again, desperate to get some distance, she managed a small smile. "Then I guess it's a good thing Eryx didn't show up. Hey, look, it's been real nice to meet you, and like I said, thanks for saving me, and for healing me, but I've really got to get going. My mom's probably worried about me." Probably not, but he didn't have to know that.

Momentarily diverting her attention from leaving, she noticed he looked almost sad. Like he was disappointed.

"I swear I won't hurt you. I just want to talk to you."

"Why?"

"Because you're who you are. Because you're Anabo."

She'd never, ever heard of Anabo. Didn't it make sense, then, that she couldn't be that, if she'd never even heard of it? "Why do you think I'm Anabo? You've never seen me before now." She frowned. "Have you?"

"No, never until I popped into this room. You're a wonderful surprise." He tilted his head to one side and looked her up and down, his lips curving into a slight smile. "I know you're Anabo because, to us, the Anabo have an aura around them, sort of a golden glow."

"I'm glowing?"

"Trust me. You're Anabo. Even if you didn't have the glow,

I'd know you're not ordinary because you didn't freeze like the rest of them."

Her gaze fell to Alex, lying at an odd angle on the concrete floor. "He didn't freeze, either. Why?"

"He's Skia."

"If that means evil, it totally fits."

"*Skia* is Greek for shade, or shadow. Alex isn't just a lost soul. He's also immortal, with certain powers the others don't have. To us, his eyes are shadowed because he has no soul. He gave it to Eryx."

The whole concept of giving a soul away was hard to believe, but what she knew of Alex made it easier. Soulless was a good way to describe him. "If I'm Anabo, and Alex is Skia, what are you?"

"I'm Mephisto. My brothers and I capture the Skia and the lost souls, people who've pledged their souls to Eryx. Like the Ravens."

"Are you going to kill them?"

He shook his head. "Once people pledge their souls to Eryx, they give up any chance of Heaven or Hell. If we killed them, their souls would be released to him, increasing his power, so we take them to a deep cavern, carved out by Lucifer, where their spirits can't escape after they die. Our job is to find the Skia and lost souls, take them to the gates of Hell on Earth, and send them down."

So Hell on Earth wasn't a metaphor. She turned her head and saw the stones scattered across the floor and the puddles of blood.

Her blood. Then she looked at the frozen faces of people she'd known most of her life. All strangers now. Turning back, she met his gaze. "The people you capture just disappear? That's so cruel for their families."

"We stage their deaths and leave doppelgängers. Tomorrow, you'll hear about a sailing accident that took fourteen people."

She looked at Missy, her face frozen in a mask of rage. "Can't you get them back?"

"Not unless Eryx agrees, and in the thousand years of his existence, he's never released anyone from their pledge." His expression was curious. "Did you really intend to join them?"

"I figured I'd pretend, so I could find out what happened to my dad." She glanced down at the blood, almost black in the dim candlelight. Like oil. "Even if I'd been serious, it didn't matter. They asked me here because they hate me, not because they wanted me to join."

"They can't help hating you. It's not personal. It's because of what you are, because you're a threat to them and their purpose. Kasamov probably egged them on so they'd get you here tonight and he'd have a scapegoat to take the blame when you disappeared."

A shiver slid up her spine. "Did he start the Ravens just to suck in more people?"

Jax nodded. "The Skia form groups like the Ravens and teach them how to recruit. They start with two or three, make sure they get what they want so they'll buy in and understand how to play on others' wants. They go out and find new people, who in turn find other new recruits, and so on, growing converts exponentially."

She thought of Missy, losing all that weight. And skinny, short Casey Mills. He had made the football team this year and everyone had been shocked. "I wonder why Alex didn't find somebody popular to start the Ravens, someone who has some pull?"

Jax shot a disgusted look toward them. "This is the first time we've seen a group this young, which means this is new territory for Eryx. I imagine he had no clue about the best way to recruit kids and Alex's Ravens are a trial run. Wherever they try again, they'll do it better."

One of the others spoke up. "Jax, we have five minutes before the freeze fades."

He glanced away, but didn't respond, turning back to look at her with a funny expression on his amazing face.

"Why can't you freeze Skia or Anabo?" she asked.

"There are certain things we can't do to an immortal soul that belongs to Eryx, or to an Anabo soul that belongs to God."

"There are certain things we *can* do to you, Jax, if you don't hurry up," ponytail brother said, "and you're not going to like any of them."

He looked torn, hesitant. "I don't want to leave her."

"Later," the one with a goatee said. "You'll have to come back for her later. Besides, you can't just take her."

22

He frowned. "Why not?"

"Because she has to want to go. Free will, bro. Can't f' around with free will. You know that."

"But I have her scent. She's mine."

She blinked. "I'm sorry . . . what?"

"I'm Mephisto—you're Anabo. Since I'm the one who caught your scent, it means you're intended for me."

Was he serious? Why would she be meant for a guy from Hell? If there was such a thing as destiny, she was supposed to find a quiet, smart guy, one who wasn't over six feet tall, with midnight hair and a face she couldn't stop staring at. He'd be Russian Orthodox. Or Episcopalian. He might even be Jewish. But he wouldn't be from Hell.

"Maybe she's meant for you," goatee brother said, "but there are over three billion males on this planet, and she gets to pick which one she wants. Maybe that's you. Maybe not."

"Remind me to kick your ass when we get home."

Sasha looked from his beautiful face to the others, lined in a semicircle behind him. "Do you mean . . . are you wanting to . . . if I went with you, would we be going to Hell? The real one?"

His smile was incredible. "We don't live in Hell. We live in Colorado."

"Come on, Jax. Erase her memory and let's get on with it."

"You can erase my memory?" She was alarmed all over again.

"Only the memory of me. Of us. You'll remember every-thing until the Ravens froze."

23

"Why can't I remember you?"

"Because I don't want you to. If I have any chance at all with you, it'll have to be as a normal guy." He nodded toward the Ravens and his brothers. "This is not normal."

"Jax, shut up already and put her to sleep before we lose the freeze."

"Dammit, Phoenix, I can't leave her! What if I can't find her again? What if she dies before I can come back?"

"It's a risk you have to take."

His expression was frustrated and desperate. "Do you have a boyfriend?"

In her dreams, Tyler Hudson asked her out and they fell madly in love. In real life . . . she shook her head.

"So, when I come back, even though you won't remember me, do you think . . . would you . . ." He stopped and swallowed. "If you thought I was normal, and I asked you out, would you say yes?"

He was terribly earnest, actually looked worried she might say no. That a guy like him had even the tiniest bit of self-doubt blew her mind. "I'm sure I would, but how do you know I wouldn't say yes now?"

Surprising her, he stepped back, his expression anxious. "Are you saying you'd go out with me, knowing what I am?"

She hesitated, not willing to lie, but not entirely sure of the truth.

"No," he answered for her, "you wouldn't. Of all those three billion guys, why would you pick me? I'm a freak."

"Maybe we wouldn't even like each other, so it wouldn't matter."

"I like you now, so really, it's all about you."

"How can you like me? You don't even know me."

"I know enough." He was thoughtful for a moment, then said, "What's the one thing a guy could say to you that would be irresistible?"

"I don't know. It's never been said, because I've never met anyone irresistible." Although, if Jax was a regular guy, she'd find him irresistible. He was beautiful, with silky black hair, a perfect face, 'tall and broad, wearing way cool clothes. But those eyes. They were so dark, and she couldn't say why they made her think of Hell, but staring up at him, her mind went places it had never been before. Tucking her hair behind her ears, she focused on his chest. "Why is me being Anabo such a big deal?"

His voice was so low, so quiet, she had to strain to hear. "Our father is Mephistopheles, a dark angel who answers to Lucifer. That makes us sons of Hell. Only a girl with a pure soul can love a son of Hell. If you were ordinary, you'd be fainting, or screaming while you ran away."

"Why me? Why not another Anabo?"

"There isn't another one. At least, not that we know of. In a thousand years, we've only found one other, and she . . . well, she . . ."

Jerking her gaze to his, she asked, "Where is she?"

There was a long silence before he finally said, "Eryx killed her. If he knew about you, he'd kill you, too."

She went cold. "That's why Alex was taking me to him."

He looked like he felt sorry for her. Like he felt bad for what he was about to say. "So long as you're alive, there's a chance we could find you, that you'd become Mephisto, that you'd have Mephisto children. The more of us there are, the more lost souls and Skia we can find, which makes it harder for Eryx."

So there was a downside to being Anabo. A big one.

"Time's up, Jax," ponytail brother said. "Put her to sleep and erase her memory. *Now.*"

Sasha tried to duck and run when he moved, but she'd barely begun to turn before his arms closed around her and everything went dark.

TWO

SHE WOKE UP WITH THE MOTHER OF ALL HEADACHES. Blinking as awareness filtered in slowly, she saw the flicker of candlelight on a metal ceiling and sat up so quickly, her head swam. Looking around hurriedly, she saw no one. The Ravens were gone. Rocks and dark splotches littered the floor, barely illuminated by the guttering candles. It all came back to her— leaving the apartment with Missy, coming to the Embarcadero, the Ravens' hatred. The stoning.

What had happened? Had she blacked out and they all hit the road? Did they leave her for dead? A shudder ran all along her body, and she rubbed her arms as she stood, anxious to get out, away from this horrible place. Suppose they came back and realized she was still alive? Rushing for the door, she ran into the warehouse and stumbled toward the exit. Where was Alex? The last thing she remembered was seeing him laugh while the Ravens tried to kill her.

Dawn was just breaking when she ran into the narrow alley and sprinted for the street. The sound of a fishing boat horn drifted across the water, followed by the rumble of a bus as it passed where she stood on the sidewalk, waiting to cross. She was so glad to be outside, alive, free to go home. She didn't want to think about later, what would happen when she saw the Ravens again. Her stomach heaved as she ran across the street, and she barely made it to a bush before she threw up. How could they do that to her? How could they hate her enough to want her dead? She'd never been in so much pain, every part of her body bruised, her face and head bleeding.

Straightening from the bush, it struck her all of a sudden that she had no pain now. Except for the headache, she wasn't hurting anywhere. Holding out her hands, she saw that they looked just like always. She touched her face, her head, her arms—nothing.

Whoa. After being pelted with stones, how could she have not one bruise or scratch?

She began walking, faster and faster, trying to put as much distance, as quickly as possible, between herself and Pier 26. Ten blocks later, she spied a cab and ran out into the street, waving like a maniac. He pulled over and she got in, breathing hard while she gave him her address. Then she settled back and stared out the window, trying desperately not to cry.

Anabo. Alex had said she was Anabo, that it meant light, that she was a descendant of Aurora, the daughter of Eve. She hadn't known Eve had a daughter. Before Cain and Abel, she had Aurora. Before she ate the apple and tempted Adam. Was it true? She'd always wondered if Adam and Eve were real, or just a story to explain the beginning of sin.

No way. Alex was not only a lowlife scumbag, he was crazy. There was no such thing as Anabo. If there was, she'd have heard of it. If Eve had had a daughter, wouldn't there be something, somewhere, that mentioned it?

Maybe she'd look it up. For now, all she wanted was the safety of her own room and a hot shower.

By the time the cab delivered her at the curb outside her building, she felt only slightly better. Inside, she nervously waited on the old elevator. Mom would be up by now, and maybe these days she didn't care where Sasha went, but she was bound to want to know why Sasha was coming in at six thirty in the morning.

She opened the door, trying to be quiet, thinking maybe she could sneak down the hall to her room if Mom was in the kitchen, or her own bedroom, but no such luck. Mom was right there in the living room, sitting on the sofa, looking way pissed and even a little scared. She launched off into a long tirade, all in Russian, most of which Sasha couldn't understand. She knew enough Russian to carry on a simple conversation, but when Mom got cranked up like this, forget it. Not that it mattered. Sasha was pretty clear on the message: Mom was furious.

She stepped into the room, and that's when she saw that some-one else was there. An enormous man sat in Dad's favorite chair, staring at her from folds of fat, his small eyes never blinking.

"Mom," she interrupted, "what's going on? Who's this?"

Her mother didn't answer.

He sighed, setting his belly to jiggling. "I'm your uncle, Tim Shriver."

Couldn't she have come home, had a shower, and faked being sick so she didn't have to go to school? Why did a fat guy who claimed to be her uncle have to show up right now? "I don't have an uncle."

"I'm married to your father's sister, Melanie. Mike and I worked together for many years. Trust me, I'm your uncle."

No way Dad had a sister and never told her. "Why weren't you at his funeral? If you worked together, shouldn't you have been there? And if Dad had a sister, she'd have been there." She wasn't about to trust anyone at this point. "Who are you really?"

"He tells the truth," Mom said, now staring at the coffee table. In the background, the local news was on. "There was bad blood."

Moving farther into the room, Sasha stared at Tim. "If you worked with my dad at the same insurance company, did you go to Russia? Do you have any ideas about who killed him?"

He darted a look at Mom, who was still focused on the table, motionless as a statue, before he looked again at her. "Mike didn't work for an insurance company. He and I were with the CIA. Someone ratted him out."

Oh, God. Never, ever in her wildest imagination had she thought of something like that. "Mom, is it true? Did Dad really work for the CIA?"

Her mother nodded, looking miserable. "It's how we met, when I was still in Russia. The situation in Moscow was terrible for me. I wanted to live in the United States, but they said no, until Mikhael said he would help me."

"Why did they say no?"

"Because of my family. My grandfather was head of the KGB under the Soviets. His son, my father, became almost as important in the new Russian government, but everything was chaos, lots of scrambling for position, and an old enemy accused him of selling arms to rebels in Chechnya. He was imprisoned for treason."

Sasha stared at her mother as if she were a stranger. Never in her whole life had she heard any of this. Mom had talked about her life in Russia as if it was idyllic. They had lived in the country, in the Ural Mountains, on a sheep farm. Mom's mother died when she was little and she lived with her grandfather and father and a housekeeper named Marta. Was it all a lie?

Did she know her parents at all? She felt betrayed, like a dupe.

"I also worked for the Russian Security Council," Mom said, "which is like our State Department, and it frustrated me as much as it did my father. There was so much corruption, so much suffering of the Russian people, all because of greed and power plays. Eventually, my father was exonerated, but he died not long after his release. I was bitter and wanted to leave, to move to the United States. Mikhael convinced the State Department I could be helpful to them, because of my background, so they hired me as an analyst, and I'm sure they hoped I'd pass along information as it came my way. Even after I arrived in the States, I continued friendships with people in Russia."

Sasha's hands were clenched into fists, and her whole body was stiff with anxiety and fear. "Was it one of your friends who killed Dad?"

If possible, her mother became more pale, looking up at Sasha as if she had cut her to the core. "No one knew he was with the CIA. He went to Russia as an insurance adjuster, and everyone believed his cover."

"Obviously, someone knew, Mom. All this time, you knew he died because he was a spy, but you never told me. Why? And why won't you tell me who killed him?"

"Why does it matter so much, Alexandra? He's *dead*! Knowing who shot him won't bring him back. You have to *let it go*!"

"I want a name, Mom."

She deflated and looked down at the coffee table again, tears spilling across her cheeks. "A Russian operative. Yuri Andreovich."

Finally, she knew, but it was a stranger whose name meant nothing at all, a Russian whose job was to assassinate foreign spies. He probably shot Dad, then went home to his family and had dinner. Just another day at the office for Yuri Andreovich. "How did he know? Who told him Dad was a spy?"

Mom didn't say a word.

"The CIA is still investigating," Tim said. He shot a look at Mom again. The tension in the air was thick with hostility. Her mother and Tim Shriver evidently despised each other. A lot.

Sasha sank down into the chair opposite his. "Why are you here?" she asked Tim.

"Katya, do you want to tell her?"

Slowly, her mother shook her head. Her hands clutched the folds of her robe, her knuckles white.

"Your mother has been fired from the State Department and is being deported to Russia. She has two hours to collect her things before an INS officer arrives to take her into custody."

Sasha felt like her shoes were on the wrong feet, her hair was parted wrong, the sky had just turned green—everything in her world was becoming more screwed up by the second. "But she's a citizen. They can't deport a citizen, can they?"

"Actually, she's not a citizen. The United States allowed her into the country, and the State Department hired her because they wanted her knowledge of the Russian government, but they never trusted her enough to grant her citizenship."

"She and Dad were married! Doesn't that give her automatic citizenship?"

"Usually, but in her case, no. You have to understand, your

mother's family were prominent in Russia, people with money and influence. The United States didn't trust her reasons for defecting and have always been suspicious of her motives. It's odd for someone to walk away from that kind of money and position."

"If they don't trust her, why did they hire her to work at the State Department?"

"Because she understands the inner workings of the Russian government, and she has important contacts there that are helpful to the United States. She has very minimal security clearance, so it's not as if she can access state secrets."

"What happened, Mom? Why did they fire you?"

Her answer was so quiet, Sasha barely heard her say, "Because of Alex Kasamov. He was sent here to get something from me, and when I refused to hand it over, he threatened to get me into trouble. I'd done nothing wrong, so I told him he didn't scare me and he needed to go away."

Sasha waited for her to finish, but Mom just sat and stared. And cried.

Tim sighed. "Kasamov is a Russian operative. He told the State Department that Katya was the one who ratted out your father. His proof was all hearsay, and Katya denied it, of course, but the accusation was enough to get her fired. And deported."

She wished Alex would go back to Russia and get lost in Siberia. She hoped God could forgive her for hating him so much. "Mom, what did he want that you wouldn't give him?"

Her mother looked up at her. "When my grandfather was head of the KGB, he collected personal information about all kinds of people—heads of state and other key political figures from around the world. My father continued the tradition when he was a senior administrator in the Russian Security Council. He was a rich man with many friends, and he gathered information about all of them. He made copies of private letters and memos, took pictures of them in compromising positions, recorded their private conversations. He and my grandfather saw this not as an invasion of privacy, but as insurance for the future. Favors, they called them, but it was only a nice name for blackmail. If they needed something—classified information, or the name of an arms dealer, or even a restaurant reservation in Paris—they called up these favors. When my father died, he left me all of the information. It's in a safe-deposit box in Geneva, and I intend to die without ever seeing it again. The number of the box and its contents will be buried with me."

"Why does Alex want it?"

"He said his supervisor in the Russian Security Council found an old file of my father's with a list of the contents of the lockbox. He wants it and sent Alex to get it."

"Why didn't you give it to him, Mom? What could be in that box that's so important, you'd risk everything?" Sasha was unaware she was crying until tears splashed against her hand.

Her mother stood. "I wasn't willing to hand over detailed, personal information about important people to anyone, least of all his boss, who is a bully and a criminal. Even if I'd known what

35

would happen, that Alex would accuse me and I'd be deported, I wouldn't have given him the box number. Some things are bigger than ourselves, Alexandra. Doing the right thing always comes with a price."

"I'm glad you feel so virtuous, Katya," Tim said, sounding bitter. "Maybe if you weren't selective about when to be noble, everything would be different."

Sasha wondered what he was talking about. Her mother looked like she'd just been punched, shock and pain reflected in her expression. She opened her mouth as if she would say something, but instead, she stormed away to the kitchen, cursing in Russian while she slammed cabinet doors.

What had happened to make them hate each other this much? Sasha wanted to ask, but Tim was red in the face, his breathing very labored, and she was afraid he'd have a heart attack if she upset him further.

She swiped at her tears and wondered what it would be like to live in Russia. Could she finish high school there? Just the thought of being a new kid in a school where she barely spoke the language made her dizzy with anxiety. "Where will we live?" she asked Tim. "Moscow? St. Petersburg?"

It was a little while before he said in a quiet voice, "You can't go with her, Sasha. You're a U.S. citizen, so you have to have a visa to enter Russia."

Her dizziness moved closer to a full-on panic attack. "How long does it take to get a visa?"

Tim looked away from her, clearly uncomfortable. "Not that long, but there won't be a visa for you. Not yet, anyway. As much as the United States doesn't trust Katya, the Russians are angry with her for defecting. Until she has a feel for how things are, it's too dangerous for you to be with her. Kasamov's boss still wants the contents of that lockbox, so he could use you as leverage to get Katya to turn it over. It's not a risk Katya wants to take."

Fear nearly ate her alive. "Will he do something to Mom?"

"It's possible. I won't lie, Sasha. The next few months are going to be very difficult for your mother. The best thing you can do is stay here, out of harm's way, so at least she doesn't have that worry on her shoulders."

"I guess I can stay with a friend until it's safe for me to go."

"No, Sasha. That's why I'm here. For now, you're going home with me."

She blinked. That sounded just terrible. "Where do you live?"

"In Colorado. Telluride. Your mother will get things sorted out, and in the meantime, you'll live with us and get to know your aunt and your cousins. I have two boys, close to your age."

A couple of teenage boys and a stranger who had bad blood with her father wasn't going to make being separated from her mother okay.

Tim sighed again. Or maybe he was just sucking in deep breaths because of his size, because it was hard for him to breathe.

One thing was sure—he didn't look like a spy. "You work for the CIA, which is part of the State Department. Can't you help Mom?"

"I'm not CIA anymore." His scowl was hard to recognize, his face was so flabby. "I quit after your dad was killed and they tried to pin it on me. They thought I was the one who ratted him out. There wasn't a shred of evidence, because it wasn't true." He cleared his throat and dropped his gaze to the floor. "He was my best friend, until I married his sister. Melanie always resented Mike, but I didn't realize how much she hated him until . . . later."

He didn't say "until it was too late," but Sasha heard it in his voice. Her aunt sounded like a witch. And she was going to have to live with her. "Did Dad hate her?"

"No, but he avoided her because she became so angry and hostile whenever he was around. After we married, I thought I could help mend fences and invited him to meet us for dinner in D.C. Big mistake. It ended in a loud, embarrassing fight, and she stood up and accused him of trying to ruin my career. It got around, because things like that always do, and when he was killed, I was the first person they looked at. I was in Russia at the time, had been doing some recon on Yuri Andreovich, but there was nothing they could find that proved I was the snitch."

"If it wasn't you, then who was it?"

He met her gaze, his small eyes hard with anger. "If I knew, I'd do everything in my power to bring that person down. I'd take away everything important to them." His voice shook with passion and rage. "I'd make them *wish they were dead*."

Something crashed to the floor in the kitchen. "Mom? Are you okay?"

Her answer was another string of Russian curses.

Sasha stared at the television, trying hard not to fly into a million pieces. In the middle of her total freak-out, she saw Missy's face on the screen, followed by Amy Lee, then David Hollister. Casey Mills. All the Ravens, one by one, with a line at the bottom that read: *Fourteen local teens drown in sailing accident.* She leaned forward, straining to hear the newscaster.

". . . aren't sure why they were out so late, on a stolen sail-boat, but a Coast Guard spokesman says they were involved with a secret club at St. Michael's prep school known as the Ravens. None of the fourteen was wearing a life jacket when the Coast Guard answered the Mayday."

⁓

By the time Jax and his brothers were done with the Ravens, it was close to six in the morning in California, seven in Colorado. Along with his brothers, he transported back home to the Mephisto Mountain, to the grand hall of the house. The scent of food, particularly bacon, was heavy in the air.

"I'm starving," Phoenix said. Everyone but Jax echoed him and walked toward the dining room, shrugging out of their trench coats as they went. Halfway there, Phoenix stopped, turned, and looked at him expectantly. "You planning to eat, bro?"

"Not yet. I want to call Mallick and see how it went with Sasha."

"You have to eat, Jax. You'll run out of energy, and it'll be that much longer before you can see her."

"I'll eat as soon as I talk to him."

Phoenix turned away while Jax pulled out his iPhone. Mallick answered on the second ring. "How did it go?" he asked, without preamble. His impatience was killing him. He wanted to go right then, wanted to see Sasha again. He was still floating on a cloud of euphoria, still stunned that he'd found an Anabo, one meant for him, still fighting the overpowering instinct to snatch her up, bring her here, and never let her go.

Yeah, he got the purpose of free will. It was what they lived for, what they fought for, but at the moment, he wished there was no such thing. They were forbidden to interfere with free will, so he'd have to win Sasha like any other guy, which wasn't going to be easy. He knew as much about romance as he did about knitting, which was exactly zero.

"She's still asleep," Mallick said.

Jax frowned, his eyes on the portrait of Jane, the only other Anabo they'd found, hanging close to the front door of the mansion. He was concerned that Sasha had stayed asleep this long. "No movement?"

"None. Seems strange. You put her under, right?"

"Yes, at about midnight. Unless I'm close by to keep her under, she should have woken within a couple of hours."

40

"Maybe she's just really tired," Mallick said. "Or her body's forcing her to rest because of what she went through."

"But I healed her. She shouldn't have any need to recuperate."

"You healed her body, Jax, not her mind. It's pretty horrible what those kids did to her. I think her brain is working to process it."

Mallick was a smart guy, one of the finest among the people who worked with the Mephisto. Since the beginning, they'd recruited humans to help, always on the lookout for the best of mankind. They had found Mallick in the mid-1700s, the only holdout on a ship full of Eryx's followers. After Jax and his brothers took the lost souls and the Skia to Hell on Earth, they asked Mallick if he would accept immortality, become a Lumina, and join them in their never-ending war against Eryx. He agreed and turned out to be one of their best recruits. Jax trusted him completely, which made him the logical choice to watch over Sasha, then follow her home to find out where she lived. But he couldn't do that if she didn't wake up.

"I'll be there as soon as I knock back an energy drink," Jax said. "I'm running on empty."

Mallick didn't say anything.

"Hello? Mallick? You still there?"

"I think she's about to wake up. Hang on."

"Are you cloaked so she can't see or hear you?"

"Of course. Hold on, Jax."

Jax paced the perimeter of the circular hall while he waited.

"She's blinking. Now she's sitting up, looking around at the stones and candles. She sees the blood. She's confused. It's all coming back to her. Poor thing looks scared to death."

"Dude, you're killing me."

"She has to work it out, Jax. I think now she's wondering why they left her here, why they didn't finish her off. Okay, she's realizing someone might come back. I gotta go. She's running now, into the main warehouse, toward the exit."

"Call me as soon as she gets home."

"Done." The call ended.

Jax slipped the iPhone into his pocket and strode toward the dining room, where he wolfed down a plate of food in record time. The oldest of them, Key, the de facto leader, was eyeing him with that big brother look on his face.

"May I suggest you take your time with this, Ajax? A plan seems in order, instead of your running off half cocked."

Around a huge bite of biscuit, Jax said, "When you find your Anabo, tell me how patient you feel, how interested you are in waiting for a plan."

"If it meant the difference between keeping her forever and losing her because I rushed in without a clue what I was doing, I'd wait."

"Of course you would, Kyros. If only the rest of us were as perfect as you."

Key frowned and returned to eating his eggs. "Fine. Go now. But don't come crying to me when it all goes south."

Jax wiped his mouth, tossed his napkin to the table, and stood. "I'm outta here." He wanted to take a shower and put on some clean clothes before Mallick called. He didn't plan to talk to her today. Just follow her around to see where she went to school, what she did, who she hung out with. He needed to decide how best to approach her, so a little reconnaissance was in order.

As he walked toward the hall, his brothers yelled out random advice. Zee said, "You should give her a present. A piano would be nice."

Ty said, "Bring her a puppy. Or a kitten! Girls love little animals."

"No way," Denys, the youngest, said. "You should give her a pair of shoes. Colin Firth did that in a movie and the chick loved it."

"I suggest a tree," Key said. "You can take one of my dogwood saplings, if you like."

Jax wasn't absolutely sure, but he suspected Sasha would be underwhelmed by all of their suggestions. From what he saw in movies and on TV, girls seemed to enjoy getting jewelry, not pianos and trees. Maybe Phoenix had some ideas, since he'd had Jane for a little while, but as usual when it came to females, he said nothing.

Just as Jax reached the dining room door, the emergency alarm began to blare, its wailing siren resounding through the great hall, all through the mansion, all across the mountain. Jax froze in the doorway. Didn't it just figure? He was minutes from leaving, and now this. No telling what the alarm was for, but it was never sounded except in serious crisis. He had no choice but to stay until he knew if he was needed. Sucking in a deep breath in a vain attempt to corral his frustration, he popped down to the basement, to the war room, where he found Brody, the newest Lumina, looking very freaked out.

As soon as all the brothers were there, Brody said, "On my way to Denver, I stopped in Ridgway for gas, and while I was filling up, I saw Boggs climb out of the back of the Land Rover and take off."

Denys was still eating a biscuit. "Who's Boggs?"

Key, ever the calm leader, said patiently, "Frank Boggs, from Boston. He's the Purgatory that came to us a few days ago. His son murdered him and is now spending all of Boggs's money. He must have hidden beneath the blankets in the back when Brody left the mountain."

Jax's frustration boiled over. "Why the hell did we get *another* Purgatory? We all decided not to take on any more! Babysitting pissed-off ghosts is not what we're about, not what we're here for."

"We didn't *all* decide," Key said, scowling at him. "You got mad, just like you are right now, and *you* decided there'd be no more Purgatories. As usual, you failed to notice nobody agreed with you."

"How about if I skip the search?"

Key immediately shook his head. "You know the rules, Ajax.

We all go, or no one goes. That's not an option, because the guy's headed for Boston to get his revenge and kill his son. Then he for sure won't make it to Heaven. Our father will immediately take him to Hell."

"This is exactly why we need to stop accepting Purgs. If Boggs had been sent to Purgatory, instead of here, he'd never have had the chance to escape and be in the real world again. I don't remember the last Purgatory who didn't manage to escape. They all do it, and we spend way too much time hunting them."

With his hands clenched into fists, Key was close to losing his temper, which was rare. They all walked a thin line between the dark side they inherited from Mephistopheles, and the purity of their mother's Anabo soul. Dealing with M was difficult at times, impossible at others. A long time ago, Lucifer intervened and told M to stay out of what they did, to provide doppelgängers and let his sons take care of hunting the lost souls. But he was their father, and even if he was a dark angel, he was compelled to give advice, offer help, tell Key what to do.

Key was still glaring at him, visibly trying to get a handle on his anger. Before he could say anything to Jax—before they could get into a fight—Ty said, "Whether we take on any more Purgatories is a moot point right now. We need to get going."

Key nodded, even as he gave a hard look to Jax. "Let's head out front." As one, they transported outside, to the steps that led down to the drive. The Luminas, all 122 of them, stood in knee-high snow, waiting to hear what the emergency was. Key told them quickly, and Phoenix gave instructions and directions for the search. Within five minutes, everyone except the remaining Purgatories were gone from the Mephisto Mountain.

Jax hoped they'd find Boggs soon. He wasn't sure how long he could last before his frustration caused him to do something really stupid, like abandon the search. Key would kick his ass, then call a council, and his brothers might give him six months of solitary on Kyanos, the tiny island in the north Atlantic where they grew up. Still, it might be worth the risk, just to see Sasha again. He had a sense of urgency that began as soon as he heard the alarm, almost a premonition. He needed to get to Sasha as soon as possible.

⤜⤚

Time passed in fast-forward, every second bringing Sasha closer to the moment when she'd have to say good-bye to Mom. She had to pack anything she wanted to take to Colorado and box up what wouldn't fit in her suitcase; the boxes would be shipped to her later by a friend of Mom's.

Numb, her mind strangely blank, Sasha jacked up the volume on her iPod and packed as fast as possible. When she was done, she went to her mom's room and helped her, listening to her sing songs she'd learned as a child in the small village in the Urals where she grew up. She'd been singing those songs to Sasha since she could remember. They usually made her happy, but today they made her angry. "Was it all a lie, Mom? Did you really grow up on a sheep farm?"

"Yes, Sasha. My family owned several properties, but I spent most of my childhood there, with the housekeeper, Marta."

"How did you meet Dad?"

"I applied for a visa to the United States and was denied. He knew about it, and contacted me, to see if I'd be willing to help him in exchange for him seeing that I got the visa."

"Did you love him, or did you only marry him so you could become a citizen?"

Mom dropped the sweater she was folding and turned to her, looking hurt. "How can you ask? Of course I loved him! Would I have stayed married to him if I didn't? It's not as if our marriage made any difference to me becoming a citizen."

Sasha picked up another sweater and folded it, trying hard not to cry, wishing none of this were happening. She waffled between anger at her mother for not telling her about Dad, and feeling sad and afraid for her. If Mom had told her, she wouldn't have gone to that stupid meeting last night. She wouldn't have been nearly killed. But listening to her mother cry softly, she felt horrible for her. "Maybe you should have gotten rid of the lockbox. Taken all the letters and memos and pictures and destroyed them."

"I know that now, but I never dreamed anyone even knew about it. Until Alex showed up, I hadn't thought about that lockbox in several years. Now, it's too late. If I were to go to Geneva, I'd be followed and the papers and photographs would be taken from me before I could destroy them. All I can do is refuse to hand over the box number and code." She looked up from the trunk she was packing. "Someone may come to you and ask to have the box number, but you'll know nothing, and this is how it should be."

"I just don't get what could be so bad about what's in the box."

Mom sat on the edge of the bed. "I don't remember a lot of what's there, but to give you an example, I recall a taped phone conversation between a man in Afghanistan and a man in Britain who gave him the name of an arms dealer in exchange for fifty thousand pounds. When the tape was made, the British man was a low-level staffer for a member of parliament." Mom turned to look at her. "Now, years later, he's planning to run for prime minister. Can you imagine if that tape fell into the wrong hands?"

Sasha sank to the bed. "Maybe it'd be good if people know he's a scumbag. Or maybe the British police would arrest him."

"I doubt there's anything else that would provide enough solid evidence to arrest him, but if it hit the news, of course he'd be ruined. If he's elected prime minister, Alex's boss would threaten him with the tape to force him into policies favorable to Russia, even if they were bad for Great Britain. And that's just one example."

"If you can't go to Geneva, maybe I could. No one will be following me."

Mom shook her head vehemently while she got to her feet. "Out of the question, Sasha. It's far too dangerous."

"If it meant keeping you from getting hassled by Alex's boss, or anyone else in Russia, wouldn't it be worth it?"

"I can handle them. What I could never handle is something happening to you. It's not a solution I'll consider, ever, so let it be." She bent to the floor and opened the air return for the heater, pulled out the filter, then reached into the wall to withdraw a white plastic tube, maybe two feet long. Standing, she turned to Sasha and handed it to her. "This is the painting I found in Vladivostok. Keep it safe and don't ever show it to anyone, especially not to Tim. He'll sell it, or give it to a museum, and that cannot happen. Do you understand?"

Sasha nodded, grasping the tube in both hands.

"When I showed it to Alex, I noticed it was beginning to flake, so I had it sealed in this tube to protect it. It's best if you don't take it out. Find somewhere safe to hide it."

"If it's valuable, why don't we sell it? We could go somewhere and be together, like South America."

"We can never sell it. The value of it to us isn't the art." Mom drew her close, shaking with emotion. "I love you very much, Alexandra."

With the tube in one hand, she clung to her mother, her heart breaking into a billion pieces. She was so afraid—for herself, for Mom. What would happen to her in Russia? "I can't believe this is happening."

Mom hugged her more tightly before she dropped her arms and turned away. "It's only for a little while that you'll be with

Tim and Melanie. After you graduate next May, I'll have something worked out and we can spend the summer together . . . somewhere. Then you'll be at university." She reached into her purse and withdrew an envelope. "This is cash I keep in case the bank goes from business. It's almost two thousand dollars, all I have to give you on this short notice, so keep it safe and spend wisely. If you need something, Tim will get it for you, and I will pay him back as soon as I'm able."

Sasha folded the bills in half and shoved them into her pocket. "Why was there bad blood? Why did Dad and his sister hate each other?"

Her mother looked down at the white tube in Sasha's hand. "Your papa never hated her, because he couldn't hate. He was born that way, a good soul." She raised her gaze to Sasha's. "But some are born with darkness they can't escape. Mikhael tried to be a brother to her, but she was jealous and angry of anything he did, always looking for some way to hurt him. It's why she seduced his best friend to marry her, to drive a wedge. Tim was once a handsome man, but marriage to her and his lost friendship with Mikhael made him what he is now."

"She'll hate me."

Mom flinched and turned away, toward the bedroom door. "She may resent you, Sasha, but no one could hate you."

Remembering the Ravens' rage against her, Sasha knew that wasn't true. They hated her so much, they had wanted her to die.

In the living room, Tim was watching TV. As they came

in, Sasha saw another familiar face on the screen and heard her mother gasp. Alex Kasamov's car had been found idling on the Golden Gate Bridge, his cell phone, laptop, and briefcase still in the seat. Alex had vanished.

The police assumed he was a jumper.

~~~

By the time they found the spirit of Frank Boggs, it was past three o'clock in California. With anxiety practically choking him, Jax hurriedly showered and put on clean clothes, then popped himself to Oakland.

In the lobby of her building, he looked at the mailboxes and ground his teeth in frustration. No names. Mallick hadn't come inside, just followed and watched Sasha. While Jax stood there debating whether he'd have to pop into every apartment in the building to find her, the elevator doors opened and a guy with a load of furniture on a dolly wheeled out. His uniform was marked with a thrift store logo. Jax didn't pay him much attention, until he noticed one of the boxes had the name Annenkova written across it.

"Hey," he called out to the guy, "let me get the door for you."

"Thanks."

As soon as they were outside on the sidewalk, Jax asked, "Somebody moving? I'm looking for a place, and it's slim pickings."

"Two-bedroom, up on five. Weirdest thing, man. Like they took off in a hurry. All this nice stuff, left behind."

Jax's heart stopped. "Yeah, that is weird. Wonder where they went . . . ?"

"Beats me, but maybe that lady up there could tell you if the apartment's available."

"Lady?"

"Yeah, she's the one who called us to pick this stuff up. Number five-twelve."

Jax went back inside and dematerialized, popping up to five. The apartment was at the end of the hall, last one on the right. The door was open and a woman stood in the empty living room, writing something on a clipboard. "Hello," he said after rapping on the door, "I'm looking for Sasha Annenkova. Is she around?"

"I'm sorry, no," the woman said, looking uncomfortable. "Sasha moved away today."

Damn and hell. Thinking fast, he walked closer to the woman, but not too close. He had on shades, but humans didn't need to see his eyes to be afraid. They could sense it, knew instinctively that he was dangerous, something dark and evil. She looked tense, though not quite frightened. "She didn't tell me she was moving. Isn't this kinda sudden?"

"Yes, it was very sudden. Something of a family emergency."

"Are you family?"

"Oh, no, I worked with Sasha's mother. I'm just closing up the apartment for them."

Why had she left in such a hurry? Was it because of what happened last night? Had the Ravens' stoning scared her enough that she moved? This was his worst nightmare. He found an Anabo, one meant for him, and now she was gone. No wonder he'd felt so unsettled all day.

His entire life, he'd been susceptible to premonitions. It was part of the reason he was the one who led his brothers during takedowns. He knew before they popped into a situation if something was off, which is why he'd gone ahead of everyone last night, because he'd felt edgy. They'd planned the Ravens takedown for over a week, ever since Zee saw a lost soul at a concert in San Francisco, followed the guy home, then to school, where he discovered thirteen others. As soon as they'd found the group's Skia, Phoenix worked out a plan to take them out, but just before they were set to leave the Mephisto Mountain, Jax was hit by a bad vibe. He told them to give him ten minutes, and went ahead.

The instant he landed in that warehouse, he saw the golden glow of Anabo surrounding the blonde girl in the center of the room, and a nanosecond later, he was awash in the sweet, salty scent of her. He'd found his Anabo, a moment he'd anticipated for over a thousand years.

Now, she was gone, and he'd do whatever it took to find her.

Quickly assessing the situation, he knew this called for some serious acting. And lying. He shoved his hands into the pockets of his trench coat to keep himself from grabbing the woman and scaring the information out of her, and said hesitantly, "I, uhm, go to school with Sasha. We, uh, well, we go out, and . . ." He forced a look of total confusion and distress to his face. "I don't get why she didn't call, didn't tell me."

"She didn't have time, but I'm sure she'll call you once she gets where she's going."

"I hope so. We have tickets to a concert tonight."

"Oh." The woman looked conflicted. "Actually, I don't think she'll be there. She didn't move somewhere else in town. She moved to Colorado, to stay with her aunt and uncle for a while."

"Do you know where in Colorado? My family owns a house in Telluride, so maybe when we go for Christmas, I can see Sasha. Is she anywhere close to Telluride?"

The woman smiled then, obviously pleased. "What a happy coincidence! That's where she's staying."

He didn't believe in coincidence. Everything was connected, everything happened for a reason. Sasha moving to Telluride, only twenty miles from the Mephisto Mountain, was a sign from God, a return on the deal he made with Jax and his brothers so many centuries ago. The Mephisto Covenant. If they kept Eryx from taking over Hell, they would each find an Anabo, and if each could win his Anabo—if she stayed and became Mephisto—they would have what they wanted more than anything: peace in their restless, angry souls and the same chance of Heaven as every other human.

Elation made him return her smile, watt for watt, before he turned and left the apartment, went to the end of the hall, and disappeared. Seconds later, he was back in Colorado, bugging the new Lumina, Brody, a major computer geek, to find out the name of Sasha's uncle.

⁓

Sasha remembered breaking her arm when she was twelve, during a volleyball game. At first, she hadn't felt anything but a jarring sensation, then it was a couple of minutes later before the pain of the break hit her.

Flying into Telluride on a dinky puddle jumper they'd caught in Denver, she stared out at the mountains and wondered if this was like when she'd broken her arm. She felt nothing now, but it couldn't last.

Tim never said much at all, didn't speak unless she asked him a question, then answered in short, curt sentences.

They got off the plane, collected her luggage, and went out to the parking lot, to a Toyota sedan. The drive into town was as silent as the flight. She stared straight ahead, uninterested in the houses, the turn-of-the-century buildings, the quaint shops. Once or twice, the memory of last night came to mind, but she shoved it away and concentrated on the clouds overhead. They were thick and dark, turning everything gloomy.

Her mother's voice was in her head, making her throat tight with unshed tears, but she wasn't going to think about it right now. She wondered what her friends at school were doing, how everyone took the news about the Ravens. They'd never know Sasha went to that meeting. Not that it mattered now. She'd probably never see any of her friends again.

Tim eventually turned off of the main street and drove through a neighborhood of old Victorian houses, until he pulled into the driveway of one that was painted green, maroon, and pale pink. Most of the houses on this street were nice, but the Shrivers' paint was peeling, the yard was overgrown with dead weeds, and the front porch sagged on one end. The detached garage wasn't in any better shape.

Tim parked in the drive next to a Hummer and opened his door. "Let's go in and I'll send the boys for your luggage."

She followed him to the back door, then inside, into a kitchen that smelled like burned coffee. Dirty dishes covered the countertops, and M&M's were scattered across the floor. "*Melanie!*"

His shout startled her, but she didn't move from where she stood, just behind and to the right of him. Footsteps approached, and she prepared to meet her aunt, who was bound to hate her.

Instead of a woman, a guy with spiky blond hair and a Jay-Z T-shirt came around the corner of the entryway into the family room. He looked straight at Sasha and frowned. "Who the hell are you?"

Tim grasped her arm to pull her forward. "This is your cousin, Sasha. She's going to be staying with us for a while. Sasha, this is Brett, my oldest boy."

"Hello," she said without smiling. Why would she smile at a guy who just gave her the once-over, stopping to stare at her boobs before he met her gaze and grimaced, making it clear she didn't measure up? What a tool.

"Go get her bags and take them up to the guest room," Tim said.

"Is her leg broken? I'm not the f'ing bellboy." He turned and left the kitchen.

Expecting Tim to go after him, or at least yell for him to come back, she couldn't believe it when instead he walked to the refrigerator and said over his shoulder, "Wait for Chris to get home and he'll get your bags."

"I can do it, if you'll just tell me where to take them."

With a slice of cold pizza in his thick fingers and the first bite in his mouth, he walked past her toward the family room. "First door on the left at the top of the stairs."

Ten minutes later, just as she reached the landing with her second bag, the front door opened in the foyer below and she heard a woman say, "Is she here?"

Tim, who was parked in a gigantic recliner in front of the TV, said, "She is."

"You lousy bastard, I can't believe you'd bring that son of a bitch's kid into my house. You have no right!"

"It's my house and my best friend's daughter. If you don't like it, leave."

"Maybe I will."

"Don't let the door hit you on the way out."

Sasha had turned to look down, but Melanie never noticed, moving out of sight and into the family room without glancing up. The door remained open, until a guy with dark hair walked in, closed it behind him, then looked up and saw her. He darted his eyes toward the angry voices in the den before he headed up the stairs. "You must be Sasha."

"You must be Chris."

He took the bag from her hand and walked toward the guest room. She followed and watched him set it on one of the twin beds before he turned to look at her. "Dad said he was bringing you here to live with us. Bummer about your mom."

Sasha only nodded.

"Well, I've got some stuff to do." He walked past her into the hall and then through the doorway just next to hers, and closed the door behind him. A few seconds later, she heard the familiar sound of a video game intro.

She reached to open the first bag and start unpacking, but hadn't even begun unzipping it when Melanie stormed into the room. "Do *not* unpack! You won't be here that long."

Sasha stared at her, not really sure what to say. She'd expected the woman to hate her, and the way things were going, she'd probably be sleeping in a cardboard box tonight.

Melanie moved farther into the room, to the edge of the bed. With jerky movements, she unzipped the largest of Sasha's bags and started yanking everything out, throwing the items to the floor. "Where is it? I know that bitch gave it to you and I want it, *right now.*"

"What are you looking for?"

"My father's ring! Mike ripped it off after he died, but now

Mike's dead, too, and I mean to have it. It's *mine*."

"I don't have the ring. My mother took it to Russia."

"Liar. You're a liar, just like Mike." She reached the bottom of the bag, then turned to the other. Sasha watched her empty everything to the floor, then caught a fearful breath when she pulled out the white tube.

"What's this?"

"A portrait of my mother," Sasha lied.

Melanie dropped the tube as if it burned her hand and kicked it beneath the bed. "If you hang it up, if you even take it out, I'll light it on fire. You got it?"

"Yes." Sasha tried not to look relieved that Melanie hadn't opened it. She forced herself to have no expression at all, hoping Melanie would finish searching and go away.

When it became clear that Sasha wasn't a liar, that she really didn't have the ring, Melanie went off on her. "I'm glad your mother was deported. The only thing better would be if the Russians executed her. She was always so high and mighty, looking down her nose at me, thinking she was something special. Just like Mike. Mr. Perfect, could do no wrong. But he got what was coming to him. I was never so happy as when I heard he'd been shot. Arrogant bastard, always—"

"Stop," Sasha interrupted, thinking Melanie was scary as hell and it was no wonder Tim was miserable, and Brett was a total douche, having a mom like this. "I get that you hated his guts, but he was my father and I loved him. I can't listen to—"

"Don't you dare talk back to me!" Melanie moved closer, her eyes wild with fury, and Sasha stepped away, seriously afraid she was about to be slapped. "It's bad enough I have to put up with you at all, but I'll be damned if I'll tolerate your talk!"

Wow. Hypocritical much? "I'm sorry to be an inconvenience, but it's not like I have a choice. Can't we just get along?"

"I can't look at you without thinking about my brother."

"What did he do to you that made you hate him so much?"

"He was born! He lived, he breathed, and he was so perfect, so much the golden child, it's like I stopped existing."

Dad had done nothing to deserve her fury. This woman was insane with jealousy, paranoid, and eaten up with bitterness: a victim of her own twisted mind. There was something else about her, something scary evil that went beyond her hate and rage, but Sasha couldn't pin it down.

"I don't want you here, don't care if you live or die. Push me *just once*, and you'll be out in the street. *Do you understand?*" When Sasha said nothing, she moved closer and shouted, "Answer me! *Do you understand?*"

Tim said from the doorway, "Back off, Melanie."

Melanie wheeled around to face him. "You're taking her side over mine?"

"She hasn't done anything except tell you to lay off of her dad. Go take your meds and shut up." He glanced at Sasha, then looked at the pile of clothes, books, and toiletries on the floor. His small eyes ended up at his wife. "Either treat her right, or I'll make that call so fast, your head will spin."

"You wouldn't dare!"

"Don't kid yourself. I'll make sure they lock you up and throw away the key."

Looking as if she might explode, Melanie stormed out of the room, shoving Tim aside as she went.

Sasha was curious who Tim could threaten to call that would freak Melanie out enough that she would lay off and leave the room. A doctor? A hospital for psychos?

After giving her a slight nod, Tim turned and left as well.

Alone again, she closed the door and began picking up her things. When she was done putting her stuff away, she slumped into an old wooden chair in front of a small desk and stared at the ugly wallpaper. She'd known it would be hard to live with Dad's sister, but the reality was so much worse. Intuitively, she knew it wouldn't get better, that Melanie was never going to accept her, much less like her. The best thing to do was avoid her, as much as possible.

Reaching for her backpack, she pulled her laptop out, powered up, and signed onto the Internet. Her habit was to hit Facebook first, but she avoided it for now. Seeing everyone's status was bound to bum her out, and she didn't want to read about the Ravens. She wondered if anyone was talking about her, about why she hadn't shown up at school today.

Probably not. Her best friend, Marley, had moved to Portland almost a year ago, right after her dad had died, and after that, she hadn't really hung out with anybody in particular. She ran with the cool kids at St. Michael's, but always just as part of the group.

After her father's murder, it took her a while to realize she didn't see things the same way anymore. The endless talk about music and clothes and who said what and who lost the V and who was smoking weed in the parking lot seemed really pointless after Dad was shot.

But she wasn't a loner, so she stuck with the group of kids she'd known her whole life, mostly out of habit. Which was why, she guessed, she'd taken the risk of going to the Ravens' meeting last night.

Shaking off thoughts of St. Michael's, she went to Google and typed in "Anabo," just to see what came up. There were lots of hits, but nothing related to descendants of Aurora. She typed in "Aurora" and "Eve" and hit thousands of sites, most of which were escort services and porn outlets. Then she added "biblical" and "Eden" to the search, and found a Princeton grad student's thesis on the story of Aurora, a daughter born of Eve before she fell from grace. In his footnotes, he cited a book by a guy named Giardna, a Renaissance man who spent his life writing about biblical characters no one had ever heard of, including Aurora, the daughter of Eve. He died penniless and unknown, until someone named Bennington found his papers and published them in England in 1853.

So Anabo wasn't real, but the idea existed, and that must be where Alex got it. He'd picked it up and claimed it was true, then made up the mysterious Eryx and got a bunch of wrongheaded kids to follow along, like a cult. She wondered why. Was he a twisted, sick pervert? Why did a grown man start a secret club with a bunch of high school kids?

She shuddered, remembering their rage, the hate, the violence of the stones coming at her, over and over.

Closing her laptop, she stretched out on the closest twin bed and stared up at the ceiling. She'd never felt so alone. The enormity of it all hit her hard, dissolving her numb cocoon. Turning to her side, she gave up trying not to cry.

⚬⚬⚬

"How'd it go? Did you find her? Was Brody right about the Shrivers?"

Jax walked into the TV room and plopped down to the leather couch. "Yeah, he was right, and yes, I found her."

"Then why do you sound so bummed out?" Phoenix gave him a look. "Did you talk to her?"

"No, because she didn't see me. I went to the house where she's living with her aunt and uncle and checked it out."

Phoenix sat up and turned toward him. "You better be real careful, Jax. If she ever finds out, she'll hate you for being an invisible creeper who spies on her when she's alone."

"I won't do it again, but I had to see if she's all right after what happened last night."

"And?"

He looked toward the gigantic television, at the guys on SportsCenter. "She cried. A lot."

"Girls cry a lot. Get used to it."

"Did Jane cry a lot?"

"More than I thought possible, for random reasons, not always because she was sad."

"I'm pretty sure Sasha cried because she's sad." The sound of her crying made him feel very weird. "I was hanging around outside, looking for any sign of her, when Tim Shriver pulled up and there she was, in the car with him." He told Phoenix everything, including what Melanie had said about Sasha's mom being deported.

"That's why she moved in such a hurry." Phoenix turned down the volume on the TV. "No wonder she cried."

"You're not gonna believe this, but her aunt and one of the cousins are lost souls." He leaned his head back and studied the Greek key design carved into the crown molding. "After I left Sasha, I went all over Telluride, looking for more. I found two at the coffeehouse, both kids." He closed his eyes. "I hit pay dirt in the bookshop."

"You found the Skia?"

"He's a teacher at the high school."

"Damn." Phoenix leaned back again, quiet and thoughtful for a while before he said, "Right in our own backyard. How'd we miss it?"

"I asked Key to check dates, and he found out the Skia has been here since the start of the school year, but he got his first pledge, which was Melanie Shriver, about two weeks ago. His second was Sasha's cousin, Brett. The kid's not a good student, so his chances of getting into any college were zilch. After he pledged, he was accepted at Colorado in Boulder." He glanced at Phoenix. "He also won a sweepstakes and used the money to buy a Hummer."

"He pledged his soul for college and a freakin' car?"

"M says he resisted, but Eryx wanted him to be first because he's the most popular kid at Telluride. The Skia went for his mother, and after she pledged, she talked the kid into it."

"So much for maternal love." Phoenix sighed. "What about the others?"

"Right now, there are two, a guy who's friends with the Shriver kid, and his girlfriend. From what I could see at the coffeehouse, these aren't outsider nerdy kids like the cell we found in San Francisco."

"Eryx learned a lesson from that. To entice others, he needs the most popular kids to pledge first."

"I guess this is his newest strategy, suckering young people into following him."

"I'm only surprised he didn't do it sooner."

Jax wished he could focus on something else, but the sound of Sasha's crying was stuck in his head, all mixed up with the horrible things her aunt had said to her. Not that he was surprised. Melanie Shriver couldn't help being a bitch. Lost souls took a long time to learn how to manage their resentment toward people who still had control of their lives—their souls. They acted out, were mean and hateful, and frequently became violent. If they managed to avoid capture by the Mephisto and stayed out of Hell on Earth long enough, they eventually figured out they could win a lot more souls for Eryx if they weren't total assholes. But in the first year or so of a lost soul's new reality of belonging to Eryx, they were generally horrible people.

"Don't sweat it too much, Jax. We'll start first thing in the morning on reconnaissance, and I'll have a plan to take them down within a couple of days. Once her aunt and cousin are out of the picture, Sasha won't be so unhappy."

"That'll help, but I can't lie, Phoenix. I have no idea how to do this or what to say to her."

"Well, there's the direct approach, but you run the risk of her telling you to leave her alone. Hard to get a girl to like you if you can't come near her. I think you should hang out where she does and try to act like a normal guy. Get to know her on her own terms, and maybe tell her bits and pieces as you go, sort of ease into it."

"She's curious, at least. She was Googling 'Anabo' before she started crying."

"Did she find Bennington's book?"

"No, but I did and left it on her computer. She'll see it when she wakes up." He rubbed his eyes. He hadn't slept at all last night. "I guess what's freaking me out most is that I have one shot. If it doesn't work, if she decides she can't stand me, that's it. Game over."

"Just go slow, and try to be patient."

"Hard to be patient when she's living with two lost souls. I'm scared shitless they'll find out she's Anabo and tell the Skia, who'll take her to Eryx immediately."

"We'll work as fast as we can to get rid of them. In the meantime, no matter how hard it is to resist, don't sleep with her. Don't mark her before she's all in and f' it up like I did."

It had been over one hundred years since Phoenix found Jane, only to lose her when Eryx kidnapped her, then waited until they arrived to rescue her so he could kill her while they watched. Phoenix went crazy, eaten up with grief and guilt. They didn't know exactly how things worked with the Anabo, because they'd never found one before, so it was a huge surprise when they all suddenly sensed Jane, just as they sensed one another. Even if the six of them were thousands of miles apart, they knew exactly where the other Mephisto were located. Phoenix told them he'd slept with Jane, which was how they figured out the correlation between sex with an Anabo and the sensing mark.

Unfortunately, they also shared that same sense with Eryx, so by the time they realized that if they could feel it, so could Eryx, it was too late. He came to London to see why he sensed someone other than his younger brothers, and found Jane. He couldn't allow her to stay with Phoenix and eventually become Mephisto, or give birth to children who would grow up to be Mephisto, so he killed her. Phoenix still grieved and lived with constant guilt.

They watched football for a while, until Phoenix said in a dead voice, "You have to protect her from something she doesn't know exists, and at the same time convince her to love you. You're going to get to a point when you believe having sex with her will seal the deal, but it won't, Jax. She won't look at it like you do, and all you'll be left with is a marked woman who has no choice but to come here, the only place she can be safe from Eryx. Never forget, even if she's forced to live here on the mountain so Eryx can't find her, she doesn't have to become Mephisto. She doesn't have to accept you, even if she carries your mark. She could become a Lumina and marry one of them. Think about that more than you think about getting her naked."

"Thanks for the advice, bro, but you're way ahead of me. First, I have to figure out how to meet her."

THREE

HER CELL PHONE WOKE HER UP. TIM WAS CALLING FROM downstairs, she guessed because it was hard for him to climb the stairs.

"Are you hungry?" he asked.

"Uh, yeah, I guess so." What time was it? She sat up and looked across the room. Hadn't she closed her laptop?

"Come on down for supper. Mel's cooking steaks."

Her stomach growled, and her mouth watered. She decided she might as well get it over with now. It wasn't like she could completely avoid Melanie, living in the same house. "I'll be right there."

Ending the call, she got up and went to the computer, rubbing sleep from her eyes while squinting at the screen. She hadn't pulled up this Web site. It was a pdf file, pages from a book. The one compiled by Bennington.

Staring at the screen, wigging out because she had no idea how the pdf file had gotten there, a few of the lines popped out at her. *Aurora left Eden, God sent her a mate of pure spirit, and a line of descendants began, the Anabo, people of light, and theirs was perfect and harmonious, a nation as God intended.* She paged down and read more. *Lucifer sent his minion, Mephistopheles, to insinuate evil into the hearts of the Anabo, as he had done in Eden. The mightiest escaped his influence and scattered across the Earth to bear the fruit of their light. And so it followed, they would be known by the mark of Aurora, a sunburst of the Alpha, the beginning as God planned when he created the world and man in his own image.*

Stepping back, she rubbed the rest of the sleep from her eyes and wondered all over again how that file had come to be on her screen. Maybe it was somehow attached to the Princeton guy's thesis paper and had opened automatically.

All the way down the stairs, she thought about her birth-mark, an elaborate, swirly *A*, very tiny, with a sunburst around it . . . *the mark of Aurora, a sunburst of the Alpha.*

For the first time, she wondered if the Anabo was real.

She took her place at the table, an oak oval in the kitchen, and noticed everything was clean. No dirty dishes, no M&M's on the floor. Melanie didn't speak, never looked at her as she scurried around, setting a bowl of English peas and a basket of rolls next to Tim's plate. He reached for one, buttered it sloppily, then shoved half of it into his mouth.

Melanie finally landed, eyes averted, looking into the family room toward the stairs. "I hope they come soon. Brett doesn't like his food to be cold."

Amazing. She was worried Brett would be unhappy with cold food, even though it was his own fault if he didn't come when it was ready. Sasha stared at her aunt, trying to make some connection between her father and this psycho woman. How could siblings be so 180 from each other?

The doorbell rang, and Melanie popped up to get it. Moments later, she reappeared, a dark-haired man just behind her. Hands clasped in front of her, cheeks pink, eyes bright and lively, she was like a different woman.

Sasha stared, wondering what was up.

"Tim, look who's come to join us for dinner!"

Tim glanced up, barely nodded, then reached for another roll.

Melanie waved the man toward the chair next to Sasha, but he hesitated. His dark eyes narrowed slightly, like he was checking her out. She shivered and looked away.

"Sasha," Melanie said breathlessly, smiling like she would if Santa Claus had come for supper, "this is Emil Bruno, Brett's history teacher."

Mr. Bruno moved closer, skirting the table to walk behind her, coming to stand just to her right. He was scary. Not violent scary—something darker, more sinister.

Like Alex.

Her whole body was covered in goose bumps.

He took the chair and sat down, entirely too close for comfort. Out of nowhere, completely unbidden, the Lord's Prayer began in her head. *Our Father who art in heaven, Hallowed be Thy name.* It freaked her out almost as much as this dark man sitting next to her. *Thy kingdom come. Thy will be done on Earth, as it is in Heaven.*

She startled when he said in a smooth, silky voice, laced with the underpinning of an accent, "It's a great pleasure to meet you, Sasha. What a delightful name. I once knew a Sasha. She was almost as beautiful as you, but dark-haired, and older."

A flatterer, just like Alex. He was always telling her she was beautiful, bright, and talented. He'd look at her sketches, because Mom showed them to him, and go on about how brilliant she was. She knew it was all fake. She never understood why her mom couldn't see through his BS. Evidently, it wasn't until he started pressuring her to hand over the stuff in the lockbox that she told him to get lost.

Melanie said in a hushed voice, "Sasha's mother was deported back to Russia, and Sasha wasn't allowed to go with her, so we're stuck with her until—"

"That's *enough*," Tim said. "It's no one's business why Sasha is with us, and we're not *stuck* with her. She's our guest. Family. Back off."

Melanie smiled at Mr. Bruno. "As I was saying, that's why Sasha is staying with us. She has no other family."

"Family is all around," Mr. Bruno said. "The world is our

family. Friends are our family. Don't you feel friends are one of life's most important elements, Sasha?"

"Yes," she murmured, trying desperately not to look at him, not to meet his eyes.

Tim said, "We're out of rolls," and Melanie hopped up to fetch more. Footsteps sounded on the stairs. Brett and Chris were on their way.

Incredibly, Sasha was glad. Anything to take Mr. Bruno's focus off of her. Every muscle in her body was tensed, ready to catapult her out of her chair, away from this scary man.

"Hey, Mr. Bruno!" Brett was clearly glad to see his teacher.

Chris was less vocal. "Hey," he said, jerking his chin up before he focused on the table. Sitting down, he reached for a baked potato.

Tim ate another roll.

Sasha watched Melanie deliver a fat, juicy steak to Brett's plate. He cut into it and scowled. "It's too done, Mom. You know I hate my meat too done." He speared it with his fork and tossed it to the floor.

Staring, Sasha was shocked.

Melanie went to the stove and clucked while she set about preparing another steak, occasionally mumbling apologies. Un-freaking-believable! After Brett's second steak went under the broiler, she came to the table and laid one on Mr. Bruno's plate. She followed suit with Tim, then Chris. As she turned away the last time, she said, "Sorry, Sasha, I guess you'll be a vegetarian tonight."

Give us this day our daily bread.

All she had to eat were peas. There weren't enough potatoes, and no one offered to share with her. The rolls were all gone. Melanie ate some kind of weird hot cereal that looked like brown mush. *And forgive us our trespasses, as we forgive those who trespass against us.*

Her stomach growled, the scent of the steak making her mouth water. *And lead us not into temptation . . .*

"So, Chris," Mr. Bruno said, "are you coming to the meeting tonight?"

Chris never looked up from his steak while he shook his head and mumbled something about homework.

"Come on, now, it's Friday night. Why don't you join us?"

Sasha ate her peas, despite feeling light-headed and sick. Just like when she was around Alex.

"How about you, Sasha? Would you care to join us tonight?"

"Uh, no, I don't think so. I'm pretty tired."

"It'd be a good opportunity to meet some of the other students. Might make your first day less stressful. We have a small group right now, but that'll change, right, Melanie?"

"Definitely. Kids these days have so many distractions, it's great for them to join a group where they can find some common ground and have a little fun. I wish you'd come, Chris. You'd like it, I know you would."

"Leave him alone," Tim said around a bite of steak. "He's not interested in your silly secret club."

74

Mr. Bruno didn't look the least bit insulted. He said smoothly, "I can understand your prejudice, Tim, but don't you agree that joining something, feeling a part of a group, is good for young people?"

Tim ignored him. The tension in the air was thick and painfully awkward.

Melanie filled the uncomfortable silence with a little speech about how hard it was to be a teenager these days. She looked at Sasha and said with a fake smile, "You should go and try to make friends. Telluride High is tiny, and there are already cliques in place. You'll have no friends at all."

"Thanks for your concern. I know just how much my happiness means to you."

Melanie dropped the act and scowled at her. "Fine, you little ingrate, stay here and hang out with Tim. He's a laugh riot. Or Chris. He's tons of fun, his nose always stuck in that stupid video game."

"Melanie," Tim said in a low, menacing voice, "I know that phone number by heart."

Who was Tim threatening to call? Sasha couldn't imagine anyone other than some kind of doctor or mental institution. Whoever it was, the threat worked. Melanie glared at Tim, but didn't say anything else.

Mr. Bruno appeared unaffected by the tension and ugly words, continuing to eat as if nothing was wrong. Brett devoured his dinner, also oblivious. Chris didn't eat all of his food before he shoved back from the table, got up, and left.

Sasha hurriedly finished the rest of her peas, then scooted her chair back and excused herself.

"Melanie," Mr. Bruno said, "surely you can find something more for her to eat? We can't have our new student fainting from hunger, can we?"

"Would you like some flaxseed cereal?" Melanie offered, halfheartedly.

Yeah, and maybe a side of dirt to go with it. "No, thank you."

"It was a great pleasure to meet you, Sasha, and I look forward to getting to know you better. I take special pride in my friendships with my students. It's the whole reason I organized the Ravens."

. . . but deliver us from evil.

She ran for the stairs, taking them two at a time to the landing, then down the hall to her room. She barely made it to the bathroom before she lost the peas, his voice repeating in her head. Ravens. Ravens. *Ravens.*

❧

She had strange dreams that night, one about food—tables and tables of delicious food that disappeared before she could touch it—and one about her mother, knee-deep in snow, wandering around, looking for a place to hide from giant Russian soldiers. Then she dreamed about the Ravens, the cold, smelly warehouse, and the stoning. She relived every second, up until the last thing she remembered—when she prayed to God for help, to save her.

After that, the dream became strangely hazy and discordant, like so many dreams that make no sense. The Ravens suddenly froze in place and only Alex remained, threatening her, about to kill her, until he disappeared and there was someone else, a dark, evil figure whose words were indistinguishable, but strangely calming. She wanted to wake up, but dreamed on, and her fear morphed into anticipation, as if something amazing was about to happen.

Just about the time she was enjoying the dream, weird as it was, she woke with a start and squeaked in alarm because someone was standing next to her bed, a looming shadow in the darkness.

"Calm down, willya?" Brett said, clearly annoyed. "Dad's making me take you skiing, so get up and get ready."

She didn't want to go anywhere with Brett. Not only was he a tool, he was a Raven. It hit her all over again, the freakish coincidence of another secret club in a town hundreds of miles from San Francisco, also called the Ravens, also led by a grown man who scared the crap out of her. Which totally made her think it wasn't coincidence. "I don't ski."

"I know you don't, and it's not like I want to teach you, but Dad won't give me lift-ticket money unless I take you with me. He says if you're going to live here, you have to ski. It's what people do in Telluride."

She considered giving Brett the money so she wouldn't have to go. "How much are lift tickets?"

"A day pass is a hundred bucks."

Oh, man. She couldn't part with that much money. "This sucks."

"No shit." He moved away from the bed, toward the door. "You'll have to use Mom's ski stuff. It's in the closet at the end of the hall. Hurry up. We'll leave in thirty minutes and hit the Bluebird before we head for the lifts."

"What's the Bluebird?"

"Breakfast." He walked out.

She resigned herself to a miserable day, but at least she'd get to eat.

～

"Sasha's going skiing."

Jax sat up in bed with the phone to his ear. "She just got to Telluride, but she's going skiing?"

Mallick said, "She left the house dressed in a ski suit, and there are two pairs of skis on the roof of her cousin's Hummer, so that's my best guess. Right now, I think they're headed for the Bluebird."

Jax ran a hand through his hair, then rubbed his eyes. "Wonder if she knows how to ski."

"Not sure, but I can find out. You want me to follow her up to the slopes?"

"Yeah, keep an eye on her, and I'll call in a bit to see where you are."

"If she doesn't know how, maybe that's your entry. You could offer to help her learn."

"Yeah, maybe." He frowned. "Kinda awkward, though."

"Could be, but at a minimum, you can follow her around a little today and watch for an opening."

"Thanks, Mallick." He hung up and headed for the shower.

~∽~

Brett barely spoke to her in the car, and when they arrived at the café, he went to sit in a booth with three other guys and blew her off. Not that she cared. She sat at the counter and spent fifteen bucks on a ginormous breakfast platter, enjoying every bite.

When they left and were out in the parking lot, Brett introduced his friends. There was Thomas Vasquez, a tall guy with dark red hair who seemed nice, and Mason Dixon, a stocky guy who kind of reminded her of Charlie Brown. The last guy, Kelley Easter, very hot with blond hair and green eyes, whom Brett called East, looked her over and said, "I bet you give good head with those puffy lips."

There were guys at St. Michael's just like Kelley Easter, guys who said totally inappropriate things and thought they were being cool—or übermanly or something—never realizing how stupid they sounded. She'd learned from experience, the only way to deal with guys like East was to dish it back. "I bet you've always been a douche."

Instead of taking the insult the way she intended, he only laughed. "Shriver, why didn't you ever tell me you have such a hot cousin?"

"Didn't know. Her dad and my mom hated each other, so we never hung out."

East turned away and headed toward a small white SUV. "We'll see you at the lifts."

Brett turned toward his Hummer, and Sasha followed. He said as they got closer, "Don't get any ideas about East."

"You're kidding, right?"

"I saw how you looked at him, checking out his package."

If it weren't so insulting, it'd be funny. "Is it a happy place over there in Fairy-Tale Land?"

"So don't admit it, but I saw you. Maybe he'd take you up on it, but he goes out with a girl named Julianne, and she's superjealous. Also a bitch."

He was serious, which blew her mind. "Yeah, okay, whatever."

He looked disappointed, she guessed because he hadn't gotten a rise out of her.

Halfway up the mountain, he said, "It's gonna be rough at school, Sasha. I checked out your Facebook page last night, and it looks like you had a lot of friends at your old school. You should know it's not going to be like that at Telluride. It's really small, just thirty seniors."

Sasha looked across at him, wondering why he was suddenly being nice to her. "I'll be fine, but thanks for the info."

"You know, if you'd join the Ravens, things'd go a lot easier for you."

Her memory instantly kicked in, and she was right back at

Pier 26 with that group of Ravens throwing rocks at her. "I'm not much of a joiner."

"At least think about it. I get extra points for every member I recruit."

Now she knew why he was being nice. "Points? For what? Is there some kind of prize?"

He didn't answer for a while, then finally said, "I guess you could say I get more privileges."

She remembered David Hollister bragging about how he'd moved up the ranks. Not that she had known what he meant, not like she cared. "There were Ravens at my school in San Francisco, but they all died in a sailing accident, night before last."

He jerked the wheel so that they fishtailed in the snow. When he had the Hummer under control again, he said in a rough voice, "What's your point?"

"I know what's up with the Ravens, about Eryx and the oath. Like I said, it's not for me."

"What kind of kids were the Ravens at your school?"

"Mostly loners, or a little too weird to exactly fit in."

"Is that why you don't want to join? Because you think the kids in our group are losers?"

"I don't know who's in your group, so no, that's not it. It's just not my thing." End of story. She wished he'd leave it alone.

"Maybe if you knew more about it, you'd change your mind."

She knew enough. "I doubt it, Brett."

He was quiet again, until he said, "It's gotta be tough having your mom shipped off to Russia, and you being left behind, but Eryx could fix it for you. Come to our next meeting, on Monday, and you'll see why it's so great. We don't invite just anybody."

"Who is Eryx, anyway? Where did he come from, and why does he want people to pledge that they'll follow him? I don't get what's in it for him."

Brett shrugged. "He just has a different way of thinking. It's not like a religion. More like a way to live life that makes you happier."

She didn't remember the Ravens at St. Michael's being happy. They were always getting into fights, pulling detention for playing seriously mean pranks on people.

"He can do things that erase bad stuff in your life, like your mom leaving."

"What did he do for you?"

Brett gave her a slight smile. "My GPA and SAT scores are pretty bad. College was looking like a no go for me, until Eryx helped me out. I got an acceptance letter from the University of Colorado a week ago." He glanced at her. "Plus I needed a new car, and right after I pledged, I won a fifty-thousand-dollar sweepstakes. Mom took me to Colorado Springs, and I got this Hummer."

Was this what it was all about? Giving people what they wanted most, so they'd say an oath? She remembered Missy losing all that weight, and scrawny Casey Mills, making the football team.

"East is a Raven," Brett added. "So is his girlfriend, Julianne."

"What did Eryx do for them?"

"East won a writing contest for a short story and got a scholarship. Julianne got into modeling school."

"How does Eryx make these things happen? Why is getting people to pledge an oath such a big deal to him that he'd do so much?"

Brett shot her a sober look. "Do you believe in Hell?"

She stared ahead at the snow-covered road and halfway wished she hadn't asked. "Yeah, but it's not something I think a lot about."

"Eryx isn't exactly human, Sasha. His father is a dark angel who takes people to Hell after they die." He must have seen the look on her face, because he quickly added, "I know it sounds bizarre, and unbelievable, but I swear, it's true. Eryx wants to take Hell away from Lucifer and change things in the world."

She really wanted to think Brett was crazy, but after what had happened in San Francisco and the things Alex had said to her, she was terrified it might be true. "What would he change?"

"He'll make Hell more like Heaven. If people aren't scared of death, they'll be different. There won't be as many wars, or murders, or bad people in the world."

There was something flawed about the idea, but she couldn't wrap her head around it.

"The only way Eryx can take over Hell is if he has enough people following him. Think of it like a petition, where the more people who sign, the more weight it carries. If he has millions of followers, if a huge percentage of the world believed in him, he'd be all that matters, the only thing that counts. Hell as we know it would cease to exist, and Lucifer would become just another soul, unless he apologized to God and got back into Heaven."

Her mind was officially blown. Brett was passionate about this, and he didn't strike her as a guy who got all worked up about much, especially anything spiritual. "How do you know he is what he says he is? Maybe he's just a wack job."

"I thought the same thing, Sasha. Then I met him, and he's obviously not normal. He looks . . . different, and he can do things no ordinary human can do."

"Like what?"

"I can't tell you. It's one of the secret things about the Ravens, and we're sworn not to tell. If you'll come to a meeting, you can see for yourself."

"You mean Eryx will be there?"

"Maybe, but even if he isn't, Mr. Bruno can show you some stuff that'll make you think real hard about what you believe, and what it'll take to change things."

She'd never follow Eryx after seeing what his followers were capable of. People who would stone another person weren't interested in making the world better.

What if the Ravens in Telluride found out about her

birthmark? Did Mr. Bruno know about the Anabo thing? If he did, and if he knew about her birthmark, would he talk the group into killing her? It wasn't a risk she wanted to take.

"Will you come to a meeting and check it out?"

She knew he wouldn't stop pestering her if she stuck with no, so she opted for a noncommittal, "I'll think about it."

~~~

After promising he'd teach her to ski, Brett ditched her at the top of the lift when he spied some girl with long auburn hair. "Holy shit, that's Reilly O'Brien. Hey, Reilly, wait up!" He skied off, leaving Sasha to career down the tiny lift slope. She barely made it out of the way before the people behind skied off.

When she could stop, only by crashing into a snowbank, she saw Brett chasing Reilly, who was glancing over her shoulder at him like she was scared.

It took a while to extract herself from the snowbank, and she wobbled back toward the lift. The slope ahead looked more like a sheer drop than a ski run, and her stomach did a flip, just looking at it. No. Way. She'd have to beg the guy to let her back on the lift, to take her down to the base. Her humiliation would never end.

While she stood there, trying to work up the nerve to ask if she could ride back down, a guy came off the lift, alone, and skied right up to her. "Are you okay?" He had an accent, a little bit British.

"Fine. I'm fine."

"Are you sure? You look kinda lost." He grinned at her. "It's okay if you admit you got on the wrong lift. People do it all the time. The green runs are just over that way. This one is a black diamond, for experts. Have you ever skied before?"

"No, never." His voice was familiar. He was familiar. But she had no clue who this guy was, and she decided he must remind her of someone back in San Francisco.

His eyes were covered by mirrored wraparounds, and he wore a red ski cap that didn't quite cover his black hair. His face was so perfect, so beautiful, she couldn't stop staring.

"Let's head that way," he said, nodding to the north, "where there's an easier run, and I'll help you get down."

"I really appreciate it, but I don't want to hold you up. I'll just ask if they'll let me back on the lift."

He shook his head. "Most times, they won't." He skied away a few feet. "Come on, it'll be okay. I'll stay right with you."

It was almost as mortifying to follow this incredibly hot guy, clearly an expert skier, as it would have been to beg a ride on the lift. But he was waiting for her, smiling, being all nice about it.

When she was finally even with him, he nodded approval. "You can do this, no worries." He smiled. "I'm Ajax DeKyanos. Everyone calls me Jax."

"I'm Sasha Annenkova. It's nice to meet you." She smelled cinnamon, like hot-spiced tea, warm and wonderful. How could he smell this delicious? And how was it possible for one human being to be this good-looking?

She was startled to realize he was staring back at her, his smile gone. "Sasha," he said softly. "Beautiful."

Did he mean her name was beautiful? Or was he talking about her? "Ajax is an unusual name. And DeKyanos—is that Greek?"

He nodded. "But I'm not Greek. I'm a mutt, from all over."

"Do you live in Telluride, or are you here to ski?"

"I just moved here, to live with my dad until I graduate in May. I was at a boarding school in England, but they kicked me out when I mooned the queen."

England. No wonder he had a little bit of a British accent. She caught a slight twitch at the corner of his mouth. "Oh, go on."

He grinned then, showing perfect white teeth. "Okay, so I didn't, but the truth is so much more boring."

"Try me."

"I thought I should come home and hang with the old man before I head off to college. How about you? I'm guessing you didn't come to Telluride to ski."

"Good guess." They both laughed. "I'm staying with my aunt and uncle because my mom . . ." She didn't want to say why, so she lied. "My mom's out of the country for her job."

"So you'll be going to school in Telluride?"

"Right."

"Cool. Now I know at least one person." Pointing ahead with a ski pole, he said, "Come on, and I'll teach you how to ski. You'll get the hang of it in no time."

Yeah, and maybe later she could build a space shuttle. "Good luck with that."

"Hey, now, no being negative. You're built for skiing."

"I am?"

"Totally. You have two legs and two arms."

"Are you trying to be a smart-ass?"

There was that grin again. "Better than being a dumb-ass." He skied ahead and waited for her to catch up, pointing out where she screwed up, praising her when she got it right—which wasn't very often.

For a painful half hour, he coached her down a green run, and when they reached a small plateau, he held her arm and directed her into the forest edging the run, to a fallen tree. She took off her skis and sat down gratefully, watching him do the same.

"Now, then," he said with a wide smile, "that wasn't so bad, was it?"

"You're all kinds of awesome, but I'm not gonna lie—I'd rather sit for the SAT again than ski another inch."

"As bad as that?"

"How much farther to the bottom?"

"About the same as what we just did."

She was so toast. "Just curious, but if you didn't have me with you, how long would it take for you to ski from the top to the base?"

"This run?" He was cheeky. "Ten minutes. Maybe eight if it wasn't snowing."

She groaned. "I'm so sorry. And so embarrassed."

"It's okay, and don't be embarrassed on my account. Like I said, people get on the wrong lift all the time."

"I didn't, actually. I'm up here with my cousin, Brett. He said he'd teach me to ski, and took me on the lift with him, then ditched me as soon as we got off."

"Even though he knows you've never skied before?"

"He saw some pretty girl and instantly forgot me."

Jax leaned forward, elbows against his knees, and looked out at the run, at the skiers as they passed. "Here's the thing about skiing. You have to loosen up, take it easy, and relax. Look around at where you are, feel the mountain, the snow, and love the wind against your face. You'll fall, sure, but when it happens, roll with it. Don't fight it." He turned his head and gazed at her solemnly. "Think you can do that?"

"I'll try."

"Good." He pulled a small flask out of his pocket, unscrewed the lid, and took a swig before handing it to her.

"I can't drink. I tried it once, just a little bit, and spent the whole night driving the porcelain bus."

"It's not alcohol. Just some spiced cider."

No wonder he smelled so good. She took a drink and didn't want to give it back. Warmth spread through her like melted butter. She sipped again. "This is incredible."

"Drink the rest. It's nice, yeah?"

Her whole body was infused with warmth. "Are you sure this is just cider?"

"Real sure." He was cheeky again. "And maybe a little magic."

"Will it get me arrested?"

"Nope. Drink up, Sasha, and we'll have some fun on the way down."

She polished it off and handed him the flask. "Thanks, Jax." He was so nice, which was unexpected. Most guys who were built and hot were way too into themselves to have a clue anyone else was alive, but he didn't give off that vibe at all. He seemed almost humble, and just so . . . kind. The combination of his looks and his thoughtfulness was powerful, and she couldn't help being a little bit attracted.

Who was she kidding? She had to make herself stop staring at him. And how weird was that? He wasn't her type, at all.

Her last crush had been a thin, wiry blond guy with glasses: a band geek who played the clarinet and shared a lab table with her in chem 2. Tyler Hudson. No matter how much she tried to flirt with him, he never flirted back. They were great friends—and that's all they were.

Tyler was the kind of guy she was attracted to. She didn't go for big, muscular jocks.

Until now.

Standing, she put her skis back on and followed him out of the forest, concentrating very hard, determined to loosen up, like he said. Incredibly, she managed to ski at least a hundred feet before she fell. Remembering to roll with it, she was back up and on her way pretty quickly. It got easier and easier.

They were close to the bottom when he called, "You wanna ski another run?"

She couldn't believe it, but she said yes. *What* was in that cider?

～～

If Jax had ever had a better day, he couldn't remember. Sasha was beautiful, funny, and she never gave up. Watching her gain confidence, discover that she could ski like anybody else, that she didn't suck, and seeing the pure joy in her lovely blue eyes—it was perfect.

After the third run, she became very brave. Too brave. She took it into her head to ski off the main run, through a narrow loop in the trees that wound back to the main. He followed, freaking when he saw her get enough speed that she couldn't take a turn. She fell and tried to roll with it, but she crashed against a boulder at a weird angle, catching her leg in the twist of her skis. He heard the bone snap, knew she'd broken it even before she did.

With his heart in his throat, he nearly hit the boulder himself, he was so frantic to get to her. Hurrying out of his skis, he rushed to kneel next to her and yanked his gloves off so he could gently untangle her skis, poles, and legs.

She lay in the snow, her gold hair spilling all around her, blinking up at him, obviously scared and fighting back tears. "I think maybe you should go for the ski patrol."

"Maybe not." He concentrated carefully before he laid his

hands on her, just where her left fibula had snapped. Slowly, the bone knitted back together. When it was done, he looked into her face and saw exactly what he expected. Shock. Amazement. And fear.

"How did you do that?"

He'd have to erase the memory, as soon as possible. She'd forget the break and the healing, would think she'd simply fallen. She'd also forget seeing his eyes if he took off his shades.

Tossing them aside, he bent low, slid his hands into her silky hair, and kissed her. She tasted like caramel—salty and sweet.

It was several heartbeats before she kissed him back, and it dawned on him she was following his lead, mimicking him—just as she'd done all morning. She was as much a novice at kissing as she was at skiing. Seventeen, almost eighteen, and she'd never been kissed.

He hated himself for being such a sap, but there was something about being her first kiss . . . innocent, fantastic, beautiful.

Kissing her, being this close to an Anabo, he knew for the first time how it might feel to be at peace. It was intoxicating. Impossible to move away. It took tremendous willpower to break the kiss, but he allowed himself to stay close and stare into her incredible eyes, the color of the sky at dusk, dark blue, lit from within by the light of her soul. She stared back at him without flinching, without judging. Just like in San Francisco, she saw what was in his eyes and had no fear. Curious, maybe confused, but not afraid.

"Jax, who are you, really?"

They were inches apart. "Who do you think I am?"

"I . . . I don't know, but lots of things in my life are very strange right now, and I'm wondering if meeting you wasn't just lucky coincidence, like I thought at first."

"What if I told you I've been looking for a girl like you my whole life?"

"I'd think you're either really corny, or you know something about me that makes me . . . uhm, different than other girls."

He lowered his head until his lips were just next to her ear. "You're Anabo."

She stiffened and turned her head so they were nose to nose. "How do you know?"

"Knowing the Anabo is part of who I am."

"Do you . . . is there any reason you have something against Anabo?"

He understood, then. She was worried he might take her to Eryx, if knowing who she was made him an enemy. "Because of what I am, the only girls I can be with are Anabo. Finding you is huge for me."

She frowned a little. "So that's the only reason you're hanging out with me?"

"That's the reason I approached you. I'm hanging out with you because I want to."

They stayed like that, lying in the snow staring at each other, for a long time, until she whispered, "So Anabo is real?"

"Very real."

Sasha kissed him again. She liked him, he was sure of it. If he stuck to the plan, would she like him more tomorrow? And the day after? Would she eventually fall in love with him? Could he ever love her the way he was supposed to?

He let his thoughts run wild, pushing forward to the day she'd accept him, claim immortality, and become Mephisto.

Like him.

Tearing his mouth away from hers, he scrambled to his feet and stared down at her, his breath coming sharp and fast.

She struggled to sit and blinked up at him, clearly confused. "Jax, what's wrong?" Her gaze fell away, and she blushed. "It's because I'm terrible at kissing, isn't it?"

"No, Sasha, it was perfect." She was perfect, a child of light. One in a billion. That he'd found her was amazing. That she was meant for him was a miracle. But in all his years of wishing and hoping to find an Anabo, he never once considered what had to happen for him to keep her. She had to become Mephisto, so the very thing that allowed her to be with him, he'd have to change. When it was over, when she was Mephisto, she'd be like him, always dogged by the dark side. The peace she knew now would be gone. How could he do that to her?

And yet, how could he not? His dark soul recognized the light of hers, craved it like a drowning man yearns for air. Every instinct drove him toward one goal—to claim her, keep her, make her his, and ultimately turn her to Mephisto. But instinct didn't take into account emotion. He hadn't considered, even in his wildest imagination, that he'd have any hesitation.

Still, looking down at her lovely face, her wide, clear eyes, he couldn't deny he felt like a monster, set upon sullying the princess, dragging her down to live in the muck with him.

What the hell was wrong with him? He couldn't get all mushy and emotional about this. There was a lot more to her becoming Mephisto than just his own redemption. They needed her. More Mephisto meant fewer Skia and lost souls. She also had the ability to produce sons and daughters who would grow up to be Mephisto. If he couldn't pursue her for his own sake, he owed it to his brothers, to humanity, to follow through.

His elation completely gone, he grimly made himself set aside guilt and put on his shades, then he cleared her memory of the last ten minutes.

She blinked rapidly, her expression bewildered. Looking down, she touched her leg, then her lips before she turned her face up to look at him. "I just had the weirdest déjà vu. Like I forgot breaking my leg, and you healing it, but then I remembered." She shook her head as if to clear it. "You said, 'Forget all after you fell,' and I did, until I didn't."

He was short of breath, panicky and confused. Why hadn't she lost the memory? This had never happened before. "I . . . you . . ." How could she still remember? She didn't remember him from San Francisco, he was sure. If it had worked then, why didn't it work now?

"How did you do that, Jax?" She stared up at him with wide eyes. "*Why* did you?"

Great. They'd been together all of three hours, and already he'd screwed it up.

FOUR

SASHA WAS SERIOUSLY WIGGED OUT. JAX'S ABILITY TO HEAL her leg with just his hands made him extraordinary, but after he took off his shades, there was no doubt he wasn't like other humans. Looking into his ebony eyes made her think about sad and scary things. Then he kissed her and she was so caught up in it, she thought only about how much she liked him, how perfect it felt to kiss him back.

Evidently, he didn't feel the same way, and she was hurt and self-conscious. "Why did you try to mess with my head and make me forget? Was kissing me so awful, you wanted to erase my memory so I wouldn't expect you to do it again?"

His brows raised above his shades. "Is *that* what you think?"

If she weren't more wounded than confused, she wouldn't

have said it. "What else can I think? You freaked out, like you regretted it, like you wished you could take it back."

Stepping closer, he grasped her arms and pulled her to her feet, instantly warming her in the freezing snow. "If I regret anything, it's that you think I'm a freak."

"I know you're not like other people, but you're not a freak."

Dropping his hands, he stepped back. "I'm sorry, Sasha. I was hoping you and I . . . that we could maybe . . . look, I suck at this, okay? All I know for sure is that I like you and I won't try to make you forget anything again."

"Why should I believe you?"

He looked away from her, toward the ski run. "You probably shouldn't."

She waited to feel righteous . . . compelled to put on her skis, head down the mountain, and never look back. He was bad news, she was sure of it. Why, then, did she stay right here, staring at him and thinking he was absolutely irresistible? Why did her mind keep replaying lying in the snow, his warm body against hers? Maybe because it had been her first kiss. Watching him turn to look at her again, she wondered if it really had been as amazing as she remembered.

Only one way to find out. Closing the distance between them, she bent her neck to look up at him. "Will you kiss me again?"

"If you'll let me."

She reached up, slid his shades from his face, and dropped them to the snowy ground.

He rested his hands against her shoulders and looked as though he was at war with himself before he pulled her toward him, bending his head until his mouth was close to hers. "Remember, you asked," he whispered, right before he settled his lips against hers.

Just like before, his taste was the same as his scent—sweet, tart, and spicy, like mulled wine, spiced cider, hot tea—everything warm and wonderful.

But this kiss wasn't like the first. Not sweet. Not gentle.

Maybe he wasn't the boy next door, maybe he wasn't even a real boy, but holy smokes, did he know how to kiss. This wasn't his first rodeo. His hands slid into her hair to hold her head, angling her so he could deepen the kiss. His lips were so warm—almost hot. She stepped into him, her arms sliding beneath his jacket, around his back to cling to his red sweater.

"I never knew kissing could be this incredible," she murmured against his mouth. The first one was perfect, but there'd been no open mouths; he'd not been so close that she could feel his chest rise and fall against her.

"It's you, Sasha. You're incredible."

Her body took on a will of its own, pushing against him, aligning with his, trembling. Beneath her palms, the muscles in his back stretched and moved when he lowered his hands from her head and wrapped her up in his arms. He broke the kiss and pressed her head to his shoulder, resting his cheek against her hair. "I don't know why you asked, but I'm glad you did."

She sighed, standing there next to him, inhaling his scent, and admitted she'd hoped it wouldn't be good, that kissing him wouldn't be amazing, that she had thought so only because it had been her first time.

Instead, she didn't want this to end. "Tell me who you are, Jax."

"Are you afraid?"

He had the strangest eyes she'd ever seen, he could heal with the touch of his hands, and he could make people forget things, but not once since she'd met him at the top of the lift did she feel afraid. The opposite really. Being with him the past few hours had made her feel everything in her life wasn't so depressing.

"You're not answering. Does that mean you *are* afraid?"

"No. Should I be?"

He kissed the crown of her head. "Never, Sasha. Never, ever be afraid of me."

"Has this ever happened before? Someone not forgetting?"

"You're the first. But really, honestly, it isn't something I do very often. I fixed your leg so you wouldn't have to start school in a cast. I kissed you because I wanted to, and I took off my shades so I could see your eyes better. I don't know why I couldn't make you forget, but I swear I'll never try it again."

She wanted to believe him. "I should let go of you and walk away."

His lips traveled across her face, kissing her forehead, her nose, her temples. "Yes, you should."

She didn't.

They stood together, arms wrapped tightly, listening to the wind through the pines while snow fell softly all around. This was one of those moments in life she knew she'd never forget.

He moved his head so that his lips were close to her ear. "Run, Sasha. If you can do it, run like hell and don't look back."

Her breath came in short little gasps. "I don't want to run."

He kissed her again, holding her so closely, her heels lifted from the ground. She felt his desperation, knew that whatever was happening wasn't a simple guy and girl thing. It scared her, but she felt so alive and in the moment, she was hyperaware of everything around her—a bird calling from overhead, the soft crunch of snow at their feet, the way his body moved beneath her palms, the taste of his mouth, even the warmth of his breath.

When he lifted his head and looked down into her eyes, she nearly drowned in the emotions rolling over her. His eyes made her feel like she was someone else, as if she knew things it was impossible for her to know.

"You didn't run. Does that mean you're going to give me a chance?"

"If I do, will you tell me who you are? Why your eyes are so different?"

"I'll tell you." He released her and stepped back. "Just give me a week and I'll tell you what you want to know."

Part of her wanted to know right this minute. Another part didn't want to know ever. But she nodded anyway and said,

"Will you tell me how you know about the Anabo thing?"

He bent to pick up his shades and slid them back onto his face. "I'll tell you everything."

While they stood there staring at each other, a terrifying scream carried across the mountains in an echo, startling her. "That sounded like . . . someone falling."

His expression grim, Jax nodded toward the run. "Let's go."

Ten minutes later, when they reached the base, she saw a crowd gathered close to the cluster of buildings that made up Mountain Village. Skiing to the edge of the group, Sasha asked a woman if she knew what happened.

"Someone went off Devil's Ridge. The ski patrol just radioed that she broke her neck."

A tremor of premonition slid down her back. "Who was it?"

"A senior at Telluride High. Reilly O'Brien. So sweet, such a great kid. It's awful."

Sasha heard a familiar voice and turned just as Brett and East skied to a spot several yards away. They were grinning, and she stiffened when they knuckle bumped.

"What's wrong?" Jax asked from just behind her. "Did you know Reilly?"

Turning around, she leaned close and whispered, "No, but she's the reason my cousin ditched me up there. He skied after her, and she was looking over her shoulder at him like she was afraid. Now look at him. He's smiling."

"Are you saying you think he had something to do with her accident?"

Sasha looked up at his mirrored shades, at her distorted reflection. "Would you think I was crazy if I said yes?"

⁓

Jax took her to a nearby restaurant, and they were eating dessert before he finally coaxed everything out of her. She told him about her mom being deported, about the Ravens and Alex Kasamov, about meeting Mr. Bruno, and about what Brett had said to her on the way up the mountain that morning. The idea of her sitting down to dinner with a Skia scared the hell out of him, but he kept calm. She trusted him, and he needed to protect that, but he also needed to protect her. He would tell her as much as possible without revealing anything that might scare her off.

He decided to start with Anabo. "So what you're wondering is if Brett thought Reilly was Anabo, and if that's why he maybe pushed her over the edge."

"I know it sounds ridiculous, but he believes this Eryx guy is where it's at. He said he gets credits if he gets people to join, so maybe he thought he'd get credit if he killed somebody he thought was Anabo."

"Why would he think that about Reilly?"

"I don't know. Maybe she was scared to death of Mr. Bruno, like I was afraid of Alex Kasamov. Alex said that was why he suspected about me."

Jax knew Reilly wasn't Anabo. He'd seen her around town. So had his brothers. She was gorgeous, and if she was Anabo, they'd have known.

"Or, maybe Brett hit on her," he suggested, "and she blew

him off and he was pissed enough to kill her. Maybe he didn't mean to shove her off. Maybe he didn't do it at all."

"You're right. I'm jumping to conclusions, I guess, because I'm still so freaked out about what happened in San Francisco." She dropped her gaze to the table, a world away. "It doesn't seem real. I don't know how they could hate me enough to want to kill me."

Jax was still worried about his inability to clear her memory, mystified that it had worked before but not today. "You say you passed out and when you woke up, it was early morning and they were gone. If they meant to kill you, why didn't they?"

"I think they must have thought I was dead."

"And no one checked to make sure?"

"It seems stupid, now that I think about it. If you're going to kill somebody, then leave her alive, she's an eyewitness, right? Why weren't they worried about me going to the cops?"

"Maybe because it would be your word against theirs. You said you had no wounds, no bruises."

Her expression became more confused. "I don't get that, Jax. I didn't dream it, wasn't hallucinating or anything, because when I woke up, there was blood all over the floor, and those rocks . . ." Her eyes widened. "I did dream about it last night, but it was weird, like dreams usually are. All the Ravens froze in place, and this guy showed up, out of nowhere. He stabbed Alex, then he heal—" She stopped and stared at him, seconds ticking by before she finished. "He healed me."

Jax took another bite of cheesecake, pretending not to notice her pause, or the way she was looking at him. "What did the guy in the dream look like?"

"I don't know. His face was blurry, and his voice was muffled. He was dressed all in black."

It was there, the memory of him that night, waiting to surge to the forefront of her mind. For whatever reason, maybe because she was Anabo, her memory couldn't be erased like other humans'.

He had no way of knowing when she'd remember, but until then, he'd stick to the plan of telling her everything in a week. He didn't know if he could make her fall in love with him if he had a year, but all he had was one week. Unless she remembered sooner. Then all bets were off. Courting Sasha would be difficult, the hardest thing he'd ever done, but it'd be a million times harder if she knew what he wanted from her. "What else did Brett tell you about Eryx?"

"He wants people to pledge their souls to him, because when he has the majority of humans following him, he can take over Hell. Ordinarily, I'd think Brett's a lunatic, but after what happened in San Francisco, and now, meeting you . . . with your eyes . . ." She tilted her head and studied him, the wheels in her mind turning so fast he could almost see sparks.

Before she could ask if he had been in that old warehouse, if he had saved her and healed her, he set down his fork and said, "Just for the sake of argument, suppose Eryx isn't a nut job.

The girl who took you to the meeting said people who join the Ravens give up God and pledge to follow Eryx. If he's not about God, he'd see anything that is about God as a threat, and Anabo is as close to God as a human can be."

She looked across the table at him, curiosity all over her beautiful face. "You know the truth, don't you, Jax?"

He kicked himself again for taking off his shades before he kissed her. "I don't know the truth about your cousin, if that's what you mean."

"You know that's not what I meant. Just tell me, is Eryx who Brett thinks he is? Is any of this real?"

"What if it is? What would it change? If you find out Eryx really is an immortal who collects souls, if he already has your cousin's and your aunt's, what can you do to change it?"

Her expression was stunned. "Oh, my God," she whispered, "it *is* true."

"I didn't say that. I said *if* it were true, there's nothing you can do about it."

"I could keep other people from pledging. Mr. Bruno was nagging my other cousin, Chris, to go to the meeting last night."

"If you knew for sure, and told people, hoping to keep them from going through with taking the oath, they wouldn't believe you. They'd think *you* were the nut job."

"Maybe you're right, and maybe I can't change anything at all, but if I knew the truth, I'd understand why the Ravens tried to kill me."

Sitting back in his chair, he glanced around the busy restaurant, watched waitresses scurry back and forth between the tables and the kitchen, saw a family laughing while they ate spaghetti, noticed a young couple holding hands across the table. Everything was all so normal. This was Sasha's world, what she understood. It seemed the greatest sin to drag her into his world, to show her what existed on the other side.

He turned his attention back to her, studied her lovely eyes, her anxious expression, the way she tugged at her bottom lip with her teeth. He wished he had what it took to get up and leave and never see her again, to let her live a normal life.

But he didn't have what it took to leave her alone. He couldn't even stop staring at her. He wanted her, and the first step to having her was raising the curtain, bit by bit, giving her glimpses of the world she'd live in if she became Mephisto.

With a deep, heavy sigh, he ripped away the first layer of her innocence. "Yes, Sasha, it's all true."

~~~

Deep down, she'd known, but she wanted it to be a lie: the Ravens, a cult begun by a Satan worshipper with an ego as big as the universe; the Anabo, only the wayward imaginings of some crazy Italian guy, back in the day. "How do you know, Jax?"

"I thought you were going to give me a week."

"You could tell me how you know without telling me who you are."

He tossed a few bills to the table and stood, holding out his hand for hers. "Let's get on a lift." They walked out into the cold and snow and put on their skis. There was a line at the lift, so they waited, and as they moved forward, he looked down at her. "What do you like to do?"

"I love art. I like to go to museums. Sometimes I sketch what I see."

"Do you want to be an artist?"

"I'm not good enough, and not really. I'd like to learn how to restore and clean paintings, maybe work in a museum."

"So you plan to go to college?"

"Yes, but now, with Mom in Russia, I have no idea where I'll go. Maybe I'll look at schools in Europe." She wished she were a better artist. She'd sketch him and maybe capture the perfection of his face. "What do you like to do?"

"I read a lot of history books, biographies and stuff. I love to play basketball." He smiled. "And ski."

Finally, they were up, and as soon as the chair took off, he leaned close and said, almost in a whisper, "Do you believe in God?"

"Of course I do. Why would you—"

"So you believe in Heaven."

"Absolutely."

"Then you must believe in Hell, and Lucifer."

She nodded.

"It's pretty simple, how it works. People are born, and their whole life, they try to do the right thing, to be good, to resist the temptation of evil. They're angry and jealous and spiteful and vain and all those things, but they try hard not to be. When they die, they're measured up and they either go to Heaven, or to Hell. Right?"

"It's what I was taught, what I believe, but no one can know for sure."

"Okay, well, what if the rules changed? What if people knew they were doomed to Hell, that the end of life would be the beginning of eternal misery? Without any chance of Heaven, who'd try? It'd be a free-for-all, and the world would be a dark and horrible place."

"That'd never happen. God wouldn't let it."

"He said he'd never again interfere with the world, with mankind's free will. Lucifer tempts humanity, but he also doesn't get in the way of free will. It's up to each person to make his or her choices and accept the consequences. Eryx wants to change all that. He wants to grow powerful enough to take out Lucifer so he can be in charge of Hell. If he ever succeeds, mankind won't have a prayer."

"Brett said he wants to change Hell to be more like Heaven, so people won't be afraid of dying and going to Hell. He says it will make the world a better place."

Jax frowned and shook his head. "It's a lie they tell people they want to recruit. Eryx isn't about changing things for the better. He's worse than Lucifer, who began as an angel but whose pride got him kicked out of Heaven. He still has a slice of light in his soul, has some dim hope of redemption. Eryx has none. He's without the smallest bit of compassion. God could get rid of him, because nothing and no one is more powerful than God, but he won't interfere. The world is what it is, and Eryx's existence is one part of it."

"Who is Eryx? Where did he come from?"

He reached up to pull a strand of hair away from her mouth. "His father is the dark angel whose job is to take souls to Hell. A thousand years ago, Mephistopheles fell for an Anabo named Elektra, which was not cool because they're like living angels, and he's a guy who works for Lucifer. To keep God and Lucifer from knowing, Mephistopheles took Elektra to a small island in the north Atlantic, which he hid behind a fine blue mist. In Greek, the word for blue is *kyanos*, so that's what he named the island: Kyanos. Elektra had seven sons, and the oldest was Eryx."

"Eryx has *brothers*?"

Jax nodded, looking at her from behind those mirrored shades. She wished he'd take them off. Even though his eyes were strange, it bugged her not to see his expression.

"As Eryx grew older, he became obsessed with jumping off the cliffs of Kyanos, even though he knew it would kill him. Mephistopheles told his sons they were destined for immortality, and when they were grown, instinct would compel them to die."

"Why would it be anyone's instinct to kill themselves?"

"They had to die to become immortal. Since their Anabo mother was mortal, Eryx was afraid the part of her that was in them would die forever, and in immortality, they would be all darkness, with no light in their souls. He prayed for help, but God and Lucifer didn't know they existed. He asked his father to come clean with Lucifer, but Mephistopheles told Eryx not to worry, that he would come back just the same. Eryx didn't believe it."

As the lift took them higher up the mountain, it began to snow, and she watched each perfect flake that hit his shades, there for a nanosecond before it melted.

"He became more certain as he grew older that he and his brothers would become immortal monsters, so the day he turned eighteen, when he couldn't fight the instinct to die any longer, he killed Elektra. Her death was the only thing that would make God and Lucifer aware of his brothers, and he hoped sacrificing her would save them."

"He killed his own mother?"

"Yes. Then he jumped, and just as he had feared, he came back as an immortal without compassion, with no conscience. His brothers hated him for what he'd done, even after he told them why, but he didn't care. He left Kyanos and found other people. He was charismatic and discovered people would follow him, would do what he told them, hoping for his favor. They pledged their lives to him, and when he asked for their souls, they willingly said yes."

"What happened to his brothers?"

"Just like Eryx, they were compelled to jump to their deaths, but because God was aware of them, he blessed each of the others before they died, so when they came back, they weren't like Eryx."

"Where are they now?"

"They were charged by Lucifer to fight Eryx, to keep him from becoming powerful enough to take over as the gatekeeper of Hell. If he did, he wouldn't care about free will. He'd snatch every soul as it leaves its host."

Sasha looked down at the trees, dusted with snow, at boulders and crags and outcroppings where trees couldn't grow. It was so quiet, noises muffled by the snow, the voices of skiers ahead and behind them muted and distant. All she could hear with any clarity was the constant hum of the lift cable. And Jax's low, deep voice, telling her things she didn't want to believe. "You realize this all sounds like BS?"

"I wish it was." He looked ahead. "But it's all true, Sasha. Eryx exists. He tricks humans into pledging their souls to him, and when they die, he takes their spirit and absorbs it into his own, which makes him stronger."

"If he's been doing this for a thousand years, he must have collected millions. How many is enough?"

"When the scales tip in his favor, when more of humanity belongs to him than to God, he'll be strong enough to take on Lucifer. But he doesn't have millions. Nowhere close. He can't take a soul if something blocks it, so Lucifer carved out a pit, deep underground, then surrounded it with the darkness of Hell.

When one of Eryx's lost souls is thrown into the pit, he dies, but his spirit can't escape. So yes, Eryx has collected millions of followers in a thousand years, but a lot of those people are decaying inside the Earth, their spirits blocked."

This was like a show on the SciFi Channel. Or a horror movie. She thought of zombies and ghouls and ghosts. But she was a logical person, and the physical parameters didn't make sense. "If the pit is deep underground, how do his followers get in there?"

"The entrance is hidden on the other side of the world, in a place no one ever goes. Beneath a certain spot is a long chute that leads to the pit. It's called Hell on Earth. It's said no one ever lands and lives. The fall kills them."

"Who says that? Who takes them there?"

With his face turned away from her, he looked down at the mountain as they moved above it.

"Jax?"

Slowly, almost hesitantly, he raised his head, turned toward her, and carefully slid the shades from his face. "I do."

Holy God. She almost couldn't breathe, she was so stunned. "*You're* one of his brothers?"

Slowly, he nodded.

Blinking back tears, she sat there in the lift chair and connected the dots. "It was you in that warehouse, wasn't it? You came to take the Ravens to Hell on Earth, and there I was, half dead. Before you took them, you healed me. That's why I had no wounds or bruises when I woke up. You stabbed Alex to keep him from taking me to Eryx. He wasn't a jumper. You took him, didn't you?"

He didn't nod, didn't answer. Just stared at her with his weird eyes.

"You work for Lucifer. You're a dark angel."

Still, he didn't say anything.

"Did you come to the ski runs today to take Brett?"

"I came to find you."

"Why?"

"I went back to San Francisco to see you, to make sure you were all right. I found out you moved here."

She sucked in a deep breath and looked ahead again. The top was close. They'd be there within five minutes. "No wonder your eyes are different."

He said nothing. She had suspected he was different, but hearing it out loud wasn't the same as wondering. Not only was she insanely attracted to him, she liked him . . . but knowing he was something from Hell, that he killed people, even if those people were lost and evil, made her skin crawl. Did he go home from a hard day's work killing people and hang out in Hell?

She moved a little, pressing closer to the edge of the chair. It wasn't that she was afraid. She wasn't. But he'd gone from being a guy she wanted to know a lot better to a stranger she'd like never to see again. "What happened with the Ravens? How did they wind up in San Francisco Bay, instead of Hell on Earth?"

"The bodies in the bay were doppelgängers. Mephistopheles provides bodies that are exact copies of the people we take to Hell on Earth. If all those people disappeared without a trace, people would panic."

"Were your brothers with you that night?"

He nodded while he pulled his gloves on and readied his poles for the ramp. "We planned that takedown for over a week. You being there wasn't in the plan. I didn't know what to do about you. I couldn't take you with me, but I couldn't leave you there to bleed to death. I healed you and put you to sleep, and we left."

"But not before you erased my memory of you."

"I had no choice. We're not supposed to interact with humans unless it's necessary to our job, and if we do, we're supposed to erase their memory of us."

"Then why are we here, interacting? You know I'll remember you."

A muscle worked in his jaw, so she knew he was clenching his teeth. Had she made him mad? "It's not like you'll tell anybody. No one would believe you."

"Why could you erase my memory of you then but not today?"

"I don't know. It's never happened before with anyone else."

"Aren't I the lucky one?"

His sigh sounded sad. "Just forget it, Sasha. This is hopeless. I see that now."

"What's hopeless?"

"You and me. I thought . . . I wanted to . . . you're beautiful, incredible, and you're Anabo. Regular people are afraid of me, but you're not like ordinary people. Your soul is pure, without original sin."

"I'm not without sin. I'm just like everyone else."

He shook his head. "There's nothing about you that's like others, Sasha. You don't realize what lies within other people, so you can't know how different they are."

"If I'm Anabo, does that mean my parents—"

"No, it doesn't work that way. What Aurora was can't be quantified like DNA—something that determines if you have blue eyes or blond hair. It's a spiritual thing, something unique to a person's soul. The Anabo are rare, but all could be traced back to Aurora."

"How do you know I'm Anabo? Did you see my birthmark?"

"I didn't need to. It's in your face, your eyes. To me, you have a certain glow, almost an aura, around you."

She remembered Mercy Jones said her aura was pure and beautiful, with the light of divinity—the most perfect she'd ever seen. Mercy said she was destined for an extraordinary life, one that would make a difference. Sasha had thought she was a wack job. Now, she wasn't so sure. "Give me an example of how I'm any different from anyone else."

He was thoughtful for a minute, then said, "You're not mad at your mother for not giving Alex's boss what he wants.

You're bummed about it, sure, but not angry. You're stuck living with strangers—a woman who hates you and a guy with no conscience—making you vulnerable to all kinds of bad consequences. Anyone else would be mad as hell, but all you think about is where your mother is, if she's safe, if she's going to be okay."

Slumping back in the chair, she stared down at her ski tips. "She said the information could cause problems bad enough to start a war."

"And you bought it without question. You trust her completely, because it's not in you to distrust anyone you love. It never dawned on you that the information is worth a lot of money, that maybe she'd rather sell it than just hand it over."

"She's never been the same since Dad was murdered. If I got mad at her, what purpose would it serve except to make her feel worse?"

"Thanks for making my point. With you, it's always about the other guy. You think everyone else is like that, Sasha, but they're not. Trust me."

"There are millions of compassionate people in the world."

"Sure there are, but even the kindest people have a dark side, a part of their soul that tempts them toward evil. They have to make a choice to resist it. You don't, because it's just not there. It's why you're not afraid of me, because I'm no threat to your peace of mind. You have no idea how appealing that is."

"So you came to find me because I'm Anabo."

"I came to find you because I wanted to know you, because I hoped we'd become friends. I've never . . . I don't have any friends."

"But you've been with a girl before."

He jerked his head around to look at her. "How would you know?"

"Because you knew exactly what you were doing when you kissed me."

"Oh." He relaxed and turned away again. "They weren't friends. Just shadowy faces in dark places."

"Hookups? Is that what you're about, Jax?"

He tapped his pole against his ski, clearly upset. "Maybe I'm not a regular guy, maybe you think I'm repulsive, and hell, I guess I am, but I've never felt like this. I'm alone, all the time. I just thought that maybe, for a little while, I could be with you, and it'd be okay. But like I said, I see now it's never going to work. When we get off in a minute, I'm going to ski the black run and go home. I won't bother you again."

He sounded so sincere, so dejected, she almost asked him to stay, but she couldn't get past what he was, what he did. This wasn't for her, no matter how hot and nice he was, no matter how great he was at kissing. She wanted to be like everyone else and go out with a normal guy, one who didn't know anything about Anabo, or Eryx. Besides, where could this lead? He wasn't human. She was great with embracing cultural differences, but hanging out with a guy from Hell? Yeah, not a good idea. So she didn't ask him to stay, or say she still wanted to give them a chance. Instead, she asked, "Where is home?"

He pointed to the west with his pole. "About ten miles that way."

"You live *here*?"

"Ironic, isn't it? You moved where I live the day after we met."

"I thought you must live . . . I assumed because of where you're from, that you live there."

"No, I live in the real world, in a real house. I eat and sleep and take showers and watch TV and play basketball. I need . . . want all the same things any normal guy wants. I'm bound to Earth until the end of time, or until we have what we need to kill Eryx."

"What's that?"

Turning to look at her, he said softly, "Redemption."

"If God blessed you before you became immortal—"

"It kept my brothers and me from becoming like Eryx, but we're still sons of Hell, Sasha. We can't stand on holy ground. If we pray to God, he doesn't hear us. When the end of the world comes, we're all bound for Hell, unless we've been redeemed."

The idea of praying and not being heard was so awful, so sad, she teared up again. "I can't believe someone like you could be ignored by God."

"You don't know me, don't know what I'm capable of or what goes on in my head."

"I know you're kind."

"Only to you, Sasha. It's so hard to keep myself from being sucked under by the dark side. All that keeps me focused is fighting Eryx. If all of us were redeemed, if we had the same chance of Heaven as anyone else, if God could hear us, we could finally take Eryx out, and the war would be over."

"Because you'd have God helping you?"

"Because we'd only be fighting Eryx." He looked away from her. "As hard as we try to keep up, even though there are six of us and only one of him, we lose ground every day because of who we are. We have to fight ourselves as much as we fight him. He has no fight. He's completely focused on his purpose."

Sasha wished with all her heart she could help him, but this was all way bigger than her. The hopelessness in him was so sad, she teetered between staying away from him and wanting to know him better.

Maybe that's why, when he turned and bent his head to kiss her, she didn't pull away.

It was bittersweet, kissing him now, but no less amazing.

Then, in the middle of the kiss, Jax disappeared, and she was alone.

FIVE

AS SOON AS JAX WAS BACK ON THE MEPHISTO MOUNTAIN he changed into sweats and headed for the old stone dairy that was now a gym. He pounded up and down the basketball court, dribbling a ball, dunking it over and over, working himself into a sweat, trying the only way he knew to forget her.

An hour into it, he was still thinking of Sasha, still pissed that he had told her so much. His careful plan, the one where he would go slow, let her know a little at a time, was history, and he went over every second he'd been with her, trying to find where it had all gone so wrong.

Somewhere between half-court and the basket, it hit him—his failure to erase her memory was the sticking point. She had watched him heal her leg, then saw his eyes, and her ability to remember all of it sent everything south. Her questions had to be answered, and he couldn't make himself lie to her. Weird for him, because he lied without a second thought, but he was looking ahead to the time when he'd need to tell her everything, and she'd never trust him if she realized he'd lied all along.

Why couldn't he make her forget? What was different today than before, in that old warehouse?

He went to the intercom at the back of the gym and hit the code for Phoenix's room. "Are you there?"

His brother answered immediately. "What's up?"

"Come play horse with me."

"I hate basketball."

"Heathen. Get your ass out here and talk to me."

Phoenix didn't respond, but a second later, he appeared, barefoot, wearing only a pair of jeans. "Make-it-take-it or one-on-one, but no horse. You always do a reverse layup, and I'm screwed."

"Make-it-take-it." Jax shot the ball at him and like Phoenix always did, shot from center court, and made it.

Jax retrieved the ball before it hit the floor and shot it back to his brother. "Aren't you going to ask?"

"No point. You look like hell, so it obviously didn't go well." He missed his next shot, and Jax dribbled it back to half-court. Phoenix was all over him, but he still managed to get a shot off. He missed. His brother took the ball, and no matter how closely Jax guarded him, he still made his shot.

"It's the worst of your sins, hating basketball when you're so damn good at it."

"Jealous?" Phoenix sank another one.

"If I could kill you, I would."

They played without talking for a while, until anger and frustration took their toll. Jax lost focus, and the ball.

Phoenix didn't go after it. He stared at Jax. "You better tell me what happened."

Breathing hard, fingers splayed across his hips, Jax did, then ended by saying, "I couldn't make her forget and that screwed everything."

Phoenix turned and went for the ball, brought it back, and began twirling it on one finger. "How many times did you kiss her?"

"What the hell difference does it make?"

"It's the spit, bro. If an Anabo drinks after you, kisses you, shares your saliva, it's in her bloodstream, and her body goes on notice that it needs to change. She's going to be hungry all the time, get stronger every day, gain powers like the ability to see Purgs, resist your memory blocks, and recognize Skia. She's also going to be more like you."

"She'll lose Anabo?" That was his worst nightmare, what had freaked him out on the slopes. Now, Phoenix was telling him he'd already caused it to happen.

Without losing his command of the twirling basketball, Phoenix looked at him and lifted one dark eyebrow. "She'll never completely lose Anabo. If she becomes Mephisto, she'll be both. She'll have incredible mental and physical strength; she'll despise the Skia and lost souls even more than we do; she'll be more prone to anger and less forgiving than she is now, but she still won't know what it is to be tempted. Everything she does will be focused on taking out Eryx."

"How do you know all this?"

Phoenix looked at the ball. "After I found Jane, I asked M, and he asked Lucifer." He looked at Jax again. "You don't have a clue how this works, do you?"

"How the hell could I, Phoenix? You never told us anything about what happened with Jane." His brother flinched and dropped the ball. They both watched it roll toward the double wooden doors of the dairy.

"It doesn't happen in one moment," Phoenix said quietly. "She doesn't remain pure Anabo until she becomes immortal, accepts your ritual, and bam, she's Mephisto. It's already happening. By the time she jumps to immortality, almost all that's left is to mark her, if she isn't marked already, and exchange ritual to make it permanent."

"You're lying. You have to be lying. Otherwise, she has no choice, and how can she make a decision if she doesn't even know about Mephisto? What about free will?"

"I assume she kissed you back?"

"Only a lot."

"She knew who you are when she saw your eyes. Maybe not in words, but she knew, and kissed you anyway, of her own free will."

"But later she didn't want to touch me. She thinks I'm disgusting."

"Her mind thinks you're disgusting. How she was raised, what she knows, her whole worldview forces her to think you're repulsive. But her soul doesn't think so. It'll just take some time for her soul and mind to come to terms. In the meantime, she's going to change, whether she realizes what's happening to her or not. If you don't kiss her again, the process will go a lot slower, but it's way too late to keep it from happening."

She drank after him, the cider in his flask, all of it, and they didn't just kiss—they stood there in the snow and gave each other mouth-to-mouth for at least twenty minutes. He'd never been kissed like that. He'd never loved it that much. "You didn't say anything about spit. You said not to sleep with her so she wouldn't be marked."

"If sex can mark her so we can find her *anywhere in the world*, doesn't it follow that your spit is bound to do something to her?"

Dammit. If he repulsed her before, she was gonna hate his guts now. "Is it permanent?"

"It is unless M can convince Lucifer to reverse it, and you can guess the odds of that happening. He wants her to be Mephisto more than you do."

"I doubt that." This was blowing his mind. "What if she really does hate me? What then?"

"If she decides to remain human, she can walk away, Lucifer will return her to what she was before you kissed her, to pure

Anabo, and she won't remember you or anything she learned about Eryx and the lost souls. Lucifer will be furious with you for failing, but it's not like he can do anything about it. Women don't always do what you want, even if you're Lord of the Underworld."

Jax headed for the weight room, housed in what used to be the creamery.

"Where are you going?"

"I've got to come up with a new plan. Right now, she can't stand the sight of me."

Phoenix fell into step beside him. "She must like you a little, or she wouldn't have kissed you."

"I kiss girls all the time, and it's not because I like them."

"Yeah, but you're a guy. It's different for girls. They don't kiss guys as a prelude to sex."

"It's not like I kissed Sasha for sex."

"Right. Same goes for her. She's freaking on everything you told her, Jax, but let her get used to it for a few days, and she'll be more open to seeing you again."

Sighing heavily, Jax ran a hand through his hair and stopped before he made it to the weight room. "I just can't figure out why I told her so much, Phoenix. It was like I started yapping and couldn't shut up."

Phoenix shook his head. "Don't go there, Jax. What's done is done, and trust me on this—you're not done doing it wrong. We're immortal sons of Hell, but at the end of the day, we're just like every guy out there. We can control every move we make in basketball, but get us around a girl we want, and all bets are off."

"We're doomed to screw it up?"

"Yeah, pretty much."

❧

Two hours into upping his bench press weights until he was shaking with effort, Jax was wrung out and exhausted, but no closer to a plan. He had no clue how he could approach Sasha again. He told her he'd leave her alone, which he realized now had been hasty and stupid, but it was way too late to take it back.

He showered and dressed, then got on the Internet, looking for anything that might help him. He felt superlame, but he searched on google for "romance," "how-to," and "what girls like."

In the middle of an article about matching flowers to a girl's zodiac sign, which he found as unhelpful as the article about how to make the most of meeting a girl's dog or cat, someone knocked and he was glad for the interruption.

Key came in, looking serious like always. Jax quickly closed his laptop and watched his brother take a seat next to the fire. "What's up?"

"I came to ask how it went today."

"You can crow all you want, because I screwed it up, just like you said I would."

Settling back in the chair, Key rested his elbows against the armrests and steepled his fingers. Jax hated when he did that. It made him look so pretentious, as if what he was about to say was of great importance. It didn't matter that this was usually the case. It still bugged the hell out of him. "Say whatever it is you have to say, then leave me alone."

Key stared into the fire. "Phoenix's plan for Sasha's cousin, the Easter kid, his girlfriend, and any other young ones who pledge between now and the takedown is to stage an accident on that old mine road between Telluride and Ouray. He says we'll wait for a heavy snow, they'll go up there to party, get drunk, go off the road, try to hike back to town, become lost in the snow-storm, and freeze to death."

"I wish it could be sooner, like tonight. What about Bruno and Sasha's aunt?"

"Melanie Shriver will freeze to death while she's searching for Brett." Key raised his gaze to Jax's. "As for Bruno, Xenos has had a Lumina tailing him since last night to get a line on his hab-its, find a way to stage his death that'll be logical and not subject to speculation."

Jax waited. "And?"

"It's easy enough. Zee says he's a closet smoker and eats garbage. If he wasn't Skia and immortal, he'd be a heart attack waiting to happen, so we're going to give him one."

It sounded like a decent plan. A simple one. Capturing him might be a little tricky, but he lived alone, so a surprise attack would work.

Why, then, did Key look so serious? So worried? "I'm wait-ing to hear the downside."

Key leaned forward again. "M says Bruno's been Skia almost

two hundred years—the oldest we've ever found. I was curious to know more about him, so I had Zee check him out. He and Brody hacked into his computer last night and found hundreds of photographs and all sorts of documents, like letters and memos, credit card statements, and pages from personal journals. All of it's incriminating, and every bit belongs to people in the government. It's huge, Jax. Congressmen, senators, even a Supreme Court justice."

He thought of the lockbox in Geneva, with all kinds of incriminating information about important people all over the world. Alex said his boss wanted it, but Jax realized now, he didn't mean his boss in Moscow. He meant Eryx. "Not all of them will take the oath to avoid exposure."

"No, but some will. Can you imagine what would happen if people with power and influence, who actually run the United States, lost their souls to Eryx?"

It was depressing and disheartening, but cleaning up the government would have to wait. "Let's concentrate on Washington after Bruno and the others are gone. As long as they're around, we run the risk of their finding out Sasha is Anabo."

"Why leave her in unnecessary danger? Bring her for a visit and don't take her back."

"Great idea, Key, except she can't stand the sight of me."

"Did you tell her?"

"Not everything, but just the part she knows was enough to scare her off."

"Maybe later she'll feel differently."

"It's a big maybe." Nice girls, even if they were Anabo, didn't go out with sons of Hell. "The forecast calls for lots of snow next week. Let's get this done so Sasha can move on and not worry about Brett and Melanie, or Mr. Bruno."

"We can't," Key said, his expression grim. "Not yet."

Cold dread settled in his gut. "Why?"

Key stood and went to the fire, stoking it with the poker. "Zee found some notes Bruno made about a Skia meeting. He couldn't find anything about a date, or a location, but sometime soon there'll be a large group of Skia, all in one place. It's a perfect opportunity for a huge takedown, something we can do in less than a day that would otherwise take months." He set the poker back in its stand and turned to look at Jax. "We need Bruno around until that meeting, whenever it is, so he can lead us there. You're still planning to start school on Monday, right?"

"I'll be there."

"Good. We need you to keep an eye on Bruno and find out what you can about his plans. He may mention a trip, or something that would give us a clue."

Great. Not only did he need to find a way to approach Sasha again, he needed to play I-Spy for the Mephisto.

Key walked toward the door. With his hand on the knob, he looked over his shoulder at Jax. "By the way, I'm not crowing over your failure. I want this to work out with Sasha, but I'm just as clueless how to go about it as you are. I admire you for trying."

Then he looked embarrassed and was gone before Jax could reply.

⤬

After Jax disappeared, Sasha spent the next few hours skiing by herself, trying hard not to think about him. Didn't work, but at least she got a little better at skiing.

Back at the base, she realized Brett had left her. In the parking lot, holding Melanie's skis over one shoulder, she walked all around, looking for his yellow Hummer, but it was gone. Part of her was glad, another part wondered how she was going to get back down to Telluride, and the last part wished she could get on a bus to Colorado Springs and never look back.

"You look lost," a tall, dark-haired man said, standing on the driver's side of a black Mercedes. "Is something wrong?"

He was an older guy who looked like a movie star, he was that handsome. Maybe he was a movie star. He looked really familiar. Afraid he'd offer her a ride if she told him her dilemma, she managed a smile and shook her head. "Just waiting for my cousin to take me back to town."

He nodded and returned her smile. "If you get tired of waiting, you can take the gondola." He pointed behind him. "It'll take you a block from Colorado Avenue."

"Thanks."

"No problem." He got into his car and drove away, waving as he went. She noticed he had vanity plates with only one letter, an *M*.

As soon as he was out of sight, she took off for the gondola; thirty minutes later, she was walking down the main street of Telluride, headed for the Shrivers'. In no hurry to get there, even though it was past four and already starting to get dark, she looked in all the shop windows at the Christmas displays. The street-lamp posts were wrapped in garland with twinkle lights, and the little insets of the sidewalk with park benches were decorated in red bows and ribbons. A thick blanket of snow covered the ground, turning Telluride into a holiday greeting card. If things were different, if she were here with Mom, staying in the hotel across the street, or in one of the pretty condos, shopping for Christmas things, maybe buying a tree, she'd think this was about as awesome as it could get.

But Mom was a million miles away, and Sasha was staying in a ratty house with the most dysfunctional family in America. Melanie was a lost soul, so the chances of there being a Christmas tree at the Shrivers' were slim to none.

She was standing in front of a gift shop when her cell rang. Figuring it was Tim, she almost didn't answer. Then she wondered if it was Mom and hurriedly pulled the phone from her jacket pocket to answer.

"Sasha," a deep voice said, "this is Phoenix DeKyanos."

Blinking, she leaned forward until her forehead was resting against the wooden edge of the shop window. "Why are you calling me? Where's Jax?"

"He's gone out. I'm calling because my brothers and I are

concerned for your safety, so we've come up with a way to protect you. If you look to your right, you'll see a dog on a leash, tied to a park bench. His name is Boo. Do you see him?"

He was the ugliest dog she'd ever seen, medium-sized, with a patchy gray coat and a face only a mother could love. He was looking at her, tongue and tail wagging. "I see him."

"Take him home with you, remove his leash, and leave him outside. When you're in your room, say his name and he'll appear. Don't worry about feeding or walking him. When you leave the house, he'll be outside waiting for you. Don't go anywhere without Boo. Take him to school with you and leave him outside. If you find yourself in a situation that calls for help, say his name, and he'll be there."

"No offense, but he doesn't look like much of a guard dog."

"He's not an ordinary dog."

"Of course he's not."

"Sarcasm, Sasha?"

"It's new. I made it myself."

He was quiet until he said, "How do you feel right now?"

"Fine."

"Don't lie. How do you feel?"

She rested her head against the window again. "Sad and confused."

"Just like Jax."

"If you're trying to make me feel guilty, I—"

"What purpose would that serve? I'm only stating facts. He

133

likes you, you don't like him, he's upset about it. End of story. Take the dog and go home."

Before she could say another word, the call ended. She shoved the cell back in her pocket and walked away from the shop, away from the guard dog she didn't need, didn't want. Brett and Melanie didn't know she was Anabo, so she'd be just fine. Miserable, but fine.

She'd barely gotten past the next store before an older man in a red cap and rainbow suspenders came up beside her, holding out the leash with the ugly dog attached. "Excuse me, but you left your dog."

"He's not my dog."

The man bent and looked at the collar tag. "Sasha Annenkova. Is that you?"

"Yes, but that's not my dog. Somebody's playing a prank on me."

The man cocked his head to study the homely thing. "He is kinda ugly, but he looks like a friendly sort. And it's awfully cold. Maybe you could take him with you, just until you can give him back to your practical-joker friend." He held out the leash.

She didn't take it right away, and the dog whined, hanging his head, looking even more pitiful. Good grief. Huffing out an irritated breath, she took the leash from the man and glared at the dog. "Just until my *friend* comes to get you, understand?"

Perking up, the dog came to sit at her feet, resting his paws on the toes of her Uggs while he gazed up at her adoringly. He was missing half of one ear, and his right eye drooped.

"There now, see? He likes you." Rainbow Suspenders smiled like he'd just found the solution to world peace. "It's got to be hard for this little guy, being so ugly, but he's all heart. Who knows? Since he likes you so much, maybe you'll warm up to him."

She was struck by his unintentional analogy. So maybe Jax was lonely and wanted to be her friend; maybe he was hot, smart, funny, and kind. Maybe he was sad because she didn't want to be his friend. It didn't change what he was, just like this little dog's obvious affection didn't change that he was a creature of Hell. All she wanted was for everything to go back to how it had been before, when she was normal and ordinary, like everyone else. How could she do that if she dated a dark angel and had a hellhound for a pet? Suddenly very tired, she said, "Good night," and turned away, the leash in her hand.

"Good night, Sasha," Rainbow Suspenders cheerfully called after her.

She trudged down the street with Boo alongside, suddenly painfully hungry, and wondered if she should stop somewhere to get a sandwich before she went to the house. If all she got for dinner tonight was a plate of peas, she'd die of starvation.

Deciding to take her chances, mostly because she didn't want to spend any more money today, she headed toward the Shrivers', noticing when the people she passed took one look at Boo and grimaced.

The sun had set and twilight lay across Telluride, casting everything in gray and black. Away from the main drag, it was quiet and much darker. Not until Boo began growling low in his throat did she realize someone was following her. She didn't hear anything, but she knew someone was there. When she sped up, the feeling of someone right behind her didn't fade.

Boo suddenly lunged away from her to turn all the way around, baring his teeth and growling ferociously at whoever was behind her.

Oh, crap.

Jerking on his leash did no good. He was glued to the spot, body quivering, back legs bent as if he was set to pounce.

Fear made her look over her shoulder; horror made her heart race and her breath hitch.

Reilly O'Brien stood less than five feet away, a look of rage on her beautiful face. "I'm going to kill Brett Shriver, and you're going to help me."

❦

Standing on the sidewalk outside of St. Patrick's Cathedral in New York, Jax watched people come out after mass. He tried to see inside, just as he'd done a thousand times before at a thousand different churches, but the small glimpses he caught were as satisfying as a drop of water to a guy in the desert. Just enough to frustrate him.

He wished he could go inside, kneel at one of the pews, and ask God for help. He'd be able to think and come up with an idea about how to win Sasha, even though he'd maybe screwed it up beyond hope.

He'd just managed a good look at a row of candles close to the doors when Phoenix appeared next to him. "We have a situation."

"I don't give a damn."

"It's Sasha."

The church forgotten, he jerked his head around to look at his brother. "Tell me."

"M brought a new Purg to the mountain a few hours ago, that red headed chick from town, the hot one. The Shriver kid shoved her off Devil's Ridge, and she's hard-core pissed at God for not protecting her. Reilly hadn't been there an hour before she escaped."

For once, Jax didn't go off about the Purgatories. "What's this got to do with Sasha?"

"She's with Reilly, right now."

"Reilly *abducted* her?"

Phoenix nodded. "Almost thirty minutes ago. Boo gave chase, making his tag go so haywire, it set off the alarm. Ty lost the signal when Boo made it to Last Dollar Road, so he popped over to see what was going on. Reilly has Sasha in the woods outside the old Taylor house, where the kids go to party. It's Saturday, so a lot will be there tonight. We think Reilly's waiting for Brett to show up."

"Why did she take Sasha?"

"That's the freaky part, Jax. We don't know. Key told me to come after you, because of the rule that we all go, or no one goes, but also so you can make sure Sasha's okay."

Jax turned away from the church. "Let's go."

❧

"Do you know what it's like to try to live up to perfect parents? They're both doctors, working in third-world countries to save all the poor people. They left me with my grandparents so they could be saints, but what does that say about them, that they left me here with a couple of old people who never know where I am or what's going on?"

Sasha couldn't think of anything to say to that. Her mother had ditched her for what she said was a higher purpose, but it didn't feel good. It didn't make it okay. Especially now, considering all the weird stuff that was happening to her. Tonight was the icing on the cake. She still wasn't exactly sure how she had gotten here, in this little snowy clearing behind what appeared in the half-light of the overcast sky to be a small cabin. One minute she was wondering if she was hallucinating Reilly O'Brien, and the next, Reilly had her hand while they flew over the treetops so fast she couldn't breathe. She heard Boo barking his head off below them, until his barks became more distant, then stopped altogether.

She kept trying to get her hand loose from Reilly's, but she couldn't. It was as if they were fused together.

"Give up!" Reilly said. "I'm not letting go until after Brett shows up and you tell him I'm the one who's going to kill him."

"Why won't he know it's you?"

Reilly shot her an impatient look. "He can't see me!"

"I can see you."

"Of course you can, because you're an angel, but Brett's only human, so he can't."

"I'm not an angel."

"You're glowing, and every angel I've seen since I died glows like that." She frowned. "Until the dark angel came. He didn't glow, but he was super-good-looking. Strange, right? He said I'm too angry at God to go to Heaven. He took me to this huge, spooky castle and told me I'd have to stay there and work through things before I can go to Heaven." She smiled. "But I escaped and saw you, and you're going to be there when I pay back Brett for what he did."

Sasha suspected, but now she knew for sure, Brett really was a murderer. Justice needed to happen, except if Reilly killed him, Sasha would get the blame. Who'd believe a ghost had done it?

But all her attempts to talk Reilly out of killing Brett were ignored. Instead, Reilly talked and talked, venting her anger and sorrow.

Would Sasha ever get to go home? Would life ever go back to normal? Her whole life was unraveling. Everything had changed within the space of two days, and it had all started when she went to that stupid Ravens meeting, which she did because Mom had given up trying to find out who had killed Dad. Then she left her with Tim Shriver, and now this.

Yeah, she knew all about being abandoned. But she didn't say so to Reilly. Even if she wanted to, she'd never get a word in edgewise.

"I'm dead, and everything I looked forward to will never happen." She shook with fury. "I never even had sex! I didn't have a boyfriend because it took too much time away from school, and volunteering to save the whole freakin' world, and being an example to everybody. My mom was always telling me that, to be an example. I was an idiot! I should have gotten a tattoo, pierced my nose, and slept with that way-hot guy who works the lift at Revelation Bowl. I wasted all my chances, and now I'm dead. Brett shoved me off that cliff, and I want revenge."

"He's a lost soul, Reilly. Do you know about the lost souls, about Eryx?"

"The death angel told me, and that only makes me more determined to off the bastard. He won't be sucking anyone else into that stupid club, and he won't be around to kill again."

"He'll be taken away soon. Anything you do to him will only interfere."

The girl's face morphed into an expression of tremendous pain. "I never knew what evil looked like, until today. I was so scared, and prayed for God to help me." She choked on a sob. "But he didn't! He let Brett Shriver kill me, and I can't forgive him for it."

"Look, Reilly, I understand how angry you are, but if you

kill Brett, I'm going to prison. That's not fair. I hate the guy, but I wouldn't kill him. And what will it change if *you* do? You're still going to be dead. Please, let me go and—"

"Shh! A car's coming up the road."

Panicking, Sasha fought hard to get away from Reilly, but it was no use. The girl jerked her arm so hard, her shoulder wrenched and she cried out in pain.

"Shut up! They can't hear me, but they can hear you. I have to be able to surprise them."

When Sasha heard voices and car doors, she shouted, "Brett!"

Reilly clapped a hand over her mouth, but it was too late.

"Sasha, is that you? What are you doing up here? Who told you about the ghost house?"

Ghost house? That might be funny someday. Right now, she was terrified he would come to the back of the cabin, looking for her. Wrestling with Reilly, she finally got her mouth free and yelled, "I met a guy on the slopes, and he said you'd be here. I came to tell you about Reilly O'Brien."

Instantly, Reilly stopped trying to cover her mouth. "What are you doing? He'll kill you, too!"

"Just wait," she whispered.

"What about Reilly?" Brett called out.

"Did you hear? Reilly didn't die. Her neck's broken, but she's going to live."

All was quiet until Reilly said, "He'll never buy it. The news is all over town."

Sasha didn't respond. She was hoping Brett would be worried enough to head back into town and find out for sure.

Then she heard footsteps and knew it hadn't worked.

"Where are you, Sasha?"

Reilly was dragging her backward, into the forest, when giant shadows appeared with them in the small clearing behind the cabin, two of them moving toward her so fast that she didn't have time to scream. One of the shadows grabbed her wrist, the other grabbed Reilly's, and immediately, her hand was released. Then she was enveloped within something that smelled of leather and spiced cider, and everything went dark.

⁓⁓⁓

Unable to think of a place to take her where they could talk about what happened without interruption and eavesdroppers, Jax decided to take her to his room at the Mephisto house. When they arrived, he released her and stepped back, watching while she blinked in the light and looked around her. "Where are we?"

"In my room. I'll take you home in a while, but I thought you might want to know what's up with Reilly, and we can talk here without anyone overhearing."

"How did we get here, Jax?"

"I can transport myself and anything I can carry anywhere in the world in just a few seconds. It's kind of necessary for what I do."

She looked at him as if she expected him to sprout wings and fly. "You are one spooky dude, Ajax DeKyanos. What else can you do?"

"I can hear things ordinary people can't, my sense of smell is almost as good as a dog's, I can see in the dark, and I sometimes have premonitions. I'm also pretty good at basketball."

Her attention returned to her surroundings. "So this is where you live. Our whole apartment in Oakland would fit in this room."

He looked with her, seeing things for the first time in decades. He lived here—day in, day out—so he scarcely noticed the paintings in gold-leaf frames; the twelve-foot ceilings; the massive furniture, blood-red silk against dove-gray walls; his gigantic desk; the black marble fireplace; or the things he kept in his bookshelves, besides the books.

Sasha walked away from him, circling the room, stopping to stare at the paintings, craning her neck to see the upper bookcases. She asked about a few things, like his dueling pistols and his British helmet from Waterloo. She knew of the artist who had painted him and his brothers in the gardens of their house in Yorkshire in 1803. What she didn't know was that the artist had become a Lumina. His paintings were all over the house.

She was still studying the portrait when she said, "I don't want to know how you found me. Don't tell me where Reilly went, and I'll die happy if I never have to know how she intended to kill Brett, because I'm pretty sure I was crucial to the plan." Turning, she met his eyes. "All I want to know is why she came after me. Is it because Brett's my cousin?"

He shook his head.

"Yeah, I was afraid of that. It's because I'm Anabo, isn't it?"

Now was probably not the best time to tell her it was because she was changing to be like him, which enabled her to see ghosts, so he simply said, "Yes."

Moving away from the north wall, she went to the windows on the west wall and cupped her hands to look outside. "I can see the shadow of the mountains. You must wake up every morning to an awesome view."

The door opened, and Mathilda came bustling in, a large tray in her pudgy hands. "I was told you won't be coming down for supper, Master Jax, so I've brought you a wee bite." She set the tray on the table beneath the portrait and turned to look at Sasha. "How'd'ye do, missy? I'd be Mathilda, the housekeeper."

Turning, Sasha smiled. "It's nice to meet you. I'm Sasha."

"Well, of course you are. Are you hungry?"

"Yes, ma'am."

"Then have a nibble, and don't let Master Jax talk yer ear off." She turned toward the door. "If you need something, just give us a ring."

When she was gone, Sasha looked at him with curious eyes. "Is there a reason you have an English housekeeper who dresses in clothes from the 1800s?"

He explained about the Purgatories before he said, "Mathilda's twelve-year-old daughter was attacked by her employer. Trying to protect her child, Mathilda killed the man. He was an aristocrat, an earl, and she was a housekeeper; justice in England in those days was always skewed. Her daughter died, and she couldn't get past her anger at God for letting that happen. She was executed before she could resolve it. She's been with us since 1852."

"How did Reilly escape?"

"We're not sure yet, but she won't try again. She'll either agree to stay with us and work to get past her anger, or be sent to Purgatory to figure it out on her own." He caught the scent of meat, and his stomach growled. He noticed she kept darting glances toward the table. "Would you like to eat something before I take you home?"

"I shouldn't, but I'm not sure there'll be anything to eat at the Shrivers'."

"Why shouldn't you?"

She looked exasperated. "I don't want to be here, Jax. I don't want to talk to you, or know you. I just want my old, normal life back."

Now was the time he should tell her it was too late: that she might be able to go back to normal someday, but not anytime soon. Not as long as she looked at him with that paradoxical expression of desire and loathing. Maybe she didn't want to talk to him, but he'd bet anything she wanted to kiss him.

He ended up saying nothing at all, but walked to the table and held out a chair for her. When she was seated, he took the chair opposite and prepared to eat without talking. Maybe it would help if he didn't look at her. He focused on his plate, which was filled with pot roast, potatoes, roasted butternut squash, and fresh green beans, but he couldn't avoid looking at her. She was gorgeous, her long blond hair pulled back into a braid, some of it escaping to tease her jaw. Her nose was pinked by the outdoors, and her lips were slightly chapped.

"You're staring."

"So are you."

They both dropped their gazes, and he ate a little before he couldn't stand it and looked up again, catching her doing the same. So it went, and her demand for no talking went south when she said, "My favorite dessert is chocolate mousse."

"Mine, too."

"You're just saying that."

"Mathilda will back me up. My favorite color is red."

"Mine, too."

"Now you're teasing me."

"No. If you looked in my closet, you'd see how much I like red." She reached for one of the apple dumplings and took a bite.

Sasha didn't eat as much as he did, but she ate a lot for a girl. He wondered if she was stronger. Did she think about things she'd never thought about before? He hoped not. That she was changing without knowing it bothered him, but the idea that she'd be dogged by dark thoughts and negative emotions nearly broke his heart.

And he had done it to her.

When they were finished, he said, "Unless you have more questions, I'll take you home now."

She stood and moved away from the table to put on her ski jacket, then went to the center of the room, turning all around to look at it once again. "I can't believe you live here. It's like a palace or something."

What would she think if she saw the rest of the house: the paintings, the library, the front hall? He might never know. She had made it really clear how she felt about him. His earlier depression slid further down, into despair. If only he hadn't told her so much.

He stood and walked to the wingback before the fire to get his trench coat, planning to pop her back to town, to the Shrivers' curb, where they'd find Boo and he would leave her. But when he turned around, she was right there, so close he could smell the caramel salty sweetness of her. It made him crazy, looking down into her beautiful eyes, at her creamy soft skin, knowing he couldn't touch her. "Ready?"

"Yes," she whispered, staring at him.

He thought he was imagining that her body swayed toward his, right up until her soft breasts pressed against his chest. Never, in his whole life, had he wanted anything more than he wanted to touch her, to kiss her until she couldn't breathe. But knowing the consequences, that it would speed up her transformation, he ruthlessly squashed the desire and stepped back to pull his coat on, ignoring the look of confusion and disappointment on her face. She wanted to kiss him, even though she despised him.

If she knew that kissing him would turn her into what he was, what disgusted her, would she still want to? Not a chance.

Taking a deep breath, reminding himself over and over that kissing her wasn't a good thing, he moved close again and slipped his arms around her. She was so small next to him, her hair so soft against his cheek. When her arms slid around his back beneath his trench coat, he almost caved. Not kissing Sasha was the hardest thing he'd ever done. A few seconds later, they stood on the street in front of the Shrivers' house and he let go of her immediately.

"Jax, I don't feel right about any of this. I like you, I do. I want to be with you, so much, but I . . . it's such a strange thing, what you do and who you are. Please understand."

"Sasha, all I've ever wanted, since I was old enough to know what was what, is to be like everybody else. I understand. It's killing me, but I understand."

"I guess after this, unless I'm abducted by another rogue Purgatory, I won't see you again."

"You'll see me Monday, at school."

"*What*? Why? I thought you lied about boarding school and all that about your dad."

"I did, and it's not like I need to go to school. We have tutors who teach us constantly, so we can keep up. I've been educated my entire life, and I've lived through a lot of written history, so nothing taught at school will be anything I don't already know. But my brothers want me to go so I can keep an eye on Bruno and the Ravens. Planning their takedown has become compli-cated." He could see the panic in her eyes. "I'll stay away from you, and we can pretend we don't know each other."

"Yes, that's what we should do. Maybe we won't even be in the same classes."

"You won't let on to anyone who I am, will you?"

"Like you said, who would believe me?"

"Be careful around Bruno, Sasha. Try not to be so afraid of him, like you were of Alex Kasamov. Don't give him any reason to suspect you're Anabo. He's much older than Alex was, with years of experience, so he's triple the threat."

"Older? He looks about the same age."

"Eryx makes some of the lost souls immortal, then sends them out to recruit. Bruno has been Skia for over two hundred years, which means he's extremely cunning and clever, because he escaped our notice until now."

"What does Skia mean?"

"In Greek, it means shade, or shadow. The eyes really are a window to the soul, and Skia eyes are in a dark shadow to us because they have no soul. Unlike the lost souls, who keep their spirit until they die and it's released, the Skia give it to Eryx when they become immortal, so they're like an extension of him, almost like a clone, or a robot."

"So that's how you know someone is Skia, but how do you know someone is a lost soul?"

"Their eyes are also slightly shaded, just not as much as the

Skia. They're almost always part of some secret society that's supposed to look appealing to outsiders, like it's special to be invited to join. And they hang around the Skia, looking for favors. Once someone pledges, they regret it immediately, because they understand they were tricked and lied to, they can't go back, ever, and whatever chance they had for Heaven is history. Even Hell looks pretty good to a lost soul. Knowing you'll be obliterated when you die is a hard truth, and their only goal becomes to be made Skia, so they'll live forever. The more people they get to pledge, the more they're noticed, and the better their chances that Eryx will make them Skia."

"So that's why Melanie was trying so hard to get Chris to become a Raven. Wow, that's severely sick and twisted. Her own child."

"They have no conscience, Sasha. Just be careful, okay?"

"I'll be careful." She shot a nervous glance at the house.

Jax whistled, and Boo came bounding out of nowhere, tail wagging as he loped to Sasha's feet and sat, gazing up at her like she was his own personal goddess. "If anyone bothers you, he'll be there to help. He's a good dog, and his only purpose is to keep you safe."

"Where did he come from?"

"My brother, Titus, who we call Ty, found him in Mexico. He was bait for the dogfights."

"You mean, he's not . . . he didn't come from—"

"No, he's just an ordinary dog, but Ty has a way with animals, and he uses a little magic to get them to do what we need." Moving farther away, he said, "Good night, Sasha."

"Jax, wait. I . . ."

He waited, but she couldn't finish the thought, so he said good-bye again and disappeared, headed for home to find Key and request that someone else be assigned to go to Telluride High and spy on Bruno. If he had to see her all day, every day, knowing it was hopeless, he'd go insane.

SIX

AFTER RETRIEVING MELANIE'S SKIS AND BOOTS, WHICH she'd dropped when Reilly grabbed her hand, Sasha walked back to the house, Boo trotting along beside her. She was nervous when she opened the front door, unsure what she'd find, but was relieved when she discovered Tim snoring in his recliner, no sign of Melanie, Brett still not home from the party at the ghost house, and Chris, as usual, in his room playing a video game.

She stowed Melanie's ski stuff back in the hall closet, then prepared to take a shower. When she heard a soft whine from outside, she whispered, "Boo," and there he was, wagging his crooked tail, looking up at her like she was all that. She bent and scratched behind his lopsided ears, surprised he was soft instead of wiry.

Fifteen minutes later, dressed in a robe with a towel on her head and Boo curled up at her feet, she sat at the little desk and logged onto Facebook. Just as she'd suspected, everyone from St. Michael's was talking about the Ravens. There were all sorts of wild theories about what had happened. Some swore they were Satan worshippers, others said they were a coven of witches, while still others said they were just a group of losers who invented the Ravens so they'd have at least the illusion of cool. But pretty much everyone agreed, they'd committed suicide. The lack of compassion made her a little nauseous.

Lots of her friends had written on her wall, asking why she wasn't at school yesterday, and was it true she'd moved, because somebody overheard the headmistress talking to the librarian about it.

She replied to a few and ignored the rest, then opened the Word doc that was her college essay about her intention to study art history and become an expert at restoration. It was something she had to do in order to apply, but her enthusiasm was zilch.

Wiped out, she gave up and closed the laptop, ready to go to bed. As she lay down and turned off the bedside lamp, her thoughts inevitably turned to Jax, imagining he was just an ordinary guy, that they went out, that he kissed her—lots of those amazing kisses—that they started school and everyone knew they were together. It wasn't fair at all that she met a guy she liked this much and he was someone she could never be with.

Boo curled up at her feet and sighed, like he was happy, and that was the last thing she remembered before she woke up the next morning to find Brett standing next to her bed. Boo was gone, hiding somewhere, she supposed. "I'm not going skiing again, so save your breath."

Unlike yesterday, when he woke her when it was still dark, the sun was up and she could see him clearly, standing there in a pair of black boxers, his hair sticking out at weird angles, his eyes swollen with sleep, and his color just to the left of green, almost yellow. She decided he was hung over. Or his kidneys were failing.

He also looked severely pissed. "What were you doing at the ghost house last night, and why did you say that to me about Reilly? Where did you go?"

She stared at him as if she had no idea what he was talking about. "Ghost house? You've gotta be kidding. I never saw you last night, *or* yesterday afternoon. Thanks a lot for leaving me. If a guy I met hadn't offered me a ride, I'd have had to walk back to Telluride from Mountain Village."

"Where were you last night?"

"I went to dinner with the guy who brought me back to town." She'd never been a good liar, because she didn't lie much, but she told this whopper and almost believed it herself. "Somebody must have played a prank on you, and you were too drunk to know it."

"Julianne did go up with East, earlier. That's something she'd do, for sure." Brett stepped back to sit on the other twin bed.

154

"Swear you weren't up at the ghost house last night?"

She rolled her eyes and huffed out a breath. "No, I'm lying, because I totally know about a ghost house, since I've lived here all of one day and made so many friends who'd tell me about it and take me there." Staring up at the ceiling, she wished he'd go away. Knowing he was a murderer made her skin crawl. She remembered how devastated Reilly had been, her whole life over almost before it started, all because Brett Shriver was a guy who couldn't stand that she'd said no. He'd have dealt with her rejection before he pledged his soul to Eryx, but now that he was lost to God, he had no conscience, nothing to keep him from acting on his impulses. Reilly had told him she wouldn't go out with him, and he'd shoved her off of a cliff.

He evidently bought that Sasha hadn't been at the ghost house. He relaxed a little, looking around the room. "Have you thought some more about joining the Ravens? We have a meeting tomorrow night."

"I'm not sure. On Facebook, kids at my old school are talking about the Ravens who died. They think they committed suicide."

"Are you afraid we have a suicide pact?"

"Maybe."

He laughed. "I can promise you, the last thing we'll do is off ourselves. Why would we? It's like we have everything we want, whatever we have to have. I was flunking biology when I pledged. Now I have an A. I've got a perfect life, so why would I kill myself?"

Sasha could see how someone who didn't know the truth would think it all sounded awesome, a gimme for anything they wanted, without all the work, or the sacrifice. She'd thought it was BS, but she still went to a meeting, thinking she'd say the oath so she could get what she wanted: to find out who had killed her dad.

Looking at Brett, at his expectant expression, she wondered if he knew about Jax and his brothers. Did Mr. Bruno tell the Ravens about Hell on Earth? "I'll let you know tomorrow."

He stood and went to the door. "Don't mention it at school where other teachers can hear. There's a rule that we aren't supposed to have secret clubs, and Mr. Bruno could get fired for starting the Ravens."

When he left her room, she let out a long breath, unaware until just then that she'd been holding it. Boo came out from under the bed and jumped up to lie on her, half on, half off, his front paws on her chest. It was Sunday, and she was thinking about what she'd do today, wondering if she should get up and go to church, when she drifted back to sleep.

When she woke up again, she heard Melanie shouting and Tim speaking in his low, even voice. Throwing the covers back, she crept to the door and opened it a crack to see what was going on. Melanie stood outside their bedroom door at the end of the hall, dressed in some serious hoochie-mama jeans that had cutout diamonds across the backside, showing lots of skin. Her blouse was low cut, showing cleavage so deep, she could hide a small child in there.

"I want her out of this house. It's only a matter of time before they start snooping around, looking to see if that bitch is communicating with her."

Who was *they*?

"Of course she'll communicate with her. Sasha is her daughter. Your paranoia is getting on my nerves, Melanie. Take it somewhere else, and for God's sake, wear something that doesn't announce to the whole town you're a cheap tramp. Everyone knows you have a thing with Bruno. Leave Chris some dignity, at least."

"Chris! *Chris*! It's always about Chris with you. Have you forgotten you have another son? Remember him? You never even look at him, much less speak to him."

"I could say the same about you and Chris."

"You know exactly why, you son of a bitch! Don't go laying some guilt trip off on me, not when we both know who's the guilty one when it comes to him. You think you can look down your nose at me, when you were over there in Moscow, with that—"

"Enough! I've had enough, Melanie. Shut up or leave."

Turning, she stalked away from Tim, toward the stairs, which meant she had to pass Sasha's door. Sasha hurriedly pulled it closed, then stood there, breathing fast, waiting for Melanie to pass before moving an inch. Except Melanie didn't pass. She flung open the door and shoved it so hard, it banged against the wall, then she got in Sasha's face. "In case you missed any of our private conversation, I'll fill you in. Tim got an e-mail this morning from his old boss at the CIA. They want to know if your mother has contacted him, because they've lost track of her. They think maybe she's *dead*."

Tim filled the doorway with his huge bulk, glaring at Melanie. "It's like you enjoy being a nasty bitch." He looked at Sasha, his eyes softening. "No one said anything about your mother being dead. It's standard to keep tabs on someone like Katya after deportation. They wanted to know if we'd heard from her, and I said no, but that I'd ask if you have."

Slowly, Sasha shook her head, hands clenched into fists at her side. The impulse to punch Melanie in the face was as foreign as it was overwhelming. She'd never felt moved to violence like this. "I'll let you know when I hear from her."

Melanie was still less than a foot from her, close enough to punch, close enough to see the glue sticking her fake eyelashes to her real ones. She leaned in just a little and whispered, "Go on, I dare you. I can see you want to."

"So you can have me arrested?" Sasha pinged back. "Yeah, I don't think so."

Melanie turned on her micro heels and left the room, shoving Tim as she went.

When she was gone, he said, "Get dressed and we'll go out for lunch."

Food was Tim's answer to everything. Sasha felt bad for him, so she nodded.

❧

"What are you reading?"

From a side chair, Jax watched Phoenix walk into the library and take a seat on the low leather sofa in front of the fireplace. "What are you, the book police?"

"I take it, then, that you're reading something you're embarrassed about. So what is it? *Harry Potter? Eragon? Lord of the Rings?* Or are you going through another childhood phase, where you read books for little kids? Is it *Old Yeller? James and the Giant Peach?*"

He may as well fess up. Phoenix would drive him nuts until he did. Holding up the book, he showed it to his brother and waited.

It didn't take long. "*How to Win Friends and Influence People.* Now that's just fascinating, but maybe you should read the Sons of Hell edition, *How Not to Scare the Shit out of People and Alienate Everyone You Meet.*"

"They were out of that one, so I settled."

"And?"

"It's geared toward salespeople, but it fits, I guess. I'm trying to sell myself as a regular guy. If I do what this book says, I should have people eating out of my hand."

"What does the book say?"

"Flattery will get you everywhere. Remember to say people's names, because they love to hear it. Ask them what they're up to, make it all about them. Show genuine interest in them and their life. Make like you think they're the only person on the planet."

"Okay, I'll buy it, but what about before all that? How do you get close enough to show interest, genuine or otherwise?"

"M got me some contact lenses, made out of glass because the plastic ones melted. They do an okay job of making my eyes look normal, but I'm going to wear shades as much as I can get away with. I'm working on thinking about pleasant, positive things, so maybe I won't come across like a psycho. But my ace in the hole is Brody. He's going with me, posing as my twin brother. Fraternal, since we look nothing alike. We'll hang together, and maybe the vibe he gives will counterbalance mine."

"That's pretty brilliant. Did you come up with the idea?"

"In a roundabout way. I told Key that I wouldn't do this, that he had to find someone else to go to school and spy on Bruno. I suggested Brody, since he was nineteen when he crossed over and looks like he's seventeen. Key said no, that it has to be one of us, and he's hell-bent on it being me. So I said I'd go if Brody goes with me."

"The girls will be all over him like syrup on pancakes, and what happens if he finds one he likes extra special? Under the Lumina rule, he can't date a human, or expect to bring her here. Maybe you should pick a Lumina who's already mated."

"He's a geek. Okay, so he's a Lumina and people are naturally attracted to him, but these are teenagers, Phoenix. His being a nerd will override his being a Lumina."

"Says you. I predict disaster, unless you keep a close eye on him."

"We'll be together all day. No worries."

Phoenix stood and went toward the doorway into the front hall.

"Are you going out to the shop?" Phoenix built choppers as a way to pass the time, to have something to occupy his mind so he wouldn't think about Jane so much. Jax didn't think it worked out like that, but his brother did spend a lot of time out there. He'd built a bike for each person on the mountain. Some had two.

"No, I'm jonesing for bangers and mash."

"London?"

"Where else?"

Standing, Jax tossed the book to the library table and followed his brother. He didn't really want bangers and mash, but whenever Phoenix went to England by himself, it was because he was feeling Jane. He'd visit her grave, and bad shit was sure to follow. Last time, he went in a pub and picked a fight with a big bruiser of a guy. Nearly killed the man, hurt several others, including a couple of bobbies, and the damage to the pub was in the thousands of pounds. M had punished him with six months of solitary on Kyanos.

"You don't have to go with me."

"Yeah, I do." In the front hall, they asked Deacon to bring their trench coats, and two minutes later, they were standing at the foot of Jane's grave, in the dark. It was eight o'clock at night in Yorkshire.

One minute after they arrived, Eryx materialized at the head of Jane's grave. He placed one booted foot on the stone marker and looked at them, a sardonic expression on his face. "I always thought it was touching how you planted Jane outside of holy ground so you could visit her without burning to a crisp. Wonder if her parents ever figured out they were visiting a weighted casket over in the St. Stephen's churchyard?"

Phoenix kept his eyes on the headstone, never acknowledging Eryx was there.

Jax turned his collar up to the cold and damp, noticing when it began to snow. He didn't ask Eryx why he was here, or what he wanted. He didn't care.

Eryx made a few more remarks about Jane, hoping to get under Phoenix's skin, but when he failed even to get him to look up, he sighed and dropped his foot to the ground. "One of my immortals, who you took out last week, bought a painting for me in San Francisco. I sent someone to collect it from his possessions, but it wasn't there. I need to know if you took it."

Mildly curious now, Jax said, "What the hell would we want with another painting? We have hundreds already."

"If you have it, if you'll give it to me, I'll return the favor."

A favor? This was a first, making all kinds of alarms go off in his head. Eryx wanted it bad enough to offer a favor, and Jax wondered why. "You're outta luck. We don't have anything of Kasamov's."

"He bought it from a Russian woman who's since moved back to Russia. She insisted, even under specific questioning, that she didn't sell it to him, but she doesn't have it. And the painting wasn't in his things."

Specific questioning meant she'd been tortured. It had to be Sasha's mother. She was Russian, had just moved back to Russia, and she'd gone out with Kasamov. Jax had wondered if she took the oath, and had sent Mallick to find out. He'd returned early this morning to report that no, she hadn't, but things were pretty bad for her. The Russian Security Council had her quarantined, pending reentrance to the Russian population. She must have been released and immediately picked up by one of Eryx's goons.

Then Eryx said, "There's a child, a daughter, who may know something about it."

In a thousand years of trapping unsuspecting lost souls and Skia, Jax had perfected the ability to mask his emotions. He shrugged indifferently while inside he was losing his mind. Was someone there, right now, questioning Sasha about this elusive painting? Did she know anything about it? Would her interrogator torture her, as her mother had been tortured? Would he see her birthmark?

His face remained impassive when he glanced at Phoenix, who was still staring at Jane's headstone as if he had no clue what was going on around him.

"Since when are you such an avid collector?" he asked Eryx.

"I don't give a damn about art. The painting is significant because of the subject matter. Kasamov described it, and I want to see for myself if what he said was accurate."

He wished God would break his promise not to interfere and kill Eryx right now.

Instead, their father's first son once again set his foot on Jane's headstone and leaned over to rest a forearm on his knee. "Maybe you'll find it as intriguing as I do. Kasamov claimed the painting renders God and Lucifer working in tandem with each other. There is an Anabo receiving the darkness of Lucifer, transforming her to Mephisto."

"We've known that can happen since we started."

"The Mephisto in the painting receives God's blessing, which would suggest he's redeemed. You'd have to agree that's intriguing, Ajax. If you were redeemed, God could hear you, you'd have a chance of Heaven when he decides to call it a day, and you could stand on holy ground. If all the Mephisto had that ability, you'd win this little war we've been waging for a thousand years, and that's something I can't allow. I want that painting, and I'll do whatever's necessary to get it." He stood straight again and disappeared.

Panicking to the point of hysteria, Jax was about to return to Colorado, until Phoenix grabbed his arm and said in a fierce whisper, "No! Stay!"

"I'll kick your ass if you don't let go of me."

"It's a trick," his brother whispered to the ground. "Just stay here for five minutes."

"They tortured Sasha's mother. If he sends someone to see Sasha, they'll—"

"Realize she doesn't have the painting and leave."

"What if she does have it?"

"Then she'll give it to them. Or not. If you show any anxiety about that painting, it tells Eryx there's some merit to what he was told by Kasamov, who probably didn't buy the painting—he just saw it."

"I don't care about the painting. I'm only worried about Sasha."

"You should care about the painting. Unless Kasamov was lying, or misinterpreting what he saw, the painting depicts the Mephisto Covenant. If Eryx discovers we can be redeemed through an Anabo, he won't stop at trying to abduct and kill the ones we find. He'll have every Skia and lost soul on the planet actively looking for them. We'd never have a prayer of finding one again."

"If such a painting exists, why would Sasha's mother have it?"

"We can't be sure she does, but we need to find out. And we will, but not until we've stayed here a while longer. I guarantee Eryx is watching us, right now. If we leave too soon, he'll follow. Do you want to lead him right to Sasha? Just stay calm and wait a few more minutes, then we'll go home and get a Lumina to check on her."

Jax waited, but it was the longest five minutes of his life. At one point, he said, "What would happen if I just took Sasha to the mountain and told her she has to stay?"

"You'd pay the price for interfering with free will. Don't think

Lucifer will forgive you for breaking the rule, just because he wants this to happen between you and Sasha. Not to mention, she'd hate you for sure, and if you two don't hook up, it's all pointless anyway. I understand the temptation, but don't go there, Jax."

"Can we leave now?"

"We can leave as soon as you shut up and let me say good-bye to Jane."

Turning on his heel, Jax walked away, toward the old elm Key had planted after Phoenix found Jane. He said when it was very tall, he'd put a big swing in it for their children. Looking up into the naked, gnarly branches, none of which supported a swing, Jax remembered Jane's smile, her blue eyes, her musical voice, and the last thing she said before she died.

When they rushed in to rescue her, she looked toward Phoenix, her beautiful face bruised and bleeding, Eryx's dagger just above her heart, and called out to him, "Bring me back! Bring me to life!" Phoenix was already running and caught her before she hit the stone floor.

Eryx watched, and when it was obvious she was gone, that Phoenix couldn't bring her back, he said, "She doesn't respond because she no longer carries your mark. She has mine. Only I can gift her with immortality. Maybe I should, and she could give birth to *my* sons."

With cold fury on his face, Phoenix stood, Jane cradled in his arms, and disappeared from the ancient castle Eryx called home.

Looking toward his brother now, seeing his slumped shoulders and bowed head, Jax clenched his jaw, an old familiar frustration settling over him. Over one hundred years had passed, but it was still all Phoenix thought about. So many things they hadn't known when he found Jane, and their worst ignorance was the rules of the Mephisto mark. They didn't know Eryx could read it as they could, didn't know he also had the ability to mark an Anabo. He'd raped Jane, leaving his mark in place of Phoenix's. It was horrific enough to live with her death, but burying her with Eryx's mark still inside her body elevated Phoenix's crushing guilt and grief to helpless rage.

Finally, when Jax didn't think he could stand waiting even one more second, Phoenix turned and said, "I'm ready."

∽∾

After lunch, Tim drove Sasha and Chris back to the house. He went immediately to his recliner to watch football, and Chris said he was going to a friend's house to play a video game. Brett and Melanie were gone, so Sasha decided to stay in her room and work on her college essay.

Until she got to her room. It was like a war zone, minus the shrapnel and dead bodies. Every drawer had been emptied onto the floor, and all the clothes she'd hung in the closet were strewn across the room, along with bedcovers and sheets. Her sketchbook had been ripped to shreds, and the MacBook she'd gotten for her birthday last April was in pieces, the screen separated from the computer, both sides smashed and broken. So much for her essay.

Walking through the mess, she realized her clothes weren't just thrown all over the floor. They'd been ripped, cut, and torn, completely destroyed. She went to the bedside table to look in the drawer, not at all surprised to see the plastic tube was missing.

"Sasha, can you come downstairs? There's someone here to see you."

Shaky and close to tears, she stumbled across her ruined clothes and went to the hall, then down the stairs. A skinny guy with dark hair and geeky glasses stood in the foyer, smiling at her. Tim said, "Why don't you take Brody up to your room where you can visit? I wouldn't want to bug you with the game."

Which was his way of saying, Don't bug me while I'm watching the game. "Sure, Tim." She waited until he was back in the family room before she turned to her visitor. "Do I know you?"

He shook his head. "Jax sent me."

She didn't recognize him from the family portrait she'd seen in Jax's room, but asked anyway, "Are you one of his brothers?"

"No, I work for them. I just need to ask you something, if you have a minute?"

Maybe he was a hard-core nerd, but there was something about him she liked immediately. He had the kindest eyes, and he seemed so calm. She could use some calm right now. Still, she wasn't big on trusting strangers at the moment. "How do I know you're who you say you are?"

He flipped out a cell phone and dialed a number before handing it to her. Jax said, "Is she okay?"

She met the eyes of her visitor and said, "She's fine."

"Sasha? Is Brody there?"

"Yes."

"And you're okay?" He sounded positively panicked.

"I'm okay. What's going on?"

"Talk to Brody, and I'll be there in just a little while."

She ended the call and handed the phone back to Brody. "Come on up."

At the doorway to her room, she stopped and waited for him to catch up. "We went to lunch about two hours ago and had just gotten home before you came."

He took one look and said, "Is anything missing?"

"I had a plastic tube with a pencil sketch portrait of my mother inside, and it's gone."

He walked into the room, stepping over the piles of clothes. "Looks like you'll be doing some shopping."

She closed the door, went to the closest bed, and sat on the bare mattress. Brody took a seat on the other and pushed his glasses up to the bridge of his nose. He told her a story about Eryx, and Alex Kasamov, and a painting he had supposedly bought from her mother. "Jax is concerned a Skia may show up, looking for the painting, and you might be questioned in a way that would hurt."

"You mean, like, tortured?" She swallowed before she glanced at the curtain rod, then focused on her MacBook. "Would someone torture me just to find out about some old painting?"

"Eryx wants it bad. We don't know why, or what it means, but he's really anxious to get his hands on it."

"Does he want the painting so he can sell it?"

"No, he doesn't need money." Brody reached down and picked up a small strip of paper that had a sketch of an eye. "You said you've been out for a couple of hours. Do you think whoever did this was looking for the painting? Because I'm not sure someone in a hurry to find something would take the time to destroy all your stuff."

"I think my aunt did it, because she hates me. And she probably took the tube just to be extra mean. She knew it had a portrait of my mother inside, and she hates my mom even more than she hates me. She said if I took the picture out of the tube, she'd burn it."

Brody gazed at her with sympathetic eyes. "I'll do all I can to help you get things set to rights, but first, it's really important that you tell me the truth. Do you have the painting?"

She glanced away and said, "No."

Just then, Jax appeared in front of the windows.

Her heart sped up, and she wished she didn't feel this happy to see him. He hadn't shaved, and the dark stubble made him look older, more masculine, more dangerous. He immediately focused on her, his concern obvious. "Are you okay?"

"I'm fine, but my stuff is toast. I think Melanie did it."

He looked around the room, his body tense, hands clenched into fists.

"If one of Eryx's people came looking for a painting, why would they stick around long enough to mutilate my clothes, rip up my sketchbook, and smash my computer? She's the only one who'd be this personal about it."

"Since Melanie lives here, she was the one chosen to search, and she went a little crazy." He glanced at the MacBook. "Or a lot crazy."

Moving close, he sat next to her, his thick thigh pressed against hers. "Sasha, you know you can trust me, so tell me, please, do you have the painting Eryx is looking for?"

She didn't answer, staring down at his boots. "Where'd you go to get so muddy?"

"England. Phoenix wanted to visit Jane's grave."

"Who's Jane?"

He looked down into her eyes and said softly, "She was his fiancée, an Anabo he found in London, over a hundred years ago."

"How did she die?"

"Eryx killed her."

A shiver ran up her back. "And Phoenix still visits her grave?"

"Not as often as in the beginning, but yes, he still visits, and grieves. In all this time, he's never looked at another girl. We go out, my brothers and I, but Phoenix never does."

"How did Eryx find her? Did a Skia discover her and take her to him?"

He shook his head, looking down at his muddy boots. "Are you sure you want to know?"

"Of course I do, so maybe I can learn from it and not do whatever she did."

"She carried Phoenix's mark, something that could help us find her anywhere in the world. It's a protective thing. Like last night, if you had been marked, we could have found you, even if Reilly had taken you a thousand miles away. The thing is, we didn't know Eryx can also sense the mark. He took her the night she and Phoenix were going to elope, and we went after her, but by the time we got there, it was too late."

"What a terrible, horrible story. On her wedding night." She imagined it, a girl packing her bag, excited to run off and get married, then taken by a stranger and murdered. "What does that mean, she was marked? How? Where?"

Surprising her, he leaned close and whispered, "If one of us has sex with an Anabo, she's marked."

She blushed and hated herself for it.

He grinned, and she knew she must be completely red, but she couldn't look away from his eyes. They seemed a little different today, brighter or something. Good Lord, he was beautiful. She seriously considered sitting on her hands to keep from touching him.

Instead, she made herself look away from him, and that's when she noticed Brody had carried the desk chair to the window and was now standing on it, removing the ball finial from the end of the drapery rod, which was actually a section of PVC pipe covered in dusty, faded fabric. "What are you doing?" Panic made her sound shrill. "Get down from there! Oh my God, don't do that!"

She flew off the bed and ran at him, reaching for the rolled-up canvas when he pulled it from inside the rod, but he held it too high. "You can't take it! You've got no right!" She'd taken it out of the protective white tube to make sure Melanie never found it, which turned out to be a smart move, because the white tube was gone. Now she was about to lose the painting anyway. She'd promised Mom to take care of it, and she was desperate to get it away from Brody. "Give it back! Jax, make him give it back."

Jax was there, reaching for the canvas. "You'll get it back, I promise, but let us take it for a little while so we can figure out why Eryx wants it so much. There's a Lumina on the Mephisto Mountain who's an artist, who's cleaned and restored our paintings for years. He'll take a look, and I'll return it to you in a few days, I promise."

"Where's the Mephisto Mountain?"

"You've been there. We live on the Mephisto Mountain. It's surrounded by the same blue mist that hides Kyanos, a barrier that makes all of us and all the buildings invisible to the real world. And to Eryx. No one can breach the mists unless they're Lumina or Mephisto, which is me and my brothers. The mists are what keep the Purgatories from escaping. So trust me, if this painting is on the mountain, no one can get it."

"Even me?"

"You can pass through the mists, because you're Anabo. And if you were marked, you'd be safe there, where Eryx couldn't get to you."

So if she ever had sex with Jax, she'd be confined to living on a mountain behind some blue fog for the rest of her life. Looking up at his perfect face, the concern in his eyes, she wished that he wasn't a dark angel, that he was just a regular guy. She'd already be crazy in love with him.

But he wasn't a regular guy. All these feelings she had were wrong. She had to stop staring at him. Stop wanting him.

Swallowing, she looked away from his eyes and focused on the rolled-up canvas in his hand. "What about this artist? You said he's a Lumina. What's that?"

"I'm a Lumina," Brody said, stepping off the chair, then carrying it back to the desk. He looked at her and smiled that sweet, calm smile. "We're ordinary people recruited by the Mephisto to live on the mountain and work for them. If we agree, we become immortal, and have certain abilities that help us do our job."

"Like what sort of jobs?"

"Anything the Mephisto need to plan one of their takedowns. We have a whole group that does nothing but place records, so if someone needs to go out in the real world and prove they're a real person, there's paperwork to back them up. Jax has everything he needs to start school tomorrow because the records Luminas took care of it. He has a birth certificate on file at the courthouse, and a transcript in his student file at a boarding school in Dorset, England."

"What do you do?"

Brody grinned. "Hack into computers, invent better tools for the Mephisto to use when they're out in the field, and just generally be awesomely smart. I looked all over this room to figure out where you might hide a painting, and I caught your quick glance up at the curtain rod. Pretty smart, yeah?"

"You're humble, too."

He blinked at her from behind his nerdy glasses. "I'm not conceited, if that's what you're saying. But God gave me certain talents, and I'm all about using them to do my job better."

"You're brilliant," Jax said. "We all think so. Tell you what, why don't you take the painting to Andres, and I'll be along after a while. I'm going to help Sasha put things back together."

Brody took the canvas from Jax, then smiled at her again. "I'm glad to know you, Sasha. I'll see you tomorrow." He disappeared.

"Tomorrow?"

"He's going to school with me. I'm hoping it will make me less scary."

"How? If he's an immortal, like you, and lives with you and does what you do, how will he make you less scary?"

"He's the polar opposite of what I am. My brothers and I are the only ones who can take the lost souls to Hell on Earth. The Luminas are support people who take care of the details when we need them. We recruit the best people, who're always happy and upbeat, and it's really helpful if they have some special talent or skill that will help us with what we do. If they agree to join us, they leave the real world behind. Some marry, some don't, but they're always happy and extreme in their faith in God. Luminas are living angels, with all the characteristics of humans, except they don't grow old or die."

"What happens to them when the end of the world comes?"

"They go to Heaven. In fact, if they decide they're tired of working, if they want to leave, they can ask and be sent anytime."

"Do many of them do that?"

He smiled at her. "None. Ever. It's a nice life on the mountain, Sasha. We build cottages for them, and they can have anything they want. About the only thing they can't do is mingle among humans, but that's mostly because we worry they'll fall in love with someone and it could only lead to heartbreak. I'm taking a risk bringing Brody to school with me, but I can't get anything accomplished if everyone's scared to death of me."

"So they like working for you, helping plan how to take people to Hell on Earth?"

"I think so. They see, all the time, what Eryx and his Skia do to humans, how it wrecks whole families and ruins lives. And they know that the more there are, the more there will be. The only hope is to keep the numbers down."

"Why couldn't the Luminas be out among humans and maybe convince them not to pledge their soul?"

"Because we can't interfere with free will. People have to make their own choices, without any intrusion from Heaven or Hell, or from living angels, dark or otherwise." Moving a pile of clothes with his boot, he frowned and changed the subject. "Did she destroy everything you own? Will you have something to wear to school tomorrow?"

"What I have on."

He looked her up and down. "Nice, but you need other clothes, Sasha. Let me take you shopping. We'll go anywhere you like and get anything you want."

"I don't have much money."

"I'll pay. No strings, I promise."

"I could tell Tim, and he'd buy me some new stuff. If it wasn't for him, I'd be living on the street because Melanie would kick me out. She's brutal, Jax. She told me this morning that the CIA thinks my mother is dead. I feel sorry for him, because he has to be married to her."

"Then don't make him feel worse. Let me help you, and he won't have to know what Melanie did."

She didn't see that she had much of a choice. Telluride was superexpensive, and it wasn't like she had any way of getting to another town, one with stores that real people could afford. Unless she wanted to wear the same clothes every single day, she had to accept Jax's offer. Looking up into his black eyes, she was struck all over again by random, vivid, unfamiliar emotions, but somewhere in the depths of those eyes, she also saw sincerity . . . and genuine affection. "All right, Jax, but let's call it a loan. Even if I'm never able to pay you back, it'd make me feel better about being a mooch."

"You're not a mooch, and you can pretend you mean to pay me back if you want. I'll even pretend that I'd accept." He moved closer and slid his arms around her. "Where do you want to go?"

She tried not to slip her arms beneath his trench coat, or spread her palms across his broad, muscular back, or inhale the delicious scent of him, or rest her cheek against his hard, warm chest. She tried. And failed. "San Francisco," she finally said. "It's where I know how to find things. Start at Macy's in Union Square."

A moment later, they stood in the men's department. Glancing around, astonished that no one appeared to notice they'd materialized out of nowhere, she said, "I was kinda thinking about jeans and sweaters, instead of a pinstripe suit."

"I need something to cover my eyes." He dropped his arms and stepped back, then reached for a pair of sunglasses from a rotating display. Sliding them onto his face, he said, "What do you think?"

They were dark wraparounds. In his black trench coat, with his black hair and dark stubble, he looked awesome. She resisted the urge to melt into a puddle at his feet. "They'll do."

From behind her, someone said, "Hey, Sasha! What's up, babe? Somebody told me you moved to Colorado."

With her heart in her throat, she turned just as Smith Hardwick swooped down to plant a kiss on her lips. It didn't mean anything. He did it to every girl who ran with their group, because that's just who he was.

Before she could say a word, or decide whether or not to

introduce Jax, or formulate some kind of lie about why she was in San Francisco, Smith was on his back, sliding across the slick wooden floor toward a rack of polos. Jax stood just next to her, looking like a demon from Hell, his hands clenched into fists.

SEVEN

HE DIDN'T PUNCH THE GUY. JUST MENTALLY SHOVED HIM as hard as he could to get him away from Sasha. He saw him kiss her and instinct took over, but the second he saw the guy hit the rack of shirts, he knew he'd gone way overboard. The look on Sasha's face verified it. Man, was she pissed.

She started to run to the guy, but he couldn't let her do that. Too much explaining. She'd demand he apologize; many lies would follow. Best to make a clean break. So before she'd taken two steps, he hauled her back, erased the guy's memory of them, and popped them to another part of the store.

Jerking away as fast as she could, she turned on him and said in an angry whisper, "Why did you do that? Smith is a friend! A nice guy!"

"He kissed you."

"So? It's not like you own me! And it wasn't a kiss. It's just how he says hello."

"Are you in love with him?"

Rolling her eyes, she turned to the display of socks next to them and said to a pair of argyles, "Jax, I've known him since I was four years old and started preschool at St. Michael's. He's like a brother or something. I would have liked to see him, to visit a little. Why'd you have to go and shove him like that?"

"Too hard, huh?"

"You shouldn't have shoved him at all."

"But he kissed you."

She shot him a look, then said to the argyles, "When I start school tomorrow, if I meet somebody and he asks me out, if he touches me, are you going to be there shoving him across the floor?"

Just the idea made his stomach hurt. "I hated that, Sasha. A lot."

Her sigh was heartfelt. She turned to face him and said in a really sad voice, "Don't worry too much about it happening in Telluride. Guys don't like me. I mean, I've always had guy friends, but none of them have ever liked me. Not *liked me*, liked me."

"You're wrong. You have to be wrong. You're so beautiful, such an incredible person, how did you not have a million boyfriends?"

"I don't know. It's not as if I didn't try. But it's like I'm a nun or something. Like I'm untouchable."

"Maybe because you're Anabo. Maybe human guys can sense it, and they know you're never gonna be easy. I don't know a whole lot about humans, but I do know guys, and they're all about easy. You get what I'm saying?"

"I get it. And I guess you'd know, Mr. Gets It in the Dark with Strangers."

"It's not like that with you, Sasha."

"If you say it's because I'm Anabo, or that you respect me too much, or something stupid like that, I'll kick you in the nuts and laugh."

He said to the argyles, "You are Anabo, and I do respect you, but I'd still like to see you naked. In fact, I'd be working on it right now, if success didn't mean you'd be forced to live on our mountain the rest of your life. Also, there's that pesky problem that you think I'm repulsive."

"Not that way. I wish it wasn't true, because I'm really not okay with who you are, but no way do I think you're repulsive."

"So you'd like to have your way with me, even though you don't respect me."

He was teasing her, but she didn't realize it. She blushed, looked away, and said to the panty hose, "I just keep remembering what it was like to kiss you. I've never felt like that before."

He moved a little closer and touched her hair, so soft and silky. "It's powerful stuff, Sasha. Don't beat yourself up about it.

You can feel like that and still think I'm creepy. It doesn't make you less of a person."

"I don't think you're creepy."

"Then what's the problem?"

"I . . . I don't know. You're immortal, for one thing. What happens if we stay together? I'd be an old lady, wearing these support hose, and you'd still be a hot eighteen-year-old."

"Maybe you'd become immortal, too."

Looking up quickly, she was clearly stunned. "Are you serious?"

"Well, yeah. It could happen, if you wanted."

She stepped back, staring at him with wide eyes. "No, I wouldn't want that! Live forever? It's not right. It's weird. And what would I do for all eternity? Sit around and wait for you to get home from killing people?"

Jax was tired. She was never going to go for this, so why the hell did he try? "If you were immortal, you'd be with me when I go to . . . to . . . ."

"Kill people?"

"Stop saying that! Why can't you see them for what they are? It's a bigger deal to step on a bug. And what would you have me do, let guys like Kasamov and Bruno stick around to trick more people into losing their souls?"

Great tears welled in her eyes and slowly rolled down her cheeks. "I don't know," she whispered. "I don't know what I want you to do. I want you to be different. I want you to be

183

normal and not from Hell. How can I do this? How can I be with you and still believe in God?"

"Do you think I don't believe in God?"

"I know you believe there is a God, but you're not about Heaven."

"Only because I can't help it. I was born this way, and maybe Heaven's not in the cards for me, but it doesn't mean I don't want it."

Swiping at her tears, she moved close and slid her arms around him. "I'm sorry, Jax. I wish it was different."

He circled her shoulders and dropped his cheek to her hair.

"I'm not really in the mood to shop, after all. Let's just go back to Telluride."

"You need some clothes, and we're going to get some. We'll just try to avoid anyone you know, deal?"

She nodded against his chest. "Deal."

❧

Shopping for clothes wasn't something he did. Ever. All of their clothes were bought for them by the Luminas, or handmade by the Purgs. He'd shopped before, but always for things like books, or ski equipment, or liquor. Sometimes cigars. But shopping for clothes was a whole new thing, and hanging around in the girls' department was an experience like no other. The scents were intriguing, the dyes and fibers from the clothes mingling with perfume and skin and assaulting his nose. Above it all, he never lost Sasha's scent, even after she disappeared with an armload of clothes through a doorway to the dressing room and said she'd be right back.

She didn't come right back. She was in there forever, until he began to worry that something was wrong. Maybe she was choking on something, or had tripped and hit her head. When he couldn't stand waiting any longer, he cloaked himself to invisible and popped to where her scent was strongest, which was inside a tiny cubicle with a mirror.

She stood there in a pair of jeans and nothing else.

Nothing. Else.

He stared. Reality was so much better than imagination, he was speechless with wonder. He saw her birthmark, just below her right breast.

Crossing her arms over her lovely breasts, she glared at him. "You can't be in here!" she whispered. "No guys allowed."

"No one can see me. I'm invisible."

"I can see you!"

And so she could. The reminder of how she was changing made him anxious, so he looked once more at the swell of her beautiful breasts, then popped out. He regretted that. A lot. The image of her soft skin and perfect pink nipples was burned into his brain, making him all the more bummed that she couldn't get past what he was and be with him.

Finally, after another ten minutes of watching giggling girls and tired mothers wander through the racks, he was relieved when Sasha reappeared, several items in her arms. He went with her to the register and paid cash, bemused as they walked away and she was freaking about how much it cost. "It's nothing, Sasha. We're very rich, and this is like . . . nothing. Say thank you and stop talking about it."

"Thank you, Jax."

∽∾∾

Jax didn't take her back to Telluride until after dark. Before they were done, he'd bought her tons of new clothes, underwear, perfume—because a saleslady had accosted them and he decided she definitely needed to smell like what was on that little white card—a new sketchbook, a watercolor of the Golden Gate Bridge he bought from a woman on the street, and a top-of-the-line MacBook with a pink carry case. His generosity was huge, and when she protested, certain he'd regret dropping so much cash, he said, "You're fun to buy stuff for because you get so excited about everything. Let me do this. Let me have some fun. Fun isn't something I get to have much of."

He finally agreed to stop buying her things and they returned to Telluride, to her room, just after seven o'clock. He wanted to stay and help her clean up, but she said, "I'd rather do it myself. Thanks, but you go on home and get ready for school tomorrow."

"Will you be okay? What about Melanie?"

"I'm going to avoid her as much as I can, but if she comes in here and hassles me, I'll deal. Don't worry about me."

"You might as well tell me to stop breathing." He looked around at the mess and shook his head. "This blows, but I'm glad it was her, searching, and not a Skia, asking you questions."

"You'll take good care of the painting, won't you?"

"It'll be safe, no worries."

"Will you tell me what it is? My curiosity was killing me, but Mom said it was starting to flake, and I was afraid if I unrolled it, tons of paint would fall off."

"I'll tell you. In fact, after Andres has had a chance to look it over, I'll take you to see it."

"You'll give it back, won't you?"

"Of course I will. Put it out of your mind." He went to the desk and picked up the half of her broken laptop that contained the hard drive. "I'll see if Brody can get the files off this, if you want."

"That'd be awesome. My college essay is on there. Applications are due in a week, so I kinda need to get on that."

He stood straight, and she knew he was about to disappear. She didn't want him to. She wanted him to wrap his arms around her and kiss her again. In fact, she wasn't sure she'd ever wanted anything so much. What was wrong with her? How could she want him like this, knowing what he was?

Almost as if he could read her thoughts, he said quietly, "The ball's always in your court. I'm here, and ready, if you ever change your mind. Good night, Sasha. Don't forget to call the dog." He faded away, and she was alone.

∽≈∾

"For a girl who hates you, Sasha sure hangs with you a lot." Phoenix was in Jax's room when Jax came home, playing Demon

Slayer on the screen behind the Mephisto portrait. "Brody says you ran him off, and here you are, six hours later."

"She needed some clothes, so I took her shopping."

"Bummer, man. Hate shopping. And major bummer that her aunt isn't just a lost soul, but a crazy-bitch lost soul. There's something extra weird going on with that family."

"Sasha says there was bad blood between her father and Melanie, and she thinks her mother and Tim hate each other."

"Yeah, that's a lot of hate and animosity for no apparent reason. There's something more to the story." Phoenix shut down the game and hit the remote that lowered the portrait over the screen before he got to his feet. "You need to see the painting, Jax."

"Okay." Something in his brother's expression forewarned him this wasn't going to be good, so he was primed for the worst, that the painting really did depict the Mephisto Covenant.

At least, he thought he was primed for the worst. He was wrong. Way wrong.

In a document lab in the basement, a small room within a whole network of offices and workspaces, files and computer banks, Andres sat at a tilted table, a lighted magnifying glass between his face and the canvas. When Jax came in, Andres pushed the glass out of the way and rolled his stool back so Jax could see the picture.

It was a portrait of a couple, standing atop a giant boulder in the middle of the mountains. Beneath them was Hell, Lucifer reaching up to touch the girl's bare foot. Above them, God peeked through the clouds, surrounded by angels, extending his hand to touch the guy's hair. She was blond, with blue eyes. He was dark-haired, with dark eyes. They stood together, facing the valley below, arms around each other while the wind blew the fabric of their long robes back, outlining their shapes, lifting their hair to wave behind them. In the far distance, a lone figure in black stood on the bank of a river, staring at the couple, his expression frustrated and angry, unable to cross because of the raging fury of the water.

Eryx. The guy was Eryx, and he couldn't reach the couple because they were together, united, with God and Lucifer protecting them. The Mephisto Covenant.

Jax stared at it, the implications running through his mind, shaking him all the way to his bones. It wasn't an anonymous couple standing on the boulder, which was exactly like the one on the northern slope of the Mephisto Mountain. It was he and Sasha.

"The artist's name is Andolini," Andres said. "He was an apprentice to Leonardo who claimed to be visited by angels in his sleep, given visions by divinity. He was executed as a heretic in 1505."

The painting was over five hundred years old, yet the woman had Sasha's face. It was her—there could be no mistake. Thank God she hadn't unrolled the canvas. "If Kasamov saw the painting, and he must have, since he described it to Eryx, why didn't he tell him about Sasha? He knew her, so he had to know this is her in the painting."

Andres pointed toward the woman's face. "She was different before."

"Before what?"

"Before I cleaned the dried and flaking paint from her eyes and cheeks. Someone altered her face, so she looked different." Andres looked up from the painting. "And there's something else." He rolled closer and pushed the magnifying glass over the section of the river where Eryx stood. "I noticed right away that the river runs in the wrong direction. You can see it's our own brook, at the base of the northern slope, swollen with snowmelt. The water should flow to the west, this way, because we are to the west of the Continental Divide. But as you can see by how the water breaks against the rocks, it flows to the east. When I looked closer and discovered someone had painted over the original, I cleaned this part and found a number beneath. Very tiny, so you can't see it without magnification. We think it's identifying information for a deposit box in Switzerland."

No wonder Sasha's mother was so adamant about keeping the painting safe. He told Andres about the lockbox, how Katya's refusal to give the contents to Alex Kasamov ultimately led to her deportation. "That must be why she left the painting with Sasha, to keep the account information safe."

Phoenix was staring at the tiny black dots that were numbers and letters. "She obviously showed this to Alex Kasamov, but why?"

Andres turned his stool to face both of them, his French accent more pronounced. "She was in love with him, and a woman in love wants to share everything, will trust even when she shouldn't. As Skia, Kasamov was a master manipulator. He seduced her, hoping to cajole the papers from her, as well as win her as a new follower for Eryx. When he began pressuring her, she saw he wasn't real, that it was all lies, and she told him to go away, but by then, she had shown him her whole world, including Sasha. She trusted him, which is how he was able to steal into Sasha's room and look for her birthmark."

Jax thought about yesterday, when Sasha told him all her secrets: about what frightened her, about her mother's deportation, about her birthmark. She trusted him, without really knowing him, because she liked him. He hadn't realized what it meant at the time. Now he did, but it made no difference. He'd blown it on the ski lift.

He looked at Phoenix. "Did Jane tell you all her secrets?"

He sighed and nodded, still staring at the painting, at the little black dots. "I think before Kasamov told Katya he was after the lockbox stuff, she showed him the painting because it's a remarkable piece of art. She probably told him about the numbers hidden beneath the paint because it's a clever thing to do, and she would've wanted him to know she can be clever." He looked at Jax. "That's why Eryx wants this painting so badly. It's not the picture he's interested in. It's those tiny numbers. If what Katya said was true, there are all kinds of incriminating things in that lockbox about some important people. Eryx could use it to blackmail them into pledging. Heads of state, corporate directors, people who can make a big difference in the world."

A cloud of dread settled around Jax. "You're right, which means he's not going to give up. If Katya won't give him what he wants, he'll make her life a living hell."

"And if she still won't cave, he'll go after what's important to her."

The cloud of dread zapped him with a lightning bolt. "He'll come after Sasha."

The three of them stared at the painting, thinking. Jax focused on Sasha's beautiful face, trying not to overthink why a painter five hundred years ago had envisioned them together. "The only thing to do is give the painting to Eryx, but we'll give him a fake. Andres, do you think you could reproduce it, but change it so it doesn't portray the Mephisto Covenant? Paint God touching her head, instead of mine. Also, paint Sasha's face so it isn't Sasha."

"Child's play," Andres said, smiling and looking eager. "And the numbers?"

"Reproduce those, too. Eryx is after the code to the box, and Kasamov told him it's on the painting, so we'll give it to him. By the time he sends someone to collect the contents, we'll already have Katya's papers and pictures and whatever else is in there. We'll replace them with other stuff her father and grandfather might have left to her, like jewelry and maybe some Russian icons. I'll send Boris to Moscow to pick up some things from an antique dealer."

"Genius!" Andres exclaimed.

Jax shoved his hands into his pockets so they wouldn't see how badly he was shaking. "We'll see how genius I am when Eryx gets the painting—if he buys that it's authentic, if he never suspects the contents of the box have been switched."

"Maybe by then, Sasha will be here, with us, and out of danger."

Turning on his heel, Jax left the document room, unable to tell Andres that Sasha would never be with them.

⁓⁓

After Jax left, Sasha went downstairs to look for trash bags. Tim was asleep in his recliner and Chris was eating a bowl of cereal. "Where've you been?" he asked. "Mom was looking for you. She's pissed that your room is such a mess."

Talk about adding insult to injury. What a bitch. "I'm about to clean it up. Where can I find some trash bags?"

"In the laundry room."

When she'd found the bags, she went back upstairs and started stuffing them with her ruined clothes, Boo hopping around in the middle of things, thinking she was playing with him. Poor dog was as dim as he was homely. But he was sweet, which trumped dumb and ugly. A few minutes later, he dove under the bed when someone knocked and she said, "Yeah?"

Chris opened her door and watched for a while before he asked, "Why are you throwing them away?"

She held up what used to be her favorite sweater. It had two holes cut out, right where her breasts would be.

"What happened?" After a minute, when she didn't answer, he pushed off the doorframe and stood straight, frowning. "She did it, didn't she?"

It had to be rough having a mom like Melanie. Sasha didn't have the heart to say what she really thought, so she just shrugged and continued stuffing the trash bag.

"I don't get why she hates you so much."

"She hated my dad and hates my mom, so I guess it's hate by association."

"I'm sorry, Sasha. Did you tell my dad? He'll buy you some new stuff."

"No, I didn't tell him. It's okay, Chris. I got some new things this afternoon."

"Do you want some help?"

She shook her head. "Thanks anyway."

He said good night and went to his room. Seconds later she heard his video game.

When she was done, she hauled the garbage bags outside, then went back to her room and put away her new clothes, thinking all over again how awesome it had been of Jax to take her shopping. She was anxious about starting at a new school tomorrow, but at least she wouldn't be wearing the same clothes every day this week.

She powered up the new MacBook and almost cried—it was so perfect. She checked her e-mail before logging onto Facebook, and nearly jumped for joy when she saw a message from her mom. Eagerly opening it, her happiness deflated as fast as it had arrived. Short and curt, all Mom said was, *I am in St. Petersburg, looking for a place to stay, then find a job. Love you.*

She replied and told her mother all about Telluride, and skiing, not saying much about Tim and Chris, not mentioning Brett and Melanie at all. Why whine about it? Besides, it wasn't like she could tell her about the Ravens. Mom wouldn't understand. She'd think Sasha was making it up, then would tell her she needed to pray for their souls.

Like that would do any good.

EIGHT

THE NEXT MORNING WAS MONDAY, HER FIRST DAY OF school at Telluride High. Sasha dressed in jeans, a red sweater, and the new black boots Jax had insisted on buying for her. She had a new black leather coat that wasn't as long as his trench coat, but almost. Looking in the mirror on the back of the bathroom door, she thought she looked different, older maybe. She'd taken extra care with her hair, pulling part of it into a clip, instead of her usual ponytail. She wore a little more makeup, and she went ahead and used the perfume. Today, she needed all the help she could get. This was freaking her out way more than she thought possible. She shoved a twenty into her backpack and looked at Boo. "I'll see you outside, buddy." He wagged his tail and disappeared.

Downstairs, Melanie was cooking breakfast. When Sasha

walked into the kitchen, she turned hostile eyes toward her. "Where did you get those clothes?"

"I found them at the Mountain Village Spa in the lost and found. Amazing what people leave behind at spas."

"Liar. You probably conned some dirty old man into buying them for you."

Was it any wonder there was bad blood between Melanie and Dad? Sasha strongly suspected she had always been like this, even before she gave her soul to Eryx.

Melanie pointed toward the table. "There's a muffin. Take it and get out."

The scent of bacon made her mouth water, but she obviously wasn't getting any of it. Without a word, she took the muffin and left. Outside, the weekend's heavy snow had moved out of the canyon, leaving behind a winter wonderland, blindingly bright in the morning sun, the sky so blue, it made her smile. Living with the Shrivers sucked, but Telluride was awesomely beautiful. Boots crunching in the snow, with Boo trotting along beside her, she walked to the end of the block, past other colorful Victorians, turned right, and passed a row of town houses, then some condominiums, until she was on Colorado.

Traffic was light at seven thirty, but a lot of cars were parked along the curb outside some eatery to the east. If she had time, she'd go down there and order a humongous breakfast platter. Instead, she bit into the stale muffin and decided sawdust would taste about like this.

The high school was at the far northeastern edge of Telluride, only a few blocks from the Shrivers'. Everything was only a few blocks from the Shrivers'. Telluride was very small.

She reached the school grounds at quarter to eight. Crossing the wide expanse of snow that led to the building, she smiled at Boo, jumping along beside her, looking like a canine Santa Claus when the snow gathered in his beard. She looked ahead, toward the school—a beautiful, modern building—and was actually excited to get there, only because she'd see Jax again.

She'd dreamed about him last night, and had woken up thinking about him. Her whole plan to stay away from him was going to be a lot harder if she couldn't get thoughts of him out of her head. The anticipation she felt right now was also not a good sign. She shouldn't be this excited to see a guy she planned to avoid.

At the front doors, she took Boo off the leash and said good-bye, watching as he ran around the corner. She admitted she was glad to have him. If anything got weird today with Mr. Bruno, or the Ravens, it was comforting to know the dog would be there to help.

But she hoped she wouldn't need him.

Taking a deep breath, she opened the door. The office was inside, just to the right. A young woman with spiky hair, the roots dark and the tips bleached white, looked up from where she sat behind a long counter. "Good morning. May I help you?"

"My mom had to leave the country on business and will be

gone at least until next summer. So I'm staying with relatives, Tim and Melanie Shriver, and need to enroll in school."

Looking sympathetic, the woman nodded and opened a file drawer. "We've actually got less than two weeks before Christmas break, so it's probably going to be hard to get up to speed, but we have great teachers, and they'll help all they can. What's your name?"

"Sasha." She watched the woman lay some papers on the counter. "Thanks, Mrs. . . . ?"

"I'm *Miss* Rose, but everyone just calls me Rose. Fill these out, and we'll get you set up. Mr. or Mrs. Shriver will need to come by and sign something, and I'll need your transcript from your old school. Oh, and a birth certificate."

"I have my transcript, but not a birth certificate. Can I get that to you later? This all happened kinda quick."

"No problem."

The sound of a motorcycle made them both look toward the windows. Make that motorcycles, plural. Jax rode up to the building on a chopper, no helmet; beside him, Brody rode a smaller, different bike, his head covered in a helmet with a dark face guard that had a whole Darth Vader thing going on.

"Wonder who that is," said Rose.

Sasha said nothing, just bent her head to fill out the paperwork.

A few minutes later, she looked up when Jax came in, assaulted by his scent, dizzy just looking at him. Instead of his trench coat, he wore a black leather bomber with a black henley underneath and a pair of faded, ragged jeans. His eyes were covered by black-rimmed Wayfarers.

Brody stood beside him, dwarfed by Jax's size, wearing his geek glasses and a green-checkered flannel over a *Star Trek* T-shirt.

Neither of them looked her way, but walked to the counter and focused on Rose. Brody did the talking. "We just moved to Telluride last week, to live with our dad, and he didn't agree with us to start school after the holidays, so we need to sign up. I'm Brody Hewitt, and this is my brother, Jack."

Rose went through her spiel, then took all three of their transcripts and disappeared into a smaller office.

While she was gone, Sasha stared at a photograph of Telluride in fall that hung on the wall above a filing cabinet, listening to the front doors open again and again, and the sound of kids as they came inside. She could feel them staring, no doubt wondering who they were.

Brody said under his breath, "Relax, Sasha."

"Easy for you to say."

"Not really. I got the crap kicked out of me all the time in high school. I was kind of a dork."

Kind of? She looked over Brody's head at Jax, who said, "I'm almost looking forward to this. It's *Revenge of the Nerds* in real life."

Brody actually blushed. "Jax thinks the girls are going to like me."

"If you don't start speaking in Klingon, or wax poetic about

Battlestar Gallactica, I'm thinking he's right." There was something awesomely appealing about Brody.

The door into the smaller office opened, and Rose reappeared, holding out papers to each of them. "Here are your schedules. It's so close to semester's end, Mr. Mooney put all three of you in the same classes. If we need to tweak for next semester, we will, but to get started, we thought you'd like to be together, being the new kids and all."

So much for not sharing classes with Jax. She'd be with him all day, every day. But there wasn't anything she could do about it, so she'd just have to sit as far away from him as possible. She took the schedule from Rose and gave it a quick look, her eyes immediately drawn to one name—Emil Bruno. "Can I request a different history teacher?"

Clearly surprised, Rose asked, "Why, Sasha? Mr. Bruno is everyone's favorite."

Of course he was. He'd want that, wouldn't he? Thinking fast, she smiled, trying to hide her revulsion. "Oh, uhm, well, he's a friend of my aunt, and I wouldn't want anyone to think I have an advantage . . . or anything."

"Don't be silly! Brett is in his class, and Mr. Bruno certainly doesn't grant him any leeway. If anything, he rides Brett harder than anyone else."

Rose was plainly a card-carrying member of the Mr. Bruno Fan Club, which made sense, she guessed. Jax said the Skia were experts at attracting admirers and followers, drawing them in, looking for their vulnerabilities, playing to their wants and desires so they'd take the oath.

Looking at Rose, who seemed like a nice woman, it struck her that she might not be so nice if she kept hanging around Mr. Bruno. What did she want that Bruno would promise?

In most things, Sasha tended to give in, go along, avoid confrontation. But this wasn't something she could swallow. "There's gotta be another history teacher." She ignored Jax's sudden hyperactive boot, tapping against the counter. He was telling her to cool it, but she was compelled to do this. She'd never pass history if she had to be in the same room with Creepy McFreakypants. The man made her sick.

Rose lost her smile, beginning to look annoyed. "Only for freshmen and sophomores. You don't need to repeat history, Sasha, so if you intend to graduate in May, you'll need to sit in Mr. Bruno's class."

Sasha's palms broke out in a sweat and her stomach griped, threatening to toss the awful muffin. Evidently, Bruno freaked her out even more than Alex Kasamov. Just thinking about Bruno was enough to make her sick. Grasping the schedule in clammy fingers, she turned and hurried from the office, needing a bathroom. Humiliated, rushing down the hall past staring faces, she wondered if she'd make it. *God, please don't let me hurl right here in the hall on my first day.*

There, just ahead—she could make it. Maybe. Already, her stomach was heaving.

Then the impossible happened. Mr. Bruno appeared in front of her, blocking her way, his smooth voice with its weird accent dooming her quest for a toilet. "Why, hello, Sasha. I was hoping I'd run into you."

She couldn't help it.

She threw up on his shoes.

~

The only thing he had told her was not to act afraid around Bruno. So the first thing she did was throw up on the guy. Jax started after her, until Brody grabbed his jacket sleeve and stopped him. "Leave it alone. You've got to play this cool, or the whole deal's blown before we've been here an hour."

He was right, of course, so Jax was bound to stand there with all the other kids, staring at Sasha, powerless to help her. He saw Bruno's superfast expression of fury, quickly replaced by a totally fake smile. He reached out to touch her, but she jerked away from him and booked it to the girls' room. Bruno stared after her, obviously curious why she had had such a bad reaction to him.

"Dammit, Brody, what are we gonna do with her?"

"Not a lot we can do except keep an eye on her. And make sure we sit next to her in Bruno's class. Did you see how he looked at her?"

"I saw." Jax glanced around at the faces of the others, almost moved to throw up himself when he saw how they fawned all over Bruno, saying how sorry they were that that chick had ruined his shoes, and man, was she a loser, or what?

Mr. Bruno gave them a patient look. "She's just nervous because she's new. You guys need to cut her a break."

To which they all acted like that was their plan, all along.

"He could tell them to eat dirt and they'd do it," Jax said to Brody.

"It was pretty genius of Eryx to place him as a teacher. Give him another week and he'll have at least twenty more Ravens. It doesn't look as if they're the outsiders here like they were at Sasha's school in San Francisco."

"Yeah," Jax said, the old familiar instinct washing over him, "genius." It took discipline not to rush at Bruno, get him in a headlock, and pop him around the world to the patch of ground that opened to Hell on Earth.

The suck-ups followed Bruno when he walked toward the boys' bathroom, while the rest of the kids turned to look at Jax and Brody. For the first time in his long life, he knew what it was to feel awkward. But he didn't show it. Remembering what he'd read in that book, he looked at the closest kid, a tallish guy with dark red hair and some intense green eyes, and jerked a hello nod. "How's it goin'?"

"Okay." The kid glanced at Brody before he said, "I'm Thomas Vasquez. So you guys are starting today? This close to the break?"

Brody nodded and made a face, like it was so lame. "We moved to live with our dad last week, and he insisted."

"Wait," Thomas said, looking between them rapidly, "you mean you guys are *brothers*?"

"Fraternal twins," Jax said. "I'm Jack, and he's Brody." Noticing again how tall Thomas was, he asked, "Do you play basketball?"

"Point guard. How about you?"

"I play a little."

Brody said, in a perfect he-always-shows-me-up voice, "He's lying. He plays a lot. He was center at the school we went to in England."

"Hey, cool," Thomas said, smiling now. "We could use a center. Show up in the gym after school and talk to Coach Hightower."

"Okay, yeah, I'll do that." Perfect. If he had an excuse to stay after school every day, he could go through Bruno's things without worrying so much about getting caught. And in the bonus round, there was basketball.

Brody, he noticed, was staring at a girl walking toward them. She was seriously put together, walked like she wanted it bad, and gave a look to every guy she passed, ignoring the girls. The only thing marring her perfection was the vague shadow around her eyes. That a beautiful girl like that was a lost soul only served to piss him off more, and his instinct to go after Bruno almost choked him.

"Who's she?" Brody asked, although he knew exactly who she was. He'd worked on the takedown plan with Phoenix.

Thomas looked over his shoulder, then frowned. "Julianne Oliver. She goes out with Kelley Easter, who everybody calls East. She may look like your best wet dream, but stay away from her. She's a bitch on wheels. East loves beating the hell out of anybody who looks at her, which is why she makes every guy she passes think she wants some."

Jax watched Julianne go into the girls' room. Sasha was in there. He felt really hot all of a sudden and realized it was fear. This was going to eat him up, watching Sasha navigate her way around people who'd want her dead if they knew what she was. At least she'd lost a little of her naïveté, a silver lining to the transformation he'd inadvertently started. And she knew who they were, the threat they posed.

But nothing would make him feel better about all this until the Ravens and Mr. Bruno were history, dead or dying in that pit of bodies deep underground.

~

After tossing her cookies all over Mr. Bruno's shoes, Sasha had wanted to climb in a hole, curl up in a ball, and die. "I'm so sorry," she'd said to the floor, unable to unbend and look at his face, to see the dark shadow around his horrible eyes. She sensed a deep, dark fury, directed at her. She shook with terror.

But his voice was calm, composed, gentle even. "It's quite all right. You're nervous, it being your first day." He reached out and grasped her arm. "Let me take you to the nurse."

Unbending, she jerked away from him, fear overriding

mortification, blocking the faces of the others who stared at her like she was a freak. Without a word, she had rushed to move around him to go to the restroom, where he couldn't follow.

It was crowded, most of the girls standing in front of one long mirror that hung above a row of three sinks. They brushed their hair, applied lip gloss, chattered, and laughed—until she came in.

Dead silence. They all turned to look. None said a word.

Then a plain sort of girl with brown hair and nice eyes stepped forward. "Hi," she said, her expression concerned. "Are you okay?"

Sasha swallowed uncontrollably, praying she wouldn't cry.

God was on a coffee break or something, because he didn't help her out of this one, either. One tear escaped and rolled across her cheek. May as well go ahead and speak up. They'd all know as soon as they walked out into the hallway. On a slight hiccup, she shook her head and said in a tight voice, "It's my first day, and I just threw up on Mr. Bruno's shoes."

Instantly, there was an audible gasp. It echoed through the bathroom. From inside one of the stalls, a voice said, "That blows."

Someone giggled. "Literally."

Laughter ran through the whole group.

"Poor thing," the brown-haired girl said, moving closer. "Hey, Rachel, get a wet paper towel, wouldja?"

A tall girl with skinny glasses, a sheepskin vest, an itty-bitty skirt, and cowboy boots came forward with a soppy mess of brown paper.

"Squeeze it out," Brown Hair commanded. "She doesn't need to take a bath."

They all moved closer, staring curiously, watching while she dabbed at her mouth and the sweat on her forehead. "I'm Erin," said Brown Hair. "This is Rachel." She pointed to Cowboy Boots. "That's Amanda." She nodded toward a girl with dark hair, sad eyes, translucent skin, and some serious *I Love the Eighties* glasses. "And Bree's in the potty."

The toilet flushed, the door opened, and a tall, thin girl in stacked boots and a filmy, flowing black dress appeared. She wasn't exactly Goth. More like the runner-up for Miss Transylvania. Coal-black hair so long it touched her backside, blood red lips, snow-white skin, and dark eyes lined with dark shadows.

"Bree's into vampires," Rachel said while Bree washed her hands. "Ever since she read *Flashlight*."

"*Twilight*," Erin corrected, smiling at Sasha. "Now you know who we are, you gotta dish. What's your name, why did you move to Telluride, and why were you calling Ralph on Bruno's shoes?"

They all smiled encouragingly. These didn't seem like mean girls, and she was enormously grateful. "I'm Sasha Annenkova, from Oakland, staying with my aunt and uncle until next summer because my mom had to go to Russia on business."

"Who are your aunt and uncle?"

Her insides clenched, and she answered quietly, "Tim and Melanie Shriver."

"*Shut! Up!*" Rachel's eyes sparkled. "You're *living* with Brett Shriver?"

Astonished, Sasha nodded slowly.

"Ohmigod," Rachel gushed, "he's so hot! I'm going to be your new BFF and come over all the time."

Did she not realize what kind of guy Brett was? She obviously didn't know he was a murderer, but couldn't she at least see that he was an asshat?

Amanda shuffled her feet and cleared her throat. "Chris isn't so bad to look at, either."

Never in her wildest dreams did she think her living arrangements would be considered something that worked in her favor, especially since Melanie was apparently the town ho.

Erin patted her arm. "Are you feeling better?"

She smiled. "Yeah. I'm just really hungry, and nervous, I guess."

Rachel nodded, as if she knew exactly what she meant. "I throw up all the time."

Bree tossed her hair back over her shoulder, silver bangles tinkling. "It's called *bulimia*, honey, but I don't think Sasha's a hurler."

Rachel looked insulted. "I do *not* have bulimia!"

"Okay, whatever. Next time you toss up a whole pizza, go ahead and blame it on the flu." She reached toward the counter and picked up a black backpack, embroidered with a set of fangs. Withdrawing a wrapped bar, she handed it to Sasha. "Granola and honey and little pieces of pineapple. Delicious! And it's got something that'll make your boobs grow."

They all looked at the bar in Sasha's hand, quiet and serious.

Starving, she wanted to open and eat it in three bites, but she was afraid they'd stare at her boobs to see if they grew.

"Well," Rachel said, "welcome to Telluride. If you need something, like a study partner, or a housemate, let me know."

Curious, Sasha asked her, "How long have you had a crush on Brett?"

"Since sixth grade. He still doesn't know I'm alive."

"That goes for all of us," Bree said. "We're not cool enough or hot enough to be on his radar."

Relief made her smile. Rachel had a thing for a guy she didn't know at all. If she came over, if she did get to know Brett, she was bound to discover who he was, and that would be the end of her crush.

The door opened behind her, and someone walked in. Sasha tensed, watching the faces of the others become shuttered, all of them looking away, gathering up backpacks from the counter and floor, hustling to leave.

A blonde stepped around Sasha. "You must be the one who barfed on Mr. Bruno's shoes." She looked right into her eyes, and Sasha recoiled. "I heard you came on to East yesterday."

This must be his girlfriend, Julianne, who pledged her soul to Eryx so she could get into modeling school. Sasha didn't know there was such a thing as modeling school. "That's a lie."

From behind the new arrival, whose orange sweater announced she had absolutely no need of boob-enhancing granola bars, Erin made a slicing motion across her neck, and the others all shook their heads, mouthing the word *no*.

Julianne jerked around and glared at them, until they all scurried out of the door. When the girl looked at her again, Sasha told her, "East said I look like I'd give good head, and I called him a douche bag. If that means I came on to him, then yeah, totes."

Julianne tensed up, like she was about to haul off and slug her, but Sasha didn't flinch or move a muscle.

"I've heard nothing but your name all f'ing weekend. East and Brett think you're a good candidate for the Ravens, but I don't. You're a goody-goody; I can see it in your eyes. I bet you've never even given a guy head. I bet you don't even know what it means."

Sasha decided to cut her losses. She opened the granola bar and was just about to take a bite when Julianne grabbed it out of her hand and tossed it into the closest toilet. "Answer me!"

Harsh. Way harsh. Sasha was so hungry, she was dizzy. Turning her back on Miss High and Mighty with Terrible Taste in Boyfriends, she walked out of the girls' bathroom and ran smack into Jax.

"Are you all right?" His hands against her arms were warm, even through her coat, and she suddenly felt so much better.

Looking up at his shades, she nodded slowly. "You saw what happened, I guess."

"I did. I came to see if you're okay."

She noticed out of the corner of her eye that a janitor was cleaning up the horrible mess. "I'm okay. Just humiliated and feeling like a fool for being so obvious. I couldn't help it, Jax. He freaks me out."

"Did Alex make you sick like this?"

"Pretty much, yeah, but only when he was actually there. Just thinking about Bruno made me sick, and when he touched me and I saw that shadow around his eyes . . ." She frowned. "I never saw a shadow around Alex's eyes."

"Anybody else make you sick that you remember?"

"Mom took me to a new dentist when I was about ten, after our old dentist died, and as soon as he touched me, I threw up. I cried and told him to stay away from me, so Mom took me to somebody else. There was also a lady in the shoe department at Macy's who made me feel sick. I finally had to go somewhere else to buy shoes."

"They were undoubtedly Skia, and freaky to you because of instinct. Some part of you knows that if they discover what you are, they'll want you dead. They're uncannily intuitive, so try to think about something else when Bruno's around. Something nice that makes you happy."

She didn't tell him that would be him. No matter how hard she tried, he was all she thought about.

Without any warning, someone yanked her hair so hard, her head snapped back and her eyes instantly watered.

"Listen, *bitch*, you're gonna talk to me. Turn around and—*ow!*"

"Let go of her hair," Jax said in a low, menacing voice, "and I won't break your arm."

The tension was gone, and she was suddenly spinning around, held against his side to face Julianne, who looked very afraid. She stared at Jax, moving backward. "Who are you?"

She sensed danger, Sasha was sure. She might not know what he was, but she knew he posed a serious threat to her.

"I'm the new guy, Jack. Mean people piss me off, so how about you leave Sasha alone?"

Julianne became a little braver, farther away, rubbing her forearm. "Yeah, well, wait until I tell my boyfriend what you did."

"Should I wait here?"

Turning, she hurried off down the hall.

"I'm sorry, Sasha. That looked like it hurt."

"It did. She's hard-core mean."

"Even if she wasn't a lost soul, she wouldn't like you. She's one of those queen-bee girls who hate anybody who might steal some of their spotlight. Just stay away from her."

"Not a problem." Her stomach growled.

"Are you hungry?"

"I'm starving. Melanie was cooking a big breakfast, but all I got was a stale muffin. I've never been so hungry as I have the past couple of days. Maybe it's the altitude?"

"Come with me, and I'll give you some oatmeal cookies Mathilda sent."

When they were outside the back door, standing on a small stoop that led down to the sideline of the soccer field, Jax reached into his backpack and pulled out a large ziplock bag. She was eating her third when he said, "You're more hungry than usual because of me. As long as you're around me, you're going to change. You're getting stronger all the time, and that requires calories, so you want to eat more. You may notice other things that might seem a little weird, like the ability to see things in the dark and some telekinetic abilities. You can probably turn off a light just by thinking about it. The changes are the reason you can see the shadow around Bruno's eyes, and why I can no longer block your memory."

Now she knew why she felt out of sorts. Why was she surprised? Everything was happening so fast, her world turning upside down, and she couldn't stop it. She wanted to get off and stand still, to catch her breath and have time to think things through before something else hit her broadside. She didn't want to be like him. She just wanted to be herself, like she was last Thursday, before getting into Missy's car. "Did it happen when you healed me?"

"When I kissed you."

"Is that why you did it, Jax? So I'd change to be like you?"

"I kissed you because I wanted to. I didn't know until later that it would do anything to you."

"If you'd known, would you have kissed me anyway?"

He reached up to brush a crumb from her lips, then traced them with his warm fingers. "I don't know, Sasha. Maybe. Don't hate me for that."

She stupidly wished he'd kiss her right now. "Will I stay like this?"

He shook his head. "After the Ravens and Bruno are gone, when I go back to the mountain and you're not around me at all, you'll change back to how you were before. You'll also forget about me, and Eryx, and all you know about the other side."

She was relieved to know she'd go back to normal, but the idea that she'd never see him again, then forget him, bugged her. It shouldn't. She should be glad. "Will I still be Anabo?"

"The only way you can lose Anabo is if you ask Lucifer to take it. If he did, you'd be like everybody else."

"That's all I want, Jax, to just be a regular person so I don't have to worry about someone finding out what I am and wanting to kill me for it."

"You need to think very hard about that, Sasha. Your whole life since you were born, you've been Anabo. If you lose it, you'll know what it is to be tempted to sin. Maybe you think of sin in terms of the big stuff—like stealing, or murder—but most humans deal with the daily pull toward rage, jealousy, hatred: things you have no idea about because you've never felt them. Losing Anabo also means you lose what's basically a free ticket to Heaven. You'll have to earn it, like every other person on Earth."

He put the bag of cookies back in his pack, then held the door for her. "But it's always your choice. Nobody can screw with free will, so bear with me for a little while longer, then I'll be gone and you can stay Anabo, or be as ordinary as you want. Either way, you won't be like me."

As soon as she was inside, he walked past her and down the hall toward the front of the school, to the staircase that led up to the high school. Downstairs was for middle school, along with the cafeteria, library, and gym. Staring after him, aware that other people were watching her, she swallowed hard and squared her shoulders. This was how it should be, she was certain. There would be other Anabo girls he could meet, and maybe they'd be okay with dating a guy from Hell, becoming immortal, and doing what he did.

She just had to stop thinking about Jax all the time. Once she did that, everything would be fine.

Upstairs, she saw Brody meet him in the hall, and they walked together toward the other end, to English lit. A girl with long blond hair and pretty blue eyes hurried past Sasha, all the way to Jax's side, looked up at him, smiled, and chattered away like they were long-lost friends. He was right about bringing Brody. That girl wasn't scared of Jax at all. She was so not scared, she kept touching his sleeve and laughing, like this was the happiest day of her life.

Sasha watched while she followed, trying as hard as she could to be glad for him, that he could maybe hang out here for a while and not feel like a freak, even make some friends. But somewhere deep inside, she had a very strong urge to rush up from behind, shoulder that bubbly blonde out of the way, and grab Jax's warm, strong hand—to announce to everyone in the hall that he was taken.

The English teacher, Mrs. Redmond, wore a gray sweater and gray pants that exactly matched her gray hair. She smiled at Sasha and handed her the class syllabus. "Take a seat anywhere you like."

She saw Erin wave at her, so she took the seat just behind her and across from Rachel. Jax and Brody were on the other side of the room, next to Thomas and Mason, the friends of Brett's she'd met Saturday. Bubbles the Blonde sat right next to Jax, smiling at him like he was a new toy. She kept touching him, plucking at his sleeve, resting a hand on his shoulder when she leaned over to whisper something. Maybe it would have bothered Sasha more if Jax looked like he was interested. If anything, he looked aggravated. And that made her enormously happy.

Making her less happy, Brett and East sat at the back of the class, slumped down in their chairs, arms over chests in the classic I'm-all-that pose, surrounded by the beautiful people. Sasha didn't need to ask Erin and Rachel if these were the kids everyone wanted to hang out with. Queen Bee Julianne was there, along with all her little worker bees, dressed in 7 jeans and Tory Burch flats, carrying Hermés bags and wearing überbored looks on their perfect faces. When she risked glancing back at them, East was staring a hole through her, and she quickly looked away, toward the front.

Erin said in a low voice, "I heard East plans to fight that new guy, Jack, because he did something to Julianne."

"The only thing he did was make her stop pulling my hair. She was all up in my face because I supposedly came on to East." She told Erin and Rachel what happened.

Rachel shook her head, like she was disgusted. "Boy, East needs some desserts."

"*Just* desserts," Erin said.

"Right. Only desserts. Nothing else. That Jack guy is way hot, but a wild child. I heard he got kicked out of boarding school in England for smoking weed in the library."

Sasha almost laughed. It was amazing how gossip got started and spread. Just for kicks, she asked, "What about his brother, the nerdy guy? Did he get kicked out, too?"

"I think their dad makes him stick with Jack, to try and keep him out of trouble." Erin was looking across the room at them. "He *is* a geek, but he's kinda cute, in a way."

"Yeah," Rachel said, also looking, "he is sort of cute. And it's so sweet that he looks after his brother."

Jax and Brody would love this, Sasha was sure.

Then she remembered that she wasn't going to talk to them, or hang out at all, so she'd never get to tell them.

"I hope we're not going to read any more Gomer," Rachel said, reaching for her backpack.

"Homer," Erin corrected, "and I think we're done with him. Today, we're starting *The Metamorphosis*."

"Is it about butterflies?"

Erin shot a God-give-me-patience look at Sasha before she said, "Sort of. A guy wakes up one day, and for no apparent reason, he's been turned into a giant bug."

"You mean a butterfly."

"No, a bug. And everyone hates him."

"Duh. Bugs are gross."

Then the bell rang, and Mrs. Redmond welcomed the class back from the weekend. "I've been asked to announce that anyone feeling the need to talk about Reilly O'Brien's unfortunate accident this weekend can do so by signing up to meet with a counselor, who'll be in the library all this week."

Sasha stiffened when she heard Reilly's name and, without thinking, turned to look at Brett. He caught her look, then leaned over and whispered something to one of the bees. She leaned forward and whispered something to another one, and so on, until, within seconds, they were all looking at her like she was dirt. Brett was grinning.

Turning to face the front again, she was chilled to the bone, and it had nothing to do with temperature. What had Brett said to make them look at her like that?

The hour dragged on, Mrs. Redmond calling on different people to read aloud. Sasha noticed Amanda sat by herself, never looking up from her book. She suspected she wasn't reading, just avoiding eye contact with anybody.

When the bell rang, Sasha followed Erin and Rachel into

the hall, feeling like a hanger-on, but powerless to stop herself. That they didn't seem to mind, and even included her in their conversation, made them just about her most favorite people ever.

She watched Jax walk away with Brody on one side and Bubbles stuck like a burr to the other. Another girl had attached herself to their little group, smiling shyly at Brody, who looked surprised. Thomas and Mason brought up the rear.

"Wouldja look at that?" Rachel asked, staring after them. "Thomas and Mason have jumped ship."

"Who's glad?" Erin asked, also staring.

"You are." Rachel turned her bright, smiling eyes toward Sasha. "Erin's had it for Thomas since forever, but he's always hanging with Brett and East. Totally unapproachable."

Sasha wanted to say there was a way bigger and better reason to be glad about Thomas not running with Brett and East, but she only nodded.

"Don't act like I'm the only one," Erin said. "You'd go for Mason in a heartbeat if he asked."

Rachel grinned at Sasha. "She's right. I know he's sort of a big lug, but he can be really sweet—and funny."

Proving, Sasha thought, that there really is someone for everyone.

Julianne came out of the room, followed by the lesser bees. As they passed, every one of them gave Sasha that awful look again, like she was disgusting. If they'd slammed a fist into her gut, she wasn't sure it would have made her more breathless. *What* had Brett said to them?

He was smirking at her as he came into the hall. East came up from behind, grabbed one half of her backside, and squeezed, saying against her ear, "I knew it was all an act." Then he walked away with Brett, both of them laughing.

"What was that about?" Erin asked, her face a little less friendly.

Feeling already shaky ground begin to crumble, Sasha made a desperate attempt at damage control. "Brett told him some horrible lie about me."

"Why would he do that?" Rachel asked, also looking suspicious. "He's your cousin."

They wouldn't believe her over Brett, she realized to her horror. He was Mr. Popular, what every girl wanted, no matter if he was an ass with an ego bigger than Alaska. And he was her cousin. Family. Blood. Why would her blood spread a lie about her?

He wouldn't, if he was just a guy. But Brett wasn't. He was driven by something dark and evil, without a conscience. He was a cold-blooded murderer. But they didn't know. They couldn't know. Looking between the two of them, she finally said, "I don't know why he'd tell a lie about me, or even what it was. He likes to play practical jokes, so he's probably thinking this is way funny."

They didn't look completely sold, but they relaxed a little before Erin said, "We're going to biology now. What about you?"

Pulling her schedule from her pocket, she looked and wished like everything it said biology. It didn't. "Calculus."

"We'll see you later, Sasha," Rachel said, already turning away.

She watched them catch up to Bree, who said something, then they all turned to look at her with the same expression as the bees. Like she was something nasty.

⁂

To Jax, calculus was as boring and never-ending as English, made worse by the blonde who didn't take a hint. He kept forgetting her name, even though he was trying like hell to follow the rules of the making-friends book. Her constant giggling and silly chatter made him nuts. He tried ignoring her, but that only seemed to egg her on. He told her he had a girlfriend already, but she only laughed and said, "Her loss."

Brody was enjoying himself hugely, even though Jax kept reminding him this was all temporary, that he needed to find a girl on the mountain.

"I will," he said, "but for now, this is pretty awesome. Jenny is a nice girl, and she has the entire first season of *Star Trek*, with outtakes. Her granddad used to be a producer, so she has all kinds of cool stuff."

"You can't go to her house, Brody. Don't say you will."

"I won't."

Always, he was hyperaware of Sasha, never lost her scent, his sixth sense kicking in so he knew where she was at all times, even when he couldn't see her. When he could see her, he knew she was miserable. The other kids were avoiding her, and he didn't know why.

He wanted to talk to her, to say he was there for her, that he'd be her friend—he and Brody—and she wouldn't be all alone. But she didn't want that; she'd made it really clear. So he stayed away and felt her misery, his heart breaking a little more every time he looked at her.

The tall guy, Thomas, was the only thing even mildly interesting to Jax about Telluride High. He was good like the Luminas were good, a guy with deep compassion and a certain intuition about people that made him extremely well liked. He'd evidently been running around with Brett and East and Mason since junior high, but after Brett and East took the oath, everything had changed.

"Now they're all about this new club, the Ravens," Thomas told him while they waited for third period to begin. "If you're not interested, it's like you're dead to them. Which is fine by me, because I don't like hanging with them anymore. I mean, I'm up for a good joke on somebody, but the stuff they pull isn't so much a joke as it's sadistic. Brett's even doing it to his cousin. Who does that? Maybe I don't hang out with my cousins, but they're family. You don't hose your own family."

Belying his sudden fury, Jax kept his face impassive, leaning across his desk with one forearm resting on his Spanish book, forcing himself not to look across the room at Sasha. "Yeah, my brothers and I get into it all the time, but that's us. When it comes to outsiders, I'd kick anybody's ass who messed with any of them. So what's Shriver doing to his cousin?"

Thomas shot a glance at Brody, who was deep in conversation with Jenny, before he said, "He's telling everybody that his cousin was kicked out of her old school because she let her boyfriend make a video of them having sex, then put it on the Internet. Maybe she did, maybe she didn't, but why the hell would he tell people something like that? If it's true, maybe she wanted to start new and leave that behind her. If it's a lie, then he's even more of a prick than I thought."

Jax couldn't help it. He looked across the room at her, sitting alone in her pretty new sweater, her soft, gold hair hanging down her back, her eyes on her notebook while she sketched and waited for class to begin. He remembered that guy in Macy's, Smith Hardwick. He'd been really glad to see her. She was somebody at her old school, with lots of friends. She should be somebody at this school, and every damn kid should be fighting over who'd be her friend. Instead, she was all alone, a pariah, because Brett was a lost soul. Brett was a lost soul because Bruno conned him into it. And Bruno was a con man because Eryx tricked him.

He hated Eryx with every cell in his body.

He wanted to go after Brett, Bruno, and all the others, take them away from here, out of her life. The unfairness of what was happening to her nearly strangled him.

"Dude, stop staring," Thomas said. "She's gotta feel like shit right now. Don't make it worse."

He caught Brody's look and knew he'd heard everything. His calm, kind eyes never changed, but he sent a message all the same. *Patience. Have patience. They'll be gone soon.*

Clearing his throat, Jax looked again at Thomas. "No way that girl would do something like that. She looks like one of those straitlaced British girls I knew in boarding school, who go off to university to become a doctor or a teacher or something, and marry a nice guy like my brother here. Check her out. Does she look like she'd let some joker videotape her having sex?"

Thomas glanced over his shoulder at her, then looked at Jax. "You're right, but it doesn't matter now. It's out there, and no matter what she does, or even if Brett admits he made it up, there'll still be people who believe it. I guarantee, some guys will be all over the Internet as soon as school's out, looking for that video. And I can also guarantee that Brett will think that's funny, because he's twisted."

"But he didn't used to be twisted?"

"No way. He was a cool guy. It's that stupid Ravens club that did this to him. I don't know what they do there, but it almost seems like a cult, where they brainwash people. Brett and East do and say the weirdest things. It's like I don't know them at all."

"Who else are members?"

"I'm not sure because it's supposedly a big secret. They're into the secret thing, probably trying to make it sound cool. I guess some think it is, because a lot of other kids are saying they plan to join, if they get asked. Brett and East kept bugging me about it until I finally told them I'd become a priest before I joined the Ravens."

Jax was confused. "You have something against priests?"

Thomas cocked a smile. "I'm Jewish. You do the math."

Genuinely interested, and slightly amused, Jax asked, "How does a Jewish guy have a name like Vasquez?"

Thomas's smile became a grin. "By having a mother named Roth who married a red-headed Spaniard named Vasquez."

Class started then, and all through Spanish, Jax tried to think of some way to fix things for Sasha, but came up with nothing. Every idea involved himself in some way, and she'd said, multiple times, she wanted nothing to do with him.

Finally, Spanish was over, and it was time for lunch. He went to the cafeteria with Brody, Jenny, and the blond girl he couldn't shake. Thomas and Mason went along as well, and when they had their food and looked for a table, he became aware of the hierarchy that was high school lunch. The first tables were filled with Brett's group, the next tables were some guys who looked like jocks and girls who looked like their female counterparts, probably on the ski team. One of the guys, he noticed with a sinking heart, was a lost soul. A new one.

After that was a group of kids dressed in lots of black, with multiple piercings and some interesting tattoos. Jax immediately thought of his brother, Zee. Then there were some girls who looked more shy than anything else, checking them out as they passed, especially Thomas, but trying hard not to be obvious. Behind their table was a group of guys and girls who reminded him of Brody, the supersmart nerds. After that were several tables with only a few people at each one, all sitting apart from the others. Alone. These were the kids nobody wanted to hang with, even the geeks.

Sasha sat at the last table, sketching in her notebook, not one bite of food in sight.

Jax wanted to sit by her and ask why she wasn't eating, because he knew she must be starving, but he remembered what she'd said earlier, about just wanting to be a regular person. She wouldn't welcome him, or his concern.

So they walked past her table and went to the other side of the cafeteria.

He ate the food, which was maybe one step up from terrible, ignored the blonde's constant chatter, and tried not to watch Sasha, but he totally failed when the newest lost soul left his table and walked back to sit next to her. The way he looked at her made Jax's skin itch, but he stayed where he was. Whatever the guy said upset her enough that her face flamed, and she turned a little so her shoulder was between them.

Then the guy leaned close, said something in her ear, and slipped his hand into her lap.

Jax waited for her to shove the guy away and punch his lights out. She could do it, easily, because she was stronger, but instead, she began to cry while the son of a bitch moved his hand farther up her thigh and said God only knew what kinds of horrible things to her.

No one was looking. No one appeared to notice except him.

Which was, he suddenly realized, exactly what she wanted. They all believed she was cheap goods who had sex in front of a camera. To keep at least some of her dignity, she wanted to hide in plain sight, and for sure she didn't want to make a scene.

She batted at his hand beneath the table, crossed her legs so he couldn't get closer, and cried all the while, biting her lip so she didn't make any noise.

Jax had a thousand years of self-discipline behind him, but nothing had ever been as hard to resist as the overpowering need to rip that guy's head right off of his body. He clenched his jaw and watched, silently shouting at her to fight back.

Then the guy slid his hand across her back and reached beneath her arm to grab her breast; she looked at Jax, her eyes gigantic.

That's when his self-restraint went right out the window.

⌘

She tried so hard not to let this jerk wad get to her, to convince him to leave her alone and go back to his table. She tried even harder not to look to Jax for help. What right did she have, when she'd told him to stay away from her?

But all she wanted, more than food, more than her next breath, was Jax. She wanted his deep voice, telling her everything would be okay. She wanted his warm arms around her, protecting her from this creeper—from Brett, East, and all the others. She wanted his advice about how to fight the lie Brett had told about her.

She managed not to look at Jax when Scott said he knew what girls like her wanted, then proceeded to tell her, in graphic detail, just what that was, making her feel like yesterday's garbage. He said if she'd do him and let him film it, he'd hang with her and maybe she wouldn't have to eat lunch alone. His words made her cry, not from shame or fear, but from frustrated rage against Brett. He'd told her after calculus that if she'd join the Ravens, he'd make all this go away. She could hang with him and East and Julianne. She'd be like them.

Scott's words made her cringe, made her cry, and his hand between her legs made her so mad, she wished she had longer nails so she could scratch hard enough to draw blood. She tried not to draw any attention, hoping and praying no one would notice what was happening, wouldn't see Scott's hand between her legs.

Then he grabbed her breast, and she gave up trying to get out of this without making a scene. An impulse she didn't understand made her look toward Jax, and the instant she saw his face—his expression—she turned on Scott. Five seconds later, he was flat on his back, the metal lunchroom chair legs trapping his arms against his sides while she knelt on the seat and leaned over to say in a surprisingly even voice, "Touch me again, and I'll chop off your hands. Ask me again to do you or to blow you, or even say hello to me, and I'll chop off something else."

He stared up at her with shock on his weasel face and fear in his eyes. "Jesus," he whispered.

"Go back to your ski buddies and leave me alone." Sasha shoved off of the chair, gathered up her backpack, and turned toward Jax, who looked ready to rip into Scott. Maybe he would have if Scott hadn't already gotten out from under the chair, scrambled to his feet, and walked very quickly back to his table.

By now, everyone was staring, the whole lunchroom so quiet, she could hear the clink of forks and plates in the kitchen. Looking straight at Brett, she said, "You can spread lies about me, do whatever you want to me, but I'm never, *ever* going to join your stupid Ravens."

He looked around at his friends and slowly shook his head, like he was trying hard to be patient. Leaning back so his chair was balanced on two legs, he said, "You're dreaming if you think we'd let you join. The Ravens aren't into skanks, Sasha."

She wanted his chair to go over backward. So much she wanted that.

She almost jumped when it did. From behind her, Jax whispered, "Atta girl."

"Did I do that?" she asked over her shoulder.

"Damn straight."

Nervous laughter trickled through the lunchroom, until Brett was on his feet and glaring at them. Then everyone became real interested in their lunch. A second later, the juniors rushed into the cafeteria and the moment was over. She was still a leper, but she decided she didn't care. In the end, Brett would be gone, no longer able to seduce people desperate for someone, *anyone* to like them.

Turning, she moved a few inches closer to Jax.

"Why did you look to me if you were going to handle it yourself?" he whispered.

"I didn't intend to do it myself. I didn't know I could." She touched his arm. "When I finally looked at you, I thought you were telling me to take him down, like you gave me permission." She heard his quick intake of breath. "What?"

"It's what I do, Sasha. My brothers always look to me for the go-ahead."

Remembering that she didn't consciously decide to look at him, that it was more an impulse, like holding her breath when she dove into a swimming pool, Sasha knew exactly what he meant. She didn't like it, but she got it. Not only was she taking on some of his physical characteristics, she was becoming attuned to him the same way his brothers were. She wasn't just growing stronger and gaining the ability to make a chair fall backward. She was becoming Mephisto.

Taking a step back, she said quietly, "How soon will they be gone, Jax?"

With a deep sigh, he said, "I don't know yet. We need Bruno around until he can lead us to a Skia meeting, but no one knows when that will be."

"I hope it's soon."

"Yes," he said in a tired voice, "I'm sure you do."

"This is so hard, Jax. I don't know how much longer I can stand it."

He had no expression at all. "Am I that repulsive to you?"

"You're that attractive to me. I can smell you from across the room, like hot cider with cinnamon and cloves. I can hear you breathe. I see every hair on your head, every breath you take, every time you clench your jaw. My mind imagines you kissing me, and it doesn't stop there. I want to be with you all the time. I know this is all some kind of spell that'll disappear when you're gone. If that takes a long time, I'm not sure I can hold out."

"Suppose this isn't some kind of magic, that you actually like me, even just a little?"

"I don't have to suppose. I do like you, a lot more than a little."

"But you don't want to be with me because of what I am," he said dully. "Even if what I felt for you was real love, not lust or infatuation, you could never accept me."

"Do you really understand what that means? Because I'm not so sure I do. My dad loved my mom with all his heart, accepted her just as she was, but I don't know that she loved him the same way. It seems to me it can't be real if it's not returned."

He looked genuinely hurt. "You're right. Forget I said anything."

Turning, he began to walk away, but she hurried to catch up and grasped his arm, moving to stand in front of him. "I didn't mean I could never love you, Jax."

"I know."

"Then why are you walking away from me?"

"Because it's hopeless. I've known since the second I laid eyes on you that this is a pipe dream; that even if I figured out how to love you, there's no way you'd ever feel that way about me. You could. It's possible. But you won't. Why would you?"

She had no answer for that.

"Let it go, Sasha. I'm here to find out what I can from Bruno so we can move ahead. I'll work as hard as I can to get it done as soon as possible, then I'll be gone." Reaching into his pocket, he withdrew a twenty and pressed it into her hand. "Get yourself some lunch, and tomorrow, put your money in your pocket instead of your backpack so nobody can steal it."

"How did you know it was stolen?"

"Why else would you not have any lunch? I know you're starving, and it's important for you to eat. Until I'm gone, and you go back to how you were before, you'll continue to change. You're incredibly strong already, and that kind of strength requires lots of calories. If you don't eat enough, you'll begin to have trouble doing simple things, like walking. It'll happen fast, so remember to eat every meal. Lots of protein." Stepping around her, he walked away without looking back.

◦◦◦

"Are you okay?" Brody asked him on the way to biology. "You look pretty rough, Jax."

"I'm okay," he lied, mostly because no way did he want to

talk about it. Hearing Sasha say she could never love him cut deep. He'd known it, thought he'd accepted it, but he guessed there was some part of him that still harbored hope.

"Don't lose faith, and don't give up."

Jax stopped in the hall and looked at his favorite nerdy Lumina. "How many times could you hear a girl say she doesn't want you, that she can't wait for you to get out of her life, before you'd give up?"

Brody blinked at him from behind his geeky glasses. "If she looked at me the way Sasha looks at you, I could hear her say it a million times and I still wouldn't give up."

Jax was eaten up with frustration, grief, and rage. "She looks at me like that because of lust, little man. It's got nothing to do with anything real, anything that lasts."

Instead of looking offended, Brody said calmly, "Isn't that how you look at her?"

"No!"

"Right. You also look at her as a means to an end. She can get for you what no other human can. Maybe you're trying too hard to get her to change the way she thinks, when it should be you who changes."

Jax turned away and began walking toward biology. Brody fell into step beside him. "I don't know how," Jax admitted. "You don't have a clue what it's like, Brody."

"Your father managed to love someone." He caught the dark look Jax shot at him, but carried on anyway. "She's been gone a thousand years, and he still grieves, still misses her, still regrets he didn't see what would happen to his son, didn't step up and protect her by making God aware."

What Jax felt for M was complicated. Having the dark angel of death for a father wasn't easy, but he admitted Brody was right. And as much as M had loved their mother, she'd loved him. One of the Mephisto abilities was a photographic memory. They could remember everything that had happened since the very beginning, which was helpful at times, painful at others. Jax remembered exactly what his parents had been like with each other. They were polar opposites, and yet it had worked. "How do you suppose he convinced her?"

Brody shrugged. "Maybe she just accepted him as he was; or because he loved her, she saw something there that no one else saw."

They reached biology and the conversation was over, but Jax continued thinking about it. He blew through the lab assignment, most of his mind occupied with what Brody said.

The rest of the day passed slowly. He and Brody sat next to Sasha in history, to make sure Bruno didn't freak her out too much. The change was happening so quickly, she was already to a place where being around a Skia didn't make her sick so much as angry. She sketched during his lecture, keeping her head down, but when he called on her to answer a question, Jax saw the look of hatred in her eyes.

He passed her a note. *Curb it, or he's going to be suspicious.*

She nodded and went back to her sketch.

History was the last class of the day, so as soon as it was over, he headed for the gym and went through a quick tryout. Coach Hightower said, "Did you play basketball at school in England?"

"Yeah," he lied, "and I've been playing with my brothers for a long time." Since the game was invented, actually.

"Pretty impressive, Jax. We need a center. Interested?"

"Sure thing, Coach." And just like that, he was on a team.

For two hours, he was all about basketball, and when practice was over, things didn't look quite so gloomy. If Brody was right, maybe all hope wasn't lost.

Before he left the building, he went to the office where Bruno had a desk and quickly looked through it, but he found nothing about the Skia meeting.

Part of him was glad. Until they found the information they needed, he could stay at school, be around Sasha, and maybe, just maybe, figure out a way to keep her.

NINE

THE ONLY HIGHLIGHT OF THE REST OF SASHA'S BUMMER FIRST day of school was when she got back to the Shrivers' and Tim said from his recliner, "You'll probably be happy to know, Melanie has gone to Colorado Springs to do some shopping. She'll be home on Wednesday."

Sasha was more than happy—she was ecstatic. She'd dreaded seeing her aunt again, but now she had a two-day reprieve. It seemed Tim was just as happy about it. Looking at him, so huge and miserable, she asked, "Why do you stay married?"

He sighed, making his belly shake. "It's complicated, kiddo. A long time ago, before I knew about her mental problems, I loved her. She really can't help how she is, and I used to think it would get better, but it never did; then one day I realized I just didn't care anymore. But I'm almost fifty, and I have so many health issues, it's easier to stay. Even if she has her spells, she takes care of me. Besides, she's the boys' mother, and they need her."

If her day hadn't been depressing enough, it was now.

Tossing her backpack to the couch, she sat down and looked at the TV, tuned to CNN. "Did Mom give you a copy of my birth certificate? They need it at school, and I don't have one, so I was wondering if you do."

He didn't answer, and she turned to look at him, noticing he seemed more red in the face than usual. "Everything okay?"

"Fine, fine. Just feeling a little under the weather today." He glanced at her before returning to the news. "Don't worry about the birth certificate. I'll go by the school and square things away for you."

"So you do have a copy?"

He cleared his throat. "I'll get it."

She wondered why he was being so weird about it. "Thanks, Tim. The secretary also said you need to sign some stuff for me to be officially enrolled, so it'd be great if you go by."

"Consider it done." He cleared his throat again but didn't say anything else.

When the silence grew awkward, she gathered up her backpack and headed for the stairs.

"I'm making chicken and rice for dinner, so be down here at six."

"Okay." She went to her room and started on homework,

glad that Brett was at basketball practice so she could put off seeing him for a while.

When she went back down for dinner, she was ready for a showdown, but he wasn't there. Tim said from the stove, "Looks like it's just you, me, and Chris. Brett went over to the Easter kid's house for dinner."

She was almost disappointed, instead of relieved. She had wanted to see if Brett would be bold enough to stand by his lie when she confronted him about it at dinner, in front of his dad, who she was quickly learning didn't get along with his oldest son. Chris was his obvious favorite, just as Brett was obviously Melanie's.

On the upside, his absence meant more food, and she didn't hesitate when Tim offered her a second chicken breast. She ate a lot of rice, and took a second slice of cake for dessert.

Chris didn't say much, like always, but he looked at her when he said to Tim, "Kinda nice without Mom and Brett."

"That it is," Tim said as he lifted his bulk from the table and went back to his recliner.

That night, her dreams were once again filled with Jax, but they took a darker turn, strangely dangerous, more erotic, and she woke up blushing.

Tuesday came, and she was so glad to see him again. "Hi, Jax," she said, standing next to his seat in English.

He looked up at her and smiled. "Hey, Sasha." He looked like he was waiting for her to say something, but she was suddenly tongue-tied, and she walked away, to a seat at the front, as far away from Brett as she could get.

She didn't listen when people read aloud from *The Metamorphosis*, dwelling instead on Jax, fighting with herself over whether she should try to talk to him, to apologize for what had happened at lunch yesterday.

By the end of class, she'd convinced herself she should say something, but when she headed toward him, he turned away and walked out with Thomas and Brody, Bubbles the Blonde hot on his heels.

Watching him leave, she realized she'd definitely burned the bridge. She felt way more sad about that than she did about being Superloser at Telluride High, although the shunning was getting to her.

At her locker after English, she heard Julianne tell her bees, "Brett says she got a backstage pass at a Kings of Leon concert and did every one of them in the dressing room."

"Ew, gross! She's gotta have a disease," one said.

"She *is* a disease," another said.

Brett enjoyed her misery, it was clear. She'd humiliated him in the lunchroom, and publicly announced she was a "no way" on the Ravens, so she was now subjected to nonstop insults and taunts. When she walked past him in the hall after Spanish, he said, "Hey, Internet Inga, who're you filming with today?"

She ignored him, but her anger simmered. Just the sound of his voice made her angry. He was a murderer, a robot with no conscience, yet he was held up as some sort of demigod by most everyone at school. Even the teachers obviously adored him.

She, on the other hand, was less than dirt.

At lunch, Jax stared at her for such a long time, she thought for sure he'd come over and say something. But he didn't. He talked to Bubbles and, when he was done eating, left the cafeteria without looking at her again.

The day just got better and better. Scott the Molester was waiting at her locker after lunch. He smiled at her, but it was more of a leer, and he didn't hide that he was checking out her boobs. She looked closely and could swear she saw a slight shadow around his eyes. "You're a Raven, aren't you?"

He looked very proud. "Sure am. Too bad you won't be joining."

No wonder he was such a tool—he was a lost soul.

"How would you like to catch a movie up at Mountain Village?"

Waiting for the insult, she stood there and stared at him.

He lost his smile and took a step closer. "Always wanted to do it in a theater." He added some details, not bothering to lower his voice, so everyone around heard everything he said.

Shouldering past him, she opened her locker and nailed him in the back of the head with the door. "Gosh, so sorry," she said sweetly.

Holding his head, he glared at her at the same time he crowded her against the wall of lockers with his body. "Bitch, you really need somebody to—*umph!*"

Scott didn't finish his thought on what someone should do to her. He was doubled over, holding his privates.

Sasha bent low and whispered, "I warned you not to touch me again. Back. Off." When she straightened up, Jax was watching her, a slight smile playing around his lips. She shot a look at all the staring faces before she turned back to her locker and calmly took out her biology books.

It was harder to sit through history, not only because Brett kept throwing insults at her, but because Bruno allowed it. By the end of class, she was boiling mad. She went to her locker, anxious to get her stuff and get the hell out of the building, but drew up short when she saw that someone had stuck a sign on her locker: HOT RUSSIAN: WHORE: FREE SEX—JUST ASK.

She opened it and was loading her backpack with the books she needed when she felt a tap on her shoulder. Turning, she saw Rose standing there, looking irritated. "Hi, Rose."

"I'm still waiting for your birth certificate, Sasha."

"I told my uncle, and he said he'd bring it by and sign the papers."

"He didn't. You need to remind him. Without proper enrollment, you can't sit for finals."

"I'll remind him." She closed the locker and noticed Rose's eyes widen when she saw the crude sign.

"Who did this?"

"Somebody who believes my cousin's lie about me, I guess."

Rose looked away, clearly embarrassed.

"You've heard it, I'm sure."

."Well, I did hear . . . something."

"It'd really be great if you could call the headmistress at St. Michael's and get the real story."

"It's not proper protocol for me to discuss something like this with another school administrator. If you were expelled from St. Michael's, unless it was for a legal reason, it has no bearing on your enrollment here at Telluride."

Sasha turned away from her and ripped the sign off the locker, wadded it up, and dropped it to the floor before she walked away from Miss Rose.

Back at the Shrivers', it was a repeat of the night before, the only difference being the food. Melanie was still out of town, Brett was having dinner at East's house, and it was just Tim, Chris, and Sasha at the table. They had pot roast, and she ate more than Chris, which might have embarrassed her at some other time in her life, but she was so down, she couldn't really focus on much of anything except how much she missed Jax.

It wasn't supposed to be like this. She was supposed to forget about him. Instead, the constant need to see him was almost overwhelming. If she knew how to get to his house, she'd take Tim's Toyota and drive there and tell him she was sorry, she was wrong, and please, could he forgive her and like her again?

No, she wouldn't. She couldn't. *He's a son of Hell. He's immortal. He kills people.* She had to keep telling herself, over and over, and force herself to stay away from him. He'd be gone soon, and she could forget. She'd be able to move on, to lose this terrible, wonderful obsession.

Just thinking about his being gone made her nuts, made her want to run to him as fast as possible and beg him not to go, not to let her forget him.

"Sasha," Tim said, startling her out of her reverie, "I've had a bit of trouble getting a copy of your birth certificate, but it should be here by tomorrow. Marin County requested a copy of my temporary guardianship papers, and they had to have those before they'd send the birth certificate."

She was so caught up in wondering how she could lose this mania for Jax, she'd actually forgotten about Rose's second request this afternoon. She nodded at Tim and said, "Thanks for letting me know. I'll tell Miss Rose tomorrow."

Sleep was elusive, and she got up twice to check her e-mail, wishing she'd hear from her mother again, but there was nothing.

She finally drifted off after midnight, and her dreams were stranger than ever. She and Jax were in the woods, running from something dark and evil, something she knew could end his immortal life. She screamed for him to run faster, but the thing that chased them gained ground, and just before it caught up to them, she woke herself up, sobbing.

She dressed for school with a deep sense of dread, and the weather only added to her depression. The sky was dark, with low, heavy clouds that promised snow before the day was out.

Trudging to school with Boo, she seriously thought about ditching. She'd take some money up to the slopes and ski all day, alone, with just the mountains and trees and the solitude of the soft, quiet snow. But she couldn't afford to miss classes if she had any prayer of passing finals. Maybe right now she couldn't care less, but later, she knew she'd regret it.

Inside the school, she immediately knew something was up. Everyone was still downstairs in the front foyer, instead of upstairs in the high school hall. When she opened the door, they all turned to look at her and stopped talking. That's when she noticed there were papers all over the floor—hundreds, maybe thousands, of pages of copier paper. Bending, she picked one up and saw it was a handwritten note on St. Michael's letterhead, sent by fax.

*Dear Mr.*_____ (the name was blacked out),

Thank you for your note. I was terribly distressed to hear that Sasha Annenkova is having such a difficult time at her new school in Telluride. I can't imagine what kind of mischief a student intended by spreading a blatant lie about Sasha. She was an exemplary student here at St. Michael's, a leader, a young woman her fellow classmates admired and respected. She is sorely missed, and most certainly was not expelled. Her mother was called to Russia on important business, and Sasha went to live with family members in Telluride. This is the extent of the story, and I urge you to put matters to rights.

Warmest regards,

Doreen McAllister, Headmistress

Looking up, she scanned the faces of the students and noticed they all looked apologetic—all except for Brett, East, Julianne, and Scott.

Brett stepped up on the stairs and turned to the group. He looked right at her, unsmiling. "Pretty cute, Sasha. What'd you do, white out a letter from your old school and write a fake note, then make a billion copies?"

"Shut up, Brett," Erin said. "The fax is dated yesterday, and it's from a San Francisco area code. Just admit you made it all up and apologize to Sasha."

He tried again. "She had a friend do it."

Someone else said, "She's your *cousin*, asswipe! What kind of loser tells gross lies about his own family?"

"Shriver does," another student yelled, and the floodgates opened, people yelling and shouting at Brett, suggesting he do all sorts of things to himself. In the space of one minute, Brett Shriver went from Mr. Popular to scumbag.

Finally, Sasha found Jax's face in the crowd. He stood at the back, taller than most, but far away, which is why she hadn't seen him right off. She walked forward, and the other students parted to let her through. When she was just in front of him, she reached for his hand.

He turned toward the stairs and walked with her up to the high school hall. The others followed, and just as they reached the landing the bell rang, sending everyone scurrying for class.

When the hall was empty, she looked up into Jax's wonderful face. She wanted to kiss him. "How'd you do it?"

"I had one of the Luminas hand deliver a note to her."

"From who?"

He squeezed her hand. "James Hewitt, whose sons, Jack and Brody, are friends of yours. Mr. Hewitt was worried his children might be running around with the wrong kind of people. He sent a note and a donation for the school to Mrs. McAllister, hoping she'd be so kind as to tell him if there was any truth to the story about his sons' new friend."

Sasha grinned. "And she answered right away."

"It was a very big donation."

"And you made a zillion copies."

"Actually, Brody did. Key's Xerox machine freaks me out. We came up at four this morning and scattered the papers all over."

Sasha sobered, gazing up at him. "Thank you, Jax."

He leaned down and whispered, "Whatd'ya say we ditch English and go out for pancakes?"

She nodded, and they turned and walked back down the stairs and right out the front door; no one made any move to stop them.

❧

They came back for second period, and the rest of the morning, Jax enjoyed every moment of what was happening to Sasha. It was as if the lie had never existed—kids talking to her, hanging around her locker, accepting her. She never strayed far from him, though, and if she looked around and didn't see him right away, he saw a look of panic in her blue eyes.

"She's falling for you," Brody said after lunch, on the way to biology.

"It's the change in her. She's feeling weird, and I'm stability."

"What you did was genius. Much more effective than beating the crap out of Shriver. Whatever influence he had is history."

"Yeah, I guess, but that's not why I did it."

Brody gave him a cagey look. "Why did you do it?"

Watching her walking ahead of them, surrounded by the girls who'd befriended her the first day, before Brett's bullshit lie, he said, "She was suffering."

She glanced over her shoulder, checking to see if he was there before she continued on toward biology.

"What's next?" Brody asked.

Jax smiled at his pretend twin. "I was thinking about a moonlight drive up the Mephisto Mountain."

"That'd be nice. Or you could take her over to Jenny's house to watch *Star Trek* outtakes."

"And I suppose you'd be there, too?"

"Naturally."

"You're getting attached, man. Don't do it to yourself, Brody."

"I'm okay."

"If it's the damned outtakes you're after, I'll buy them for you."

Brody didn't answer, which was Jax's first clue that his little nerdy friend was way more into Jenny Brown than was advisable.

Today, the biology teacher, Mr. Hoolihan, wasn't at all friendly to her. Sasha was handed the day's lab handout without even a hello. He pointed toward the back of the room and said curtly, "Sit down."

She and Brody were assigned as lab partners, and Jax was with Thomas, who was without a lab partner since Reilly was gone. When Sasha slid onto the stool next to Brody, he leaned close and whispered, "How're you feeling?"

"Okay, but kind of wobbly, or something." She looked at him. "Was it weird to become immortal?"

"Very weird."

"How did you do it?"

"Just like the Mephisto. I jumped, and when I woke up, I was immortal. Some people they recruit lose faith on the way down, so when they wake up, they're in their own bed, and they think they dreamed of falling." Brody blinked at her from behind his dorky glasses. "Are you thinking about it, Sasha?"

She sat up straighter and shook her head. "I told Jax I don't want to be Mephisto. I'm not even sure I want to stay Anabo."

"I don't understand. It's a blessing, a gift—something so unique and rare, hardly anyone is ever born Anabo. Why would you want to give that up?"

"I don't want to spend the rest of my life worrying about being killed because of what I am."

Class began, and Mr. Hoolihan passed out dead frogs. She'd

dissected a frog just last month at St. Michael's, so she knew what to do. Brody was staring at his frog, not making a move to touch it. "What's wrong?"

"I was just thinking about this frog. He was born to be a frog. If he'd had the opportunity to become, say, a turtle, or a fish, or a horse, do you think he'd have gone for it?"

"Lay off the analogy, will you? I'm not a frog, and I don't want to be a horse. I'm a girl with a weird birthmark who's thinking about getting rid of it."

"Did Jax tell you how rare it is to be Anabo?"

"He said there aren't many."

"As far as we know, there are none. Except you. In a thousand years, the Mephisto have only ever found one other. Does that not make you think twice about giving it up?"

"I have thought about it, and it's what I want. I'm not cut out to be Mephisto."

"You don't have to become Mephisto to make a difference, Sasha. Your whole life has made a difference to so many people, all because of what you are. You're a light in the darkness, something to give people hope. Can you really give that up with a clear conscience?"

"Yes, I can, and laying a guilt trip on me isn't going to change my mind."

"I never pegged you for a coward, Sasha."

Was she a coward? Did she owe something to the world because of the way she had been born? It didn't seem fair. Why couldn't she just be ordinary?

She dissected her frog, labeled all the organs on the frog-diagram worksheet, then sat back to wait for Mr. Hoolihan.

He gave her a C. As he moved toward Brody's frog, she asked, "Why did you give me a C? What did I do wrong?"

The man never looked at her when he said, "I don't like the way you pinned the specimen."

His dismissive tone and attitude made her furious. "You don't *like* it? What does that mean? Either I did it right or I didn't."

He turned to her, eyes narrowed, and said in a low, almost threatening voice, "You got a C. Keep this up and I'll give you a D."

She saw the shadow then, and understood why he was being such a jackass. He was a lost soul, and it seemed they couldn't help it. Her anger boiled over. "I deserve an A."

He scratched out the C and wrote a large D across her paper. "You're not at some snooty prep school anymore, little girl."

"I'm not a little girl. Explain to me why I deserve a D."

He scratched the D out so hard, he tore the paper. Then he wrote an F that covered the whole sheet. "There's your explanation."

Sasha stared hard at him, and he glared back. He was practically foaming at the mouth because he was so angry and out of control. Every part of her—body and soul—wanted to lunge across the desk and put the guy in a choke hold. She shook with the energy it took to keep herself from doing it.

Finally, he turned away and barely glanced at Brody's unfinished frog before scribbling a shaky A across his paper.

Jax was looking at her with an odd expression. He shot a glance at Hoolihan, then back at her, and mouthed the words, *Be careful.*

She nodded and focused on her paper, which she folded neatly and slipped beneath the slimy frog.

"Just curious," Brody whispered, "but have you ever had a violent thought in your life?"

"Never."

"You wanted to go after him, didn't you?"

"It hurt not to."

"You can see what he is?"

She nodded. "What I can't figure out is why he purposely screwed me over."

"Brett was their best asset for recruiting, and now he's lost his shine. I think they blame you."

"He did it to himself."

"True, but they don't see it that way. You've ruined all their plans to make a huge sweep at this school, and they hate you for it. You need to be very careful, Sasha."

Watching while Mr. Hoolihan made a big fuss over Amanda's frog, like she'd just invented the cure for cancer, Sasha saw it for what it was—base flattery meant to wow her, to make her like him, to make her more interested in joining the Ravens. Amanda fell for it, smiling happily, turning to shoot a superior look at Sasha before she looked toward Brett. He nodded his head at her, and she looked ready to pass out from sheer joy.

"He's still something cool for some, it seems. People will do just about anything to win approval," Brody whispered. "Even sell their soul."

"I wish Jax would take Mr. Bruno now, right away, before more people join."

"There's going to be a Skia meeting soon, but we don't know where, or when. Bruno is planning it, so we're waiting until he does something that'll let us know, like make reservations, or book a plane flight, or contact some of the Skia who're invited. It's a chance to take out a lot of them, all at once. Otherwise, planning for each one could take months, and as you can see, some of them work very fast."

Watching Amanda, Sasha felt all the weight of the Ravens, of Bruno and Eryx and what they could mean to this girl who looked so sad, who ate lunch by herself, who thought Chris wasn't bad to look at. She was in danger of losing her soul and becoming an empty shell, lost to Heaven or Hell. Just . . . gone. She wouldn't think Chris wasn't so bad to look at. She wouldn't think about Chris at all. Her whole focus, her every moment, would be centered around finding new people to join the club, new members to give their souls to Eryx.

"Brody, I know you and Jax and the others can't interfere with free will, or try to convince people not to join, but what about me? Can I?"

He looked at her and smiled. "You're still human, Sasha. Unique and on the edge of becoming something different, but still human." He glanced at Amanda. "But be very careful. So much of what you know, she wouldn't believe, and if for some reason she did, she might share it with someone who could screw it all up for the Mephisto. Surprise is crucial, so we can't let Bruno have any clue that we're onto him. Even if you don't tell her anything, if you start lecturing or preaching at her, she'll run straight to them."

"So what you're saying is that it's hopeless?"

"Not hopeless, just difficult. It would be worth a try, because every human who says no means one less for Eryx."

She wanted Eryx to fail, but it wasn't that so much as wanting to keep Amanda from becoming lost. There was something about losing her, in particular, that bothered Sasha. She was now glancing at Brett every so often, to see if he was looking her way. He wasn't, and she eventually slumped back in her chair to stare at the lab table, her previous excitement fading.

Sasha spent the rest of class thinking of a way to approach Amanda.

She got the opportunity during the next period, a study hall for anyone not involved in various senior activities, like yearbook or prom committee. The first five minutes, Coach Hightower joked around with everyone and talked a lot about basketball, mostly to Jax. "We've only got two more games before the break, but we'll have a full schedule in January." He looked around the room. "You'll all be at tonight's game, right?"

Everyone nodded or said, "Yes," and he looked satisfied.

Sasha sat on the far side of the room, next to Jax, glancing out the window every so often, looking for Boo. Brett and East sat at the back of the room, not talking, not joining in, not studying. They just sat and stared, mostly at her, which might have creeped her out yesterday. Today, she didn't care.

Amanda sat on the opposite side of the room, along with a couple of other girls who were quiet and probably really smart. They were actually studying. Amanda was reading *The Metamorphosis*, but Sasha noticed she never turned a page.

Then Coach Hightower said, "What we need is some cookies. Who wants to go get some?"

Immediately, Amanda raised her hand. "I'll go."

"Okay, great," Coach said, then glanced around the room until he saw Sasha. "You wanna go along and bring the cocoa?"

She nodded, so glad he'd picked her. This was her chance to get to know Amanda.

After he handed them twenty dollars, they left the room and headed toward the front of the school. Sasha waited for Amanda to say something first, but after they'd walked outside and across half the school grounds, Boo tagging along behind, she realized Amanda wasn't going to say a word.

Okay, then she'd start. "How long have you lived in Telluride?"

"I live in Placerville."

They walked on in silence for a while before Amanda asked, "Why would Brett make up that story? He's your cousin. Maybe not the same as a brother, but still, he's family."

"He wanted me to join the Ravens, and he thought if he made me miserable enough, I'd do it so he'd take it back and tell everyone it was all a joke."

"Why don't you want to join? I think it sounds awesome, and it's not like they ask just anybody."

Sasha chose her words carefully, and finally asked, "Do you know what you have to do to join?"

"Sure. You have to give up God and promise to follow Eryx."

Curious to find out how much Amanda knew, she asked, "Who's Eryx?"

"He's kind of like an angel. Whatever you want, he can get it for you."

"How come I've never heard of him? I mean, if he's all that special and amazing, why don't more people know about him?"

Amanda shrugged. "I don't know. Maybe because some people would harass his followers; that's why they just have these secret meetings."

"Whatever. It's not for me."

"Why? Are you über-religious or something?"

"I believe in God, and I hope when I die I'll go to Heaven. If that makes me über-religious, then yeah, I guess so. I'm just not down with turning my back on God and following some guy I've never heard of."

"Even if he could get you what you really wanted?"

"He couldn't get me what I want."

"What do you want?"

"For my dad to still be alive."

"Oh." Amanda looked ahead when they reached Colorado. "My mom didn't die, but she left, and I wouldn't want her to come back. She was crazy, and mean. She went out with other guys, drank all the time, and spent the grocery money on stuff she thought would make people think we were rich. Pretty dumb, since Dad is a butcher. He's a lot happier since she left."

Sasha wasn't sure how to respond, so she asked, "What do you want from Eryx?"

Amanda shrugged. "To be happy, and maybe do better in school, and get a boyfriend, and not be so shy and awkward. I hate it."

Boo ran in front of them, hopping around like he was on speed. Now that they were on the main street, Sasha decided he needed his leash. Pulling it from her coat pocket, she whistled at him, then bent to hook it to his collar.

"No offense, Sasha, but that is one butt-ugly dog."

Boo whined and hung his head. "Now look, you've hurt his feelings." She scratched behind his ears before she stood straight.

"I'm sorry. I wish I had a dog, even an ugly one." She bent to pet Boo, who licked her hand.

They walked on, looking in shop windows as they went. "I don't think you need to join the Ravens to get what you want, Amanda."

"You wouldn't understand. It's easy for people like you."

"People like me?"

"You're hot, and you have cool clothes, and you're related to the hottest guy at school. I know he's kind of on everyone's hate list right now, but that'll change, I guarantee, and he'll be what he's always been. With all you've got going for you, you're gold."

Sasha gave that a lot of thought, all the way to the bakery, where they bought cookies and cocoa, and then as they walked back toward the school. She hadn't been a loser at St. Michael's, so why would she be a loser here? Sure, there was the handicap of being new, but if what Amanda said was true, she could be okay, have friends, be somebody again.

And if that happened, she'd have Amanda right there with her, so Amanda wouldn't be tempted by the Ravens' fake promises. She glanced at her *I Love the Eighties* glasses. If she'd get some new frames, maybe wear some makeup, and ditch the whole unmade bed look, she'd be pretty.

"So I was thinking, would you want to go with me to the basketball game tonight?"

"I can't. My dad gets off work at five, and I have to go home with him because I don't have a car. Placerville is twenty miles away. And he won't let me drive back because he's paranoid about the road between here and there. It's winding and icy in places."

"Maybe he'd bring you back, if you asked."

"Maybe. He's always after me to be more involved at school. He's Mr. Friendly, so he just doesn't get how hard it is."

"My dad was like that. All my friends loved him." They had

turned off of Colorado and were close to the school when she said, "Why don't you come home with me after school? We could work on calculus, and I'd loan you something to wear to the game tonight."

"Really? You'd do that?"

"Sure, why not? I really want to go, but the idea of walking into that gym all by myself is freaky."

"Okay, I'll come, and I'll ask if my dad will bring me back for the game tonight."

Sasha was feeling a whole lot better about things when they walked back into study hall. Jax turned to look at her as she came in, but before she'd taken two steps toward him, Brett said in a loud voice, "Hey, East, did I tell you my cousin's mom was deported because they found out she's a Russian spy?"

Would he never stop? Sasha was frozen to the spot, not sure what to say, what to do.

With his dark gaze still on hers, Jax said, "If Sasha's mom was a spy, the United States wouldn't send her to Russia. They'd arrest her for treason." He turned then and gave Brett a hard look. "Back off, Shriver."

"What the hell? You think you scare me?"

"You should be scared. Lay off of Sasha."

Coach Hightower cleared his throat and waved at Sasha and Amanda to bring up the cookies and cocoa. "Come on, you guys, let's have some sugar and get along, yeah?"

Sasha moved toward the teacher's desk, swallowing the lump

in her throat. Jax had stood up for her, even though he'd said he intended to lay low, to attract as little attention to himself as possible.

≈

By the time sixth period, which was history, began, Brett's reign as Top Dog at Telluride High appeared to be officially over. Now he was the one being shunned, by everyone except the other Ravens. Brody told Jax before class started, "I overheard some kids saying you threatened to beat up Brett if he doesn't leave Sasha alone. They think it's pretty pathetic that the new guy is having to defend her against her own family."

Brett had really stepped in it, but he was a lost soul, and an arrogant, spoiled brat, so he didn't get exactly how deep he was until he said before history began, "Hey, Sasha, why don't you tell Mr. Bruno about your dad getting shot by the Russian Mafia?"

Thomas said, "Hey, Shriver, why don't you shut up? Leave her alone and go back to your cave."

Half the class followed up, telling Brett just what they thought about him.

Even Julianne's handmaidens were looking at Brett like he was something they'd scrape off their shoe.

That he looked genuinely surprised told the whole story.

Mr. Bruno was frowning at him, although not for the same reason as everyone else. Brett was his golden ticket, the guy who was supposed to attract new followers for Eryx. Instead, the kid was making huge missteps that did just the opposite and turned people off.

Jax had taken the seat right next to Sasha, hoping his proximity would remind her not to let her hatred of Bruno be too obvious. When class began, she kept her head down, sketching in her spiral while Bruno talked about the War of 1812. Just as he'd done every day, Jax paid close attention, looking for any hint the guy might drop about where he was going, where the Skia meeting might take place.

Toward the end of his lecture, he said, "The final for this class is next Tuesday, so tomorrow and Friday, we'll review the semester. I regret to say I won't be here to give the final, but Miss Rose has agreed to be here instead."

Jax glanced at Brody and caught the slight nod of his head. He'd heard, and noted it. Bruno was going to be gone next Tuesday. They had less than a week to figure out where he was going and who was going to be there, make a plan for the takedown, and ask M to provide doppelgängers.

He looked at Sasha and felt a little dizzy. Once Bruno was gone, they'd take out the lost souls he'd collected in Telluride, and after that, Jax would go back to the mountain and Sasha'd forget all about him. He'd waited a thousand years for her, and she would know him for less than two weeks. He would never forget her, no matter how much longer he lived. Another thousand years, a million years—it didn't matter. He'd never forget Sasha.

When the school day was finally over, Sasha and Amanda walked to the Shrivers', Boo trotting along beside her. "This may sound a little weird, so don't freak on it or anything, but my aunt is kind of a bitch. She and my dad didn't get along, so she sees me as more of him, I guess, and she doesn't like me. If she's rude, I'm apologizing in advance."

"It's okay. My mom was mean, so I'm used to it."

"Maybe she won't even be home. She's been out of town and may not be back yet."

Unfortunately, Melanie was back. When they came in, she was in the family room, sewing a button on a shirt. Looking up, she smiled at Amanda. "Sasha, how nice. You've brought a friend home from school. How do you do? I'm Sasha's aunt, Melanie."

"Hi," Amanda said, clearly confused. "I'm Amanda Rhodes."

"Would you care for something to drink, Amanda? A soda, or maybe some hot tea?"

"No, thank you."

Melanie never looked directly at Sasha, and the Carol Brady act was scaring the hell out of her. What was going on?

She went to the stairs, Amanda just behind her, and cringed when Melanie said, "You girls have fun up there and just give me a shout if I can bring you anything."

When they were in her room, Amanda said dryly, "Yeah, Sasha, she was really horrible."

"I don't get it. She's been awful ever since I got here on Friday."

"Maybe she's just being nice because I'm company."

"I guess so." She sat on one bed and Amanda sat on the other while they did their calculus homework. When they were done, they went to the closet and started looking for something Amanda could wear to the game.

Thirty minutes later, Amanda looked like a different person, wearing a pair of low-rise jeans and a soft white sweater that offset her dark hair and was perfect for her pale skin. She resisted makeup, but Sasha insisted, and when she was done, after she pulled part of her hair back into a loose braid, Amanda looked in the mirror and gasped. "You're a miracle worker. I've tried makeup before, and different stuff with my hair, but I never looked like this."

The glasses didn't even look that bad.

With perfect timing, Chris knocked and came in, his eyes widening. "Amanda?"

"Hi, Chris."

He gave her the standard guy once-over before he said, "I almost didn't recognize you." He looked at Sasha. "Are you going to the game?"

"Yes, are you?"

"No, I don't do sports if Brett's involved. But I forgot my chemistry book, so I was wondering if you'd get it when you're at the school."

She couldn't figure out why Chris disliked his brother so much. Jax told her Brett had been a lost soul for only a few weeks, but she thought the animosity Chris felt toward him went back way longer than that. "Sure, Chris. What's your locker number and combination?"

"I wrote them down." He handed her a slip of paper. "Thanks." After one more look at Amanda, he mumbled good-bye and left.

Sasha grinned at her new friend. "He gave you the guy once-over—twice."

"He didn't seem very enthusiastic."

"You don't know Chris. He's the quiet type, and he pops in and out of here superfast. Trust me, he was impressed." She couldn't wait to go to the game and see everyone's reaction to Amanda's new look.

At ten till five, she and Boo walked Amanda over to Colorado, to the market where her dad worked. He was the butcher, übernice and friendly, and when Amanda asked if he'd bring her back for the game, he looked like the sun had just risen behind his daughter's head. "I'd love to bring you back for the game." He grinned at Sasha, and invited her to their home to eat supper before they returned to Telluride. She wanted to join them, but she needed to find Tim and ask him about her birth certificate. Rose had reminded her twice again before she had left school. "Thanks, Mr. Rhodes, but I'll have to take a rain check. I'll see you guys at the game."

Back at the Shrivers', she was surprised, and relieved, to find that Melanie was nowhere around. Tim was in the kitchen making a ginormous sandwich.

He looked up when she came in and smiled. "Hey, kiddo, how was school?"

"Okay. Did you have a chance to go by and sign those papers and give Miss Rose my birth certificate?"

"I didn't, Sasha. Sorry. I'll do it tomorrow." He slapped a couple of slices of tomato on the towering pile of roast beef and wheat bread.

"She's kind of leaning on me for it, Tim, and finals are next week."

He carefully stacked leaves of green lettuce on the sandwich. "I don't get why they need a birth certificate. It's not like you weren't born, right?" Taking the sandwich, he went into the family room, to his recliner, and sat down.

Sasha followed, standing next to the bookcase that held no books, only video games and DVDs. "If it's a problem, Tim, maybe I should just tell Rose that we have to wait for Mom to contact us."

Tim looked really upset, his face turning red, his small eyes glancing between Sasha and the stairs. "I told you I'll take care of it, and I will."

Why did he look so freaked out? He'd forgotten his sandwich, mopping sweat from his flabby face with his napkin, mumbling something about consequences and being tired of it all.

"What's wrong? Is there a problem with getting the certificate from Marin County?"

"Why don't you tell her, Tim?" Melanie asked as she came

down the stairs. "Go ahead. Tell Sasha why you can't order a birth certificate from Marin County."

Stiffening, preparing for battle, Sasha waited.

Melanie went to the sofa and sat, crossing her legs, checking out the toe of one of her spike-heeled boots. "Go on, Tim. We're all waiting."

"Be quiet, Melanie." He was still wiping his face with the napkin. "Please, Sasha, just let me get your birth certificate."

"For God's sake, you're such a spineless worm!" She turned her hateful gaze to Sasha. "Marin County doesn't have your birth certificate. No one does. Katya found you in a slum in Vladivostok when you were two years old, probably the kid of a crack whore who ditched you."

"You're lying." Sasha looked at Tim, waiting for him to tell Melanie to back off.

He leaned his head back against the recliner and closed his eyes, the plate with his sandwich sliding from his lap to the floor, spilling tomatoes, lettuce, and roast beef across the carpet.

"You're an illegal alien," Melanie said in pretty much the same way she'd say Sasha was a crack whore. "You're not a citizen of Russia, either. It's as if you don't exist. Tim didn't know until he went to San Francisco that you're not Mike and Katya's natural child. You're not even legally adopted, so you belong to nobody. If you'd gone with your mother, having no papers, they'd have taken you away from her, and because Tim's living in some fantasy that he owes it to Mike to protect you, especially since your saintly mother—"

"Melanie, if you say *one more word*, I'll put a bullet through your head."

She stood, went to his chair, picked up the roast beef from the floor, and smeared it across his shirt; then she grasped the neck of his shirt, pulled it open, and dropped the meat inside. "This'll save time. You won't have to wait for it to show up as another bulge." Turning, she went to the foyer, grabbed her purse from the hall tree, walked out, and slammed the door.

After an eternity of staring at each other, Tim said in the quiet of the room, "Before Katya was to leave for the United States, she went to Vladivostok, to the house where her grandfather used to live, to say good-bye. She never expected to be in Russia again. The house was old and abandoned, and there you were, wandering through the debris. She took you to the police, but they couldn't find anyone who was missing a two-year-old, and when she offered to keep you, they said no and sent you to an orphanage. Things were bad for her in Russia, and she couldn't wait the months it would take for a legal adoption, so she went to the orphanage that night and took you, then caught a plane to Paris. She contacted Mike, who met her there, married her, and they flew to San Francisco. He got you through customs with a fake birth certificate, which is probably what they used to get you into school. Katya said she lost it and would send another as soon as she could, but so far, I haven't been able to contact her."

Sasha sank to the floor, crouched there with her arms around her knees, Tim's giant body a blur through the flood of tears. Mom and Dad had told the story of when she was born at least a million times—all about how Dad had flown home from halfway around the world to be there when she arrived, and how Mom had been told she could never have children, but there was Sasha, a miracle.

It was such a great romantic story. And it was all a lie.

She remembered her mother had said she'd found the painting in an old empty house in Vladivostok. Mom had failed to mention what else she'd found.

"When she received notice she was to be deported, she called and asked me to come," Tim said, staring at the floor. "She said that she had something of Mike's she wanted me to keep. I didn't expect it to be his daughter, but she asked me to take you, to protect you from what could happen if she took you back to Russia."

"Would they put me in an orphanage? I'm too old for that, aren't I?"

"It's very different in Russia, Sasha. Crime is a way of life, and the Mafia is everywhere, even in the government. The sex trade is huge. Since you aren't legally her child, Katya worried you'd be taken from her and sent to work."

Just then, Brett came down the stairs. On his way to the kitchen, he said, "So Sasha, turns out we're not actually related at all. Pretty weird how just one phone call could get you kicked out of the country."

Tim frowned. "There won't be any phone calls to anyone, Brett. Do you understand?"

"Sure, Dad. We wouldn't want anything bad to happen to Sasha, would we?"

TEN

WHEN JAX GOT HOME FROM PRACTICE, HE WENT TO HIS room to do homework, and found Phoenix playing Demon Slayer. "Didja get the memo that you have this game in your room, too?"

"I've been waiting on you, bro. I have news."

"Coincidentally, I also have news." Tossing his jacket to the bed, he went to sit opposite his brother, watching the screen while Phoenix incinerated the demons. "It's pretty sick that we have this game. Kind of latently suicidal, isn't it?"

"We're not demons."

"Semantics. So what's your news?"

"Zee's been over at Bruno's every day after he leaves for work, and today he found a list of the Skia who're going to be at the meeting. It's teachers and administrators from schools all over the country. Fifty-five of them, attending under the guise of a conference on how to stop underage drinking."

"And in the night-owl session, Mr. Bruno will teach them how to recruit teenagers."

"Right. We've got a whole crew of Luminas researching every name on the list, to get what M needs for doppelgängers."

"He's going to have to make it a rush order, because I'm pretty sure the meeting is next week." He told him what Bruno said about being out. "Makes sense they'd do it during Christmas week, when most schools have a break."

Phoenix wiped out a whole band of demons. "Right. It's just gravy that it's Christmas. Eryx does love irony." He progressed to the next circle of Hell. "So how did it go today?"

Jax leaned back and told him, but wasn't halfway done before his cell rang. He pulled it out of his pocket, surprised to see Sasha's name on the screen. He answered and knew right away something was terribly wrong.

She was crying. Hard. "Can you come over?"

"I'll be right there." He shoved the phone back in his pocket, went through his bathroom to his closet, grabbed his trench coat, then came back to tell Phoenix he was leaving.

"What's up?"

"She's crying and asked me to come over."

"I told you girls cry a lot."

"I'll be back later." He popped out of his room and into hers, cloaked in case anyone else was there. She sat at the end of her bed, tears streaming down her cheeks. Sitting next to her, he pulled her close. "What's wrong? What's happened?"

With her face buried in his shoulder, she told him around her sobs, something about her birth certificate, and being adopted, and her mom finding her in the same abandoned house where she found the painting.

It was hard to get the whole story, but he finally did, and understood why she was so upset. She felt betrayed because she'd been lied to.

"I was two years old, Jax. Why was I there, in a falling-down house, alone? Who did that to me? Why would my real mother leave me there?"

He suspected she was left there, with the painting, by someone who wasn't human. Maybe an angel. Maybe Lucifer, who asked God to send an Anabo to bring hope back to the Mephisto. Maybe God himself.

He supposed it didn't matter. Listening to her cry, feeling her shake with emotion, he was torn, wondering what to say, what she could handle.

"Jax, I want to see the painting."

He'd seen that coming, but he wasn't ready. He wanted to show her the reproduced painting that Andres was still working on. "Maybe now's not a good time, Sasha. Let's wait until you're—"

"No!" She jerked away from him and got to her feet, rounding on him. "I want to see it, right now! You said I could. You said you wouldn't take it away from me."

"You won't like it, Sasha. You'll be even more upset."

"I'm not sure that's possible. I want to know why I was there, who left me, and what it means. I'm not anyone's child, not a citizen of this country. I don't actually exist. No way can I go to school, and college is a joke. I'm going to be a homeless person, without an identity."

He stood and reached to cup her face between his palms, pushing the tears from her cheeks with the pads of his thumbs. "I'll get the Luminas to work up some papers tonight, and you'll have them in the morning before school. They'll make sure the papers are on file, wherever we tell them, so if anyone checks, you'll be as legal, and real, as anyone else."

"What about the painting?"

He sighed and dropped his hands. "I really wish you wouldn't look at it yet. Don't you have enough on your plate without that?"

She wiped her cheeks with the backs of her hands. "All you've done is make me even more determined to see it."

"All right, fine, but don't ask me questions because I don't have any answers. Deal?"

She moved close and slid her arms beneath his trench coat, around his back. "Deal."

Ten seconds later, they were in the document lab, where Andres was hard at work on the fake, the room infused with the scent of paint and linseed oil. He looked up when they appeared and smiled at Sasha. "Ah, the Anabo. Hello, Sasha. I'm Andres."

She nodded at him and said, "Hi, Andres. Is that my mom's painting?"

He pointed to the one on the left. "Yes, this one. I am reproducing it, as you see"—he pointed to the canvas on the right—"with a few changes."

Jax watched her look at the canvas, saw her eyes widen, knew her heart was racing because he could see the tiny pulse in her temple. She must be freaking out. She was going to go off about destiny, or how this made a joke of free will, or something. He watched and waited.

She said breathlessly, "Ohmigod, this is an Andolini!" She looked toward Andres. "It is, isn't it?"

The painter nodded sagely. "I was captivated the moment I saw it. Very rare, of course, and in excellent condition."

"My mother told me it was flaking."

"Not the original. Someone altered it with shoddy paint. See? Your face was painted over, and here—"

"What did you say? *My* face?"

"Yes, see? It's you in the painting. And Jax."

She leaned in and looked closely—so still, Jax was certain she was holding her breath.

Andres continued on as if he were a museum docent. "The river was redone, to hide these tiny numbers. That was the flaking paint. The original paint is pristine. This must have been kept in perfect storage for many years to be so clean and undamaged. I'm appalled someone would alter it, but I suppose your mother felt it necessary, so no one would realize this is you, and she saw this as a perfect way to hide the account number."

"The code to the lockbox in Geneva?"

"Right, and this is why Eryx wants the painting. If he could get his hands on the contents of the box, he'd have dozens of leads to people he might blackmail into pledging."

"Are you putting a wrong account number on the fake?"

"No, they're the same. We sent a Lumina to Geneva yesterday to remove the contents from the lockbox so Eryx can't get them, even if he has the account number."

"What was in the box?"

"Just what your mother said. Private letters, taped conversations, and compromising photos of lots of people we see in the news, although some of them are retired now, or dead. If Eryx had access to it . . ."

"What will you do with all of it?"

"Destroy it."

"If you're leaving the real account number, why make a fake painting?"

Andres looked at him. "Does she know?"

"Know what?" Sasha looked even more freaked out.

"I guess that answers the question," Andres said dryly.

"Sasha and I are going to my room." He hauled her close and popped them upstairs.

Phoenix was still playing Demon Slayer, now in the seventh circle of Hell. "So what was she crying about?"

"Why don't you ask her?"

Jerking around, Phoenix saw her and jumped to his feet.

"Phoenix," Jax said, watching her step back from him until she bumped against his desk, "why don't you tell Sasha why we need a fake painting to give Eryx? Tell her about the Mephisto Covenant."

"Why don't you tell me yourself?" Sasha asked.

"Phoenix tells it better." He walked to the window and stared out at the mountains. "He's also way less invested, so he can bear watching your facial expressions."

"You didn't really just say that."

"Wait until you hear what he has to say."

Dead silence.

After a while, he looked over his shoulder and saw Sasha turn on Phoenix, who was watching her with a funny look on his face. "Will you *say* something already? You're freaking me out, staring at me like that."

Phoenix stroked his goatee and said, "The Mephisto Covenant is a deal Mephistopheles made with God when we became immortal. He didn't think we could do what Lucifer wanted us to do if we had no incentive, so he asked God to give us a loophole, some way to earn Heaven. God said if we could love selflessly, we'd be at peace, and we'd have the same chance of Heaven as any other human. M agreed, but it wasn't until later that he realized his sons are unlovable. We tried to find girls to love, but it was hard to do when they ran away screaming."

"Hyperbole?"

"No, they really did run away screaming. M was bummed, but he said we had another alternative. An Anabo girl wouldn't run away. She'd give us a shot. The problem was, and still is, there aren't enough Anabo. We found one, over a hundred years ago, and now you. In a thousand years, we've found exactly two."

"The Mephisto Covenant," she said softly. "If Jax loves me, if it's real and selfless, he'll be redeemed?"

"He'll be like everyone else on earth and have the same opportunity to reach Heaven."

"But he's immortal. He'll live forever."

"Forever is relative. The end of the world will come, someday, and when it does, all of us will be in Hell, unless we're redeemed and have lived a life worthy of Heaven."

Silence fell again, until she said, "That's heavy."

"It's heavier when you consider none of us have a clue how to love someone. We don't know anything about females other than the obvious, and the odds of convincing a girl to stay here with us and join the fight against Eryx are even slimmer than finding an Anabo in the first place."

"So if I stayed, I'd be just like you and Jax and the other brothers?"

"Not just like us, no. You'd go with us on takedowns, and you'd be Mephisto, but you'd still be Anabo, which means you'd never lose Heaven. You'd also have children, someday, and they'd be born like you, a mix of Mephisto and Anabo. They'd grow up and join the fight."

Again she was quiet. Jax watched the sky finally open up and snow, the flakes falling large and thick, laying a fresh layer on the old, draping everything in pristine white. He wondered if he'd throw up. He felt sick enough. Why wasn't she saying anything?

"Only two?" she asked.

"Only two."

"And the other was Jane. She was yours."

It took a moment for Phoenix to respond. "Yes. You have no idea how great a threat Eryx is to you, Sasha. That's why we need a fake painting to give him. He wants the numbers and won't rest unless he gets them. We decided to give them to him, but we couldn't give him the real painting because, with God's hand touching Jax, and Lucifer touching you, the picture depicts the Mephisto Covenant. Eryx doesn't know that we can be redeemed by an Anabo. As it stands, he's satisfied with trying to take those who we find, to prevent them from bearing our children. If he knew we could be redeemed, he'd have Skia and lost souls across the globe actively searching for Anabo and killing them on sight."

"But there are only two. You said so."

"Only two that we know of. There could be more."

"Why aren't you hunting for others?"

"We don't have the manpower that Eryx has. There're six

of us and one hundred twenty-two Luminas, and all our time is taken up hunting Skia and lost souls. Eryx has thousands who follow him that we haven't discovered yet. We're limited to accidentally stumbling across an Anabo, like Jax did when he popped into that warehouse in San Francisco."

"Doesn't it frustrate you, knowing there may be more, but not knowing where, or who?"

"Frustration doesn't begin to cover it, but M says we need to be patient, that we're going to be here forever, and we'll eventually all have a mate, but we're not made for patience. We're sons of Hell."

"What does that mean, really? Jax tells me all the time that he's got a dark side, but I never see it. I don't understand."

"You wouldn't because you're Anabo."

"I still want to know."

Jax could hear Phoenix begin to pace.

"The dark side is just what it sounds like. It's despair, and the rage that goes with it. There's an unfairness to our existence, justice that's never served. We didn't ask to be born this way, without any hope of Heaven or knowledge of God. We know about him, of course, but we were born without his even being aware. He can't hear us, can't help us, offers no solace. All humans, whether they realize it or not, are connected to God, and that makes all the difference."

He paced some more, and Jax waited for the worst part.

"The rage sometimes takes over, and bad things happen.

We've killed men who weren't lost souls. We're punished for it, but we still do it. We fight a lot, with each other and with complete strangers and with men who piss us off. We have anonymous sex because we're eternally eighteen-year-old guys, but mostly because it's the only way we can ever feel close to a female."

"How do you do that if they run away screaming?"

"We're masters at disguising what we are. We find willing partners in dark places, like nightclubs. Back in the day, we visited taverns and back alleys. We're prone to jealousy and hate. We aren't above blackmail to get what we want, and we've stolen a few things over the years. The key here is that we don't feel remorse. The only thing that keeps us from twisting off completely is the dim hope of finding an Anabo. God said we would find love and earn Heaven if we didn't actively earn Hell. So we try to stay on the straight and narrow, but as I said, we're sons of Hell, and sometimes the rage gets to be too much."

Silence fell, but Jax couldn't make himself turn around to look at her. He couldn't stand to see the look of disgust on her face.

"Why did your father do it? If he knew being with an Anabo was forbidden, why did he seduce her?"

Phoenix replied in a low, quiet voice, "He was lonely. Mephistopheles is the dark angel of death, so when someone dies and his spirit's bound for Hell, M or one of his thousands of assistants escorts him. Mephistopheles is feared and despised almost as much as Lucifer, but Elektra wasn't afraid, and she didn't hate him. When he finally crossed the line and broke the rule, she didn't say no. He fell for her, hard."

"It must have killed him when she was murdered, and by their own son."

"He never got over it. He suffers the guilt of her death, as well as guilt over fathering a son who's the worst evil the world will ever know."

"So all this, because a man was lonely."

"Loneliness is a terrible place to live. We became immortal over a thousand years ago. We have each other, and M, and the Luminas, and the Purgatories. We have our work. We have everything we need or want, can travel anywhere in the world at the speed of light, have amazing powers, and some of us are even mildly talented. You should hear Zee play the piano, or watch Jax play basketball. What we don't have is a companion. Everyone wants someone, and maybe we're all from Hell, but when it comes to girls, we're as human as any guy out there."

Jax heard his brother stop pacing. "I hope you'll stay with us. I want it for Jax because he's my brother, and I want it for all of us on the mountain because we need your help, but as much as anything, I want it for you. This is what you were born to do, and if you don't stay, it'll be as if you never really came to life."

In the silence that followed, Jax knew he'd disappeared.

Sasha moved to stand next to him and look out at the snow. "What he told me . . . it's almost like a Greek tragedy, or an old Bible story."

He moved to stand just behind her, sliding his arms around her and resting his chin against her silky hair. "Why did you call me, Sasha? Was it just so I'd bring you to see the painting?"

She didn't answer right away. He heard the clock on the mantel tick away almost a minute before she whispered, "No."

"Why did you call me?"

Turning in his arms, she looked up into his eyes. "I've never felt like that before, completely alone, like I had no one, not even my mother. All I could think about was you, that I wanted you. I was so sad, and scared, and I felt like my whole life was a lie." She slid her arms around his waist and tilted her head back to look up at him. "I don't understand why, or how, but ever since I met you, the only time I feel right is when I'm with you. When I'm not, I feel nervous, kind of jumpy, and not exactly sad but not myself. Out of sorts."

"I'm sorry, Sasha. It'll go away as soon as I'm gone and you can forget about me. We're pretty sure the meeting is next week, so once Bruno is out of the picture, we'll take the lost souls and that'll be it. I should be gone from your life completely by Christmas Eve."

He expected her to say she was glad.

Instead, she burst into tears.

Tightening his arms, he wanted to make her stop, wanted to fix whatever was making her so miserable. But he was totally lost, had no idea why she was crying into his neck like this. How could he fix the problem if he didn't know what it was? He asked, twice, but she only cried harder. She was so despondent, so sad, he started to get choked up, and it freaked him out.

That was the only explanation he had for why he blew off his resolution not to kiss her again.

He lifted his hands to her head and turned her face up to his, intending to give her a nice, easy little kiss, to offer comfort. Maybe he even had a subconscious motive to surprise her into not crying. He had to do something, because this was killing him. Lowering his head, he barely brushed his lips across hers, tasting the salt of her tears. While he was still being amazed that anything could be this soft, he felt that same liberating sense of calm he remembered from when he'd kissed her before. Eryx, the Skia, Hell on Earth, the crazy jealousy he felt for every guy who looked at her, the rage he harbored against her family— even, ironically, his unrelieved lust for her—all seemed so much less overpowering.

With a shuddering sigh, she melted against him and kissed him back. He dropped his hands to her shoulders, then lower, across the bumps and ridges of her sweater, exploring the way her slender body curved from the span of her waist to the flare of her hips. It wasn't as if he'd never touched a girl before, but this wasn't just a girl—this was Sasha, and he wasn't in a hurry.

His nice, simple, comforting kiss turned into something else when he felt her hands slip beneath his shirt and glide across the bare skin of his back. She subtly turned her head one way, he instinctively moved the other, and without conscious decision, he wasn't just tasting her tears. Their tongues touched, and she made a funny little sound, low in her throat.

After that, he couldn't be sure how it happened, but she wasn't crying anymore and he wasn't thinking. At all. His hands were underneath her sweater, touching every inch of her warm, smooth skin; they were kissing like two condemned people suddenly given a reprieve; and his feeling of calm morphed into happiness so intense, he'd swear his blood was singing.

She broke the kiss but didn't move, blinking up at him, her eyes so blue, he decided there was nothing on Earth as beautiful. "I'm sorry I'm such a crybaby," she whispered.

"It's okay." He feathered little kisses across her forehead. "I just hate for you to be so sad. I want to make it better, make you happy."

"As much as I'm sad for me, I'm sad for you."

"Why? Are you feeling guilty for not wanting to stay? Because you shouldn't. This isn't about me. If you change your mind and stay because you feel sorry for me, it won't work. It has to be what you want."

"I'm sad that you didn't have a choice, that your mother died, that your whole life you've been something people are afraid of."

"Don't pity me. Ever. I like it better when you think I'm repulsive."

She looked surprised. "Feeling sad for you isn't pity, just like grieving for the person I thought I was isn't the same as feeling

284

sorry for myself. Sometimes, things are just really, really sad, and it makes me cry."

"What do you mean, the person you thought you were?"

Laying her head against his shoulder, she pressed her cheek to his chest and tightened her arms around his middle. "My real mother, the one who actually gave birth to me, didn't leave me in that old house. I think someone who isn't an ordinary human left me there, with that painting, knowing a woman with a big heart and no chance for babies would find me and keep me until I was old enough to understand who I am."

"None of that changes anything, Sasha. Your mother still loves you, is probably missing you awful, right this minute. And maybe you've learned things most regular people will never know, but you're still the same girl you were before that Ravens meeting. You still have a choice."

Lifting her head, she stared up at him. "Someone, maybe God, maybe Lucifer, maybe a rogue band of angels, went to a lot of trouble to leave me in that old house. I was supposed to be found by you and your brothers."

"So? Everyone bears the weight of someone else's expectations, but at the end of the day, they still have free will. They always have a choice. Maybe you don't know it, but I also have choices. I want you, Sasha, more than you can begin to imagine, but even if you were willing to stay, even if you *wanted* to stay, I'd still have the choice to say yes or no."

"Would you say no?"

Pulling away from her, he stepped back and ran a hand through his hair, all the reasons he wasn't supposed to kiss her flooding back into his mind. "It'd kill me, but I might."

"Why? Is it because you don't really like me? I'm the only Anabo you've ever found, but that doesn't mean you have to like me."

"Oh, I like you, Sasha. I like everything about you, except maybe for that crying thing. I think we'd like being together for the next gazillion years. I'd love nothing more than to wake up and see your beautiful face every morning, and go to sleep with you right there next to me every night." He reached out to smooth her hair, tucking it behind her ears. "But turning you to Mephisto means changing you so you know rage and hate, and I honestly don't know if I could go through with it. I can't stand the idea of your feeling like I do."

Her eyes were wide with surprise, and something else. Maybe disbelief. "If I become immortal, do I have to be Mephisto?"

"You can't do what we do if you're only Anabo, Sasha. Anabo is a state of being that feels compassion for every living thing, and that includes the lost souls. You can't capture a man and send him to Hell on Earth if you feel any compassion for him."

"But I don't feel compassion. I don't feel anything toward Brett and Melanie and Mr. Bruno except anger, so when I think about them being gone, I'm relieved."

"That's because you're already changing, which freaks me out like you wouldn't believe. I see your anger toward them, like yesterday with Scott, and today with Mr. Hoolihan in biology.

Your instincts kicked in and you challenged him, which is just a precursor to what comes next."

Turning away from her, he walked around the room. "If you had the ability to pick him up and take him around the world to the entrance to Hell on Earth, you'd have to fight yourself not to do it, to wait until everything was ready, until you had a plan for his fake death, until M had provided a doppelgänger. It would frustrate the hell out of you to wait, and in the meantime, you'd feel so much anger, you'd practically choke on it. You'd see how others don't know, how unsuspecting they are, and vulnerable. You'd watch those innocent kids follow Mr. Bruno, and more than it would make you sad, it would piss you off. You'd want to take him, immediately, and at the same time, you'd be frustrated with the humans. You'd have no compassion, just like me. You'd experience rage and violence. I can't stand the thought of doing that to you."

"Even though you want me to stay?"

"It makes no sense, but that's how I feel."

"Why am I the only one to change? What about you?"

He stood in front of the TV screen with Phoenix's game paused and stared at the exploding demons. "If I love you without prejudice, unselfishly, I'll have the same chance of redemption as any other human. Not a free pass, like you've got right now, but a chance. I don't know for sure, but I think that would make me different."

"Do you have to love me for me to stay, or can I become Mephisto even if you don't?"

287

"I don't have to love you, no, but if you choose Mephisto, you're stuck with me and no one else. You could become a Lumina, if you wanted, and stay here to help, but not do what I do. Maybe you'd like that. You could work on the mountain for the rest of eternity and maybe find a nice Lumina who doesn't live and breathe violence and rage."

She was quiet for a long time before she said, "That's only a theoretical possibility, right?"

He sighed and shoved his hands into the pockets of his trench coat while he turned to face her. "Yeah, pretty much. I'd want to kill anyone who touched you, even if he was a Lumina, and killing an angel would buy me a one-way, instant ticket to Hell."

She pushed away from the desk and walked across the rug to where he stood, standing so close he could feel her breathe. "See, here's the thing. I wouldn't want a Lumina to touch me. I don't want anyone else to touch me. There's just you, Jax. And what confuses me is wondering if I'd feel this way even if I wasn't changing to Mephisto."

"The changes are all about getting your body and mind ready to take on Eryx. Whatever you feel about me—good or bad—is all you. But no worries. After next Thursday, Lucifer will change you back to how you were before, and I'll be gone, so you'll forget about me."

Her eyes welled with tears again.

"Oh, God, please don't cry. What did I say? Why aren't you glad about that? It's what you want. You said so, over and over."

"Jax, you're such a . . . such a . . . *guy*." Turning, she walked away, around the room, staring at the floor, talking as she moved. "I don't want to forget you. I want to be how I was before, but I don't want to never see you again."

"I want to stand on holy ground and not catch on fire. I want to take all your clothes off and carry you to that bed over there. We all want things we can't have, Sasha. It's one of the most painful parts of growing up, the realization that we can't always have what we want."

She stopped at the end of the bed to stare at him. "Phoenix slept with her, didn't he?"

The train they were on just took a detour, and he tried to follow. "What?"

"When Phoenix met Jane, he seduced her, just like your father seduced Elektra. Why haven't you seduced me?"

"Because you'd be marked, and Lucifer can't change that. You'd have no choice but to stay here until you die. Otherwise, Eryx would kill you before the next sunset."

"But you could have what you want. I'd stay, and maybe you'd love me and could stand on holy ground. You could've had all you want, if you'd had sex with me before I knew too much. It's not like I would have for sure said no. So I ask again, why haven't you seduced me?"

"I can't interfere with free will. I'd be taking the choice away from you."

"So Elektra knew what she was getting into when she didn't

say no, and Jane was totally up on what it meant to sleep with Phoenix. Is that what you're saying?"

"I don't know, Sasha. I wasn't there when they didn't say no."

She glanced over her shoulder at the bed, then looked at him with the strangest expression on her face. "If I said I'd climb in that bed with you, right here, right now, would you do it?"

He backed up to the chair and sat, unable to answer.

She walked toward him and bent to place her hands on the arms of the chair, bringing her face close to his. "No, you wouldn't, because none of that is good enough. You want it, but not nearly as much as you want something else. It's why you'll let me go without a fight, without trying to force me to stay."

He shook his head, praying to a God who couldn't hear him that she wouldn't say it. If she didn't say it, it wasn't real. Wasn't true.

"You want me to love you. You want that more than you want me in bed, or holy ground, or anything else on Earth or even in Heaven. Your father and Phoenix didn't have to have it. Maybe they wanted it, but it wasn't a deal breaker. For you, it's all or nothing."

He couldn't swallow. Couldn't breathe. Grasping her arms, he gently pushed her away, got to his feet, and disappeared from his room.

❧

Twenty minutes later, she was almost through the eighth circle of Hell when there was a knock and Phoenix said through the door, "Jax, what's up? Don't you have a basketball game in less than an hour?"

Sasha kept her focus on the screen, grimly wiping out more demons and some weird flying monkey creatures with fire for hair and evil red eyes.

The door opened, but she didn't look away from Hell.

"Sasha? Where's Jax?"

"I don't know. He disappeared."

"Did you guys get in an argument?"

"No, I hurt his feelings." She pushed the buttons faster, wiping out the enemy with severe determination. "Completely annihilated him. You know why? Because I'm stupid. A total rube. Clueless wonder. God gave me a brain, but forgot to send the instruction manual."

Phoenix sat next to her. "I've never made it to this level."

"A friend of mine in San Francisco played Demon Slayer, and whenever I went to his house, he wanted me to try. Made him mad that I was better at it than him. Maybe because I'm Anabo, I have a natural ability."

"You sound a little bitter, Sasha."

She froze the last of the demons in the eighth circle, the screen went black, then an intricate gate appeared with an inscription across the top that read, ABANDON ALL HOPE, YE WHO ENTER HERE. "Why can't I just be normal? Why can't Jax just be a regular guy?"

"Why isn't the sky green and the grass blue? Why ask the question? It is what it is, and nothing can change it."

The ninth circle was way different. There were flowers and trees and a gurgling brook, birds singing and bees buzzing. It looked more like a My Little Pony video game. "What's this? A joke?"

"It's Eden in Hell. The evil you have to overcome isn't so obvious."

The rules for this level of the game popped up.

Welcome to the Ninth Circle, where the line between Good vs. Evil begins to blur. To make it back to the real world, you must decide who are enemies, and who are friends. You may die, but if you choose wisely, one can bring you back to life and guide you to the other side.

She looked at Phoenix, who was rubbing his goatee thoughtfully, black eyes focused on the screen. "Okay, I get it now. I'm actually dead and traveling through the ninth circle of Hell."

He turned his head and met her gaze. "What if you were? Who would you pick to be your friend?"

"I really hate rhetorical questions."

"Do you hate Jax?"

"Of course not." She sighed and slumped back in the chair, tossing the game controller to the table below the screen. "Maybe if everything wasn't happening so fast, if I just had time to get my head around it. Last Thursday, I was living my life, thinking I'd graduate in May with all the kids I grew up with, spend four years at NYU, get a job at the Met, get married, work, have a couple of kids, live to my eighties, and kick off, just like every other schmo in the world. Now, in one week, my whole life has gone one eighty, to something I couldn't make up in a million years."

"It would be nice if you had a while to get used to the idea, but you don't. And even if you did, would it change anything? You're either willing to live forever and join the fight against Eryx, or you're not. Since Jax is a basic necessity for that to happen, if you hated him, I'd say the choice is pretty obvious. But you don't hate him. You just said so."

"I don't love him, either."

"If you like him, the rest can come later."

"You don't have to answer this, Phoenix, but I really want to know—was it hard for Jane to make the decision?"

He went still, then looked away from her. "No."

"How did you find her?"

"It was like Jax found you, during a takedown." He stared at the floor with no expression on his face. "She had a twin sister who wasn't Anabo, who was . . . she had some problems. They were extremely close and did everything together. They had a dancing instructor, because in those days it was important for young women to know how to dance. Jane's family were aristocrats in England, very wealthy and influential. The dance instructor was Skia, and he promised health to Jane's sister if she'd take the oath. She did, but her recovery was only temporary, and she was angry and bitter. Jane couldn't understand why her sister had changed so drastically, or why she pushed her away.

"We discovered the Skia by chance, and found all of his lost souls within a couple of days. The takedown was at a ball. There was a fire, started by an overturned candle, and seventy-nine people died, including Jane's sister. The rest were able to escape, but they didn't remember how, because we made them forget. One of those was Jane."

"So you found her that night. Did you tell her everything, right away?"

His nod was slow. "I went to her room, to check on her, and she was crying. She freaked out when I appeared, but I explained who I was, and what happened. I went back the next day and the day after that, and every day for over a month, until she said she wanted to join us, that if someone as faithful and good as her sister could be suckered into pledging, there was no hope for anyone, anywhere."

"And she didn't hate you."

He smiled sadly. "No, she didn't hate me."

Sasha stood and walked to the windows to look out at the mountains, at the endless forest and craggy rocks, dressed in snow. She suddenly realized she could see them almost as well as if the sun was shining. Remembering what Jax said about being able to turn off lights, she turned toward the lamp on his bedside table and concentrated carefully, but nothing happened. Then she heard a guy yell from far away, "Hey! Who's jacking with the lights?"

"Probably need to work on that," Phoenix said as he stood and walked closer to her. "Tell me where you want to go, and I'll take you there. Jax obviously isn't coming back."

She looked around his room, certain this was the last time she'd see it.

"You're not going to stay, are you?"

Looking into his brother's black-as-midnight eyes, she slowly shook her head. "He wants too much. Even if I was all in, like Jane was, it would never work out between Jax and me. He'd never be happy with me, not in the long run."

"I think we both know that's not true. Given time, you have the ability to give him what he wants. You're afraid the same can't be said for him."

"So what if I am? I can't spend forever without some kind of love in my life. I *can't*. I'd want to die, but I could never die. It really would be like living in Hell, loving someone who couldn't love me back."

"What makes you so sure he can't?"

"Did you love Jane?"

That made him mad. He scowled at her. "How could you ask me a question like that? I've lived over a *hundred years* with guilt."

Sasha took a step toward him. "Guilt isn't love. You liked her, you wanted her, you lusted after her, but you didn't love her. It was all about you. Even after a hundred years, it's *still* all about you. You're so wrapped up in how she died, and how it was because of what you did to her, that you don't have room to miss her, or grieve because she's not here, living the life she was supposed to live. If you did, if what you felt for her was love, you'd have let it go by now, and made something good from her memory, instead of this whole woe-is-me martyr thing you've got going on. So the answer is no, you didn't love her. She was what you needed for redemption, a means to an end, and I'm not okay with being that to Jax. I'd rather forget all of this and live out the rest of my life with an ordinary, nice guy, who may not be perfect, but who can love me for me, not what I can get him."

"Are you done?"

"So done. Can I leave now? Or are you too mad to take me?"

"I'm not mad." He suddenly hauled her next to him, his arms around her like the jaws of life gone haywire. "Just say where."

She didn't say anything, partly because she couldn't breathe, but partly because she realized, too late, she'd stepped way over the line. Again. What was with her tonight?

"You can tell me where, or we can stand here all night."

"I'm . . . sorry," she managed to say. "Not my . . . place . . . to say you didn't . . . love her . . . and I'm . . . sor—"

"Forget it, Sasha." His arms relaxed a little, and she sucked in a deep breath. "Do you want to go to the Shrivers'? Or the school?"

"Both. Would you take me to my room to get my coat, then to the school?"

"I'm not an f'ing taxi service."

"Please? I can't face any of the Shrivers right now, but it's freezing outside, and I need my coat."

"It's a damn good thing you weren't meant for me. Nothing I can't stand worse than a pain in the ass."

"Nothing I can't stand worse than a martyr, so I guess we're even."

"You said you were done."

"I'm sorry, Phoenix. I don't know what's wrong with me. Really, truly, I'm not like this. I don't even *think* things like that, much less say them out loud."

His arms relaxed further, and he looked down into her eyes. "Did he kiss you again?"

She nodded and blushed at the same time. "It's the spit, isn't it?"

"It's the spit."

Everything went dark, and a few seconds later, they were standing in her room. Jax sat at her desk, at her computer, reading messages on her Facebook wall. He looked up and frowned. "Let go of her, Phoenix."

"Chris is right next door, and these walls are like paper," she whispered.

"It doesn't matter," Phoenix said as he released her. "We're all cloaked, so no one can see or hear us."

Jax asked in a low, almost menacing voice, "Who's Tyler Hudson?"

She looked from her Facebook page to Jax's gloomy expression. "There's this thing called privacy, and you just moved into mine and put your feet on the coffee table."

"He says he's coming to Telluride for Christmas, and he wants to see you." Jax stood, drawing himself up into a rigid giant, looking like Death on Crack. He closed the distance between them, so agitated, she could feel the vibration from his body. "He wants to take you out somewhere, because he didn't realize until you were gone how much he *likes* you."

Last week, she would have died and gone to Heaven over that message. Now, it was a nuisance, and she felt aggravated at Tyler. He'd had a zillion chances to ask her out, but he had waited until she was gone to get a clue.

Jax was waiting for some kind of answer. "What do you want me to say? I sat by him in chemistry and tried to flirt, but he treated me like I was just one of his guy friends. Now he wants to hang out. So what? It's not like I plan to go." She glanced toward her computer. "Jax, you have to promise not to do this again. It's so wrong."

"I came to load what was on your old hard drive to this one, and when I turned it on, Facebook popped up. Like I wasn't going to read your wall or your messages?"

"Are you on Facebook?"

"We all are, except Phoenix. We use different identities, obviously, but it's great for getting personal information about the lost souls. The Skia use it to troll for possible followers."

"You could have just friended me."

"You wouldn't have known who I am, so you'd have ignored me. But I'm not sorry for reading it, even if you're mad, because it occurred to me I should keep up with what you're doing and who you're talking to. If word gets out to Bruno or any of the others, we could be set up, and that's not a risk I'm willing to take."

Insulted, she glared up at him. "You think I'd sell you out? Are you *serious*?"

"I don't think you'd do it intentionally, but you might let something slip."

"That's a crock and you know it! You're just pissed off because of what I said, and now you're acting like a child, trying to get back at me."

Obviously surprised, he shot a questioning look at Phoenix.

"Don't look at me, bro. You're the one who kissed her. I'm just the sad, pathetic *martyr* brother."

"She called you a martyr?"

He nodded, then looked puzzled. "Am I a martyr?"

"It doesn't matter. She shouldn't have said that."

"Maybe if you'd stop enabling him, he could move on with his life."

"What, so now it's my fault he's like this?"

"Like what?" Phoenix looked totally shocked. "You *do* think I'm a martyr."

"It's okay, Phoenix. Nobody blames you. We just want you to stop blaming yourself." Jax paused. "And I guess it'd be nice if you'd lay off pointing out how you never go out, that you stay home and work while we're off looking for girls."

Phoenix raised his dark brows. "I always wondered if you all resented me because I found Jane, because I was first to find an Anabo. Now I know."

"No one resented you. No one blamed you. No one was anything but really sad and bummed when she died. But it was a hundred and twenty-two years ago. They invented cars and airplanes and video games since then. I know you'll never forget, and no one expects you to forget, but at what point do you stop living like it's a hundred and twenty-two years ago and live like it's now?"

Phoenix sank to the desk chair and stared at her computer screen. "I don't know. I've lived like this for so long, it's who I am. Everything seems so stupid. Like, look at this girl, writing to Sasha. She's all"—he spoke in a falsetto voice—"'OMG!' and 'LOL!' and 'WTF?' and 'Girl, you should totes go out with Tyler in Telluride!'" He looked up at her. "You're seventeen years old, and this is how seventeen-year-olds talk to each other. I'm a thousand years old, and this stuff is like alien-speak to me. If I found another Anabo, she'd be writing OMG and I'd be thinking, You're f'ing kidding me."

Footsteps stopped at her door and they all froze, turning to stare at the knob as it turned. Phoenix hurriedly shut down her computer, then went to stand next to the window. Sasha went to stand beside Jax.

The door opened slowly, and someone whispered, "Sasha?"

When she didn't answer, Brett came in and closed it behind him, very quietly, then went to her computer and booted up, evidently not noticing it was still warm. He wasn't the sharpest crayon in the box. She watched her Facebook page load, mad at herself for setting it as her homepage, the password memorized. After he read the latest posts on her wall, he went to her e-mail and read one from her mother. Jax grabbed her hand and held tight, knowing how much that ate at her. Brett the Asshat was reading it before she did.

Then he deleted it! "I hate him so much, it hurts." There was one from NYU, probably answering her question about the application she intended to send next Monday. He deleted that one, too. There were a couple from friends back in San Francisco, and one from the headmistress at St. Michael's. He deleted all of them, then went to her trash folder and deleted them from there, so she'd have no way of reading them, ever. "Why is he doing this?"

"Because he's evil. Because he can. And probably because Mr. Bruno told him to do anything he could think of to intimidate you. What happened at school today made Brett look like a loser, and Mr. Bruno can't have that. He's his prime lost soul, the one who's supposed to suck in all the others, but you put a major wrench in the works."

Next, Brett went to her document files and deleted all of them, including the new essay she'd started after Melanie trashed her computer.

Jax squeezed her hand. "I'm sorry, Sasha. But I have the backup of the old one in my pocket."

After Brett shut down the computer, he went to the dresser and pawed through her things. He took the amethyst drop her dad had brought back from Russia, the pearls her mom had given her for her sixteenth birthday, and her money.

She was verging on hysteria. "Jax, what am I going to do? I need money to apply to college."

"I'll give you money, and after he's gone, we'll get your things back. Whatever he dreams up to do to you, I can fix."

"What if he turns me in for being an illegal alien?"

"They'll laugh at him. Right this minute, the records Luminas are working on your papers. By midnight, your birth certificate will be on file, and there'll be a record of your U.S. citizenship with the government. Trust me, Sasha, there's nothing he can do to you that we can't undo. Just be patient, and soon he'll be gone." He looked down at her and squeezed her hand again. "Don't let him get to you."

He was the unlikeliest hero, but ever since last Thursday night, he'd been there to save her from one catastrophe after another. Meeting his dark gaze, she whispered, "I'm sorry, Jax."

"Don't be sorry. All you did was tell the truth."

"So what happens now?"

"You're in the line of fire, and I'm not going to let anything happen to you, so you'll just have to put up with me until Bruno and the others are gone."

His hand around hers was strong and warm, and in spite of her confusion and hesitation, she never wanted to let go.

ELEVEN

JAX TOOK HER TO THE SCHOOL AND WENT WITH HER TO GET Chris's book, then left her at the entrance to the gym before he headed off to the locker room to suit up for the game. She was surprised by the number of people already there. Teachers, parents, and lots of kids, even small ones. Younger siblings, she guessed.

She hadn't eaten dinner and her stomach hurt, she was so hungry. There were no concessions, but it wouldn't have made any difference if there were. She had no money.

The team was warming up, basketballs flying, and she had to duck a few as she walked across the gym floor. She searched for Amanda in the crowd but didn't see her. Erin and Rachel were waving at her to come sit with them.

As soon as she sat down, Erin said, "We were just talking about why Brett's turned into such a douche."

Rachel nodded. "He's turned into a creeper, and I don't get why."

Sasha could tell her why, but Rachel wouldn't believe her.

"It's that stupid Ravens thing," Mason said from above them in the stands. He went to sit behind Rachel, who sent an Oh-my-God look to Erin. "Ever since he joined, he's like a different person. East, too. And Julianne."

Erin whispered to Sasha, "Wrong. Julianne's always been a bitch."

"If being a Raven means you turn into a douche bag, why does anyone want to join?" Rachel asked.

"They tell you they'll get you whatever you want," Mason said.

"I don't want anything that much," Erin said, watching the players on the court, specifically Thomas. "I heard you have to give up God and promise to follow some guy named Eryx. Reminds me of a cult."

Rachel said, "I had a cousin who joined a cult, and my aunt and uncle had to spend a boatload of money to get her out of there."

"Blows my mind what people will believe," Mason said, glancing at Sasha. "Sorry about what happened. What's up with that? I mean, he's your cousin."

Sasha shrugged. "He wanted me to join the Ravens, because

he gets bonus points for everyone he brings in, so he made up that story and said if I'd join, he'd admit it was a lie and make like it was a big joke."

"Some joke," Erin said. "Now the joke's on him because everyone thinks he's a loser."

Amanda came through the door with her dad, and Rachel said, "Wow, check out Amanda. She looks . . . different."

"She looks great," Erin said. "I can't believe she came to the game. She never goes anywhere."

"I asked her to meet me," Sasha explained, waving at her. She watched them cross the gym floor, her dad stopping to sit with some teachers, while Amanda continued on to climb up to where they sat. She noticed Brett was staring at Amanda, and she wanted to stand up and yell at him to leave her alone.

Amanda was unaware of his attention, thank God, and she smiled at Erin and Rachel before she took a seat next to Sasha. "I was almost late because Dad took forever to get ready. He's all excited, probably because he gets to talk to Rose."

"Does he have a crush on her or something?"

"He says no, but I think he does. She's always going to the market and buying lamb chops from him, and he gives her extra."

"Aw, that's sweet," Rachel said, her eyes bright. "Your dad's awesome, Amanda."

She leaned toward Sasha and whispered, "After Dad and I got home, I had a strange phone call." She met Sasha's eyes, looking really uncomfortable. "It was Brett. He said he felt like an idiot for what he did, and was really sorry."

Alarm bells went off in her head. Why would Brett call Amanda, out of the blue? Did he realize she was maybe the only kid at school who might still be interested in him—in the Ravens? "So he called you to apologize, but never said a word to me? Why?"

Amanda looked down at her hands and twisted a silver ring round and round her finger. "He said he tried, but you won't talk to him, you're so mad."

"He's lying. The only thing he's said to me since school let out was something rude, and I did ignore him, because what do you say to someone who's mean and hateful?"

"Maybe he didn't mean to sound rude?"

"Oh, he meant it. Trust me."

"He, uhm, asked if I want to join the Ravens."

Damn. "Please tell me you said no."

"I said I'd think about it."

"Amanda, why?"

Amanda looked up, her eyes filled with pain. "You wouldn't understand, Sasha. You're pretty and smart, you were probably überpopular at your old school, and in another week you'll be all that at Telluride."

"Maybe I will, maybe I won't, but whatever I am, I want you to be my friend. We can hang out, and you could come to the house and see Chris. Don't do it, Amanda. At least think about it."

"I will, but I sort of already said I'd go out with him after the game."

Double damn. "Tell him you changed your mind. I'm going to get something to eat, and I bet everyone else will go, too. Go with us. Not Brett."

"No, I'm going to go and see what he has to say. He made a big deal about wanting to explain things, and he sounded really upset. Maybe there's something we don't know about him, a reason why he's been acting so weird lately."

Yeah, there was a reason, but she couldn't say what it was. Frustrated and not sure what she could do to change Amanda's mind, Sasha turned her attention to the game.

It was about to start, and she searched the players for Jax, which didn't take long. He was bigger than any of the other guys. Wearing a basketball uniform, his arms and legs were exposed and she couldn't help staring—he was put together like nobody's business. She noticed he had a bandage on his right bicep and wondered if he was hurt, but he didn't appear to favor that arm while they warmed up. The coach called the team to the sideline and as he went, he looked up, searching the crowd until he saw her. Then he smiled, and her heart skipped a beat.

"I think the new guy likes you," Erin said. "I heard he threatened to beat up Brett if he didn't lay off, and I'm thinking he could do it, easy."

"Wonder where his brother is . . . ?" Rachel asked.

As if on cue, Brody walked into the gym, followed by Melanie and Mr. Bruno.

Brody saw her and made a beeline, while Melanie and Mr. Bruno went to sit with Mr. Hoolihan and his wife.

After Brody said hello, smiling with his calm, sweet eyes, he went to sit next to Mason, which put him behind Erin. One minute later, the brown-haired girl Jenny came to sit next to him, all shy and awkward. Then Bree came in, dressed in black, and climbed up to sit by Amanda. Sasha had to force herself not to gape when a couple of Julianne's bees made their way over to the other side of Rachel. By the time the buzzer sounded, they had a nice little group. Sasha noticed Julianne was sitting alone. She also noticed Mr. Bruno was looking up, his face creased in a frown. He looked directly at her, and she knew, just *knew*, he hated her for screwing up his Raven plans. She looked away from him to watch the game.

Telluride got the ball first, dribbled to one end, and Jax nailed a three-pointer. Then Ridgway missed, and it was Telluride's ball again.

The rhythm of it, the sound of the players' shoes squeaking on the wooden floor, the cheers and applause from the stands—it was mesmerizing. Jax handled the ball as if he'd been born with it.

After the clock wound down the half and buzzed at 0:00, the team walked to the sideline and the coach hunkered down to talk to them. Jax looked up at her, then jerked his head around at something the coach said. He nodded, then looked toward Brett, who was scowling. He gave Jax a look—a glare—and Jax said something that appeared to make Brett even angrier. Sasha was dying of curiosity. What was going on?

The second half began, and the game took on a different vibe. Ridgway was losing, and picked up their effort to close the gap. With the shot clock almost to zero, Brett passed to East, and he missed. Thomas frowned at Brett, and Jax lifted his hands in a WTF? gesture. Sasha didn't exactly understand why Brett's pass to East was a big deal, but Coach Hightower was clearly pissed. He called a time-out, pulled Brett off the floor, and yelled at him, arms waving. Looking mad enough to eat glass, Brett shoved the coach, and an audible gasp went up in the stands. Then Melanie stood and shouted something obscene, which caused another gasp in the crowd.

"What is up with your family, Sasha?" one of the bees asked.

It hit her, all of a sudden, that they weren't her family. She wasn't related to them at all. It made her sad to know she wasn't blood kin to Mom and Dad, but knowing she wasn't related to Brett and Melanie was a silver lining. She answered the bee, "I never actually met them until last Friday. My dad and Brett's mom didn't get along."

"No wonder," she replied. "Mrs. Shriver . . . wow, I can't believe she just said that."

The coach pointed toward the row of chairs, but Brett didn't go sit down. He stalked away, through the door to the locker room, and the game resumed.

"Man, he's history," Mason said to no one in particular. "Nobody shoves a coach. He'll get kicked off the team for that."

Melanie also walked out, but not before she flipped off Coach Hightower.

"Classy lady," the other bee said. "Maybe that's why Brett's turned into an a-hole. My brother says she's doing Mr. Bruno. How gross is that?"

Amanda leaned close and whispered, "See? There's at least one reason why he's acting so weird. My mom was crazy like that, always embarrassing my dad and me."

"Did it upset you so much that you made up horrible lies about your family and spread it all over?"

"Well . . . no, but I was mad all the time. I'm just saying, Sasha, maybe he's not as awful as you think."

She looked at her new friend, wishing so much she could explain why Brett was ten billion times worse than Amanda could imagine. But she couldn't. All she could say was, "Something's wrong with him. His head isn't right. Please don't go with him, don't try to understand him, and please, *please* don't join the Ravens."

Turning away to face the court, Amanda didn't reply.

Sighing, frustrated all over again, Sasha did the same.

As the game progressed, Jax and Thomas built a rhythm, and the rest of the team took their lead, putting a lot of points on the board. But Ridgway managed to keep up, and the score was tied with five seconds left on the clock. Thomas raced the ball downcourt and dished to Jax, who launched a three-pointer. The buzzer sounded just as the ball whooshed through the net, and the crowd went wild, yelling, clapping, high-fiving one another.

"Man, he's good." Mason was clearly impressed. "First game we've won this year."

Jax was elated, beaming up at her as he walked toward the door where Brett had disappeared.

It was all so male ego and normal, she grinned back.

"He *does* like you," Erin said.

Amanda stood and said, "I've gotta catch up to my dad. I'll see you guys tomorrow."

Sasha tried to grab her arm, but Amanda was already walking away, then down the bleachers to where her dad was waiting, talking to Rose. She said something to him, he looked toward the locker room door and frowned, then she said something else and left the gym. Mr. Rhodes continued visiting with Rose, then they walked out together. Amanda must have gone to meet Brett, and Mr. Rhodes was leaving.

Feeling out of breath and a little panicky, she startled when Erin tapped her shoulder.

"Hey, Sasha, are you up for the coffeehouse?"

"Do they serve food? I missed dinner, and I'm starving."

"They have sandwiches. We're waiting for Thomas, because Mason told him we would. Maybe Jack would like to go, too?"

"I think so." She glanced at Brody, who nodded. "Yeah, he'll go."

❦

This was more like it. Jax sat next to Sasha at a long table, formed by shoving several smaller ones together, and watched her shine.

With the lie about her put to bed, the other kids warmed up to her, just like he knew they would. He was even having a good time, maybe because for the first time in his life, people weren't afraid of him. With Sasha on one side and Brody on the other, his bad vibe was counterbalanced.

He bought himself and Sasha a couple of sandwiches, some soup, and several cookies.

Mason said from his end of the table, "Awesome game, Jack. Where'd you learn to play ball like that?"

"Mostly from my brothers."

"Brody, you play basketball?" Mason was clearly doubtful.

"I'm not much of an athlete," Brody said. "Our older brothers are."

Thomas finished his sandwich and wiped his hands, looking across the table at Jax. "Sorry about what happened with Brett, but it sure was a lot more fun after he hit the road."

"I don't get that guy. Either you want to play ball, or you don't."

"He's not about the team, that's for sure. I think he thought it would impress Reilly."

The whole table nodded agreement, and Bree, the black-haired girl who looked like a vampire, said, "He must have asked her to go out like fifty times, and she was always so sweet about it, because that's who she was, but the answer was always no. Drove Brett crazy, and after a while, it made him mad. You'd think if he liked her so much, he'd be at least a little bit sad that she died."

The girl with brown hair who was kind of a plain Jane said, "I don't think he really liked her. She was just the prettiest, most untouchable girl at school, so he wanted her like he'd want a great car, or the coolest snowboard. It was never about Reilly."

Plain Jane was sharp. Jax watched her while he ate, noticed the way she looked at Thomas when she thought he wasn't looking, and in turn, the way Thomas looked at her. He gained interest as the conversation progressed. And something was going on between Mason and the girl with skinny glasses—that ironically matched her skinny body. Mason kept handing her food, and she ate it, obviously hungry. But she had no food of her own. He asked Sasha if maybe she had no money, if he should offer to buy her something to eat, and she whispered, "Rachel has an eating disorder."

"Aw, man. Bummer."

He looked around the table while he ate the cookies and watched the others, wondering what was up with Julianne's ex handmaidens. They were trying to flirt with Brody, who seemed oblivious, most of his attention on Jenny, the quiet little brown-haired girl who had the whole first season of *Star Trek*, with outtakes. Jax smiled, thinking all over again that Brody was the coolest nerd on Earth.

While he was wondering why Rachel had an eating disorder, and why Thomas didn't go ahead and talk to plain Jane—when she obviously had it bad for him and he wasn't uninterested in her—it struck him that this was a new thing for him. Other than from a purely observational standpoint, he'd never taken any personal interest in humans. He found those who'd traded their soul to Eryx and took them to Hell on Earth, then went home and hung out with his brothers. People were a job to him, another face, another lost soul.

Until today, he'd never spent much time among humans. He didn't count what he and his brothers did some nights, trolling clubs for easy sex. People were afraid of them, and only in the night, with loud music and little conversation, could they get close enough to get what they wanted. He never wondered about the girl, why she was there, what she wanted, or why she'd agree to have sex with a stranger. He asked, she said yes, then he was gone, never to think about her again.

Now he wondered who they were, all those girls, and why they allowed a stranger to take them in the most intimate way. He brushed a crumb from Sasha's lip while he whispered, "Why do some girls have sex with guys they don't know?"

"Probably because they hope it'll lead to something else."

"So it's not because they want sex?"

Her eyes met his, and she shook her head slowly. "I'm no expert, obviously, but I'm a girl, and I know a lot of girls, and I read a lot. I think for us it's more about being romantic than something physical. And I don't think they really like it unless it feels safe, and they really trust who they're with." She studied his face. "Why did you ask me that?"

"I feel different. Can't explain it, but it's like I'm noticing things I never did before, thinking about things that never occurred to me, until right now."

"And you're wondering why all those strangers let you . . . ?"

"Right. For me, it wasn't a big deal. I wanted it, so I went to get it, and I always thought they felt the same way. Now, I'm not so sure, so I wondered."

"Why is it different now?"

He stared at her, trying to figure it out. "I don't know."

"What's all the whispering over there?" Bree asked, laughing. "Would you guys like us to leave so you can be alone?"

The whole table laughed, and the conversation drifted from one subject to the next. He hoped someone would say something about Bruno, but no one talked about high school. It was all about college applications, then some more about Reilly, which led to an interesting discussion about what happens to people after they die. He listened closely, amazed and relieved at the same time. None of these kids were in any danger of pledging soon, not even Julianne's former friends.

Those girls were the first to leave, then Bree left with some guy who worked at the coffeehouse, and Brody said he was going across the street to the bookstore with Jenny. Jax gave him a look, and he nodded, silently agreeing he wouldn't do anything stupid. Like kiss her. Or go to her house to watch *Star Trek* outtakes.

That left six of them, until Thomas said, "I gotta get home and finish my history homework."

Plain Jane said, "My mom's probably mad because they're waiting on me to light tonight's Hanukkah candle, so I need to go, too."

Rachel looked disappointed. "I'm not ready to go, but I will, so I can take you home."

"If you need a ride, Erin," Thomas said, "I can take you."

Erin. Her name was Erin. She smiled and said, "Thanks," then got up to leave with Thomas. As they walked away, she turned and grinned at Rachel.

"What was that about?" he asked Sasha while Rachel and Mason went back to the counter for another round of coffee and pastries.

"It was all a ploy, so he'd take her home."

"Seriously?"

"Sure. Guys can be severely clueless, so sometimes girls have to give them a nudge. Thomas would like Erin, if he got to know her, and she already likes him, so she came up with a way to make it happen. If he really had no interest at all, he wouldn't have offered her a ride."

And Jax thought *he* was a master strategist. "Would you do something like that to a guy?"

"If I liked him and he wasn't playing along, yeah."

"Did you try it with Tyler Hudson?"

"I tried all kinds of stuff, but he never got the hint, which is how I know he really wasn't interested."

"Now he's asking you out. What changed?"

She shrugged. "Beats me, but it doesn't matter because I'm not interested. At all."

"Because of me?"

"Of course because of you."

He finished his mocha and set the cup down carefully, tracing the coffeehouse logo with his finger. "But you said—"

"It doesn't matter how this is all going to end up. Right now, right this minute, there's nobody but you."

Something bloomed in his chest, and he thought maybe it was hope. "Since we have until next week, and we're going to be together a lot anyway, maybe we could just sort of pretend everything's normal, and be together like . . . you know, like . . ."

"Like we're going out?"

That awful awkward feeling came over him, and he couldn't look up from the cup. "Yeah. Like that." If she said no, if she told him she'd rather just be friends until he was gone, he'd be sick.

"Okay, Jax."

Jerking his gaze to hers, he asked, "Really?"

"Yes, really. You're my first boyfriend, and maybe it's not what I imagined, but I'm crazy mad about you, so yeah, let's do it."

Without thinking, he leaned over and kissed her.

Maybe she wasn't thinking, either, because she kissed him back.

It wasn't until Rachel whispered behind them, "Get a room," that they broke apart.

They left right after that, and he noticed as they walked out that Mason and Rachel moved to the back of the coffeehouse, to a small sofa close to the fireplace.

He held her hand and walked her to the car Brody had driven to town from the mountain. "Let's go for a drive, then I'll take you home before I come back for Brody."

She got in when he opened the passenger door, then smiled at him when he got behind the wheel and started the engine. An old Beatles tune was on the radio.

He drove her up into the mountains and turned off on the road to the Mephisto house, parking at the turnout where they could see the whole valley below. He switched off the headlights but left the motor running for the heater. "Nice, yeah?"

"It's so weird how I can see everything, like there were three full moons, but there's no moon tonight at all."

"Does it bug you, being able to do things regular people can't?"

"It should, but no."

"So you're not mad at me for kissing you and making you different?"

"No, not mad. And since every time you kiss me it makes it happen more, I shouldn't want you to, but honestly? Right now I want you to kiss me more than I want to breathe."

He silently thanked Brody for taking Key's vintage Mercedes to the game tonight. The front seat was huge, with no console, nothing to keep him from moving away from the steering wheel

319

and pulling her away from her door to meet him in the middle. "You're sure?" he managed to ask, even though they were already wrapped together like ivy on a pole.

"Real sure." She kissed him first, and after that, the world faded away.

Coats came off, then his shirt and her sweater. He held her away from him and stared. She was wearing the black lace bra they'd bought last weekend, with little pearls where her cleavage began. "I never thought I'd get to see you in it."

"Jax, you're embarrassing me."

"What? Why? You're beautiful, Sasha." He dropped one hand from her shoulder and traced her pale skin at the edge of the lace. "I thought there was nothing softer on Earth than your lips."

He was so focused on the swell of her breasts, he almost jumped when her palm touched his chest. "What are you doing?"

"If you get to touch, so do I."

That she wanted to made him glad.

"Jax, what's this?" Her fingers brushed his bicep. "I wondered why you had a bandage, but it was to cover this tattoo, wasn't it?"

"It's a birthmark. Like your *A*, except a lot bigger."

She circled it, tickling him. "It *is* like mine, only an *M*, and without the sunburst. It's really beautiful." Her fingers moved away from his arm and back to his chest while she kissed him again.

The bra came off and he had no clue who had unhooked it.

He was lost in her, in the feel of her soft breasts beneath his palms and her cool, curious hands against his hot skin, when she shifted so that she was straddling him, one knee on either side of his hips.

This was so not a good idea.

But her taste, her scent, and her beautiful breasts against his bare chest were almost enough to make him lose all reason. He'd never felt the pull of his dark side as strongly as right now, demanding he go ahead, take her, mark her, make sure she could never leave him. It would be so easy. She was as into this as he was, would go along, caught up in the moment.

"Oh, hell!" Grabbing her arms, he lifted her off of his lap and set her on the seat away from him, then clenched his hands into fists and stared ahead, breathing hard, fighting to get himself under control. Nothing had ever been so difficult.

"Jax? What's wrong? Are you mad?"

He shook his head. "We should go now."

"I don't know why you're so upset. Did I do something wrong?"

He turned to look at her. "No, it's me. I can't . . . it's not easy to—"

She smiled at him. "It's okay, Jax."

That she wasn't upset, at all, that she understood, or at least tried to, that she was so trusting . . . he turned and drew her as close as possible, breathing in her scent, burying his face in her silky hair. "Sasha, I . . ." He didn't know how to say what he felt, couldn't put words to it, so he stopped and just held her, wishing with all his heart she wouldn't leave him.

"I know, Jax," she whispered. "Me, too."

Maybe he wasn't ecstatically happy, because knowing she would leave kept it from him, but for now, he was content. And for him, that was nirvana.

TWELVE

BEFORE JAX WENT TO GET BRODY AT THE BOOKSTORE, HE dropped Sasha at the Shrivers'. She went inside and was so glad no one was around. Brett was still gone, she supposed, because his Hummer wasn't in the drive. Melanie's car was also gone. Tim wasn't in his recliner, and the house was dark. Upstairs, she knocked on Chris's door, but he didn't answer. She opened it a crack and saw he wasn't there, so she slipped in and laid his chemistry book on his desk.

Then she went into her room and locked the door, calling Boo at the same time. He appeared and leaped into her arms, licking her face with unequaled doggie enthusiasm. She squeezed him tight and buried her nose in his soft fur. "Poor, ugly baby. You are a sweetheart, you know that?" Sitting at the end of her bed, she set him down next to her and pulled her cell from her pocket to dial Amanda's number.

Her voice mail picked up, and Sasha said, "Call me when you can." She stared at the phone for a while, wondering and worrying. If Amanda didn't call back, that wasn't a good sign.

Taking a seat at her desk, she powered up the laptop and read her wall on Facebook. She'd been friended by fifteen kids from Telluride High, including three of Julianne's bees, which made her smile. *Take that, Brett.*

Tyler had written another message. She replied and told him she hoped he had a great vacay, but she was going out with a guy she'd met at school. She didn't mention that the guy had almost no control over his insane jealousy because he was a son of Hell, but she was thinking it.

Remembering the question Jax asked her at the coffeehouse, the way he looked, the interest he had in the others, she wondered if maybe she wasn't the only one changing. If she became more like him, didn't it make sense that he'd become more like her? Later, in the car, at the end when he hugged her, she couldn't explain why it was different, but it was. She felt something from him that wasn't there before.

Her e-mail program dinged, and she opened the window, elated to see her mom had sent another message.

Dear Sasha—

Tim e-mailed to let me know about Melanie telling you what

I had wanted to share when the time was right. I'm so sorry you found out this way, and from someone who hates me and despised your father. It must have been hard for you, and I want to talk to you about it soon, but right now I have no cell phone, and very little money, so it will be a while before I can call you. Until then, always know how very much I love you, and how very much Mikhael loved you. You aren't our natural-born daughter, but no one ever loved a child so much. I miss you terribly, and worry constantly, but I know you are safe there, as you wouldn't be here.

I think I have found a way to bring you to Russia, to be with me until you go to university, but it will take some time. Be patient and do your best in school.

I love you, very much.

Mom

Did she really have a way to bring her to Russia, or was she just saying that because she felt bad for leaving her behind? She guessed it didn't matter. If Mom figured out a way, then she'd go to Russia. If not, she'd stay here with Tim and Chris, and it wouldn't be so bad. After next week, Melanie and Brett wouldn't be a problem.

She thought about Jax, not seeing him anymore, actually forgetting about him, and tears popped into her eyes. She couldn't help it. Every time she thought about it, she cried, as if someone was going to die. Knowing that she'd forget him made it only worse.

Swiping at the tears, she wondered if her mom would be able to find a job, where she was living, if the Russian government was making her life difficult because she had defected. She wanted to ask, but she knew her mother wouldn't give her real answers.

She stared at the e-mail for a while, debating how to reply. Finally, she wrote,

> *I wish you had told me a long time ago, but I guess I understand why you didn't. Knowing I'm not your biological child is hard, but it's so much weirder to know I'm not even legally yours. It'll take me a while to get used to it, but I will.*
>
> *I love you,*
>
> *Sasha*

She wanted to work on her college essay, but Jax had forgotten to give her the backup, so instead, she did the rest of her homework, then took a shower and got in bed. Tired and drowsy, she snuggled into the covers, with Boo curled up on her feet, and was almost asleep when she realized Amanda hadn't called her back.

Sitting up, she reached for her phone and called again. No answer. She told herself it could be all kinds of reasons, like her cell died, or she left it somewhere, or she had it on silent, but she knew in her heart it wasn't any of those things. Amanda didn't want to talk to her.

Lying down again, she prayed hard that Amanda wouldn't

join the Ravens, even while she remembered what Jax and Brody told her, that everyone has free will, the ability to make their own choices, even if they're really, really bad ones.

～≫

She woke with a start when Boo growled, from beneath the bed, and she turned over just as her door opened and the overhead light came on. Brett stood there in a pair of navy boxers, with a smug look, his eyes slightly shaded. "You thought you talked her out of joining, didn't you?"

Oh, no. "Amanda didn't join. You're lying."

He stepped inside the room and closed the door before he headed toward the bed. "Not yet, but she will, and so will others, but only if you back off. I think you need a little lesson so you understand who you're dealing with."

Sasha scrambled to get out of bed, standing on the opposite side. "I know exactly who I'm dealing with, but if you think you can threaten me, you're way wrong."

"Funny, you don't look stupid, but since you're not getting the idea, let me make it real clear how things are gonna be from now on. You're going to do whatever I tell you, or you'll be leaving the country within a week."

The way he was looking her over, she knew he wasn't just talking about staying out of his way so he could suck people into the Ravens.

If only she couldn't see him, those shaded eyes and the intent in his expression.

She concentrated until the light went out, but she could still see him.

She almost couldn't breathe, she was so scared. Instinct propelled her toward the door, and she let out a yelp when he grabbed her from behind. He was hauling her back to the bed, his arms hurting her, when fear overcame all else and she went wild, twisting and shoving until he fell back and stumbled. She made for the door again, but he was there first, breathing hard, glaring at her. He turned the light back on.

"You can't get away with this."

He advanced on her. "I can get anything I want, and right now, I want you." As he came at her and she backed away, he went through a list of all he intended to do—and what he expected of her.

She willed the light to turn off again, and the chair to move from the desk into his path. He fell over it and landed on the floor, cursing at her, furious as he got to his feet and kept coming.

When the back of her legs bumped the edge of the bed, he shoved her and she fell back, bouncing on the mattress. Rolling, she fought for a handhold, desperate to get away from him. He fell on her, his weight holding her down, his hands sliding beneath her, squeezing her breasts so hard, she cried out in pain. With the side of her face pressed against the sheets, she saw Boo scramble onto the bed, teeth bared, growling ferociously. He leaped across the space between them, and Brett got off of her, kicking and punching, trying to get Boo away from him. He was bleeding from scratches and bites, yelling at her to call off the dog.

Sasha hustled to get off the bed and was just about to run for the door when Boo went flying across the room and hit the wall next to the closet, whimpering as his body landed on the floor, then went still.

The door flew open, the light switched on, and there was Chris, also in boxers, his dark hair standing on end, his eyes swollen with sleep. "Jesus, Brett, what the hell are you doing?"

Brett was breathing hard, his leg bleeding all over the rug. "Get out, Chris. This is none of your business."

Chris looked at her. "Was he going to rape you?"

Silently, tears falling freely, Sasha nodded.

"Brett, you're a piece of shit. I didn't know I could hate your guts any more than I already did. Go find some of your Satan worshipper buddies, and leave Sasha alone."

"They're not Satan worshippers! It's not like that."

"It doesn't matter. You've sold your soul. You're evil."

"Come on, are you serious? You've been playing Demon Slayer too much."

"Yeah, and every day, I kill fake demons, wishing it was the real thing. Wishing it was you. Now get out, and if you lay a hand on Sasha, I'll have every cop within a hundred miles on your ass."

"She's not really our cousin. She's an illegal alien."

"I don't care if she's from Mars. You've got no right to hurt her." He advanced on Brett, raising his fists. "I'll break your face if you don't get out *right now.*"

Brett glared at him, then made a promise to Sasha with his eyes. He'd be waiting until Chris wasn't there, and he'd be back.

As soon as he was gone, Chris lowered his fists and said, without looking at her, "Lock your door, then shove that chair beneath the knob, because he can pick the lock with a paper clip. If he comes back, scream your head off."

"Thank you, Chris."

"Yeah, whatever. Don't ever be home alone, Sasha."

He was about to leave when she asked, "Why do you hate him? What did he do to you?"

Hesitating at the doorway, gazing out into the darkened hallway, he said, "He stole a story I wrote and gave it to East, who sent it in to a contest as his own and won a ten-thousand-dollar scholarship. It'll be published, with his name on it, in a science-fiction anthology. I worked on that story since I was thirteen. Three years, and I thought it would go a long way to getting me into college if I could get it published. Then East swiped it, and Mom wouldn't believe it was mine. Said I was just jealous of Brett and his friends."

"Did you tell Tim?"

He nodded. "But Dad doesn't always win their fights, and so I was screwed." He walked out and closed the door before she could say anything else.

Rushing to Boo, she lifted his limp body from the floor and

rocked him back and forth, crying. Poor, ugly, sweet dog. He died trying to protect her. She hated Brett so much, wished more than anything that she could take him away and send him to that deep, dark hole in the ground.

Someone knocked and she stiffened, worried it was Brett. "Who's there?"

Tim said through the door, "What's going on, Sasha? I heard a commotion."

How to answer? *Oh, hey, I was just fighting off your son who wanted to rape me.*

Before she could come up with a response, the door opened and he came into her room, his frown turning to a scowl when he saw Boo. "Who gave you permission to bring a dog into my house?"

Staring at his eyes in stunned disbelief and horror, Sasha backed away.

Tim had pledged his soul to Eryx.

❦

"Jax, wake up."

Instantly alert, he sat up quickly and saw Ty standing at the end of his bed. "What's wrong?"

"It's Boo. The alarm went off, and when I checked, it's because his collar went cold. It might mean Sasha took it off, but more likely, he's dead, and that can't mean anything good."

"Shit!" Jax jumped out of bed and ran to his closet, threw on a pair of jeans and a T-shirt, slid into his trench coat, then popped to her room, cloaked because he had no idea what, or who, he'd find. His relief was immediate when he saw Sasha was there, that she hadn't been taken, but it swiftly turned to pain when he took in the whole situation.

She stood in a corner, clutching Boo's lifeless body against her chest while her aunt and uncle shouted at her. Her eyes met his, but she didn't move toward him. She knew he was cloaked, that the others couldn't see him. But she also knew whatever was going down wasn't going to be as horrible as she thought, because he was there. The anxiety in her eyes eased.

He looked toward Tim and Melanie and felt the old familiar feeling of defeat when he saw Tim's eyes. He was surprised, because he hadn't thought Tim was at risk.

"You don't deserve this room," Melanie said. "I can't believe you brought that mangy thing into our house, and he attacked Brett! Look at the blood on the carpet. If he wasn't dead already, I'd take him out and shoot him. Maybe I'd miss and shoot you instead."

"You'll clean this up," Tim said, "and apologize to Brett. Then you can pack up your things and move down to the basement."

"I'll clean it up and I'll move, but it'll snow in Hell before I apologize to Brett. Did you hear what I said? He tried to *rape* me. If it wasn't for Boo and Chris, he would have."

Jax nearly passed out, the rush of blood to his head was so fast. Had he ever been this mad? Had he ever wanted to murder a human this much?

"He's an eighteen-year-old boy," Tim said, "and you're prancing around in front of him all the time. What did you expect?"

With hate in her eyes, she said in a dead voice, "I'll apologize."

They both looked like they were disappointed, like they wanted to keep berating her, but with her total capitulation, there wasn't much left to say. On their way out, Melanie said, "You could make all of this go away if you'd join the Ravens."

"No way. I'm not a sellout like Tim."

Tim, moving amazingly fast for a fat man, backhanded Sasha, knocking her to the floor. She tried to roll away, but the nanosecond between when she went down and when she realized Tim was coming at her again was enough time for him to slap her so hard, her lip busted, and blood dripped onto Boo's fur. Tim was drawing his leg back to kick her when Jax threw a freeze on everyone in the house, picking Sasha up off the floor almost at the same time. She clung to him, blinking and shaking her head as if to clear it.

"Jax, I remember something," she whispered. "You did this that night you found me in San Francisco, didn't you?"

He kissed her lip until it healed, and held her cradled in his arms against his chest for as long as it took to get a grip on his anger. Finally, when he could speak, he said, "Yes. And now we have a big problem."

"What to do with them when they unfreeze?"

"Right. Just stay with me and stay quiet, okay?"

She nodded and tightened her arms around his neck. He

popped them to the house, to the war room in the basement, and set her on her feet before he hit the intercom and called his brothers. In less than a minute, they were all there, wearing trench coats over boxers or pajama bottoms. Key gave Jax a hard look. "Talk now."

"Tim Shriver took the oath. He was assaulting her, and I froze the whole damn house. We've got maybe eight minutes before it fades."

Key looked at Sasha before he took off to pace around the long oval table in the middle of the room, pushing his long hair behind his ears. "We can't take them all, not yet. It'll alert Bruno, and the whole plan will be screwed."

Denys said from the opposite side of the room, "Let's take Tim and leave the others. He's huge, so Bruno wouldn't question if he had a heart attack."

Ty shook his head. "We don't have a doppelgänger."

"We can have one by this afternoon," Zee pointed out. "In the meantime, we could put him in a coma and get M to work on his heart, so the hospital won't question what happened to him."

"It's risky," Phoenix said. "He could actually go into cardiac arrest and die. That's a win for Eryx."

"Don't see we have a choice," Zee said, fiddling with his diamond stud. "Sasha can't stay in that house if he's going to beat up on her."

Key looked around at each of them. "Are we agreed?"

They all nodded.

He looked at Jax. "Will it work?"

"It'll work, but the son of a bitch tried to rape her."

"*Tim?*" three of them asked in unison.

"Brett."

They all looked at Sasha, who was standing there in nothing but a T-shirt and wide eyes.

Phoenix asked, "Did he see your birthmark?"

"No. Boo attacked him before . . . before anything happened. Then he killed Boo and Chris came in and threatened to pound him if he didn't leave. Then Tim came and I saw . . . his eyes, and he was mad about Boo, and about the blood on the carpet, and he shouted for Melanie. I told them why there was blood, why Boo bit Brett, and they called me a slut and said I'd have to live in the basement. Then Jax came and . . ."

She was babbling. Jax hauled her next to him and wrapped her inside his trench coat, looking over her head at his brothers. "I'm taking her to my room. If Chris wasn't already asleep when I threw the freeze, make sure he's asleep after the fade."

"I will," Ty said.

"When we're back," Key said, "we'll discuss Sasha. What happened tonight *cannot* happen again. We need something more effective than a dog guarding her."

As soon as his brothers disappeared, Jax popped her upstairs, picked her up, and laid her on his bed, drawing the covers to her chin. She blinked at him, resisting shock. Her teeth began to chatter. "I'm . . . so . . . cold."

Unbending, he went to the console against the north wall and opened the doors, retrieved a bottle of whiskey, and poured half an inch. He took it to the bed and slid an arm around her waist, pulling her to sit. "Drink this."

"It'll make me . . . sick."

"It won't, I swear." He watched her take the glass and said, "Small sips."

She drank a little and made a face. "It's like NyQuil."

He resisted smiling at the comparison of his two-hundred-dollar reserve scotch whiskey to a four-dollar bottle of cold medicine. "It gets better."

She kept sipping until it was gone and handed him the glass. "It did get better."

He set it on the bedside table, and after she was lying down again, he tucked her in. "Try to sleep. I'll stay right here until you wake up."

"Jax, I don't want to go back, but I . . . don't have anywhere else to go, and I can't leave Chris there all alone, especially now, when his dad is going to be gone."

"I know, Sasha. We'll talk about it when you wake up. Go to sleep now." He'd force her to sleep if he could, but she was way past his being able to manipulate her in any way.

"Why did he do it, Jax? He hated Melanie, never even looked at Brett, made fun of the Ravens."

"Everyone wants something, and if they want it bad enough, and if the Skia can figure out what it is, they'll cave. Tim wanted something—I don't know what—and he believed Bruno when he told him he could have it."

She was quiet before she asked, "Would you sit here with me for a while?"

He sat and stroked her hair, watching for her lids to get heavy.

They didn't. She was wide-eyed, staring up at his ceiling. She shivered.

"Are you still cold?"

She nodded. "Would you get in with me?"

Standing, he shrugged out of the trench coat and tossed it to a chair, then took off his boots and got into bed with her, still in jeans and a T-shirt. He pulled her next to him, and she laid her head against his shoulder, wrapped an arm around his middle, and was asleep in two seconds. He figured he'd stay awake until his brothers came home, then leave her there asleep while he went down to meet with them and figure out a new plan to keep her safe.

Instead, he drifted off, and when he woke up, he was on his side and she was curled into him like they were spoons in a drawer. He realized he'd woken up because Phoenix was standing next to the bed. "How did it go?" he whispered.

"We put Tim on the floor of his bedroom and set it up so he was comatose, and M worked on his heart. We put Melanie in the room so she'd see him right away. Chris wasn't asleep, but Ty fixed it so he was after the freeze faded. That's when shit got crazy."

"How?"

"Melanie saw Tim passed out on the floor, but she didn't call an ambulance. She got dressed, then went to see if he was dead yet. He wasn't, so she went downstairs and made coffee. She had a cup, went back upstairs and checked again. She was pissed off he still wasn't gone, and cussed him for living. This went on for over an hour, until Key said to hell with it and made Chris have a bad dream so he'd wake up and want to check on his dad. We were there almost two hours before an ambulance came to get Tim."

"If Eryx knew, he'd take her out."

Surprising him, because he thought she was still asleep, Sasha asked, "Why? I thought when they die, he takes their soul and it makes him more powerful."

Phoenix said, "All true, but he wants them to live as long as possible so they can recruit new followers. If a lost soul kills another, it's automatic death, and Melanie's not calling an ambulance for Tim is like trying to kill him."

Jax withdrew his arms from around Sasha, turned over, and sat up, blinking the last of sleep from his eyes. "What day is it?"

"Thursday," Phoenix said.

Glancing at the clock, Jax said, "School starts in two hours. I'll take Sasha home for some clothes and her books, then we'll come back here, get dressed, and meet over breakfast."

Phoenix said, "I'll tell Key," then disappeared.

Sasha rolled to her back and looked at him. "Jax, what am I

going to do? Maybe I'm stronger than before, but last night, he was . . . I couldn't get away from him."

The concept of being overpowered wasn't something he could comprehend, but looking into her eyes, he could see how frightened she was. "Did you eat dinner?"

"Just what we had at the coffeehouse."

He shook his head. "Not enough. You've got to eat protein. If you get in a bad situation again, if you've eaten what you need, you won't be as weak or helpless. As for Brett, we'll think of something, Sasha. He won't bother you again, I swear it."

She sat up and slipped her arms around his neck. "I wish I could stay here until they're all gone, but I can't leave Chris."

"I wish we could take them all out, immediately, so you wouldn't be in harm's way."

"I want Bruno gone so he can't take any more oaths, and I want the others gone so they can't talk people into pledging, but when I think about what happens after they're gone . . ."

He sighed. "Is there just no way you'll change your mind, Sasha?"

Pulling back, she looked into his eyes and didn't say yes, didn't say no. "We should get dressed."

❧

No one was at the house when Jax took her to get some clothes; they were probably at the hospital with Tim. She hurriedly stuffed some things in one of the Macy's bags from their shopping trip, grabbed her laptop and backpack, then he popped them back to his room.

"You can use my shower, and I'll go next door to use Phoenix's. If you need something, press the intercom button and ask for Mathilda. But fair warning, she'll pop in really quickly."

He left then, and she went to his bathroom, gawking at how huge it was. He had a ginormous bathtub, a separate shower, and a sauna. A sauna!

She walked farther and was in his closet, which was as big as the bathroom. He had a gazillion pairs of black leather boots and scads of shoes. He had at least twenty suits, all black, and dress shirts hanging in a perfect row, separated by color. He had tuxedos and flannel, sweaters and jeans, and a whole section was nothing but leathers. Standing there, looking around at his clothes, where he got dressed every day, she was overcome by his scent, that lovely fragrance of cider and spices, making her think of everything warm and wonderful.

In the middle of the back wall was a long, built-in dresser. She moved closer and noticed a small wooden box. It was rough hewn, almost primitive, but smooth and shiny from years of handling. Unable to quell her curiosity, she picked it up and lifted the lid. Inside was a small scrap of fabric, maybe linen, faded to beige, impossibly thin and worn in one place, as if he'd rubbed that spot over and over, wearing away the fibers. She lifted it out and saw a lock of dark hair beneath. It had to be his mother's. He'd had this little box for a thousand years, kept it where he'd see it, every day, took out that little bit of fabric and touched it so he wouldn't forget, so she'd never die in his heart.

Blinking, not wanting to cry again, she put the fabric back, replaced the lid, and carefully set the box back on the dresser.

She went to the shower and couldn't stop thinking about that little box. She was still thinking about it when she stood in front of the mirror in his bathrobe and blew her hair dry.

He knocked and came in with a towel around his waist. Oh, man, he was amazing to look at. "Sorry. I need to get in my closet." His gaze swept her from head to toe, not failing to notice the robe was dragging the ground, and he smiled.

"I hope you don't mind. I was wet, and cold."

He walked on toward his closet. "Of course I don't mind. What's mine is yours." He closed the door, and she went back to drying her hair, wondering if he was looking inside that little box. Did he do it every day, before he got dressed? Or at night, before he went to bed? Maybe by now he didn't take it out except every once in a while.

Why couldn't she stop thinking about it? What was it about that little box with his mother's mementos that fascinated her so much?

By the time he opened the door, dressed in jeans and another henley, this one red, she was curious enough to ask. "Don't hate me for being nosy, but I looked in your closet."

He shrugged while he took a seat on the bench close to the tub and pulled on his boots. "Not sure why you'd look. Just a bunch of clothes."

"It's a girl thing."

"Really? Girls like to look in guys' closets?"

"If it's a guy they like, they want to look at all his stuff." She fidgeted with the hairbrush. "I'm kinda curious about that little box on your dresser."

Done with his boots, he stood and disappeared into the closet, returning a few seconds later with the box. "This one, you mean?"

She nodded, not admitting she'd already looked inside. "It looks so old."

He came close, the box on his palm, and lifted the lid. "I made it when I was a kid, from an old dead hickory tree on Kyanos. Took me a couple of months of whittling." He moved still closer, to show her the contents. "When my mother died, we each took a piece of her robe and a lock of her hair before we buried her." His fingers lifted the fabric from the box, and as if by instinct, he rubbed it. "Someday it'll disintegrate, especially if I don't stop touching it, but it's funny, I can't help it." He looked up and met her gaze. "Kinda weird, huh?"

"No," she whispered around the lump in her throat, "not weird at all."

He put the lid back and returned to the closet, calling out as he went, "Are you about ready? I bet you're hungry, and Hans is making his famous pancakes, just because you're here."

"Hans?"

"He's the cook, a Purgatory that came to the mountain during World War One." He returned to the bathroom and watched

342

while she put on some makeup. "You don't need all that stuff, Sasha. You're unholy gorgeous without it."

"You're such a guy."

"I'm just pointing out the obvious."

"You're prejudiced because I'm Anabo. Also inclined to flattery." She leaned closer to the mirror to put on mascara, well aware he was watching her every move.

"That looks hard to do."

"You get used to it." She dropped the mascara into her cosmetics bag and dug around for lip gloss. When she was done, she pulled out her clothes. "I'll go in your closet to get dressed."

"Do you have to? Let me watch."

She walked away. "You're bluffing. If I said yes, you'd leave."

"You're right, but only because we need to get downstairs, and I'd be way too distracted."

"What is it with guys and naked girls?"

He was following her. "Not girls. Girl. Just you. I only want to see you naked."

She'd never understand why she did it, but she jerked the tie belt loose, flung off the robe, and turned to face him. "Okay, there. Now you've seen me naked. Is it really such a big deal?"

He wasn't looking at her body. Just her eyes. He looked a little hurt. "You don't have to make fun of me."

Everything went still. So still, she'd swear the rivers stopped running and the birds weren't singing. "I would never make fun of you, Jax."

Turning away, he walked out and closed the door behind him.

Not sure what just happened, but feeling like she'd kicked a puppy, she hurriedly got dressed, then went to find him. He was standing at the window in his room, looking out at the mountains. Moving to stand next to him, she reached for his hand. "Are you mad at me?"

"No. It's okay, Sasha. I don't know when to stop, and I forget sometimes that you're seventeen and still so innocent."

"I know what's up, Jax. It's not like I exist in a bubble."

"Sure, you know, but you haven't lived it." His hand tightened around hers. "And for all that I've been alive a thousand years, I'm about as clueless as you are when it comes to how this works." He sighed. "I want to be with you all the time. I want to know everything you do, and why. I wish I knew how to be romantic, and I think a lot about stuff they do in movies, but then it just seems so corny, and I know I'd start laughing and ruin everything."

The sun was sparkling on the snow, and the sky was so blue it almost hurt to look at it. "You do lots of romantic things, without even knowing it."

"Like what?" He obviously thought she was lying.

"Like scattering all over the school a million copies of a note that changed everything for me. Like saving me every time I turn around. Can't get much more romantic than that. And taking me shopping when you hate shopping, then buying me all those clothes, and the computer. You stood up to Brett for me at school, which made you stand out when you said you didn't want that. You're always making sure I eat, because you know I'm starving all the time." She turned her head to look up at his profile. "And you're not trying to coerce or cajole me into staying, even though it means so much to you if I do." She didn't mention the little box, or that she thought that was the sweetest, most amazing thing ever.

"So you're not thinking I'm lame because I don't bring you flowers, or write poems about you?"

"It's not romantic if it's not real, and the things you do for me are because that's who you are, so it's real." She smiled. "Like *really* real."

He squeezed her hand, then turned to walk her to the door. "Let's eat and figure out how we're going to keep you safe until next week."

The hallway was wide; the walls were painted dark red, dimly lit by candles in sconces; and every so often, they passed a door or a painting. After a while she realized the paintings weren't copies. "Jax?"

"They're all genuine, and unknown because we commissioned them when the artists were alive, and no one but us has ever seen them. There are hundreds, all over the house."

She heard a Green Day song that got louder as they approached another door.

"That's Zee's room. He's a music freak. You should see his music room. He has every instrument known to mankind and can play all of them. In his room, he has a stereo system that'd blow you away."

They turned a corner and were in another long hallway. "How big is this house?"

"It's three floors, five if you count the basement and the attic. There are six suites. You maybe didn't notice, but there's another door in my room and it leads to a little sitting room, then another, smaller bedroom that could be a study, or whatever. All the suites are like that. Then there are twenty regular bedrooms, I think, but I've forgotten."

"Why so many? Do the Purgatories have their own rooms?"

"No, they don't sleep, or shower, or do anything human."

"How old is this house?"

"Over a hundred years. After Phoenix lost Jane, we moved from Yorkshire, thinking a change would be good for him. It didn't make any difference, but here we are."

"Did you always live in Yorkshire until you came to Colorado?"

"No, we started in Greece, then Russia. We were there over four hundred years, until we moved to Jamaica, but it turns out we like snow more than sand. Then we moved to Yorkshire."

They came to a staircase, wide and sweeping down into a circular grand hall with a white marble floor, inlaid with a black M, just like Jax's birthmark. When they were standing on the M, she looked up. Far above the entry hall, the ceiling was domed, painted with sky, clouds, and angels; a round skylight was at the pinnacle. The walls were paneled in rosewood, edged in gilt, populated by portraits of men, women, and children in clothing from centuries past. There were three curved consoles spaced against the rounded walls, each one decorated with inlaid wood, topped with pink marble and a candelabra. To her right was a double doorway that led into what looked like a living room, equally as opulent and awesome as the front hall. To the left appeared to be a library. Jax steered her in that direction.

Bookshelves went from floor to ceiling all the way around the humongous room, and a narrow catwalk intersected them halfway up, accessed by a spiral staircase. An enormous fireplace graced the wall opposite the doorway, a portrait of a woman in a blue Regency-era dress hung above the mantel, and candle sconces provided soft, golden light to the dark corners where the sunlight from four large windows didn't reach. It was like stepping into the pages of a nineteenth-century novel.

"You're blown away, yeah?"

"Blown. Away."

"Thought you'd like it. When you come back, you can hang out in here and look over the books. We have lots of first editions, some of them autographed."

Still holding her hand, he walked her back through the front hall and around the stairs, toward an open doorway that led to the dining room. There was a table big enough to land a plane, gorgeous china, two humongous chandeliers, a sideboard with silver platters and chafing dishes, and five really big guys staring at them as they walked in. For some weird reason, seeing them like this, fully dressed, awake, and not in a panic, made her anxious. These were Jax's brothers, and she wondered if they would like her, if she'd like them. If she stayed, they'd be her constant companions for the next million years.

They each had the same black hair and were dressed almost identically, all in black, standing a few feet apart, obvious in an attempt to look casual, but none quite pulling it off. She felt like a specimen in a lab experiment, and these were scientists, studying her to see what she was made of.

Jax began introductions. They were the same in so many ways, yet entirely different in their facial features, in the way they wore their hair, in their personalities. Denys was the gregarious one, the life of the party, she thought, the guy who made it his mission to make people laugh. He spoke first, eyeing her red dress and Jax's red shirt. "Okay, fess up, you guys planned that whole dress-like-each-other thing, didn't you?"

Considering the five of them were all literally dressed alike, it was funny, and she laughed.

The tallest of all of them, Ty, said, "Do you ride horses?"

"No, I grew up in San Francisco."

"Then I'll get you a horse and teach you to ride." The brother next to him elbowed him, and he looked insulted. "What? I was just trying to be nice."

"Hello, Sasha," the elbowing brother who had a ponytail said with a smile. "I'm Kyros, but everyone calls me Key. We're glad you're here."

"We're glad you're alive," said another brother, Xenos, who

went by Zee and had severely short hair, a tattoo of a question mark on his neck, and a very large diamond stud winking in one ear. "And we'll be even more glad if you decide to stay. Do you like music?"

"Only a lot."

"Like who, for instance?"

She named a few of her favorites and he nodded, as if she passed inspection. "Have you ever heard of Arcadia?"

"Zee, back off," Jax said. "She's not going to like your grunge punk."

"Actually, I have. They're out of Britain, and played at the Fillmore in San Francisco. Some friends and I snuck in and saw them."

Jax looked at her as if seeing her for the first time. "You *snuck* into a concert?"

"We'd have bought tickets, but it was closed to anyone under twenty-one."

The last of the brothers was Phoenix. He didn't smile. "I have an idea about how to keep you from getting into any more trouble at the Shrivers'."

"What is it?"

"Don't go back."

Before she could respond, a deep voice said from behind her, "Breakfast is getting cold."

Turning, she had to stifle a gasp. A man with dark skin and dark eyes stood in the doorway, wearing an outfit that was straight out of the *Arabian Nights*. He looked ready to jump a horse, grab a broadsword, and raid a village in the name of Mohammed.

"Sasha," Jax said, "this is Deacon, our butler."

All righty, then. It was strange enough to have a butler, but to have one who looked like Deacon made it severely weird. "Hello, Deacon. It's a pleasure to meet you."

The man nodded slowly, just once, not making eye contact. Then he turned and left.

"Did I say something wrong?"

"No, he's old school and won't look directly at a woman who's not in his family. He's a Moor, our first Purgatory, who came to us during the Crusades. His wife and daughters were killed by crusaders, and he's nowhere close to forgiving God for letting that happen."

"Why would a Muslim man be named Deacon?"

"It's a nickname. He's been after us for centuries because we're filthy infidels who offend him, so he's forever lecturing us. One night, maybe three hundred years ago, Key called him Deacon, and it stuck."

Phoenix said, "Let's eat."

⁂

Ten minutes later, Jax wondered why he had thought it would be a good idea to introduce Sasha to his brothers. He should have listened to Phoenix, who told him to have breakfast served to her in his room, and to meet with the brothers alone. He'd warned him this could lead to disaster. At the far end of the table, Phoenix ate his breakfast without saying a word, but Jax knew what he was thinking, knew he would take the first opportunity to say, I told you so. Jax decided he'd pound him. Just as soon as he kicked the living daylights out of his other brothers.

Sasha was insanely beautiful today, her long, blond hair pulled back into some kind of apparatus so that it hung straight and silky to the middle of her back, and her slender body shown to perfection in a dress that wasn't cut too low, but just enough to show the soft swell of her breasts. She positively glowed, and like a cluster of insects stupidly beating themselves up to get close to the light, his brothers constantly tried to one-up each other in front of her.

Except Phoenix, Mr. I'm Above All of This.

Deacon was his usual stalwart, silent self, gliding around the table to serve coffee and juice, but once in a while he'd glance at Jax, silently communicating that yes, this was a debacle. Of course, he didn't help the situation. He worked for the Mephisto to learn humility, but after eight hundred years, Deacon wasn't humble. He was proud and considered himself above most everyone, especially the Mephisto. He never tired of lecturing, but today, he didn't say a word.

Although Jax admitted it wouldn't have done much good anyway. He and his brothers usually ignored Deacon's dire warnings of the consequences of bad behavior. If he called down his brothers for acting like stooges in front of Sasha, they wouldn't stop. As breakfast continued, they got louder and more obnoxious, and Sasha got quieter.

At one point, she turned to him and said, "Do you eat like this every day?"

"Not the huge selection, but Mathilda and Hans are good cooks. Do you like the squab?"

"It's a little like chicken, but different. Delicious." She ate another bite. "What is a squab, anyway?"

"Pigeon," Key said before Jax could even take in a breath to answer. Then he launched off into the culinary history of pigeons.

No sooner had he finished talking than Ty said, "I have a dovecote with homing pigeons. Did you know homing pigeons orient themselves to where they're hatched, and no matter where they are in the world, they'll try to fly back to their home, even if it's across the ocean? I bought some breeding pigeons from a guy in Brussels, but I have to keep them caged or they'd try to fly back to Belgium."

"You know," Denys said, "there's a bar in Brussels where the drinks are all free." He grinned. "But there's a five-hundred-dollar cover charge."

"The best bar in the world is the Black Orchid in London," Zee said. "Lots of bands got their start at the Orchid."

"Did you know we have a greenhouse?" Key asked. "I grow orchids." He went off about some of his experiments, how he'd developed several new varieties.

Sasha kept eating, listening as though everything they said was the most interesting bit of information she'd ever heard.

She was so not like him. She was patient and kind and considerate. He wanted to tell his brothers to shut the hell up and stop monopolizing her attention.

He became more depressed as breakfast wore on. Even if by some miracle she decided to stay, how could she survive here, with a bunch of clueless guys, angry ghosts, and a job that entailed confronting evil souls, day in and day out?

When everyone was almost done, Key said, "I've given this a lot of thought, and the best solution isn't to guard Sasha from Brett, but to keep him away from her in the first place. We need something to threaten him with."

"He killed Reilly," Sasha said. "He would probably rather not be arrested and tried for murder, so if you could make him think you have some kind of evidence, he might back off."

"I can get a picture," Jax said, thinking this just might work. "I could say I was taking pictures of Devil's Ridge with my phone, and happened to capture him shoving Reilly."

"He'd want to know why you didn't already take it to the police," Key pointed out.

"The school gossip says I got kicked out of boarding school for smoking weed. I'll say I don't want the cops looking at me, so I won't show them the picture if he'll leave Sasha alone."

"Wait," she said, "won't he want to see the picture?"

"I'm sure he will, but M can get us a picture of anything that actually happened."

Everyone agreed he should give it a try, and as he led Sasha out of the house and down the drive to the car Brody had pulled around, he hoped it would work.

He opened the door for her, and she turned to look back at the house. "It's so amazing, really like a castle: all the gray stone and the million chimneys, turrets, lead glass, and gargoyles."

On the winding drive to the highway, she looked from side to side, asking questions. He told her the small stone houses were the Lumina cottages, the big stone building was an old dairy they'd converted to a gym, and the long low building made of pink granite was where everyone on the mountain attended tutoring sessions.

Farther down the mountain, they passed through the Kyanos mists, and her eyes were wide. "It's like the fog in San Francisco, except blue."

"If people who aren't Mephisto or Luminas come up this road, it dead ends and all they see is more forest and mountains."

"What if they hiked farther up? Would they run into an invisible building?"

"No. It's hard to explain, but it's as if it's not there to anyone but us."

"Is that what Hell on Earth is like? Is that why no one knows it's there, like scientists or people who drill oil wells?"

"Yes. Our home and Hell on Earth exist on another plane of reality that only a few can see. Heaven and Hell are in another dimension, one none of us sees until it's time. I've never been to Hell, and I've never met Lucifer. M is our go-between."

He parked the car in the school parking lot, killed the engine, and handed her an envelope. "This is your birth certificate. It shows that your mom is your natural parent, and that you were born in Moscow. There are also U.S. citizenship papers and a Social Security card. It's all real, and recorded in the right files with the government."

Feeling a huge weight lifted, she wanted to tell him this was awesomely romantic, but Brody was there, so she just smiled and said, "Thank you, Jax."

THIRTEEN

SHE WAS SURPRISED TO SEE BRETT IN ENGLISH. SHE ASSUMED he'd stay at the hospital by Tim's deathbed all day, not because he was sad, but because it was a good excuse to skip school. It wasn't like Brett had any feelings for Tim. He was a lost soul, so grief was no longer part of his makeup.

He glared at her when she came into the room, and shot such a look of hatred at Jax that Sasha felt sick to her stomach. Amanda, she saw with a sinking feeling, was sitting next to Brett. She avoided looking at Sasha, staring down at her book instead, toying with her necklace, which Sasha could see was the amethyst drop Brett had stolen from her drawer.

She remembered when her dad had brought it home to her; he'd said he bought it from a yak herder in Siberia, which she knew was a made-up story, but she went along and wore it every day for a whole year.

Seeing it now, hanging around Amanda's neck, and knowing how she had gotten it, Sasha was mad and sad, all at once. Amanda didn't know. She thought it was a gift from a boy she liked, a boy she now viewed as some sort of underdog.

After they sat down, she heard Brett telling East and Julianne about Tim, laying on worry and fear with a heavy hand. Sasha knew just how that must sound to Amanda. Glancing back at her, she saw that she had sympathy written all over her face.

All through class, while different people read from *The Metamorphosis*, Sasha tried to think of a new plan, a new way to keep Amanda from joining the Ravens.

But when the bell rang, she had nothing.

The day marched on, until it was lunch, and the same group who'd been at the coffeehouse sat together, with a few additions, including a guy on the ski team who used to be best buds with Scott the Molester.

Mason and Rachel were funny together—he was so big and she was so tiny. Sasha could only guess what had happened between Thomas and Erin last night, but something, for sure. They were so into each other, they didn't talk much to anyone else.

After lunch, before fourth period began, while Jax went to find Brett, to show him the picture M had sent to his phone, and to tell him his options, Sasha hung around his locker and nervously waited for him to come back.

While she stood there biting her lip, Amanda walked up. Trying to play it low key, trying extra hard not to stare at her necklace, Sasha smiled and said, "Hey, Amanda. How's it going?"

"I wanted you to know that Brett's being supernice to me. I think he's just really mixed up. Now, with his dad so sick, like he might even . . . die, I feel like I need to give him a chance."

"I understand."

"You do?" She looked genuinely surprised.

"I get why it's cool to like a guy when he likes you back."

Amanda looked so relieved, it would be comical if it wasn't so tragic.

"But seriously, Amanda, be careful. You know I don't like him, and there's a real good reason for it. Just don't join the Ravens. Lead him on about it if you have to, but don't join."

"It's not that big of a deal, Sasha. I mean, yeah, it's kinda strange, but it's not like I have to be a member forever."

"How do you know?"

"Brett told me."

This was *so* frustrating. "What if he's lying? What if you say you give up God and pledge to follow Eryx, and it's real?"

Amanda shrugged. "It's not like I'm going to worship Satan or become a witch or a vampire or something wack like that. It's just a club, like a secret society in college." She looked down the hall, and said, "There he is. I gotta go."

Sasha slumped back against Jax's locker and stared after Amanda, watched her go up to Brett, saw him put his arm around her shoulders. How could she not see what kind of guy he was? It seemed so obvious to her, and it wasn't like she was alone. People were talking about the basketball game, and how he had acted like such a tool, shoving the coach, then storming off like a big baby. He was kicked off the team, of course, and rumor had it Coach Gill suspended him from the ski team as well. Brett's popularity had crashed and burned in less than twenty-four hours, and he'd done it to himself. That Amanda could like him . . . it blew her mind.

"It's a done deal," Jax murmured from her left.

She turned to look up at him. "Really?"

He nodded. "Brett won't bother you again. He freaked when I showed him the picture." He looked closer and said, "What's wrong?"

She didn't want to tell him, because he'd give her a lecture about free will and how pointless it was to interfere. So she straightened and smiled and said, "Nothing's wrong. I was just worried about you and hoping it went okay."

"It went even better than I imagined." He glanced around at the still crowded hall. "We've got five more minutes until class. You wanna go under a cloak and make out?"

That sounded so much better than fretting about Amanda. "Only a lot."

He grabbed her hand, they walked around the corner into an empty room, and disappeared.

<hr />

Rose came during history and waved Sasha and Brett out of class. In the hall, she said quietly, "Mrs. Shriver called from the hospital and said Mr. Shriver's taken a turn for the worse. She asked me to tell Brett, but I assumed she'd want you to know, too, Sasha."

She'd assumed wrong, but Sasha didn't say that. They followed her to the high school office and signed out for the day, then walked back out into the hall. Brett, she noticed, wouldn't look directly at her. He said in a dull voice, "Do you want to go to the hospital?"

"Only for Chris. He doesn't know what Tim did last night before he came home and smacked me around. He still thinks that's his dad in that hospital bed, so I'll go to be with him." She walked away.

"Chris joined the Ravens about three hours ago."

She stopped cold, turned quickly, and went back to him, shaking so hard, her voice came out in a weird warble. "You're *lying*. He wouldn't do that!"

"Mr. Bruno went to the hospital and told him he could save Dad's life if he'd join." He shook his head slowly, looking at her like he felt sorry for her. "When are you going to wake up and realize, Eryx always wins? He's what people want."

"Not everyone."

"Yes, everyone. People need things, want things, and you're kidding yourself if you think you can keep anyone from joining."

"I can try. I have to try."

"You might as well spit on a forest fire. No one's immune. *No one*. Even my dad, Dudley Do-Right. He ate until he was a whale, then worried he'd kick off and Mom would throw Chris out in the street. Bruno promised him he'd stay alive at least until Chris is old enough to live on his own."

"Why does she hate Chris so much?"

"Dad had a girlfriend in Russia who died having Chris, so he brought him home and told Mom she had to raise him like he was hers. People screw things up, then they want it fixed, or they want something they can't get on their own, so Eryx promises it to them. Chris pledged his soul to save Dad's life because he knows if the old man croaks, he'll be Dumpster diving for his next meal." He got right in her face. "What have you got to offer people like Dad and Chris?"

"The truth."

"You think that'll help Chris? You think the truth will save Dad?"

"It would have if they'd known it before they pledged. Eryx's promises are lies, sucker bets for desperate people."

"Where you're stupid is not realizing everyone's desperate. All Eryx has to do is figure out why, what they want, and promise it. Wait and see how many of your new friends believe the truth is where it's at."

It was as if the roof of the school opened up and a lightning bolt of rage hit her out of the clear blue sky. Reaching for his neck, she shoved as hard as she could, and they flew toward the lockers. She held him there, choking the life out of him, ignoring his clawing hands, his desperate kicks. She wanted him to die, *right now*, so he couldn't tell Eryx's lies to anyone else.

❧

When she didn't return for her backpack, Jax got up and left the room, pretending he was about to hurl so Bruno wouldn't question why he was leaving. As soon as he went into the hall, he looked toward the office and his heart stopped. Against the lockers, she had a choke hold on Brett, and he knew, like he knew his name and that the sun would set tonight, she'd crossed the line between Anabo and Mephisto. He'd known it was coming, that it was inevitable, but thought it would take longer. All those kisses from him had done this to her, and he waited to feel terrible, but it never came. Instead, he thought she was freaking glorious in her rage and determination.

Realizing he had mere seconds before someone came into the hall and saw them, he popped himself to where she was, pulled her off of Brett, and set her aside. "Be still."

Unconscious, Brett slid to the floor, and Jax bent to settle his hands on him and heal the damage to his throat and larynx. Grabbing Sasha's arm, he walked her away and took the first door he came to, which was the girls' room, erasing Brett's memory and waking him up as the door closed behind them. He'd be confused about how he wound up on the floor, but he'd get over it. He'd collect his backpack, go to the hospital, and never remember how close he had come to death.

Jax threw the lock on the door and turned to look at her. In her red dress and black boots, she stood straight and tall, blue eyes flashing with righteous fury, breasts rising and falling rapidly.

She had never looked more beautiful. "You almost killed him. You can't do that. Do you understand?"

She nodded.

"Tell me why you almost killed him."

In a low voice, she did.

He wasn't sure what surprised him more—that she wasn't crying, or that she wasn't trying to get out the door and go after Brett to finish what she'd started.

"With Chris on the other side now, there's no reason for you to go back to the Shrivers'. We'll get your things and move you to the house, to an extra bedroom."

"No. I'm staying there. I'm going to figure out Bruno's plans from Melanie. If Tim's gone, she'll be with Bruno even more. She may even go with him on his trip."

"I can't let you do that, Sasha. If they find out you're Anabo, it's all over."

"They won't find out because they won't be suspicious. I'm not afraid of Mr. Bruno. I'd like to kill him."

"He'll sense that as much as fear, and wonder why."

"I'm going to find out where that meeting is, because once you know, you won't need to keep Bruno around."

"Then what? Are you still hell-bent to lose what you have of Mephisto and go back to how you were before?"

"I don't know. I can't think real well right now because it's taking every bit of concentration not to shove you out of the way and go after Brett."

He'd spent decades learning how to control the instinct to

take the lost souls out. He realized he had a new problem with Sasha. "Go back to class, get your backpack, and leave. If he speaks to you, answer without looking at him and force yourself to think about anything but how much you hate him. Can you do that?"

"I think so."

"I'll be waiting just outside the door."

He grabbed her hand and walked her back down the hall, then waited while she went inside, hoping she could get out of there without attacking Bruno. She was incredibly strong, but no match for a Skia. As soon as she came out, he glanced around, saw no one, and hauled her into his arms. Five seconds later, they were in the war room.

"Why are we here?"

"Everything's changed, Sasha."

"By everything, you mean me, right?"

"Yeah, pretty much." He hit the intercom, and within a minute, his brothers were all there, looking from him to Sasha.

Key must have been in the greenhouse. He had soil on his hands and was brushing them together while he gave Jax a serious stare. "Talk now."

Jax explained what just happened, aware that Phoenix was freaking more than anyone else.

As soon as he finished, his closest brother said to Sasha, "*No way* are you going back to that house. It'd be like leaving a lamb in a lion's den."

"A lamb with teeth," Key said with a funny smile, his eyes on Sasha. "So you tried to kill a lost soul. How do you feel right now? Still wishing you could finish him off? Or are you having some regret about wanting to kill someone?"

"No regret." She looked toward Phoenix. "If I go back, it's a possible way to find out where the Skia meeting will be."

"We're watching every move Bruno makes, and we can do the same to Melanie. Your going back is pointless, and isn't gonna happen."

"Don't I get any say in this? What about free will?"

Phoenix came toward her, walking like he had to hold himself back. "If free will means you die, then to hell with free will. I'll lock you up and sit on you if you try to go back."

Without knowing she was stomping on the eggshells they'd tiptoed across for over a hundred years, she asked curiously, "Did Jane change like I'm changing? Did she try to kill somebody?"

He stopped in his tracks and swayed like she'd slapped him. Nobody said a word, waiting to hear what he would say. His face was chalky white. "Jane was . . ." He swallowed. "She couldn't walk. I lied about her sister. She wasn't sick. She was perfect in every way, until she pledged her soul because she was told it would heal Jane."

Jax stared at Phoenix, incredulous. His brother had never told him Jane couldn't walk. He glanced at his brothers and could see they were just as dumbfounded.

"When I found her, that night of the ball, she was in another room, with all the old ladies, sitting alone. I thought it was weird, but was so elated to find an Anabo, I didn't think so much about it. Until I told her to stand up. Everyone was frozen but her and the Skia."

"You can't freeze Skia?"

He shook his head. "Or Anabo. Later, when I went to see her, I told her I could fix her legs, but she wouldn't let me touch her, not for a long time. She was the daughter of an aristocrat, very proper, even with a guy alone in her room."

"So you didn't kiss her two hours after meeting her, like Jax did."

"No, it was a long time later, several weeks. Not only was she freaked about the Mephisto, about Eryx and all the rest, she was terribly upset that I'd taken her twin to Hell on Earth. When she finally allowed me to heal her, it was bittersweet, because she saw her handicap as the reason she'd lost her sister. I wanted her to understand that yes, her sister had done it for her, but it was so she wouldn't be something less than perfect, because they were so beautiful, made such a lovely pair. It was vanity that made her sister pledge, but Jane couldn't see it. I wanted her to. I wanted her to change, to be like me, so she'd understand. M told me I should kiss her, so I did, but like I said, it was a different time."

"Not much spit?"

He shook his head. "She hardly changed at all. Then I hit on the brilliant idea that marking her would speed everything up, and she'd get it and stop being so ambivalent about me."

"So she wouldn't let you do more than give her a honey-I'm-home peck on the lips, but she let you sleep with her?"

"There's some of the story I'm leaving out. The point is, once that happened, she died, so the answer is no, she didn't change like you, and she didn't try to kill anyone. She didn't live long enough to have a chance, to do what she was born to do. I'm not going to let that happen to you."

Sasha looked around the room, then said to Jax, "You and your brothers didn't know any of this, did you?"

Speechless, he shook his head.

She huffed out an impatient breath. "Guys. Sheesh." She looked at Phoenix. "That was really hard, wasn't it?"

"If it makes you understand why I won't let you go back, it was worth it."

"I understand." She leaned against the wall and conceded defeat. "You're right that it isn't worth the risk, not to mention that it'd be miserable. And once they're gone, I'd have to come here anyway. I have nowhere else to go."

"We could take you to Russia, to be with your mother," Key said. "You have papers now, and it might be hard to explain that to her, but you could think of something. You always have a choice. We obviously want you to stay with us, but not as a last resort."

Ty's cell rang, and he answered it quickly, nodding before he said, "Got it," and hung up. He looked around the room at all of them. "Tim's doppelgänger is ready."

Key said, "Everybody up on the plan, or do we need to review?"

They all said no.

"Then let's do it."

"What about Sasha?" Jax asked.

His oldest brother gave her a look. "Until she's all in, she can't be at a takedown."

"Then I'm taking her to the Shriver's to get her stuff."

"We all go, or no one goes. You know that, Jax."

Yeah, he knew that. It bugged him to leave her right now, but he didn't have a choice. "I'll meet you in the front hall," he told Key, already reaching for Sasha with one hand and her backpack with the other. Two seconds later, they were in his room, but he didn't let her go. Tossing her backpack aside, he pulled her into his arms and kissed her. With lots of spit.

When he stopped, she gazed up at him with bedroom eyes, until they widened, like she was surprised. "Jax, I just figured out Phoenix's problem."

"You were thinking about Phoenix while I was kissing you?"

"I was thinking that you're different, and I suddenly realized why he's so miserable. It's because he changed as much as Jane did, but when she died, he stopped. He couldn't go back to how he was before, but he couldn't move forward, either. He sees things differently, which is why he doesn't go looking for anonymous sex, because it can't be all about him anymore." She studied his face, then said softly, "Last night, you asked me that question because you're becoming like me as fast as I'm becoming like you."

He knew she was right. What he didn't know was if it was permanent. If she left and returned to how she was before, would he? Had Phoenix kept the changes because Jane died?

He thought about it and realized it made no difference. Even if his changes were forever, if he had to spend the rest of time more miserable than the past thousand years, he'd have no regrets. She was here now, and he would enjoy every minute until she wasn't.

His brothers were waiting for him, but he bent his head to kiss her one more time.

～～～

Two hours later, Sasha was working on calculus when Jax called and said he was out front, in the car. "Let's go get your stuff while the Shrivers are at the funeral home."

"I'll be right down." After she slid into her coat, she left his room in search of the stairs, took a wrong turn, and wound up in a dead-end hallway.

He called again. "Where are you?"

"Lost."

"Close your eyes and imagine you're out here, beside the car."

She stopped walking and did what he said. Damn, what a rush! When she opened her eyes, she was outside, but instead of being next to the old Mercedes, she was standing on the hood.

Hopping down to the snow-covered ground, she opened the passenger door to the sound of his laughter. She'd never heard him laugh like this, and it made her happy, made her smile, which totally killed any attempt to fake like she was mad at him for laughing at her. "I didn't know I could do that. *How* did I do that?"

He only laughed harder. "Not very well. I said . . . *beside* the car."

By the time he was halfway down the aspen-lined drive, he'd stopped laughing, but he was still grinning. "Until you become immortal, you can't do it when you're not on the mountain, or go anywhere off the mountain, but that's not a bad thing." He almost laughed again. "No telling what you might land on."

"That was way cool. I'm going to practice when we get back."

He looked across at her, his eyes still laughing. "You liked that, did you?"

"Totally loved it."

When they reached Telluride, he drove straight to the Shrivers', and she let them in with the key hidden at the back of the house.

"While you're packing, I'm going to nose around and see if I can find anything about Bruno's meeting."

It took her less than a quarter hour to pack, and when she was done, she went to look for Jax. She found him in Melanie and Tim's bedroom, poking through drawers. "Any luck?"

"Not a thing."

She looked in the closet. "She has some new stuff."

He came up behind her. "As you keep reminding me, I'm a guy. Her clothes are about as interesting to me as stale bread."

"It's not the clothes, but that they're new, still with tags, and none of it is stuff she'd wear in Telluride in December. It's all for warm weather."

"Maybe she's planning to take a cruise. Or a trip to the Bahamas. Doesn't mean she's going with Bruno."

"She can't afford to take a cruise. She and Tim argued a lot about money. That's one of the reasons she was so pissed about me being here, that it would cost them money."

He looked at the clothes again and shook his head. "It's a clue, you're right, but warm weather could be anywhere in the southern hemisphere."

Moving farther into the closet, she toed some bags, shoes, and dirty laundry out of the way, thinking about all the times she stuck things under hanging clothes to hide them from Mom, who could be way too nosy. There was a new tote bag, the tag still attached, and she picked it up to look inside. "Dramamine. Sunscreen. Paperback novel." She raised her gaze to his. "And a restaurant guide for Key West."

"Well, now, aren't you a clever girl?" He looked very pleased. "I'll get Zee and Brody to start looking through Key West reservations for next week."

"Maybe they should also look at charter boats."

"What makes you think he'd charter a boat?"

"The Dramamine."

"What's that?"

"Motion-sickness pills, for people who get seasick."

His eyes widened. "Then yeah, I'll have them look at charter boats." He glanced over his shoulder. "We should get out of here before someone comes home."

"I'm ready."

Just as they got back in her room to get her suitcases, the doorbell rang. Jax said, "Wait here," and disappeared. A nanosecond later, he was back. "It's a FedEx guy, bringing boxes up to the porch."

"It might be my stuff from Oakland."

Downstairs, she opened the door, saw her name on the first box, and took it as a sign that her things had come just as she was leaving. While Jax loaded everything in the car, she wrote a note and left it on the kitchen table. Short, vague, and simple, she said she was going to stay somewhere else until she could join her mother in Russia.

Then Jax drove her to the Mephisto Mountain, and when he passed through the mists, she wondered how long she'd be here. Less than a week? Or eternity?

He looked across the seat at her with a brooding expression, and she knew he wondered the same thing.

❧

Jax couldn't sleep, which was weird for him. He usually got into bed, rolled over, and was asleep in seconds. Tonight, he stared at the ceiling and couldn't get his brain to shut up.

Dinner had gone way better than breakfast. Sasha asked a lot of questions about how it went with Tim, and after that, his brothers relaxed. Before long, they were like always, joking around, talking about the upcoming takedown, arguing football, ignoring Deacon's lectures, and praising Hans when he came in to see if the food was good.

After dinner, he and Sasha had gone upstairs and hung out in his room for a while—he couldn't stop kissing her—until Mathilda made her go unpack, swishing after her, declaring she would help, and wouldn't that room on the third floor with the pink and brown be lovely for her?

Thirty minutes later, they were back, Deacon and another Purg named Alfred toting Sasha's things. Mathilda claimed it was just too quiet up there, and the "puir girl" wouldn't get a wink. Before he knew it, the small bedroom that was just past his sitting room—the one where he never sat—was filled with the furniture from the pink-and-brown bedroom, and Mathilda was unpacking, firing off instructions to Deacon, who looked like he always did: disapproving.

He came to Jax's room at one point and said in his usual stiff manner, "It's unseemly for a female not your wife to sleep in the same house with men who are not her brothers. I will take her to live with the Lumina woman who works with the computer."

"No."

"She should not stay on this floor of the house. I will take her back upstairs."

"No."

"This is your final answer?"

"She has a lot to deal with, Deacon. No point making her lose sleep because she's afraid. If she feels better being closer to me, so be it."

Lying in his bed, with her lying in hers, less than fifty feet and two thin walls away from him, he understood why Deacon was so insistent. He saw it as improper, but he also knew it'd kill Jax to have Sasha this close all night and stay apart. Deacon worried he wouldn't be a gentleman.

If it wasn't for the mark he'd leave on her, he was pretty sure Deacon was right.

But he wouldn't do that to her, not unless she decided to stay.

After another hour, he got up, put on a pair of sweatpants, and went to her room. He knocked, she said, "Come in," and he opened the door. She was lying in the dark, wide awake.

"Are you okay?"

"I can't sleep."

"Are you afraid?"

"No. I just can't stop thinking."

"About what?"

"You."

Surrounded by her scent, he walked close to the bed and watched her pull the covers back. He lay down, she curled into him, and five minutes later, she was asleep. Less than a minute later, so was he.

FOURTEEN

BRETT AND CHRIS WEREN'T AT SCHOOL THE NEXT DAY. ERIN asked Sasha why she was at school, and she answered honestly, "I don't like my aunt, and I'm obviously not real fond of Brett. I'd rather be here than there."

Just like she knew it would, the story went around and no one asked her again, until Amanda came up to her before calculus and asked how Brett was doing. "Okay, I guess. I haven't really talked to him since his dad died."

"Why?"

Sasha was less and less patient with Amanda's bizarre fixation on a murderer with no soul, so she was a little snippy when she said, "Because I hate his guts."

"But don't you feel bad for him that his dad died?"

"Yeah, I feel bad for him," she said with a sigh. "I feel bad for all the Shrivers."

Amanda went back to her desk.

It was Friday, and that afternoon, when they were in the car on the way to the Mephisto Mountain, Jax said, "Let's not think about school, or the Shrivers, or anything but having a nice weekend."

"Works for me," she said. "How about you, Brody?"

From the backseat, he mumbled something that sounded like *Star Trek*.

"Good Lord," Jax said.

"What?" she asked.

"Brody's got it for Jenny Brown, which is against the Lumina rule. They're not supposed to hang out with humans for just this reason. If they get attached, it's hard for them to get past it. He'll be mooning over her for ten years, and he won't look at any of the girls on the mountain because he'll be obsessed with Jenny."

She glanced at Brody, who was staring out the window, a world away. Looking back at Jax, she said, "Why can't Jenny be a Lumina?"

"She's not qualified. They have to exhibit some characteristics of Heaven. It's hard to explain, but you know it when you see it."

"Maybe Brody sees something you don't."

Jax glanced in the rearview mirror and sighed. "Maybe. I'll look into it, but don't tell him."

"He can hear you."

"No, he can't. He has in earbuds."

They reached the Mephisto house and spent the rest of the afternoon eating cookies and watching *The Sixth Sense* with Mathilda and Hans, who laughed all the way through. Later, Sasha kicked Jax's butt at Demon Slayer.

On Saturday, he took her skiing, and she was amazed at how much better she was than last time. "Must be Mephisto," she said when they skied off the lift at Revelation Bowl, an area for more experienced skiers.

"I'm pretty sure it's my expert lessons," he said, skiing away from her.

She chased and was halfway down a black diamond before she realized she was on practically a vertical incline.

That night, Zee played the piano for her and she cried because it was so beautiful.

On Sunday, she got the grand tour of the mountain, the stables, Phoenix's chopper shop, the gym in the old dairy, the tutoring rooms in the pink granite building, and, last, Jax took her to one of the Lumina cottages. A sweet, plump little lady named Tansy, who could be anybody's grandma, lived there. The cottage was like something out of Disney, wee and quaint, painted outside in a soft robin's egg blue, and the interior in but-ter yellow.

"It's a lovely life here on the mountain," Tansy said in a thick southern drawl, "but sometimes I hanker to visit Charleston, and

Denys takes me back. We go to Mirabelle's and have shrimp and grits, then he takes me out to the ocean. Do you like the ocean?"

Sasha nodded. "I grew up in San Francisco and Oakland."

"Pacific is nice, dear, but you can swim in the Atlantic. Maybe next time, you can go with us? I think you'd like shrimp and grits."

"I'm sure I would." She polished off another butter cookie. "What do you do here?"

"I'm like the Walmart greeter of the Mephisto Mountain. When we have a new Lumina or Purgatory, they stay with me for a while. I look after them until they feel at home. If you decide to come here and live with us, you'll stay with me awhile. Would you like that?"

Sasha shot a look at Jax. Tansy was awesome, but if she was made to be apart from Jax, she wasn't so sure she'd like that at all.

"Let's see how it goes," Jax said smoothly. "Sasha's just visiting right now."

"I hope you'll stay. You're very beautiful. Almost as beautiful as Reilly." She turned her head and called out, "Angel, would you like to visit?"

Sasha stared when Reilly walked in from the kitchen and smiled at her. "Hi, Sasha."

"Hey, Reilly."

The girl took a seat on the little chintz sofa next to Tansy. "I'm really sorry about what happened last week. I hope I didn't freak you out too much."

"It's okay. I understand why you did it. Are you feeling . . ." Wow, not a good idea to ask a dead girl if she was feeling okay. "Is everything going okay for you here?"

"It's getting better. I'm working on deciding what will be my job. I've narrowed it down to librarian and helping Key with his bookkeeping."

"Do you like to read?"

Reilly nodded. "If I'm librarian, I can order whatever books I want for the library."

"What's the downside?"

She wrinkled her nose. "I have to dust all the books."

They all laughed and visited a little longer before Sasha and Jax left the cottage.

That night, curled into him in her bed, she asked, "You like it here, don't you?"

"Sometimes, I imagine I would like it if I wasn't always so restless. Most of the time, the idyllic perfection the Luminas create only reminds me how one eighty it all is from who I am. Once, a long time ago, I went off and burned down a few of the cottages. Does that shock you?"

"No."

"They weren't mad, of course. They rebuilt and prayed for me while I served six months solitary on Kyanos."

She wrapped her arms around him and they lay like that until they drifted to sleep.

By Monday, she was pretty sure she was going to need a

sedative to get ready for Jax's leaving. She thought more and more about staying with him and his brothers, becoming immortal and accepting Jax as her eternal mate, but something held her back. She'd accepted what they did, even saw the necessity of it. That they were sons of Hell seemed less important than the unique ability she had to redeem one of them and give him a chance of Heaven.

She was so over the moon about Jax, she couldn't imagine ever feeling like this about anyone else.

She thought about her mom, and wondered and worried, but she'd had no more e-mails, no phone calls, nothing at all to let her know how she was. On the way to school, she asked Jax if she could see her mom if she stayed with him, and he said no, that she had to cut all ties to the outside world. That freaked her out a lot, but it still wasn't the reason she hesitated.

School started, and she went through the motions, becoming more anxious as the day passed, aware that finals began tomorrow and Christmas was three days away. The Mephisto were close to finalizing the plans for the Skia takedown, and once they did that, they'd take Bruno and his lost souls, and they'd be done. Jax would go back to the mountain, and Lucifer would clear her memory of what he was and what he'd meant to her. She'd only remember him as a guy who went to school with her for a while. If she asked, Lucifer would also take away Anabo.

Later in the afternoon, Amanda stopped by her locker and

asked if she was going to the game that night.

"I'll be there. Do you want to sit with me?"

"I'd like to, if it's okay."

"Of course it's okay."

"How is the family?"

"They're fine," she lied. She hadn't talked to any of the Shrivers since last Thursday.

"I thought I'd hear from Brett, but he hasn't called."

"You should be glad." She swung her backpack over her shoulder. "I'll see you tonight, Amanda." She realized as she walked away that Amanda was hinting to go home with her, which pissed her off. She didn't want to hang with Sasha—she wanted an excuse to go to the Shrivers' house so she could see Brett.

No one knew she wasn't living there now, and she hoped they never would. After the holidays, she'd be in Russia and it wouldn't matter, but for now, she didn't want anyone asking where she was staying.

None of the Shrivers had called since she left, so she was surprised to find Chris waiting for her outside the school. It made her sick to see his shaded eyes, so she said hello and tried not to look directly at him.

Ironically, he asked, "Where are you staying?"

"Does it matter?"

"I'm here because Mom wants to know if I can stay with you, wherever it is."

"No, that's not possible. There's no extra room"—boy, was

that a whopper of a lie—"and I'm a guest, so it'd be rude if I brought you home with me."

"Are you staying with Erin or Rachel?"

"No." She sighed and stared at the University of Colorado printed on his hoodie. "Melanie can't kick you out, Chris. If she really does it, go to the cops."

"I'd rather go with you."

"Pretty bad at the house, huh?"

"It's terrible. Dad's funeral is tomorrow, in case you wanted to know."

She didn't, and made no reply.

He reached inside his hoodie pocket and withdrew an envelope. "The FedEx guy left this for you. Mom told me to use it for an excuse to see you."

It was from her mother. She took it and kept her gaze on his hoodie.

About to turn away, he hesitated. "I wish I hadn't believed him."

"I know. Me, too."

He shrugged. "But it's not like God ever did anything for me. So Eryx doesn't, either. Same lie, different name." He walked away without saying good-bye.

She started to call after him, then didn't. He was as lost to her as if he were dead.

Looking down at the envelope, she wondered why her mother would mail a letter, instead of e-mailing. She tore it open and inside was a passport and two plane tickets—one from Telluride to Denver, and the other from Denver to St. Petersburg, Russia.

Dear Sasha,

I've made arrangements for you to come to St. Petersburg for Christmas, then to stay here with me until it's time for you to attend university. I've already enrolled you at school, and let an apartment in an old, beautiful building. Bring just one bag, and I will buy what you need when you arrive. I sold your father's ring to a collector, and it has saved us, so I hope you'll forgive me. I've also found a buyer for the painting who wants to give it as a Christmas gift, so I need you to FedEx it to me as soon as you receive this letter. I will see you soon.

Mom

It was a strange note, almost cold, and a million things chased through her mind, all at once. How did she get a passport, which looked real? How had she fixed it so Sasha could be in Russia? Mom didn't know she had papers now. Why hadn't she e-mailed, or called, to give her a heads-up? And most confusing of all, why had she agreed to sell the painting? What about Eryx? Had he given up trying to get it? Was he the one who wanted to buy it? The thought made her go cold.

"What's that?" Jax asked, walking toward her.

She held it out to him and he took it, reading quickly. Then he looked up at her with the strangest expression on his face.

"She sold the painting."

"I guess she was desperate for money, Jax."

"Yeah. I guess."

"Will we mail the fake?"

He nodded. "We can't risk letting the original back into the real world, where Eryx might get his hands on it. I'll get a Lumina to take the fake to FedEx as soon as we get home, and she'll have it day after tomorrow." He handed the tickets and the letter back to her and went around to the driver's side of the car.

She got in and looked at him, noticing his jaw was clenched. "At least now I don't have to make up a lie about the birth certificate."

He didn't speak.

"Jax?"

"Go find Brody so we can get out of here."

"Please, Jax, can't you—"

"*Now*, Sasha! Do it now!"

If he wasn't so upset, she'd tell him she didn't appreciate getting yelled at, but he looked like he was either ready to have a seizure, or to start crying, so she got out of the car and went to find Brody, who was probably hanging out with Jenny in the photography room.

～≥

As soon as she was gone, Jax pulled his cell from his pocket and almost couldn't dial, his hands were shaking so badly. When

Key answered, he said, "Is the fake ready?"

"Andres finished Friday night and it's been curing ever since. I'm planning to contact Eryx later tonight, tell him we located it, and ask what kind of favor he has in mind. Not that we believe a favor is actually on the table, or give a damn one way or the other. It's only an excuse to appease him so none of his people will hassle Sasha. He should have the fake by tomorrow morning."

"Give him the painting, or don't. It doesn't matter now."

"Why? What's happened?"

"He knows Sasha is Anabo."

The call was silent for a while before his brother asked, "How?"

Squeezing his eyes closed, fury overwhelmed him. "Katya sold her out."

❧

The ride home was tense and awful, no one saying a word. Jax was so stiff, she thought he might break right in two. Brody stared out the back window, and Sasha looked ahead at the road, which was difficult because it was snowing so hard. It had started in the higher elevations that morning and hadn't let up all day, blowing into giant drifts against houses and fences.

She had no idea how he navigated through the mists. Coupled with the snow, it was zero visibility.

When they finally arrived at the house, Deacon was there to open her car door, holding a ginormous umbrella over her head while she walked to the front entrance. Inside, Mathilda was waiting, clucking at her, following her up the stairs and down the long winding corridors to her room. She had hot cocoa and a roaring fire waiting, and asked all about her day. Sasha answered automatically, not paying close attention, her mind on Jax and his over-the-top reaction to her mother's letter. He'd known she would leave. She never wavered from it, so why was he so upset? Maybe because it was getting closer, and the tickets were a real reminder that their time was just about up.

"I always speak my mind, so ye'll forgive me if I say it's a tad strange how calm you are about leaving."

Turning from the fire, she blinked at Mathilda.

"So you'll do it, then. Leave Master Jax and the brothers, to go back to yer life."

"I have to be with my mother. Surely you can understand that. You've been here over a century because your daughter was taken from you."

"Drink yer cocoa, dearie." She took her coat and hung it in the small closet, then went to smooth the bed that was already military straight. "I know he comes in at night and sleeps here with you. I also know he's a gentleman. A child of Hell, with all that pull of the dark eating on him all the time, but he comes in here and looks after you without no touch like a man touches a woman."

"How would you know?"

"I've been looking after these lads a long, long time. I know

when they're needing, and Jax is strung tight as an archer's bow."
She fussed some more with the bed. "But he'll stay that way,
because he knows to touch you would be to keep you here forever, and he wants you to stay because you love him."

"I know."

Mathilda went to stoke the fire. "Ye're a child, yet, so you
don't know anything at all about love, or men. Not but what you
see on the movies, and the television, which is all made-up stories." She finally stopped her constant motion and took the chair
on the other side of the fire, her long skirts rustling as she sat.
"Drink that cocoa, Miss Sasha, so ye'll warm right up. I'll bring
some fresh-made oatmeal cookies after a while."

She sipped the cocoa to make Mathilda happy, but she wasn't
in the mood, and her stomach had begun to hurt.

"Have you seen the wee box he keeps, with his mother's
memory inside?"

Sasha nodded.

"He's got another, just since yesterday. Last night, while you
were in the TV room watching your show, he went out and came
back with a box like a heart. I'm a nosy woman, always was, so I
went in there just a while ago and looked in that box." Mathilda
held out her hand, palm up. Sasha leaned over and saw a ring. A
man's ring. A familiar ring.

"Go on," the housekeeper said, "pick it up, look at it, and
you'll see it's just what you think. It's your papa's ring, isn't it?"

Holding it between her fingers, she looked at the inscription inside, written in Russian, so worn it was hard to read any longer. *My heart, My life ~A*. It was given to the last tsar by his wife, Alexandra. Dad's great-grandfather had been a Russian count who had escaped the revolution to live in exile in Paris, and took with him some of the tsar's personal things for safekeeping, in hopes he'd return to Russia and give them back. Of course he didn't, and as years passed, he sold the pieces, one by one, to make enough money to feed his family. His youngest surviving son left Paris and went to America, taking the last of the pieces with him, which he sold to buy land in Minnesota. He kept this ring, and gave it to his son, who gave it to his son, and now Sasha was holding it in her hand because her mother had sold it to a collector. Who was Jax.

Tears hanging from her lashes, she looked at Mathilda.

"He sent one of the Russian Luminas to buy it from her, and paid enough so she could get all that was needed for you to be with her."

"How do you know, Mathilda?"

"I packed Boris's bag, and he told me what he was about, going to Russia. He returned last night, and Jax went out to buy the box. He will give it to you when you leave, so you can keep the ring for your son." Mathilda dabbed at her eyes with the corner of her apron. "He wants to love you, but he doesn't know how, doesn't think he's capable, so he does these things to make you happy, in hopes you will love him. He knows you'll leave, but he hopes . . . oh, he hopes."

Sasha handed the ring back to Mathilda and drained the last of the cocoa, more to hide that she was close to losing it than because she wanted more cocoa. Trying to keep it together, she set the cup on the small side table, then stood, thinking she'd go to her laptop and e-mail Mom that she got the tickets, even though she wasn't absolutely sure she'd use them. She hadn't been sure about much of anything for a while now.

The only constant in her life since everything went batshit crazy was Jax. No matter what happened, how horrible, how frightening, how sad—he was there. But it was all unconscious, some instinct in him that was as natural as breathing. Was that what love meant? That you were there for someone, no matter what it cost you? The longer he was around her and the more attached they became—so much they couldn't sleep apart—the harder it would be for him when she left. But he never turned his back, never pushed her away.

She took one step and the room began to spin. "Mathilda, I don't feel very good."

Instantly, the housekeeper was fussing and herding her toward the bed, pulling at her clothes as she went. By the time she was under the covers, she knew she'd caught something awful. Mathilda looked worried, and that was the last thing she remembered.

⁓⁓

"Is she asleep?"

Mathilda nodded, her lips pursed. "It's a bad thing I did,

Master Jax. Bad, bad, bad. Puir lamb trusted me and drank it right up."

"She'll never know. She'll wake up later tonight and think she was sick."

"I hope so. It's not something I like doing, tricking her like that, but I reckon you know best."

She left the war room, and Key said for the second time, "I don't understand why you didn't just tell her. She's going to find out. She has to find out. All you're doing is delaying the inevitable."

"He's buying time," Phoenix said. "Think of the difference it'll make if she stays because she wants to, not because she has to."

"What she wants is no longer on the table. I guess she doesn't have to accept immortality, but not staying on the mountain isn't an option. I'd think she'd want to know that. And she needs to know Katya took the oath, sooner than later. She may tell her something about Melanie's trip to Key West, which could wind up screwing the whole plan for next week. I'm ordering you to tell her, as soon as we're back after tonight's takedown."

Key didn't get it. None of his brothers did. Except Phoenix, because just as Sasha said, he was different. But he had a duty to his brothers, to the plans already under way for taking out fifty-five Skia next week. Jax nodded and said, "I'll tell her."

Her cell phone was playing an Augustana ringtone, the one she had for random calls from people not in her contact list. Groggy and feeling like someone had stuffed her mouth with cotton, she got out of bed and went to her backpack to dig around for her phone. She answered, sounding like a fifty-year-old chain-smoker, and Brett said, "Where are you?"

Aw, geez, she got out of bed for this? "At a friend's house, and the answer's still no, Chris can't live with me. Your mother needs to get over herself. Tim's barely cold."

"You don't really get how much she hates Chris."

"Yeah, I do. She was an evil bitch even before she took the oath."

"Speaking of oaths, guess who's taking hers tonight?"

"Amanda won't do it, Brett. I know she won't."

"Come to the ghost house and see for yourself." He ended the call.

She immediately called Amanda, but of course she didn't answer. She left her a voice-mail message, begging her not to do it, to wait until Sasha could talk to her.

Ending the call, she checked the time and groaned. It was past nine o'clock. She'd slept for hours and missed the game. Was Jax disappointed? Did he know she was sick? Surely he did. Mathilda would have told him.

Shaking her head to get the fuzzies out, she stood and went to the little closet to get some jeans. While she dressed and pulled her hair into a ponytail, she wondered how long she had before Amanda would take the oath. If Bruno was there, what would she do? She couldn't go commando on Brett and the others, or

Bruno would know she wasn't normal.

Maybe she could get there before anyone else, find a place to hide, then grab Amanda and take off with her.

She went through the little sitting room and knocked on Jax's door. As she expected, he didn't answer. He was probably still at the school for the game. She went through his room to the bathroom and brushed her teeth, then went back and slid into her coat. Closing her eyes, hoping she'd practiced enough that she wouldn't screw up, she imagined herself in the garage.

When she opened her eyes, she was standing on the roof of the garage, already sliding toward the edge. It was a long way to the ground.

Quickly closing her eyes again, she imagined she was inside the garage, and breathed a sigh of relief when she landed on the stone floor, just next to the side door, right beside the key rack. She didn't turn on the light, not wanting anyone to come out and ask why she was taking a car off the mountain. They'd call Jax, and he'd tell her she couldn't go, that if Amanda was going to pledge, nothing Sasha could do would make a difference.

Maybe not, but she was determined to try.

She picked a Subaru Outback, mostly because it was closest and the garage door behind it wasn't blocked by snowdrifts. Backing out, she hit the button on the visor, and the garage door went back down.

It took a while for the heater to warm, and her teeth chattered while she drove down the long drive, through the forest, to the narrow road that led to the highway. The snow had stopped, which made it easier to see, until she crossed the mists. Eventually, she broke free of the dense fog and after a few more switchbacks, she was at the highway.

Driving toward Telluride, she tried to remember how far it was to the turnoff for Last Dollar Road. She knew the ghost house was there, because she'd heard people talking about it. A family named Taylor had built the house in the seventies, then the dad went wack and killed everyone. It had been empty ever since, because possible buyers claimed there were ghosts. True or not, it had served as a party house for local kids for years.

The turnoff came sooner than she had expected, and she took the turn a little too sharply, skidded, and almost landed in the ditch. Adrenaline pumped fast and furious, making her even more anxious. She crept along while she scanned the edge of the road, looking for a turnoff that might lead to the house. There were several, but each one had a name posted, and none of them was Taylor. She was getting close to the tiny airport before she spied a turnoff with an old, rusted sign. The name had long since faded, but someone had painted GHOST HOUSE in white letters.

She shivered and turned up the heat.

The road was narrow and winding, and she came upon the house all of a sudden. There was a very small clearing in the trees, just enough for the little cabin and a tiny yard. East's car was already there, killing her idea of waiting and hiding. But there was just the one car, so Bruno hadn't arrived yet. The house was dark, except for one dimly lit window. A fire in the grate, maybe, or a candle.

Anxiety oozing from every pore, she sucked in a deep breath, killed the engine, and got out of the car. The old porch groaned and squeaked as she walked up the steps and crossed to the front door. She was about to knock, then thought, Why? This was an abandoned house. And she wasn't a guest. The knob turned in her hand and the door swung inward, revealing a small, dusty hall with a narrow staircase along one wall and a doorway into a family room on the other. She heard deep voices, and a low, pained moan.

Moving slowly toward the entryway, she cringed when a floorboard creaked, but no one came running, so she continued on. At the threshold, she froze. The room was bare, lit by a fire in the grate and three candles on the floor, each one illuminating large figures in black spray paint: 66X. Her mind wanted to go back in time, to that empty warehouse at Pier 26, to the terrifying faces of people who despised her enough to stone her to death.

Fighting back the memory, she made herself focus on the here and now, on Amanda. Naked, her arms and legs were splayed like a jumping jack in the center of the X, her wrists and ankles secured to the floor with ropes tied to tent stakes that had been driven into the wood. She was unconscious, her pale skin splotched with countless angry, red whelps. Burns inflicted on her by Brett, who was even then holding a poker in the flames, heating it up. The air was thick with smoke and the putrid smell of burned flesh.

Sasha watched Brett turn from the fire; saw East move toward Amanda, a long knife in his hand. Julianne leaned against the wall next to the fireplace, a vodka bottle dangling from her fingers. She laughed when she saw Sasha. "Wouldja lookit who decided to join us."

She remembered Reilly's words. *I never knew what evil looked like, until today.*

Taking it all in, she knew, in a defining moment of truth, she couldn't turn her back on this. Whatever sacrifices she had to make by giving up her mortality and remaining Mephisto for eternity, she had to do it. Amanda was willing to be humiliated and tortured, then hand her soul over to a liar, all so she could be somebody other than who she was. Maybe Brett was right and no one was immune. Eryx was a cancer, and if she couldn't heal humanity, she could do her best to kill the disease.

Her lingering hesitation, she realized, had been nothing more than a lack of confidence. Capturing the lost souls, transporting them around the world, then sending them to their deaths hadn't seemed like something she could do.

Looking at the evil in this room, she no longer had any doubts. She could do it. She *wanted* to do it.

They all three faced her, and she clenched her fists. "Let Amanda go. I've called her dad, and the sheriff."

Brett smiled. "No, you haven't. And no, we won't let her go. She belongs to us now, isn't that right, Amanda?" He moved close and poked her with the toe of his boot.

She roused and looked up at him with adoring eyes. "Is it time? Is Mr. Bruno here now?"

"Not yet. Soon. First, say hello to Sasha."

Amanda jerked her head up. "What are you doing at my initiation?"

"What are you talking about? There's no initiation! It's only an oath! They're torturing you because they're evil."

Brett lowered the poker and Amanda stiffened, eyes wide with terror. Just before he touched her soft, white belly with the hot metal, Sasha rushed him and shoved with all her might, gratified when he flew backward, into the wall. He hit it so hard, the drywall cracked, and he slid to the floor, stunned, his head bleeding.

Julianne stood straight and looked down at his crumpled form. "What a puss." Raising the vodka bottle, she drained it, then lifted it over her head and threw it at Sasha.

Instinct made her duck. Reflex made her lift her arm and catch the bottle in one hand. Turning swiftly, she swung it in a whistling arc and bashed East upside the head. The heavy glass shattered, and he went down like a load of bricks, the knife clattering across the floor until it came to rest at Julianne's feet. She bent to pick it up, and Sasha sprang into action, leaping across the five-foot distance to snatch the knife before Julianne was even halfway there. She turned to cut the ropes binding Amanda to the floor.

"Stop it! Julianne, she's ruining it!"

"Shut up, Geek Girl. There's no initiation. Brett and East just wanted to have some fun." She weaved a bit while she walked toward Sasha. "I hated your guts the minute I laid eyes on you."

"I'll cry about it later." Sasha threw the knife toward the farthest wall, satisfied when it plunged deep inside. Bending, she grasped Amanda's arm and hauled her to her feet. "You can get your clothes on before I take you home, or you can go naked. Take your pick."

"I'm not leaving!"

"Okay, naked it is." Dragging Amanda behind her, ignoring her useless attempts to break away, not caring when she whimpered that Sasha was hurting her, she headed for the front door.

"My glasses! I need my glasses!"

"Get some new ones." She hauled her to the door with one hand and reached for the knob with the other, jerking it open so hard, it flew back and banged against the wall. She yanked Amanda's arm and was about to step out onto the porch when Mr. Bruno appeared out of the darkness into the dim halo of light from within.

"Good evening, Sasha," he said with a pleasant smile. "Going somewhere?"

She was about to shove past him when she noticed a small pistol in his hand.

"Stay awhile, won't you?"

Backing up, she kept hold of Amanda and tried to think of what to say, reminding herself, over and over, he didn't know she was Anabo. "What's with the gun? Are you so desperate for new members, you've started threatening to kill them if they won't join?"

He came inside and closed the door, forcing her to move backward, into the room where Brett and East were still laid out and Julianne was working on another bottle of vodka. His dark eyes traveled the room in a blink before he focused on her. "Strong enough to take down two eighteen-year-old boys. I wonder, Sasha, how did you get to be so strong?"

"I was angry. Upset. Brett was torturing Amanda."

"That boy, Jack. I thought he was different, and now I know why. He's turning you." His gaze moved to Amanda, cowering behind Sasha. "Are you ready?"

It was several heartbeats before she said hesitantly, "Yes, sir."

"Repeat after me. I forswear God and Heaven."

"Don't do it, Amanda. Don't say it."

"I . . . I . . . what was it, again?"

"I forswear God and Heaven."

Sasha heard her swallow. "I forswear God and—oomph!"

Sasha elbowed her, making her double over and clutch her stomach.

The pistol was against her cheek. "Put your hands on your head and don't say another word. I have no qualms about blowing your brains out."

Of course he didn't. She prayed Amanda would cling to her hesitation, that she'd falter and lose sincerity. If she didn't mean it, she couldn't swear it.

"I forswear . . . " Mr. Bruno began for her.

She could move away from Sasha now, but she didn't. Instead, she came closer. From behind her, just over her shoulder, she whispered, "I forswear God and Heaven."

"I pledge my soul to Eryx, now and forever."

"I pledge my . . ." She drew in a deep breath, but before she could finish, Brett stirred and lifted his head.

"Jesus, what happened? Amanda, what's going on? How did you get up?" He focused on Sasha and scowled. "I should have thrown you over that cliff with Reilly."

Amanda stiffened behind her. "You mean it was your fault Reilly died?"

He blinked as if he was confused. "What? No, of course not." Trying to get to his feet, he fell back against the wall and sat there, dazed. "Bitch ignored me, dissed me. I showed her, though, didn't I, East?" He frowned. "East?" He swung his gaze to Julianne, who was sucking down vodka like it was water. "Did Sasha do that to him?"

"Yep. She's a regular Superwoman. Or part cat. Shoulda seen her move."

"Sasha?" Amanda grasped her sweater. "Can we go now?"

"Leave if you like," Mr. Bruno said, "but you'll be going alone. Sasha and I are taking a little trip together."

With the pistol resting against her temple, she didn't have much choice but to say, "Go on, Amanda. There are keys in my pocket."

"Th-thank you, Sasha. I'm so . . . sorry." She reached into Sasha's pocket for the keys, then slid around her, gathered up her clothes from the corner, and limped out. Moments later, there was the sound of an engine turning over.

"She'll go to the police."

"Maybe, but we'll be long gone, so it's no matter. Julianne, tie her up."

"Where are you taking me?"

"To Eryx, of course. Special delivery. Nice work getting her here, Brett."

He already knew she was Anabo. She'd been baited. Dread washed over her. "Why would Eryx be interested in me?"

"Oh, please, let's not play the game. You're Anabo, and I have orders from Eryx to bring you to him."

"How do you know?"

His shaded eyes were pure evil. "Your mother told him about your birthmark."

"Liar. My mother would never pledge her soul. Never."

He laughed then, like he was really amused. "Your naïveté is incredible. And misguided. Everyone is susceptible. Didn't you know?"

"She wouldn't. I know you're lying."

He shrugged. "Believe what you will." He reached out and jerked her sweater up, peering at the skin below her breast, at the little *A* that was the mark of death. "There it is, just where she said it would be."

The only people alive who knew where her birthmark was located were her mother and Jax. Now she understood why Jax had been so upset this afternoon. He had paid a lot of money for the ring so Mom could bring Sasha to Russia, which meant she had no reason to sell the painting. Jax read between the lines and knew she wasn't selling—she was giving the painting, and Sasha, to Eryx. That's why her letter was so cold, why she said to bring only one bag. Sasha wouldn't need clothes if she was dead.

Breathless with grief, she swayed, afraid she'd pass out because the rush of blood to her head was so swift. Somewhere in Heaven, Dad was waiting for his wife, and she'd never arrive. Somewhere on the other side of the world, Mom was waiting for her to be delivered to Eryx. Had she been promised immortality in exchange for Sasha?

Mother of God, she didn't know anything could hurt this badly.

Where was Jax? Would he go home, find her gone, and come looking for her? Would he be too late? She wasn't marked, so he'd maybe never find her. At least he wouldn't arrive just in time to see her die, like Phoenix had with Jane.

Unless Eryx contacted him. Would he do that, just for the twisted pleasure of watching Jax witness her death?

"Was Amanda worth it?" Bruno asked.

"I'd do it again."

"Even though she left you here?"

"She's not stupid. What could she do except get herself killed?"

He bent and picked her up, turned, and walked toward the door. "You're close to crossing over, aren't you? Another day or so and you'd be Mephisto."

Stiff in his arms, she constantly twisted her wrists, desperate to get loose from the rope. Just how strong was she?

"Escape is impossible," he said smugly, walking toward his car. "I can outrun you, and despite your unnatural strength, I could squash you like a bug. Even if you break the rope, you're not going anywhere."

In the middle of plotting her escape, and with the depressing fear that he was right and she couldn't do it, sixth sense told her Jax was near. She could feel him, out there, somewhere. Then she caught the scent of cider and cinnamon, and her heart soared. "I don't have to break the rope. You're toast."

A wall of black appeared, and Bruno stopped in his tracks.

The Mephisto had arrived.

Watching them materialize out of thin air, she remembered with perfect clarity the night she met Jax.

"Of all those three billion guys, why would you pick me? I'm a freak."

She wanted to tell him she'd never pick any of those other three billion guys, because he was all she wanted. He was her freak, and she'd love him forever.

402

FIFTEEN

MR. BRUNO TRIED TO DROP HER AND MAKE A RUN FOR IT, but he was too late. Jax flew at them, his trench coat opening wide, enveloping them in darkness. She'd barely had time to catch her breath before she was blinking in the light of day, lying on the ground. On sand. She felt it beneath her cheek. Lifting her head, she saw Jax standing over Mr. Bruno, his arms raised while he shouted toward the sky. She couldn't understand him.

Jerking her hands, she finally broke the rope, hurried to untie her ankles, then scrambled to her feet. They were in a desert, with soaring dunes, rippled by wind waves. No vegetation of any kind. A desolate place where dawn was breaking. They were very far from Colorado.

Mr. Bruno cried desperately, sobbing, begging Jax to spare him. He looked toward her, his eyes filled with tears. "Please, please, don't let him do this! Save me!"

She watched in fascinated horror as the sand beneath the man began to swirl, like a tornado, a vortex of fury. Jax kept chanting, arms raised, his trench coat flying out behind him, until the sand suddenly sucked Mr. Bruno under, and his crying pleas were silenced.

She was watching Jax's arms slowly lower when Key appeared with Julianne, Zee with East, and Phoenix with Brett. All three were thrown to the sand, and Jax raised his arms again, beginning his strange chant to the sky.

Brett looked at her, crying hard. "Sasha, help me! I'll die down there! Tell him to stop!"

East was still dazed, but managed to say, "Done for."

Julianne was drunk, not completely aware. She glared at Sasha. "I hate your guts."

Sasha watched the sand begin to swirl, then quickly looked up before they disappeared, focusing on Jax. He never looked down, didn't appear to hear Brett's cries for mercy. When it was quiet again, he slowly lowered his arms. "Are you okay?"

She nodded, unable to look away from his black eyes.

Ty appeared just then with Melanie. She didn't beg, but looked up at Sasha and said spitefully, "It won't be long before your mother joins me down there."

"What did you ask for in exchange for your soul, Melanie?"

Her eyes were wild and evil. "Your mother's complete downfall. She lost her job, her honor, and she was sent back to Russia, where she'd sworn never to return." Melanie laughed, and it sounded like a crazy person's hysteria.

"Why do you hate her so much?"

"Because Tim was in love with her. Did you know that? He would have left me for her, but she picked Mike. When he died, everyone thought Tim had done it, because he was still in love with Katya. But it wasn't Tim."

"Who was it? Who betrayed my dad?"

Jax was raising his arms.

Melanie looked at him, and the first sign of fear came into her eyes. "Make him stop and I'll tell you."

Jax continued, and she knew he wouldn't stop. He couldn't stop this any more than he could stop breathing.

"Good-bye, Melanie."

"Please, Sasha, I'll tell you, I swear. Just make him stop!"

"I can't." She scanned the faces of his brothers before she looked again at Melanie. "Even if I could, I wouldn't."

"Just like Mike, self-righteous and perfect. I hated him, all my life, but I got mine."

"What did you do to him?"

She shouted as the sand sucked her under, "It was me! I ratted out the arrogant son of a——"

Silence reigned. Now she knew who Tim threatened to call whenever Melanie went off. The CIA. He had known what

Melanie did, and held it over her head as a way to control her. Sasha moved her gaze from the innocent-looking sand to Jax's solemn face. "Didn't Melanie just take the oath a few weeks ago?"

He nodded.

"But Dad was killed last year. Why would she do that to her own brother if she—"

"Evil exists in the world, Sasha. It's why my father has a job. Not everyone who commits evil acts is a lost soul. Humans have been tempted by evil since Eve ate the apple." He smiled wryly. "Except the Anabo."

"Where are we?"

"Saudi Arabia. The Empty Quarter."

One by one, his brothers disappeared. When it was just the two of them, he took a step toward her. "You'll never know how many times I died tonight when I came home and you were gone."

"From the game?"

He shook his head. "I couldn't go to the game. We found all we needed to know about the Skia meeting, and with the heavy snow today, we decided to take down Bruno and the rest tonight. We'd placed the doppelgängers, and were about to pick them up to bring them here, but I was worried, so I went by the house to check on you. I went to your room, thinking you'd be in bed, asleep, but you weren't there. You weren't"—he swallowed— "anywhere. And I was so afraid, because Eryx knows, and you were away from . . . the mountain. I didn't know where . . ." He rushed at her and squeezed her so tight, she couldn't breathe, crying against her hair. "Oh, God, Sasha, please . . . don't hate . . . that you have to . . . stay."

She wrapped her arms around his middle and clung to him, crying because he was crying. "Jax, I had already decided to stay."

He went still. "You did?"

"I can't turn my back on all this, on Eryx and what he does to people." She moved so he had to lift his head and looked up into his eyes, surrounded by spiky black lashes. "And I don't want to leave you. I love you."

His black eyes welled with more tears.

She went on tiptoe and kissed him.

"What if I never . . . I don't know if I can love you like I'm supposed to. I'm crazy in love with you, but is it the same? Is it what matters?"

"I don't know, but we have a long time to figure it out."

The wind whistled across the dunes, blowing sand against them. "After they come back with the others, we can go home."

Home. Where she would live for the rest of time. It was way too weird a concept to really wrap her mind around, but she could at least think about the near future. "Can I stay in your room?"

"I would love that. My feet hang off the end of your bed."

"I wasn't really talking about sleeping, Jax."

He was very serious, almost frowning. "Are you sure, Sasha? Absolutely sure? There's no going back."

She nodded. "Absolutely sure."

He kissed her then, and she knew he was happy. Ecstatic, even.

She would be, too, except for one thing. When he lifted his head, she asked if she could see her mother. "I know what will happen to her"—she glanced at the sand—"but I want to see her, one last time."

"I don't think that's a good idea. It'll upset you, and wouldn't it be better if your last memory of her is how she was before she took the oath?"

"I have to know why she did it. I can't spend the rest of time not knowing. Please, Jax. Let me see her."

He sighed and pressed her head against his shoulder. "I'll ask Key."

A few minutes later, Phoenix appeared and tossed Scott to the ground, followed by Ty, who had Mr. Hoolihan. Then Denys appeared, and Sasha clapped her hand over her mouth to keep from crying out when she saw Chris land on the sand. Maybe she was changed, maybe she no longer felt compassion for the lost souls, but watching Jax send Chris to that dark pit far beneath the surface made her cry. Not for Chris as he was, but for the man he could have been.

SIXTEEN

SHE'D TAKEN A SHOWER, EATEN THE SOUP AND CRUSTY French bread Mathilda had brought, then watched the last of *Sleepless in Seattle* on the TV behind the Mephisto portrait while she waited for Jax to come back to his room and tell her whether Key had agreed to let her see her mother. She didn't remember falling asleep, but when she woke, she was beneath the covers and he was there beside her, his head propped in his hand while he slowly stroked her hair.

He was on top of the coverlet, wearing only a pair of sweat-pants. She drank him in, the shape of his chest, his shoulders, his muscled arms. She turned toward him and he kissed her, soft and gentle, murmuring words she didn't understand, his arms around her, his hands caressing her, drawing the shirt up and over her head.

He gently pushed her to her back and moved away, to join her under the covers. She knew he slipped out of the sweatpants, but she made no move to touch him, content to wait, to feel his hands against her skin, especially her breasts. "Your hands are so warm."

"Are you cold?"

"Not now."

He went to his elbow again and brought his face close to hers, so that their noses were almost touching and she could feel his breath against her lips, but he didn't kiss her, whispering instead, "Are you sure?"

She nodded.

"You're upset and grieving. I'm maybe taking advantage when you're vulnerable."

He was *this* close to sex, but he was worried she might regret it, that she was only in his bed because she needed affection. She slid her arms around his neck and slipped her hands into his soft, silky hair. "I love you, Jax."

"The first time with me isn't going to be like it would be with a regular guy. There's not only the usual complications. I think it will burn, because of the mark."

"It's okay."

He settled his lips over hers and kissed her like he meant it, slowly at first, then deeper, more seductively, drawing her to him without saying a word or making a move. Her body took on a will of its own, straining toward his, pressing against him.

While he kissed her, tangling his tongue with hers, he kept

one arm around her and let the other drift across her skin, lower and lower, until his fingers brushed against the hair between her thighs. He pushed her legs apart and touched her, so soft, so slow, until her urge to giggle passed and desire roared through her, putting every nerve on notice that something very big was about to happen. She moved constantly, her hands all over him, touching his hot skin, trying to pull him closer.

But he barely budged, stayed where he was, kissed her over and over, ran his lips down her throat and across her breasts, and through it all, his hand never left the apex of her thighs.

With no warning at all, she sucked in a deep breath and lost herself, blown away that anything could feel this incredible, this powerful—and she'd lived almost eighteen years without a clue. She was breathing as hard as if she'd run a race. "Awesome . . . that was . . . awesome."

"You liked that, did you?"

"Only a lot."

He kissed the tip of her nose before he moved to stretch above her, his weight against his arms while he nudged her legs farther apart with his knee. Then he was inside of her with one hard push, and his beautiful face had the strangest expression—like fear and joy, all at the same time. "I'm sorry . . . I thought it'd be like a bandage, better to make it quick."

"It didn't hurt, Jax."

He was surprised. Moving his body, he asked in a rough voice, "Does it now?"

She shook her head.

He moved again, asking a question with his eyes.

"No." She smiled up at him. "Do that again."

He did, and she raised her head from the pillow to kiss him. "Now do that whole thing again, but faster."

His breath quickened. "Wrap your legs around me," he whispered, just before he pressed her against the pillow and kissed her, sucking all the air from her lungs until she was gasping. Moving his mouth along her throat, he nipped at her with his teeth, then kissed that spot before traveling on to another. Her whole world narrowed to his wonderful face, his spectacular body, moving inside of her, strong and sure.

Suddenly, his head went back, his eyes closed, and his body went stiff and still. Deep inside, she felt a burn that seared and scorched and traveled all through her groin, making her flinch and try to jerk away from him. But he held her fast with the weight of his body, and when the pain was gone, she began to shake, and shudder, grasping his arms, his back, clenching his hips between her legs, holding on while she flew apart. She had no idea that anything could feel like this. It was incredible. It went on and on.

When her body finally relaxed and she drifted back to consciousness, she saw the look on his face and immediately turned her head.

"Don't look away. Why are you looking away from me?"

"Because I scratched your arms, and I know I yelled something embarrassing."

He said with a note of wonder, "The air all around you shimmered. It was . . . you were . . . the most beautiful thing I've ever seen." Shifting, he lay beside her and gathered her close, until her head was in the nook between his chin and his shoulder. "Thank you," he whispered.

"For this?"

"For staying." Lifting his head, he blew toward each candle in the room until every one was extinguished and all that remained was the soft flicker of the dying fire. "Get some sleep, Sasha. Tomorrow, we're going to Russia."

SEVENTEEN

A HUSHED NOISE WOKE HER JUST TO A PLACE BETWEEN SLEEP and awake, allowing awareness to filter in slowly. There was that noise again, the soft, gentle squeak of leather. Other noises and sensations drifted into her consciousness—Jax's even breathing, his warm chest rising and falling beneath her cheek, the ticking of the antique clock in the bookshelves, a whisper of skin against skin.

She was sprawled across him, lying on her stomach, her legs and hips tangled up in the sheets, one arm slung across his shoulder, her hand in his hair, and the other stretched across her pillow. Jax was on his back, slightly turned toward her, one arm across her body, his hand resting on her backside.

There was that weird creaking noise again. Then a soft exhale of breath. She woke further—enough to realize they weren't alone. She opened one eye and saw Zee. Turning her head slightly, she opened the other and saw all of Jax's brothers, lined up there at the end of the bed, staring at them.

Burying her face against Jax's chest, she stroked his hair and mumbled his name. He stirred and said in a hoarse, sleep-filled voice, "Again? Three times wasn't enough?" His chuckle rumbled against her chest. "And here I was worried you wouldn't like it."

She must be the shade of a tomato, she was so embarrassed. "Jax," she whispered, "we have company."

She felt him move when he lifted his head.

"Aw, come on, you guys can't be serious. What the hell are you doing here?"

Key said, "We have to go now, Jax. It's already three in the afternoon in St. Petersburg."

"Did you *all* have to come?"

"None of us had to come. We could have called, or sent Mathilda. But we wanted to make sure everything was all right. Sasha, are you all right?"

"She was fine, until all of you came in here and embarrassed her to death. Get lost."

Key said in a very authoritative voice, "You agreed not to mark her until after we return from Russia and she becomes immortal. I'd like an explanation."

"I want to be able to find her. I never want to go through what I went through last night."

"How *did* you find me last night? You never said."

"Brody tracked the GPS on the car you took."

"You marked her so you can find her, and now, so can Eryx. If anything goes wrong, she has no chance of hiding until we can get to her. This is a serious infraction, Jax. When we return, there'll be a council. If anything happens because of her mark, I don't need to tell you what we'll do to you."

"If anything happens to Sasha, I won't give a damn what you do to me."

"I've got half a mind to forbid the trip. It's a pointless risk."

"Sasha saying good-bye to her mother isn't pointless."

"Her mother is already gone. How can seeing her as she is now be anything but a terrible memory she'll never be able to erase? Better to remember her as she was."

"Are you saying Jax can't take me to Russia?" Sasha asked, still unable to look at them.

"I'm saying it's a foolish risk. You have to follow every order, do exactly as we tell you. Knowing what you do of the lost, you understand they have no capacity to feel anything for another human being except rage and hate. Your mother's love is gone; in its place is only her ambition to become something more to Eryx than another collected soul."

She knew it was true, but she also knew it would haunt her until the end of time if she didn't have the chance to ask, Why? This wasn't good-bye. This was all about an answer.

She lifted her head finally and looked at Jax. His expression was blank, so she couldn't tell if he was mad, glad, or anything in between.

He squeezed her shoulder. "Let's get dressed and do this."

∽◦∾

The decision was made for Sasha to meet her mother at the Peter and Paul Cathedral, where the tsars were buried. If her mom thought it was weird when Sasha e-mailed and asked to meet her there, she didn't let on. All attempts to pretend everything was normal were gone. She wrote back a terse, *I'll be there*, and that was it.

"She knows you're with us," Denys said, standing next to the fresh flowers in the great hall.

"How could she know?"

"Because you're marked, and Eryx told her."

"I thought as long as I was here, behind the mists, Eryx wouldn't know."

"Oh, he knows," Key said, glaring at Jax. "He just can't get to you here. The instant we leave, all bets are off. This is why you have to go inside the church immediately, and leave by the exit we showed you on the map. Jax will be there, waiting. The rest of us will be at other exits, just in case."

"In case of what?"

They all exchanged looks before Jax said quietly, "Your mother may try to kill you, Sasha." He pressed something hard and cold into her hand. "This is my switchblade." He demonstrated how to open the blade by pressing one of the jewels embedded within the ornately carved silver handle.

417

She remembered it from that night in San Francisco. This was what he'd used to stab Alex Kasamov. "Where did you get this?"

"Key had it made for me in Spain, in 1855." His smile was wry. "My seven hundredth birthday."

"Tell me I won't need it."

He stroked her hair. "I wish I could. Slip it into your pocket, just in case. Remember, you're enormously strong, far stronger than your mother, or any other lost one who might be in there with her. No matter what she says, don't for one instant believe she has your interests at heart. Never forget what you know of the lost. Of Eryx."

Key came closer. "You have five minutes, Sasha. Ask your questions, say what you have to, then leave. If you're threatened, don't engage. Just leave. And remember, if you use the blade and kill a lost soul, Eryx wins. He becomes that much more powerful. If you see a Skia, run like hell."

"Skia can be inside a church? They can stand on holy ground?"

"Yes, because they're not born of Hell. Only the dark angels and the Mephisto are barred." Key looked around at each of them. "Are we ready?"

They all nodded, and Jax slipped his arms around her.

Moments later, they stood beneath the portico at the entrance of the cathedral, less than six feet from the doors. She knew immediately something was wrong, because Jax stiffened and his arms tightened.

"I have a proposal for Sasha," a deep voice said.

She peeked over Jax's arm and saw him—Eryx. Even while she stared in stunned surprise that he was the most beautiful creature she'd ever seen, she recoiled in terror from the sight of his eyes. They didn't reflect the suffering of mankind and the secrets of the universe. They were not of Hell, but of something infinitely more disturbing: nothing. They were like a doll's eyes, dead and flat.

"Get away from the door so Sasha can go inside and see her mother," Key said.

"Of course," Eryx said in his deep, seductive voice. "But first, I'd like her to consider my offer to release her mother from her oath."

"In return for what? Her life?" Key laughed at him. "No deal."

Sasha wanted to look away from him, but she couldn't. She wanted to speak, but her throat wouldn't work. Jax's arms were like a band around her, and his body was tense, ready to disappear with her in a nanosecond. One small move from Eryx, and they'd be back in Colorado before she could blink. Eryx must have known it, because he stood completely still, just in front of the doors.

"I want the papers."

"You have the papers," Jax said.

"I have the bullshit you put in the lockbox. I want the original journals, letters, photographs, and recordings Katya's father and grandfather stored there."

"What makes you so sure there was anything else in the box besides what you found?"

"Katya knew what was inside, and she assures me the contents have been replaced with trinkets. My proposal is good for another five minutes, the time it will take for Sasha to go in there and see what her mother has become. She can have her back if I can have the original contents of the lockbox."

"It's no longer hers to give."

"Yes, I realize, but she's with you now, so let's call it a collective ownership issue. If she wants the deal, you'll all go along with it." Eryx was staring at her from those horrific eyes. "You can win your mother's soul if you'll just give me what I want."

He was a liar. She knew that. And yet, it was the greatest temptation to believe him. She turned her face into Jax's neck. "I want to see my mother."

"Yes," Eryx said, "go in and see her, know she's doomed to eternal servitude to me, to find those whose souls are seeking, and she'll give them hope, lead them to me. I've already promised her immortality, but you have the power to give her back the promise of God."

Jax began to move, walking her slowly toward the entrance, his arms still around her. Zee shouldered Eryx out of the way and opened one of the massive doors. Just at the threshold, Jax released her and she was inside, looking out. "I love you," she whispered.

"Be careful."

Turning, she moved into the elaborate, ornate cathedral, awed by its splendor, even while she searched the rows of pews for her mother. There were a few worshippers, kneeling, forearms resting against the backs of the pews, hands folded, heads down, praying. She couldn't see their faces—their eyes. Were any of these people lost souls or Skia?

"Sasha!" A loud whisper came from her right and she turned, unprepared for what she saw. Her stomach heaved and her heart broke all over again. Her mother's great, dark eyes—so beautiful—now obliterated by Eryx.

Stepping into the pew, she went toward her and sat several feet away, aware of the switchblade in her pocket and that her mother was crying.

"You hate me, don't you?"

"Mom, please, I only have five minutes."

"Did you look at the painting, Sasha?"

"Yes."

"You don't know it, because I painted over her face, but the girl in the picture is you."

She knew, but didn't say so. She also knew Key had delivered the fake directly to Eryx, so her mother didn't realize the real painting was still in Colorado. Eryx didn't know the difference, and assumed he had the original because he'd found the microscopic code numbers to the lockbox.

"I painted over your face because I didn't want anyone wondering why you were in a five-hundred-year-old painting. Even

Mikhael never knew it was you. I showed it to Alex, who told me the girl in the picture is Anabo, and what that means. He wanted the painting and offered a lot of money, but I wouldn't sell, especially after what he told me. I was so afraid for you. When I arrived in Russia, a man named Rurik approached me, a man like Alex, and claimed I'd sold it to Eryx. He demanded I hand it over. I couldn't, of course, even if I'd wanted to, because you had it."

"Melanie searched, and destroyed everything I owned, but she didn't find it. It was all for nothing that I hid it so well, because you ended up giving the painting to Eryx anyway." Not really, but Mom didn't know the painting delivered to Eryx was a fake.

"It was only a matter of time before they found out you're Anabo, either because they'd find the painting and someone would uncover the girl's face and see it was yours underneath, or someone would see your birthmark. I knew they'd kill you, so I took a chance. I asked Rurik, if I knew of an Anabo, and pledged my soul, would the Anabo be spared? He said yes, and I believed him."

She remembered Jane's sister, who appeared to give her soul as the ultimate sacrifice, and Chris, who had traded his to save his father's life—but both of them had a secret reason, hidden, and not selfless at all. "Four minutes, Mom. Tell me the real reason you did it."

"That is the real reason! But they lied to me, Sasha. As soon

422

as I pledged, Rurik made me tell him who was the Anabo and demanded I hand over the painting. The irony that you'd already been found by the Mephisto, that you'll never be in danger from Eryx, is killing me. You're safe now, but I'm not. Please give him the papers. Please help me."

She wasn't safe. Not yet. Not until she became immortal. And she knew, intuitively, there was no saving her mother. It was a lie. If Sasha agreed to give Eryx the contents of the box, he wouldn't release her mother from her oath. Sasha knew it, and so did her mom. "Melanie said Tim was in love with you. She said he would have left her, except that you picked Dad."

She'd hit a nerve, she could tell. Mom drew herself up and huffed out a breath, like she was surprised and annoyed. "It was a long time ago."

"Tell me. You can do that much, at least."

Her mother turned her face away. "I was still in Russia when I met Tim. I didn't know he was with the CIA, or that he was married. I fell in love, but when I found out he had a wife and son, I told him I wouldn't see him anymore. Then I decided to defect, and that's when I met Mikhael. He was a good man, a kind man, and after I found you, he agreed to marry me so I could live in the United States and we could raise you together."

Sasha knew where this was going, and she almost got up and ran. She didn't know if she could stand to hear it. "You didn't love Dad, did you?"

Slowly, her mother shook her head. "It was always Tim, but

423

like so many things in my life, it didn't work out. He wouldn't leave his wife and lose his son, and I wouldn't stay with him while he was married. He had a short affair after I left him, and that is how Christopher was born. Mikhael and I weren't unhappy, Sasha, and we had you, which made everything better. He loved you so much."

Sasha slumped back against the pew. "You pledged because you wanted a second chance, didn't you? You thought Tim would leave Melanie and bring Chris and me to Russia, where we'd be one big happy family."

"I knew it would never happen as long as Tim believed I had something to do with Mikhael's death. He discovered it was Melanie who had sold the information that got him killed, and she told him I provided it to her. I suffered death knowing he believed it of me."

"If you didn't give her the information about Dad, who did?"

"No one gave it to her. She was married to a CIA operative with high security clearance. She figured out his passwords and accessed his files, found out Mikhael's alias, his cover, his location. She sold the information to Yuri Andreovich for fifty thousand dollars, and after Mikhael was killed, she confessed to Tim what she had done, but instead of confessing that she accessed his files, she accused me of giving her the information. He knew she was rabid, that she'd do anything to hurt me, yet he still believed her and despised me for what he thought I'd done to Mikhael."

"So you were promised that Tim would see the truth, that he'd believe your innocence and love you again."

Her mother was sobbing now, her face in her hands. "I wanted that *so much*, was so sure it would happen. But it was a hideous lie! Tim was already dead when I pledged, and now . . ."

"Now, since you can never go back, you'd do anything to become Skia and live forever, so you sacrificed me."

She raised her head and said passionately, "I'll make it up to you, Sasha, I swear it! Please, just give him the lockbox contents and help me."

"I can't do it, Mom. I can't give Eryx what he needs to suck more people in."

"You're of the angels! Show mercy!"

Sasha stood, wishing now that she'd listened to Jax, that she hadn't insisted on seeing her mother, on knowing the reason she'd pledged. "I loved you, and I know you loved me, but it's all done now. My time's up. I have to go."

Her mom stood, too. "You'd turn your back on me? Your own mother?"

"You're not my mother. You're a stranger." Without another word —because what was there to say— she turned and walked toward the end of the pew, her hand inside her pocket, fingers wrapped around Jax's switchblade.

But she didn't need it. Her mother remained behind, the sound of her weeping carrying through the cavernous cathedral, following Sasha as she made her way to the front of the church, headed toward the Catherine Chapel, where the imperial families of Russia were entombed, toward the east exit and Jax, waiting on the other side.

⥈

Jax paced back and forth outside the church, waiting. He checked his iPhone no less than a hundred times, every few seconds, wishing she'd hurry, that she wouldn't take the whole five minutes. He regretted agreeing to bring her. Letting her out of his sight, even to go inside a church, seemed like the stupidest idea, ever. Key was right—what purpose did it serve to let her see her mother? All it could do was upset her.

Four minutes left.

Barely four thirty, and dusk had already settled over St. Petersburg, the sky turning sapphire, streaked with orange from the setting sun, the reflection turning the snow to purple. He walked closer to the door, checking the iPhone one more time.

Three minutes to go.

He stared at the door, willing her to open it.

"Do you have something to eat?" a man asked in Russian from behind him.

Turning his head, Jax said, "No."

"Spare some change?"

He handed him a twenty.

"Thank you." The man pocketed the bill, but didn't go away. "Are you waiting for someone?"

"Yes."

"Why don't you go in to wait? All are welcome."

Not all, but he didn't say so. "I'm fine."

"There are some who believe God lives in every holy place, that no evil can touch them there."

He *so* didn't need a religious fanatic bum preaching at him right now. He tried to ignore the man, staring at the door. It was killing him, the waiting. What if she didn't come out in five minutes? What if, even at this moment, someone was hurting her? He couldn't get to her, couldn't protect her.

"And some say evil exists everywhere, that only love can overcome, no matter where a man stands."

Turning his head, he looked at the old man, at his white beard and rheumy eyes. "Okay." He looked again at his phone. One minute.

"I saw the devil go inside. Do you think he intends to repent?"

Jax jerked his head around again. "What did you say?"

"Just a moment ago, up at the front of the church, I saw the devil go inside. Dressed all in black, with soulless eyes. I wonder if he's come to swallow his pride?"

It couldn't be. Eryx couldn't go inside any more than the Mephisto.

"Then again, maybe it wasn't the devil. Maybe it was just a man with evil in his heart."

"Who are you?"

The old man came a little closer. "I'm here to give you a present."

427

"Why don't you take that twenty and get yourself some supper? Go down to Anna's. They take American money."

"I'll do that, but first, don't you want the present I promised you?"

All he wanted was for Sasha to come through that door. The five minutes were up. He turned his back on the bum and stared at the door, begging God to bring her out safely. If only God could hear him.

"I love you," he heard Sasha whisper from behind him, but when he turned, there was only the old man.

Except his eyes were no longer rheumy—they were so bright blue, they twinkled. Jax was suddenly overcome by a feeling so unfamiliar, he couldn't name it.

"Go with God," the old man said before he walked away, fading as he went.

Jax blinked, wondering if he'd just seen the eyes of God. *"I'm here to give you a present."* Did he mean Sasha? *". . . don't you want the present I promised you?"* The Mephisto Covenant. God's promise of an Anabo, of redemption.

"I saw the devil go inside. Dressed all in black, with soulless eyes." Was it a warning? Was he talking about a Skia?

He'd spoken to him in Sasha's voice. *"I love you."*

His whole life had changed because of three words, spoken by a girl with golden hair and eyes the color of the twilight sky above him. She couldn't die. She was humanity's best hope. She was his only hope. He would never survive if anything happened to take her away from him. Death and eternal Hell would be better than life without Sasha.

He heard her scream, and his blood ran cold.

Swallowing hard, he sucked in a deep breath, opened the door, and rushed inside.

EIGHTEEN

SASHA DIDN'T LINGER, AND SCARCELY NOTICED THE MOSAIC ceilings, the beautiful paintings, the elaborate gilt iconostasis, grieving for her mother as if she had died. In a way, she had.

Thinking of Jax, she walked faster. He must be beside himself, worried.

She'd just passed the last tsar's marble tomb when she heard running footsteps behind her. Steeling herself, she withdrew the switchblade from her pocket and sidestepped around the tomb, hoping it was just someone running for the exit.

Instead, it was a tall man in black, his face hidden in shadow, a knife in his hand. He leaped over the tomb in one inhuman bound, and she scarcely escaped him by darting around the next one. He was Skia, much stronger than her. He was there to kill her.

She leaped across the tomb at the end, into the walkway,

booking it for the door. It hadn't seemed so far away before. Now it seemed like miles.

Her assassin caught her hair and jerked her backward. She felt his blade pierce her back, but he missed her heart, puncturing a lung instead. Time slowed to a crawl, and she prayed for her life, for Jax's soul, for an end to Eryx.

Eyes on the door, she stabbed backward with the switch-blade, but only succeeded in hitting his leg. He loosened up on her hair, and she tore herself away from him, stumbling, unable to draw a deep breath, knowing she was about to pass out. If she could just make it to the door, she'd live. Jax would heal her.

But she couldn't run, could barely move, so when the Skia caught up to her again, she knew it was all over. She would die in this beautiful church, with painted angels as witnesses.

The door opened, and she watched Jax run inside, his body and clothes instantly catching fire. He ran to her, his cries sounding as though they came from across the mountains, like an echo. "Sasha! Oh, God, no! *Sasha!*"

She felt the blade pierce her back, and this time, the Skia didn't miss. She collapsed, but not before she saw Jax reach for her, his body blistered, his clothes burning. She fell to the floor, then floated above herself, watched the Skia limp away while Jax gathered her up in his arms and rocked her to and fro, sobbing her name as he followed her into death.

Just before darkness descended, she heard him whisper, "I love you."

NINETEEN

DARKNESS SLOWLY FADED, AND KEPT FADING UNTIL HE WAS standing in light so bright, he had to close his eyes. A soft voice said, "Who are you?"

"I'm Ajax." His voice sounded strange, coming out in a whisper he didn't intend.

"Ajax was a mighty warrior. Did you live up to your name?"

He shook his head slowly. "I lost the only battle that mattered."

"Who do you bring to Heaven's gate, Ajax?"

"Her name is Alexandra. It means defen . . . defender of men." He choked on the words. "She lived beyond her name." With her sweet, soft body cradled in his arms, he clutched her against his chest.

"Will you leave her here?"

He began to cry, helpless to stop. "This is where she belongs. I can't take her . . . where I'm going. I can't take her with me."

"If you could, would you?"

Slowly, he shook his head. "She doesn't belong where I'm going. She belongs here."

"Perhaps she'd rather go with you. When she wakes, she may want so much to be with you, she'll be angry you left her here."

"It doesn't matter. I won't take her with me." Bowing his head, he buried his face against her hair. "She'd be miserable. She'd see desperation and pain and regret and hate and rage, and it would break her heart, over and over. I can't do that to her."

"So, Ajax, you'll leave her here, with God in Heaven, even though you'll never see her again. Why would you make this sacrifice, when she means so much to you?"

He raised his head and opened his eyes. "Because I love her."

Moments later, something cool passed over him. "This is the hand of God." The voice was closer now. "Take your defender of men and be at peace. For you, Ajax, son of Mephistopheles, child of Hell, the Mephisto Covenant is fulfilled."

❦

Sasha stirred in his arms, and his heart skipped a beat. Looking into her beautiful face, he saw her open her eyes and smile. "Jax, I thought I died."

His eyes welled with tears again. "You did."

"And you brought me back to life?"

"God brought us back."

Twining her arms around his neck, she moved her head to his shoulder. "I love you."

"I love you too." He glanced up and saw the icons of the Romanovs, hanging above their tombs. Turning, he saw the altar beyond the doorway of the Catherine Chapel. Looking into her lovely blue eyes, he saw his future, reflected back at him. "I talked to God, Sasha."

She blinked. "And he heard you?"

"He came to me as an old Russian beggar, while I was waiting for you, outside."

"How do you know it was God?"

"I don't know for sure, but then again, I do."

She smiled up at him. "That's called faith, Jax."

He carefully set her on her feet, to stand beside him on holy ground, and kissed her.

ACKNOWLEDGMENTS

MY SINCERE THANKS TO THE VILLAGE OF TELLURIDE, Colorado, particularly the staff at Hotel Telluride. Thank you, Principal Alex Carter and Administrative Assistant/Registrar Sharon Broady at Telluride High School, for your warm welcome and generous help. Readers please note: THS is listed in Best High Schools by *U.S. News & World Report*. Regarding Telluride and San Francisco, I took a few liberties with geography, and all mistakes are my own.

Thank you, Meredith Bernstein, agent, friend, and fellow wanderer. You are glorious.

To the staff at Egmont USA—especially my editor—Greg Ferguson, I appreciate your dedication to children's literature, and all you've done to bring this book to readers.

Enormous props and thanks to Alison Kent, HelenKay Dimon, Kassia Krozser, and Wendy Duren. I could not have done this without you. Special thanks to Jill Monroe, my favorite dreamer.

Thanks to Stephani Fry, who shared her love of YA with me and changed everything, and to Tashya Wilson for the e-mail that started it all.

Thank you, Dianna Love, for your friendship and guidance, and Trish Milburn, God's special answer to "Help me— I'm stuck!" Many thanks to P. C. Cast and Sherrilyn Kenyon for your support. Seriously, ladies, you're a gift.

My humble gratitude to the Class of 2K11 for your camaraderie and stellar books. I'm in awe of your talent and mad skilz.

Thanks to Raegan Lumpkin for keeping me on task for revisions while sailing up the Rhine in a blizzard, and a special shout-out to the crew of the *River Duchess*, who kept the light on for me in the ship's library and never ran out of hot coffee.

As always, thank you to my family. I love you. Thank you, Mike, for a thousand dinners and a million kisses. Thanks to Callie, for listening to endless plot devices and debating religion, and to Leslea, for road tripping to Telluride with me. Next time, we'll catch more fish.

WHICH MEPHISTO BROTHER WILL BE
NEXT TO FIND HIS ANABO?

Check out the sequel to
THE MEPHISTO COVENANT

Coming out from Egmont USA in Fall 2012.

ONE

KISSING MATTHEW WAS ONE OF JORDAN'S FAVORITE THINGS to do, but tonight was different. Instead of enjoying the feel of his arms around her and the slow, gentle slide of his mouth over hers, all she could think about was the argument she'd had with her father before she came to Matthew's house.

In the middle of the kiss, she sighed, and he pulled back a little, gazing at her from soft brown eyes. "It's not something you could have prevented. You didn't even see the e-mail until . . . after. Don't beat yourself up about it."

"It's not that. Not entirely, anyway. It's Dad. After the news hit about that girl's suicide, he told me I have to quit doing the TV spots for STOP, that I can't be their spokesperson anymore, and we got in an epic fight about it. Why does everything I do have to be about him?"

With long, warm fingers, Matthew smoothed the hair at her temples. "Well, he *is* the president, and you've said yourself that your family lives in a fishbowl. STOP is a great thing, but every time it doesn't work, the newspeople make a big deal about your involvement. As long as you're part of it, they're going to focus on you instead of the kids it's supposed to help."

Pulling away from him, she sat up on the sofa. Across the room, the closing credits of the movie they'd just watched rolled across the screen. "When I turned seventeen, Dad asked me to do some of the things a First Lady does, since Mom's gone. I had lessons about how to greet state visitors and which fork to use and how to talk to reporters. Dad's press secretary wanted me to get involved with breast cancer awareness, since that's how Mom died, but I wanted to work with STOP, because of Holly." Volunteering to do public-service announcements for the Suicidal Teens Outreach Program had been her way of dealing with her friend's death, and now Dad was telling her she had to quit. It felt like a betrayal of Holly's memory.

"Maybe it's not a bad idea to step back. Those e-mails eat you up, and since you aren't allowed to respond to any of them, it just frustrates you and makes you depressed."

He had a point. She'd had notes from kids that sliced her soul to ribbons. Some managed to work through their problems, but some didn't. Like the girl who e-mailed Jordan in the middle of last night and said she was all done, that she was giving up. By the time Jordan saw it, the girl was dead from an overdose of sleeping pills.

2

As the First Daughter, she received hundreds, sometimes thousands of e-mails every week. It was White House policy that each e-mail receive a reply, and most were a generic response sent by Carla, the press secretary's assistant, or one of several staffers who worked under her, but they always flagged the e-mails they felt needed a personal reply from Jordan. Since Jordan had become the public face of STOP, she also received e-mails from desperate teens, and those received a reply expressing concern and compassion, along with the phone number and e-mail address for STOP. It wasn't that she didn't want to respond personally; she wasn't allowed. The press secretary was adamant about it, because of who she was. If she counseled someone who still killed himself, it would be a PR disaster for Dad. Everything was always about the presidency. Most of the time, she didn't mind, but sometimes it really got to her. "I told Dad that the news will call me a quitter, and it'll look worse."

"And what did he say?"

She turned her head and looked at him over her shoulder. "He said it wouldn't be the worst thing said about him." Sucking in a deep breath, she let it out slowly. "It's so bad, Matthew, like everything Dad does is wrong. He said every bill he signs to fix a problem seems to create another one. Unemployment is higher than it's ever been. His approval rating is almost as low as Nixon's the day he resigned from office."

"My dad says he listened to the wrong people and took bad advice."

Just that morning, she'd noticed Dad looked really old. "After Mom died, he shouldn't have run for a second term, but he did, and now it's all wrong."

Matthew rubbed her back. "Come on, Jordan, don't be so down. Let's do something that'll take your mind off of all the negative."

"Like what?"

"We could go upstairs to my room."

"Are you serious?" She turned her head again and saw the look in his ordinarily calm eyes. "Oh, wow, you *are* serious! Geez, Matthew, way to be inappropriate. I'm supersad and bummed out, and you're saying we should have sex?"

"It's not like we haven't been going out forever, so why not tonight? It'd be something to remember from this day that isn't a bummer."

She turned away and tucked her hair behind her ears. "I just got through telling you what a bad place my dad is in. Can you imagine if I got pregnant? It'd kill him." She sighed again. "Not to mention the field day the newspeople would have with that."

"You won't get pregnant."

"Says you. Nothing's for sure, and it's not a risk I want to take." She focused on the movie credits and waited for Matthew to tell her she needed to stop running everything she did through the filter of living in the White House. Other than going off about Auburn football, it was his favorite lecture.

Instead, he asked, almost in a whisper, "Do you love me?"

Ohmigod, he dropped the L word. Out of nowhere, when she least expected it. Her friend, Tessa, said he'd do it eventually, that it was every guy's last-ditch effort to get a girl to say yes. Jordan told her Matthew wasn't like that. Sure he asked—he was a seventeen-year-old guy, after all—but she always said no, rolled out some variation of the Speech, he gave her the Lecture, and they moved on. Rinse and repeat.

Now he changed everything by asking if she loved him. Inwardly cringing, she held the do-you-love-me grenade gingerly while she debated what to say. What if she said yes, and he didn't say he loved her, too? It would be out there, with no way to take it back. She'd die of humiliation.

But what if she said she wasn't sure, and he broke up with her? She wasn't ready for life without Matthew. Other than Tessa, he was her best friend, and yes, she *did* love him, but not necessarily like that. Not enough to sleep with him.

The credits came to an end, and the menu screen popped up. Turning to look at Matthew, she lobbed the grenade back at him. "Do *you* love *me?*"

He reached for her arm and tugged until she was back against his side. "I've never known a girl like you, Jordan. You think the only reason everybody likes you is because your dad's the president, but it would be the same if he was a garbageman. It's not him. It's you, and whatever's inside you that makes everybody want to hang with you." He pulled her closer and kissed her forehead. "It's part of the reason I keep asking about sex, because it'd make me feel more sure about us, that you'd be less likely to bail on me."

Lifting her face, she met his eyes. "You worry that *I'll* break up? Seriously?"

His arms tightened. "All the time." Sincerity was all over his face, and his smile was crooked, like he was embarrassed. "I love you, Jordan."

She almost couldn't breathe. *This* was romantic. This was *awesome*. Pressing a kiss to his soft mouth, she was about to whisper, "I love you, back," but didn't get it out before there were two loud pops from the street, just outside the window, making her jump. "Somebody has firecrackers."

Looking completely freaked out, Matthew grabbed her hand while he shoved away from the back of the sofa. "Those weren't firecrackers."

A loud crash came from the front hall, and she whipped her head around just as the door flew open. Two men in ski masks rushed inside, each with an arm extended, holding a handgun.

Matthew was already lunging from the sofa, pulling her along as he booked it toward the kitchen. In those few seconds, all she could think was, *Where is the Secret Service?* There were two agents, one in front of Matthew's house, one in back, and they were constantly in contact with police patrolling the area, so help had to be on the way already. But why weren't the agents inside? Had these guys shot Maggie out there on the front steps? Where was Paul? He had to have heard the shots. He should be coming inside, right now, but as they cleared the swinging door into the kitchen from the den, there was no one.

Matthew was headed for the back door. An alley ran behind the row of town houses, and once they were outside, in the dark, they could run and find somewhere to hide until—

Her heart skipped a beat when she heard another gunshot.

It broke into pieces when Matthew stumbled and let go of her hand.

⁓

Snipping the last of the wayward tendrils from an ornamental orange tree, Key stepped back and surveyed his work. "Why won't you bloom? It's time. You need to give it up. The bees are hungry."

The tree stood there in the dark, small and silent.

His gaze moved across the lush interior of the greenhouse while he inhaled deeply of the warm, moist air, heavy with the scent of vegetation and rich earth. The greenhouse smelled like life. Situated in the rambling garden to the east of the house on the Mephisto Mountain, all but buried in late December snow, everything within the walls of glass and steel depended on him for survival, right down to the earthworms. His care was rewarded with a slight easing of never-ending restlessness.

Sometimes, when the sun shone through the glass at just the right angle, when the blue of the sky above reflected against the tiny waterfall in the middle of the south wall, he could almost forget what he was, what he did, and imagine happiness.

But those times were rare.

Tilting his head, he looked up at the bowl of stars suspended above the greenhouse and wished God could hear him.

Jax's voice on the intercom above the greenhouse door cut through the perfect silence. "We have a situation. War room in one minute."

Damn.

With a heavy sigh, Key walked toward the door, setting his green shears on the potting bench before he disappeared. A few seconds later, he stood in the room at the center of a maze of computer banks and offices housed in the basement of the Mephisto mansion. One wall of the war room held an enormous plasma screen; on another was a gigantic map of the world and a whiteboard, and the center of the stone floor was dominated by an ancient oval table, three identical chairs on either side, and a new, smaller one at the end.

His brothers were all there, in varying states of dress. Key noticed that Sasha, the latest addition to the Mephisto, wore one of Jax's dress shirts, her long, slender legs ending in a pair of white socks. She had her blonde hair up in a ponytail that somehow made her more beautiful than if she'd had it all fixed and perfect. He wished he had a girl who'd wear his dress shirts as pajamas.

He focused on Jax. "What's going on?"

Jax picked up the remote control from the table. "This was recorded about an hour ago." The plasma screen was filled with an image of the president and his daughter, standing side by side on the steps of the White House, greeting the King and Queen of Sweden. The scene changed, and Jordan Ellis was handing out Easter baskets to a gaggle of little kids. Key watched impassively, but he definitely noticed she was beautiful. Small, barely over five feet, with long dark hair and wide blue eyes, when she smiled, her lovely face lit up, and her eyes . . . he'd swear they twinkled. He enjoyed watching her, but began to wonder how the hell photo ops of the First Daughter warranted a Mephisto situation.

The voiceover reporter said, "No one has claimed responsibility, no ransom demand has been issued, but an inside source tells CNN the FBI and Homeland Security believe the two gunmen are Americans. Several militias are being questioned, particularly a group based in Texas known as Red Out."

Key felt sick. "Did the bastards kidnap her?"

From where he leaned against the map wall, Phoenix said, "They took out her Secret Service detail, broke into her boyfriend's house, shot the boyfriend, and stole the girl."

"No way. Maybe somebody could take out a couple of Secret Service agents, but they couldn't take the president's daughter farther than a few blocks before they'd have every cop and uniformed Secret Service agent in the city all over them."

"Just keep watching," Phoenix said.

The screen changed to a scene outside a Capitol Hill row house, yellow crime-scene tape blocking part of the sidewalk. Scores of people stood watching as medics rolled a gurney through the front door and into a waiting ambulance. The voiceover reporter said, "Matthew Whittaker, seventeen-year-old son of Senator Jim Whittaker of Alabama, is in critical condition at George Washington University Hospital. He remains unconscious, but FBI agents hope to question him when he wakes."

Jax fast-forwarded, then stopped when the White House press secretary was speaking. Various White House staffers stood just behind him.

"Two men affiliated with the Red Out militia in central Texas were arrested after law enforcement pursued the car seen speeding away from the Whittaker residence. Miss Ellis was not in the car. The Secret Service believes the car was a decoy and the president's daughter was taken by alternate means."

Narrowing his eyes, Key stared at the guy second to the left. "The guy second to the left is way too still. He looks like a statue."

"He's Ron Trent, the chief of staff," Jax said. "It wouldn't be so obvious if every other staffer wasn't fidgeting, or crying."

They knew the Skia by the dark shadow across their eyes, but it never showed up on TV. They had to see a face in person to know if he'd given his soul to Eryx. But there were other signs, especially with the newest Skia. It took a lot of practice to act like a human with a soul, to fashion a facial expression to fit the situation, whether happy, sad, or frightened. In a row of hyper-emotional people, Ron Trent was completely impassive, not an ounce of feeling on his face or in his eyes. "Did someone check him out? Is he Skia?"

Phoenix said, "I did, and he is. Then I called M, who found out Eryx turned the guy about six months ago."

Key instantly began to consider the difficulty of taking out the White House chief of staff. Ron Trent was a high-profile guy, closest adviser to the president. "What are you thinking, Phoenix? How can we do this?"

Jax and Sasha exchanged a look before they both turned to Key. "Taking out Trent is definitely something we need to do, but that isn't the situation."

Looking around the room at the faces of his brothers, he realized they all knew something he didn't. "Okay, then, what *is* the situation?"

"Eryx is behind the kidnapping," Jax said. "That's how Jordan disappeared. We think he staged the break-in for show, because, just like us, he can't screw too much with reality. He had those guys, who're bound to be lost souls, give the cops a good chase, and in the meantime, he transported her somewhere he can keep her until Ron Trent coerces an oath from the president. To keep that from happening, we need to find her."

Key looked around at each face, hoping to see somebody break. This had to be a joke, a prank they cooked up just to screw with him. But no, he could see from their expressions that they were dead serious. "Have you all lost your minds? We *can't* interfere with free will. If the president caves, there's nothing we can do about it. It'll be dicey to take him down, but it won't be the first time we took out a head of state. Eryx has tried to take over governments before."

11

"Not exactly free will," Ty said from the opposite corner, one of his wolfhounds sitting next to him. "The man's daughter, the only family he has since his wife died, is in danger of being killed unless the president agrees to pledge his soul to Eryx."

"Do you know for sure that Eryx is behind Jordan's abduction?"

Phoenix said solemnly, "When I went to see if Ron Trent was Skia, I popped all over the White House, looking for him. I finally found him, with Ellis, in the Yellow Oval Room on the second floor of the residence. He was telling the president—"

"Did Trent see you?" Key stopped and took a deep breath. Under a cloak, no one could see them, even the lost souls. But Skia were different. Their immortality allowed them to see past a cloak.

"Do you *seriously* think I'm that stupid?"

Feeling heated glares, aware that all of them were as angry as Phoenix, Key took one more deep breath and shook his head. "No."

"Trent was telling the president about Eryx. Why would he do that if he wasn't planning to convince him to pledge?"

"It doesn't matter. If a man will give away any chance of Heaven to become a drone for Eryx, if he'll say out loud that he forsakes God, he's without faith. He's already lost."

Ty's big hand gently smoothed Greta's fur. "He's the leader of the free world. He has power, influence. If he belongs to Eryx, it's as if our oldest brother is president. Imagine the fallout. He'll appoint Skia and lost souls to judgeships, cabinet seats, committee chairs. He'll have every agency within the federal government stacked with his followers."

"He won't be in office long enough to do any real damage. We'll take him out immediately."

Denys was staring at the screen, at Jordan in a PSA for the teen suicide hotline. "An assassination will send the United States into a tailspin."

"Then let's hope the president's faith is stronger than his love for his child."

Twirling the diamond stud in his ear, Zee spoke up from where he stood, just next to the whiteboard along the east wall. "You're pissing me off, bro. Maybe you're in charge, but last I checked, we're a democracy. Majority rules. Six to one, Key."

"Unless majority wants to break Lucifer's law, in which case it's my call." He looked at each of them, searching for any sign of dissent. One flinch and he'd send that brother to Kyanos for six months to live in solitary. Until the spring thaw, he'd starve unless he could find something to kill on the frozen North Atlantic island.

"If he doesn't pledge the oath," Denys said, "Eryx will kill Jordan."

Key looked again at the screen. Jordan was accepting a posy of bluebells from a child in a London crowd. Her eyes matched the flowers. Her smile was captivating. Thinking of her death, he felt a twinge of regret before he said, "Everybody dies sometime."

"Except us," Denys said. "And the Luminas."

"We're not human. The Luminas are live angels. Doesn't count." He watched Jordan dance with her father at some formal White House dinner. "We're not going after the president's daughter. We're not going to interfere. It's Lucifer's law, and if we break it, there'll be hell to pay."

Phoenix huffed out an impatient breath. "I told them you'd never go for this on its own merit, but they insisted we try." He pushed away from the map wall and took a chair at the table. "There's a caveat to the law. Remember?"

What did he mean, on its own merit? "Of course I remember, but the exception is only if the human is Anabo, if interfering is necessary to protect her. This isn't—" He stopped talking, suddenly feeling as if a Toyota had been dropped on his chest.

Holy shit.

Jerking his gaze back to the screen, he saw Jordan coming out of a restaurant with a lanky brown-haired guy. They were holding hands, smiling and waving at the camera before getting into a late-model BMW, followed by Secret Service, and driving away.

"She's Anabo," Sasha said quietly.